Kenneth Deighton

Macaulay, Warren Hastings

With notes and appendices

Kenneth Deighton

Macaulay, Warren Hastings
With notes and appendices

ISBN/EAN: 9783337013226

Printed in Europe, USA, Canada, Australia, Japan

Cover: Foto ©Raphael Reischuk / pixelio.de

More available books at **www.hansebooks.com**

WARREN HASTINGS.

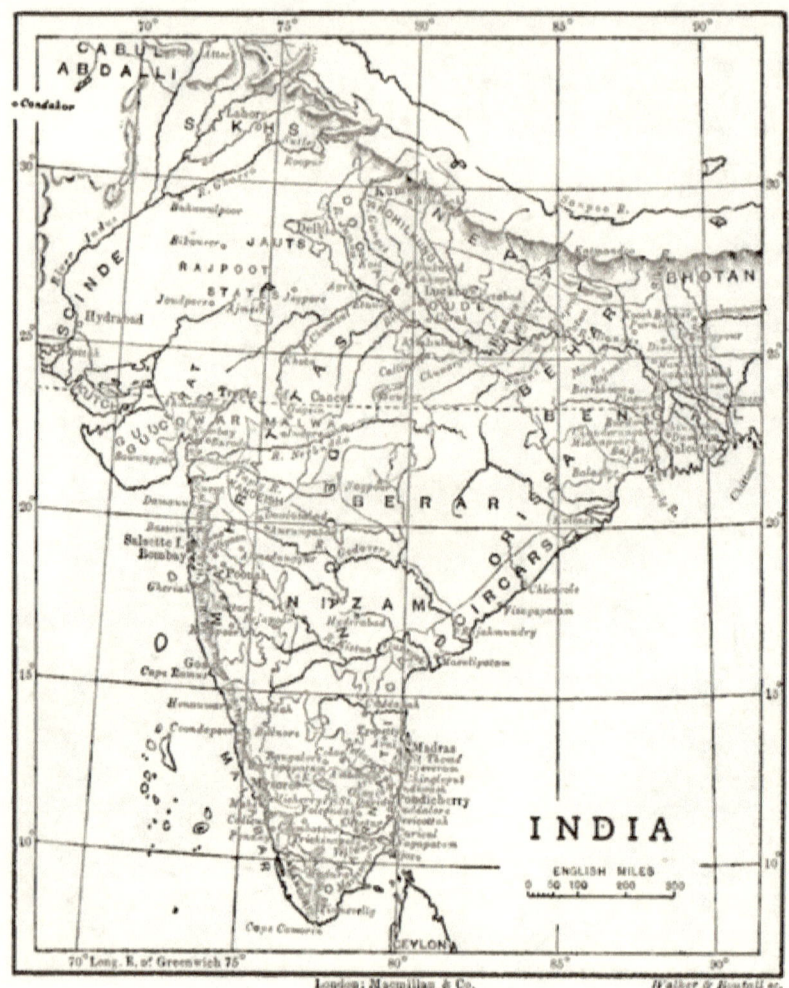

INDIA

ENGLISH MILES
0   50 100   200   300

London: Macmillan & Co.

Walker & Boutall sc.

MACAULAY

WARREN HASTINGS

WITH

NOTES AND APPENDICES

BY

K. DEIGHTON

London
MACMILLAN AND CO., Ltd.
NEW YORK: THE MACMILLAN CO.
1896

First Edition 1893
Reprinted 1896.

GLASGOW: PRINTED AT THE UNIVERSITY PRESS
BY ROBERT MACLEHOSE AND CO.

CONTENTS.

PREFACE.

In his work entitled *The Reign of Queen Victoria*, 'India,' Sir John Strachey remarks, "Sir Henry Maine has pointed out with admirable truth the consequences in India of the fact that English classical literature towards the end of the last century was 'saturated with party politics.' 'This,' he says, 'would have been a less serious fact if, at this epoch, one chief topic of the great writers and rhetoricians, of Burke and Sheridan, of Fox and Francis, had not been India itself. I have no doubt that the view of Indian government taken at the end of the century by Englishmen whose works and speeches are held to be models of English style has had deep effect on the mind of the educated Indian of this day. We are only now beginning to see how excessively inaccurate were their statements of fact and how one-sided were their judgments.' These remarks of Sir Henry Maine point to what I have long believed to be a serious misfortune—the non-existence of any history of British India, which is trustworthy and complete in its facts, and which at the same time possesses the essential quality of literary excellence. Since the earlier part of the present century the old stories of the crimes by which

the establishment of our power in India was attended
have been passed on from one author to another. . . .
These calumnies have caused and are still causing no
little mischief both in England and India. Thousands
of excellent people are filled with righteous indignation
when they read of the atrocious acts of Clive and
Hastings, the judicial murder of Nandkumar, the extermination of the Rohillas, the plunder of the Begums.
No suspicion of the truth reaches them that these
horrors never occurred, and the fear can hardly be
repressed that there may be some foundation even
now for the charges of Indian misgovernment and
oppression. . . . This false history is systematically
taught by ourselves, and believed by the educated
natives of India to be true. It is impossible that
this should not have a serious effect on their feelings
towards their English rulers." By all who are con-
versant with the progress of education in India, and
perhaps by none so readily as those who have had
a professional part in it, these words will be endorsed
as not one whit exaggerated. And if such be really
the outcome of our "enlightened policy," in the fore-
front of the band by whom misconception has been
propagated, stands Macaulay. His two celebrated
Indian essays comprehend nearly the whole of that
period regarding which, while error came so easily,
the truth—at all events till lately—was difficult of
discovery, that period for which the records were the
records of a mercantile corporation primarily concerned in making money. The fierce light that beats
upon a modern administration was unknown to the
Honourable East India Company. Its servants thought

little of posterity, cared nothing that the history they
were making should, on its transfusion into narrative,
be ordered and marshalled with the stately precision
by which a more self-conscious regime guards itself
against detraction and misunderstanding. But the
indifference of these pioneers of empire has helped to
blur and blot the fair fame of many of their own
number; and if historians have grievously caricatured
both men and measures, there is for them at least
the excuse that their distortion of objects is due in
perhaps less degree to dimness of vision than to
haziness of the medium in which the work had to be
done. That there has also been deliberate injustice
cannot, I fear, be denied. Macaulay himself was not
seldom biassed by political sympathies; though his
worst shortcomings are the shortcomings of one who
has placed unwise confidence in apparently trustworthy
guides. Mill is a much greater sinner. But Mill has
few charms, and his narrative would never stir so
much as a spasm of enthusiastic belief or kindle the
faintest glow of fervid partizanship. With Macaulay
the case is very different. The transparent lucidity of
his style, the rich colouring, the dramatic vividness,
the apt illustration, the swift assemblage of images so
various and yet so cumulative in their effect, his
learning worn so lightly and yet so massive in its
strength, the splendour with which he lights up a
battle-piece or the pageantry in which he decks some
time-honoured ceremonial, his copious vocabulary of
invective and scorn, his hatred of meanness and injustice, his lofty imagination, "that noble faculty," as
he himself says in regard to Burke, "whereby man is

able to live in the past and in the future, in the distant and in the unreal"—combine to throw over whatever he writes a glamour that no one can resist, least of all those in whom the pulse of life still throbs with full-toned animation, with whom belief is still a joy, and hero-worship a necessity. While, therefore, of those who have to study his essays the number is small as compared with the number who have to study dry histories,—and the histories of India are probably unique in their dryness, not only to English but to Indian readers,—the hold which he obtains is immeasurably greater and more enduring than that which is taken by the laborious chroniclers of weari-some detail padded with trite reflection, the compilers of narrative that has neither foreground nor back-ground, neither proportion nor perspective. A writer like Macaulay makes converts, who in their turn find disciples. To hand down his doctrines becomes a religion. His very fallacies are the shibboleth of a school. Add to this that his reputation as a scholar, as a historian, as a jurist, still looms as large as ever, and it is easy to understand that prestige of this nature should keep loyal those who might waver, and hold back those who would venture to criticize. If, then, these two essays are to be put into the hands of students and set as subjects of an examina-tion, it cannot be done with safety unless at the same time an endeavour is made to show wherein their statements are inaccurate, and how the views put forward in them assume an altered colouring from the light of fuller information. The essay on Hastings more especially needs such rectification, and this for-tunately is possible with the help of three works of recent publication, Sir John Strachey's account of the Rohilla War, Sir James Stephen's examination of the Nand Kumár myth and the impeachment of Impey, and the selections from Official Records so ably edited by Professor Forrest. From the two former works I have made copious extracts, and I wish that every student had the opportunity and the leisure to study them in their entirety. Another work which I have found most useful is Sir Alfred Lyall's *Warren Hastings*. This, if possible, should be closely compared with Macaulay's essay. It is not long,—about two hundred pages,—but it gives with unusual clearness a complete view of Hastings' administration. It has another characteristic, even more important than clearness, viz., impartiality. I do not say "studied impartiality," for the impartiality strikes one as something so natural as to be part of the man. Captain Trotter's biography in the "Rulers of India" series will also be read with much interest. If somewhat of the nature of a brief for the defence, and scarcely displaying the same breadth of treatment with Sir Alfred Lyall's work, it is fuller in detail and is based on the firm foundation of the original records which, as I have already mentioned, Professor Forrest has lately edited. Lastly, an admirable article in the *Dictionary of National Biography*, from the pen of Mr. H. G. Keene, brings into very moderate compass the events of Warren Hastings' life and official career.

In my Notes there will be found, I hope, sufficient explanation of verbal difficulties and historical references. But certain matters are too long for mere Notes, and these I have reserved for Appendices. The subjects there discussed are (1) The Rohilla War: (2) Hastings, Impey, and Nand Kumár: (3) The Impeachment of Impey; and to these I have added a short sketch of the Rise and Growth of the Marátha powers.

WARREN HASTINGS.

THIS book seems to have been manufactured in pursuance of a contract, by which the representatives of Warren Hastings, on the one part, bound themselves to furnish papers, and Mr. Gleig, on the other part, bound himself to furnish praise. It is but just to say that the covenants on both sides have been most faithfully kept; and the result is before us in the form of three big bad volumes, full of undigested correspondence and undiscerning panegyric.

If it were worth while to examine this performance in detail, we could easily make a long article by merely pointing 10 out inaccurate statements, inelegant expressions, and immoral doctrines. But it would be idle to waste criticism on a bookmaker; and, whatever credit Mr. Gleig may have justly earned by former works, it is as a bookmaker, and nothing more, that he now comes before us. More eminent men than Mr. Gleig have written nearly as ill as he, when they have stooped to similar drudgery. It would be unjust to estimate Goldsmith by the History of Greece, or Scott by the Life of Napoleon. Mr. Gleig is neither a Goldsmith nor a Scott; but it would be unjust to deny that he is capable 20 of something better than these Memoirs. It would also, we hope and believe, be unjust to charge any Christian minister with the guilt of deliberately maintaining some propositions which we find in this book. It is not too much to say that Mr. Gleig has written several passages, which bear the same

S   A

relation to the Prince of Machiavelli that the Prince of
Machiavelli bears to the Whole Duty of Man, and which
would excite amazement in a den of robbers, or on board of
a schooner of pirates. But we are willing to attribute these
offences to haste, to thoughtlessness, and to that disease of
the understanding which may be called the *Furor Biographicus*, and which is to writers of lives what the *goitre*
is to an Alpine shepherd, or dirt-eating to a Negro slave.

We are inclined to think that we shall best meet the
10 wishes of our readers, if, instead of dwelling on the faults
of this book, we attempt to give, in a way necessarily hasty
and imperfect, our own view of the life and character of Mr.
Hastings. Our feeling towards him is not exactly that of
the House of Commons which impeached him in 1787;
neither is it that of the House of Commons which uncovered
and stood up to receive him in 1813. He had great qualities,
and he rendered great services to the state. But to represent him as a man of stainless virtue is to make him
ridiculous; and from regard for his memory, if from no
20 other feeling, his friends would have done well to lend no
countenance to such puerile adulation. We believe that, if
he were now living, he would have sufficient judgment and
sufficient greatness of mind to wish to be shown as he was.
He must have known that there were dark spots on his
fame. He might also have felt with pride that the splendour
of his fame would bear many spots. He would have preferred, we are confident, even the severity of Mr. Mill to the
puffing of Mr Gleig. He would have wished posterity to
have a likeness of him, though an unfavourable likeness,
30 rather than a daub at once insipid and unnatural, resembling
neither him nor any body else. "Paint me as I am," said
Oliver Cromwell, while sitting to young Lely. "If you
leave out the scars and wrinkles, I will not pay you a
shilling." Even in such a trifle, the great Protector showed
both his good sense and his magnanimity. He did not wish
all that was characteristic in his countenance to be lost, in

the vain attempt to give him the regular features and smooth
blooming cheeks of the curl-pated minions of James the
First. He was content that his face should go forth marked
with all the blemishes which had been put on it by time, by
war, by sleepless nights, by anxiety, perhaps by remorse ;
but with valour, policy, authority, and public care written in
all its princely lines. If men truly great knew their own
interest, it is thus that they would wish their minds to be
portrayed.

Warren Hastings sprang from an ancient and illustrious 10
race. It has been affirmed that his pedigree can be traced
back to the great Danish sea-king, whose sails were long the
terror of both coasts of the British Channel, and who, after
many fierce and doubtful struggles, yielded at last to the
valour and genius of Alfred. But the undoubted splendour
of the line of Hastings needs no illustration from fable.
One branch of that line wore, in the fourteenth century, the
coronet of Pembroke. From another branch sprang the
renowned Chamberlain, the faithful adherent of the White
Rose, whose fate has furnished so striking a theme both to 20
poets and to historians. His family received from the
Tudors the earldom of Huntingdon, which, after long dis-
possession, was regained in our time by a series of events
scarcely paralleled in romance.

The lords of the manor of Daylesford, in Worcestershire,
claimed to be considered as the heads of this distinguished
family. The main stock, indeed, prospered less than some
of the younger shoots. But the Daylesford family, though
not ennobled, was wealthy and highly considered, till, about
two hundred years ago, it was overwhelmed by the great 30
ruin of the civil war. The Hastings of that time was a
zealous cavalier. He raised money on his lands, sent his
plate to the mint at Oxford, joined the royal army, and,
after spending half his property in the cause of King
Charles, was glad to ransom himself by making over most
of the remaining half to Speaker Lenthal. The old seat at

Daylesford still remained in the family; but it could no longer be kept up; and in the following generation it was sold to a merchant of London.

Before this transfer took place, the last Hastings of Daylesford had presented his second son to the rectory of the parish in which the ancient residence of the family stood. The living was of little value; and the situation of the poor clergyman, after the sale of the estate, was deplorable. He was constantly engaged in lawsuits about his tithes with the new lord of the manor, and was at length utterly ruined. His eldest son, Howard, a well-conducted young man, obtained a place in the Customs. The second son, Pynaston, an idle worthless boy, married before he was sixteen, lost his wife in two years, and died in the West Indies, leaving to the care of his unfortunate father a little orphan, destined to strange and memorable vicissitudes of fortune.

Warren, the son of Pynaston, was born on the sixth of December, 1732. His mother died a few days later, and he was left dependent on his distressed grandfather. The child was early sent to the village school, where he learned his letters on the same bench with the sons of the peasantry. Nor did any thing in his garb or fare indicate that his life was to take a widely different course from that of the young rustics with whom he studied and played. But no cloud could overcast the dawn of so much genius and so much ambition. The very ploughmen observed, and long remembered, how kindly little Warren took to his book. The daily sight of the lands which his ancestors had possessed, and which had passed into the hands of strangers, filled his young brain with wild fancies and projects. He loved to hear stories of the wealth and greatness of his progenitors, of their splendid housekeeping, their loyalty, and their valour. On one bright summer day, the boy, then just seven years old, lay on the bank of the rivulet which flows through the old domain of his house to join the Isis. There,

as threescore and ten years later he told the tale, rose in his
mind a scheme which, through all the turns of his eventful
career, was never abandoned. He would recover the estate
which had belonged to his fathers. He would be Hastings
of Daylesford. This purpose, formed in infancy and poverty,
grew stronger as his intellect expanded and as his fortune
rose. He pursued his plan with that calm but indomitable
force of will which was the most striking peculiarity of his
character. When, under a tropical sun, he ruled fifty
millions of Asiatics, his hopes, amidst all the cares of war, 10
finance, and legislation, still pointed to Daylesford. And
when his long public life, so singularly chequered with good
and evil, with glory and obloquy, had at length closed for
ever, it was to Daylesford that he retired to die.

When he was eight years old, his uncle Howard determined to take charge of him, and to give him a liberal
education. The boy went up to London, and was sent to
a school at Newington, where he was well taught but ill fed.
He always attributed the smallness of his stature to the
hard and scanty fare of this seminary. At ten he was re- 20
moved to Westminster School, then flourishing under the
care of Dr. Nichols. Vinny Bourne, as his pupils affection-
ately called him, was one of the masters. Churchill, Colman,
Lloyd, Cumberland, Cowper, were among the students. With
Cowper, Hastings formed a friendship which neither the
lapse of time, nor a wide dissimilarity of opinions and pursuits, could wholly dissolve. It does not appear that they
ever met after they had grown to manhood. But forty years
later, when the voices of many great orators were crying for
vengeance on the oppressor of India, the shy and secluded 30
poet could image to himself Hastings the Governor-General
only as the Hastings with whom he had rowed on the
Thames, and played in the cloister, and refused to believe
that so good-tempered a fellow could have done anything
very wrong. His own life had been spent in praying, musing,
and rhyming among the water-lilies of the Ouse. He had

preserved in no common measure the innocence of childhood.
His spirit had indeed been severely tried, but not by temptations which impelled him to any gross violation of the rules
of social morality. He had never been attacked by combina-
tions of powerful and deadly enemies. He had never been
compelled to make a choice between innocence and greatness,
between crime and ruin. Firmly as he held in theory the
doctrine of human depravity, his habits were such that he
was unable to conceive how far from the path of right even
10 kind and noble natures may be hurried by the rage of conflict
and the lust of dominion.

Hastings had another associate at Westminster of whom
we shall have occasion to make frequent mention, Elijah
Impey. We know little about their school days. But, we
think, we may safely venture to guess that, whenever
Hastings wished to play any trick more than usually
naughty, he hired Impey with a tart or a ball to act as
fag in the worst part of the prank.

Warren was distinguished among his comrades as an ex-
20 cellent swimmer, boatman, and scholar. At fourteen he was
first in the examination for the foundation. His name in
gilded letters on the walls of the dormitory still attests his
victory over many older competitors. He stayed two years
longer at the school, and was looking forward to a studentship at Christ Church, when an event happened which
changed the whole course of his life. Howard Hastings
died, bequeathing his nephew to the care of a friend and
distant relation, named Chiswick. This gentleman, though
he did not absolutely refuse the charge, was desirous to rid
30 himself of it as soon as possible. Dr. Nichols made strong
remonstrances against the cruelty of interrupting the studies
of a youth who seemed likely to be one of the first scholars
of the age. He even offered to bear the expense of sending
his favourite pupil to Oxford. But Mr. Chiswick was inflexible. He thought the years which had already been
wasted on hexameters and pentameters quite sufficient. He

had it in his power to obtain for the lad a writership in the service of the East India Company. Whether the young adventurer, when once shipped off, made a fortune, or died of a liver complaint, he equally ceased to be a burden to any body. Warren was accordingly removed from Westminster school, and placed for a few months at a commercial academy to study arithmetic and book-keeping, In January, 1750, a few days after he had completed his seventeenth year, he sailed for Bengal, and arrived at his destination in the October following. 10

He was immediately placed at a desk in the Secretary's office at Calcutta, and laboured there during two years. Fort William was then a purely commercial settlement. In the south of India the encroaching policy of Dupleix had transformed the servants of the English Company, against their will, into diplomatists and generals. The war of the succession was raging in the Carnatic ; and the tide had been suddenly turned against the French by the genius of young Robert Clive. But in Bengal the European settlers, at peace with the natives and with each other, were wholly occupied 20 with ledgers and bills of lading.

After two years passed in keeping accounts at Calcutta, Hastings was sent up the country to Cossimbazar, a town which lies on the Hoogley, about a mile from Moorshedabad, and which then bore to Moorshedabad a relation, if we may compare small things with great, such as the city of London bears to Westminster. Moorshedabad was the abode of the prince who, by an authority ostensibly derived from the Mogul, but really independent, ruled the three great provinces of Bengal, Orissa, and Bahar. At Moorshedabad were 30 the court, the haram, and the public offices. Cossimbazar was a port and a place of trade, renowned for the quantity and excellence of the silks which were sold in its marts, and constantly receiving and sending forth fleets of richly laden barges. At this important point, the Company had established a small factory subordinate to that of Fort William

Here, during several years, Hastings was employed in making bargains for stuffs with native brokers. While he was thus engaged, Surajah Dowlah succeeded to the government, and declared war against the English. The defenceless settlement of Cossimbazar, lying close to the tyrant's capital, was instantly seized. Hastings was sent a prisoner to Moorshedabad, but, in consequence of the humane intervention of the servants of the Dutch Company, was treated with indulgence. Meanwhile the Nabob marched on Calcutta; the governor 10 and the commandant fled; the town and citadel were taken, and most of the English prisoners perished in the Black Hole.

11   In these events originated the greatness of Warren Hastings. The fugitive governor and his companions had taken refuge on the dreary islet of Fulda, near the mouth of the Hoogley. They were naturally desirous to obtain full information respecting the proceedings of the Nabob; and no person seemed so likely to furnish it as Hastings, who was a prisoner at large in the immediate neighbourhood of the 20 court. He thus became a diplomatic agent, and soon established a high character for ability and resolution. The treason which at a later period was fatal to Surajah Dowlah was already in progress; and Hastings was admitted to the deliberations of the conspirators. But the time for striking had not arrived. It was necessary to postpone the execution of the design; and Hastings, who was now in extreme peril, fled to Fulda.

12   Soon after his arrival at Fulda, the expedition from Madras, commanded by Clive, appeared in the Hoogley. Warren, 30 young, intrepid, and excited probably by the example of the Commander of the forces who, having like himself been a mercantile agent of the Company, had been turned by public calamities into a soldier, determined to serve in the ranks. During the early operations of the war he carried a musket. But the quick eye of Clive soon perceived that the head of the young volunteer would be more useful than his arm.

When, after the battle of Plassey, Meer Jaffier was proclaimed Nabob of Bengal, Hastings was appointed to reside
at the court of the new prince as agent for the Company.

He remained at Moorshedabad till the year 1761, when
he became a member of Council, and was consequently
forced to reside at Calcutta. This was during the interval
between Clive's first and second administration, an interval
which has left on the fame of the East India Company a
stain, not wholly effaced by many years of just and humane
government. Mr. Vansittart, the Governor, was at the 10
head of a new and anomalous empire. On the one side was
a band of English functionaries, daring, intelligent, eager
to be rich. On the other side was a great native population,
helpless, timid, accustomed to crouch under oppression.
To keep the stronger race from preying on the weaker
was an undertaking which tasked to the utmost the talents
and energy of Clive. Vansittart, with fair intentions, was
a feeble and inefficient ruler. The master caste, as was
natural, broke loose from all restraint; and then was seen
what we believe to be the most frightful of all spectacles, 20
the strength of civilisation without its mercy. To all
other despotism there is a check, imperfect indeed, and
liable to gross abuse, but still sufficient to preserve society
from the last extreme of misery. A time comes when the
evils of submission are obviously greater than those of
resistance, when fear itself begets a sort of courage, when
a convulsive burst of popular rage and despair warns
tyrants not to presume too far on the patience of mankind.
But against misgovernment such as then afflicted Bengal
it was impossible to struggle. The superior intelligence 30
and energy of the dominant class made their power irresistible. A war of Bengalees against Englishmen was like
a war of sheep against wolves, of men against dæmons.
The only protection which the conquered could find was
in the moderation, the clemency, the enlarged policy of the
conquerors. That protection, at a later period, they found.

But at first English power came among them unaccompanied by English morality. There was an interval between the time at which they became our subjects, and the time at which we began to reflect that we were bound to discharge towards them the duties of rulers. During that interval the business of a servant of the Company was simply to wring out of the natives a hundred or two hundred thousand pounds as speedily as possible, that he might return home before his constitution had suffered from the heat, to marry a peer's daughter, to buy rotten boroughs in Cornwall, and to give balls in St. James's Square. Of the conduct of Hastings at this time, little is known; but the little that is known, and the circumstance that little is known, must be considered as honourable to him. He could not protect the natives : all that he could do was to abstain from plundering and oppressing them ; and this he appears to have done. It is certain that at this time he continued poor ; and it is equally certain, that by cruelty and dishonesty he might easily have become rich. It is certain that he was never charged with having borne a share in the worst abuses which then prevailed ; and it is almost equally certain that, if he had borne a share in those abuses, the able and bitter enemies who afterwards persecuted him would not have failed to discover and to proclaim his guilt. The keen, severe, and even malevolent scrutiny to which his whole public life was subjected, a scrutiny unparalleled, as we believe, in the history of mankind, is in one respect advantageous to his reputation. It brought many lamentable blemishes to light ; but it entitles him to be considered pure from every blemish which has not been brought to light.

The truth is that the temptations to which so many English functionaries yielded in the time of Mr. Vansittart were not temptations addressed to the ruling passions of Warren Hastings. He was not squeamish in pecuniary transactions ; but he was neither sordid nor rapacious.

He was far too enlightened a man to look on a great empire merely as a buccaneer would look on a galleon. Had his heart been much worse than it was, his understanding would have preserved him from that extremity of baseness. He was an unscrupulous, perhaps an unprincipled statesman; but still he was a statesman, and not a freebooter.

In 1764 Hastings returned to England. He had realized only a very moderate fortune; and that moderate fortune was soon reduced to nothing, partly by his praiseworthy liberality, and partly by his mismanagement. Towards his relations he appears to have acted very generously. The greater part of his savings he left in Bengal, hoping probably to obtain the high usury of India. But high usury and bad security generally go together; and Hastings lost both interest and principal.

He remained four years in England. Of his life at this time very little is known. But it has been asserted, and is highly probable, that liberal studies and the society of men of letters occupied a great part of his time. It is to be remembered to his honour, that in days when the languages of the East were regarded by other servants of the Company merely as the means of communicating with weavers and money-changers, his enlarged and accomplished mind sought in Asiatic learning for new forms of intellectual enjoyment, and for new views of government and society. Perhaps, like most persons who have paid much attention to departments of knowledge which lie out of the common track, he was inclined to overrate the value of his favourite studies. He conceived that the cultivation of Persian literature might with advantage be made a part of the liberal education of an English gentleman; and he drew up a plan with that view. It is said that the University of Oxford, in which Oriental learning had never, since the revival of letters, been wholly neglected, was to be the seat of the institution which he contemplated. An endowment was expected from the munificence of the

Company ; and professors thoroughly competent **to inter-pret** Hafiz and Ferdusi were to be engaged **in** the East. Hastings called on Johnson, with the hope, as it should **seem, of** interesting in this project a man who enjoyed the highest literary reputation, and who was particularly connected with Oxford. The interview appears to **have** left on Johnson's mind a most **favourable impression of** the talents and attainments **of his** visitor. Long **after, when Hastings was** ruling the immense population **of**
10 **British India,** the old philosopher wrote to him, and re-ferred **in the most** courtly terms, though with great dignity, to their short but agreeable intercourse.

Hastings soon began to look again towards India. **He** had little to attach him to England ; and his pecuniary embarrassments were great. He solicited his old masters the Directors for employment. They acceded to his request, **with** high compliments both to his abilities **and to his integrity, and appointed** him a Member of Council at Madras. **It would be** unjust not to mention that, though
20 forced to borrow **money** for his outfit, he did not withdraw any portion of the sum which he had appropriated to the relief of his distressed relations. In the spring of 1769 he embarked on board of the Duke of Grafton and com-menced a voyage distinguished **by** incidents which might **furnish matter** for **a novel.**

Among the passengers in the Duke of Grafton **was a German** of the name of Imhoff. He called himself a baron ; **but he was** in distressed circumstances, and was going out to Madras as a portrait-painter, in the hope of picking
30 up some of the pagodas which were then lightly got and as lightly spent by the English **in** India. The baron was accompanied by his wife, a native, we have somewhere read, of Archangel. This young woman who, born under the **Arctic** circle, **was** destined to **play** the part of a queen under the tropic of Cancer, had an agreeable person, a cultivated mind, and manners in the highest degree engag-

ing. She despised her husband heartily, and, as the story which we have to tell sufficiently proves, not without reason. She was interested by the conversation and flattered by the attentions of Hastings. The situation was indeed perilous. No place is so propitious to the formation either of close friendships or of deadly enmities as an Indiaman. There are very few people who do not find a voyage which lasts several months insupportably dull. Any thing is welcome which may break that long monotony, a sail, a shark, an albatross, a man overboard. Most passengers 10 find some resource in eating twice as many meals as on land. But the great devices for killing the time are quarrelling and flirting. The facilities for both these exciting pursuits are great. The inmates of the ship are thrown together far more than in any country-seat or boarding-house. None can escape from the rest except by imprisoning himself in a cell in which he can hardly turn. All food, all exercise, is taken in company. Ceremony is to a great extent banished. It is every day in the power of a mischievous person to inflict innumerable annoyances ; 20 it is every day in the power of an amiable person to confer little services. It not seldom happens that serious distress and danger call forth in genuine beauty and deformity heroic virtues and abject vices which, in the ordinary intercourse of good society, might remain during many years unknown even to intimate associates. Under such circumstances met Warren Hastings and the Baroness Imhoff, two persons whose accomplishments would have attracted notice in any court of Europe. The gentleman had no domestic ties. The lady was tied to a husband for whom 30 she had no regard, and who had no regard for his own honour. An attachment sprang up, which was soon strengthened by events such as could hardly have occurred on land. Hastings fell ill. The baroness nursed him with womanly tenderness, gave him his medicines with her own hand, and even sat up in his cabin while he slept. Long

before the Duke of Grafton reached Madras, Hastings was
in love. But his love was of a most characteristic description. Like his hatred, like his ambition, like all his passions, it was strong, but not impetuous. It was calm, deep,
earnest, patient of delay, unconquerable by time. Imhoff
was called into council by his wife and his wife's lover.
It was arranged that the baroness should institute a suit
for a divorce in the courts of Franconia, that the baron
should afford every facility to the proceeding, and that,
10 during the years which might elapse before the sentence
should be pronounced, they should continue to live together.
It was also agreed that Hastings should bestow some very
substantial marks of gratitude on the complaisant husband,
and should, when the marriage was dissolved, make the
lady his wife, and adopt the children whom she had already
borne to Imhoff.

We are not inclined to judge either Hastings or the baroness
severely. There was undoubtedly much to extenuate their
fault. But we can by no means concur with the Reverend
20 Mr. Gleig, who carries his partiality to so injudicious an
extreme as to describe the conduct of Imhoff, conduct the
baseness of which is the best excuse for the lovers, as "wise
and judicious."

At Madras, Hastings found the trade of the Company in a
very disorganised state. His own tastes would have led him
rather to political than to commercial pursuits: but he knew
that the favour of his employers depended chiefly on their
dividends, and that their dividends depended chiefly on the
investment. He therefore, with great judgment, determined
30 to apply his vigorous mind for a time to this department of
business, which had been much neglected, since the servants
of the Company had ceased to be clerks, and had become
warriors and negotiators.

In a very few months he effected an important reform.
The Directors notified to him their high approbation, and
were so much pleased with his conduct that they deter-

mined to place him at the head of the government of
Bengal. Early in 1772 he quitted Fort St. George for his
new post. The Imhoffs, who were still man and wife,
accompanied him, and lived at Calcutta "on the same wise
and judicious plan,"—we quote the words of Mr. Gleig,—
which they had already followed during more than two
years.

When Hastings took his seat at the head of the council-
board, Bengal was still governed according to the system
which Clive had devised, a system which was, perhaps, 10
skilfully contrived for the purpose of facilitating and con-
cealing a great revolution, but which, when that revolution
was complete and irrevocable, could produce nothing but
inconvenience. There were two governments, the real and
the ostensible. The supreme power belonged to the Company, and was in truth the most despotic power that can be
conceived. The only restraint on the English masters of the
country was that which their own justice and humanity
imposed on them. There was no constitutional check on
their will, and resistance to them was utterly hopeless. 20

But, though thus absolute in reality, the English had not
yet assumed the style of sovereignty. They held their
territories as vassals of the throne of Delhi; they raised
their revenues as collectors appointed by the imperial commission; their public seal was inscribed with the imperial
titles; and their mint struck only the imperial coin.

There was still a nabob of Bengal, who stood to the
English rulers of his country in the same relation in which
Augustulus stood to Odoacer, or the last Merovingians to
Charles Martel and Pepin. He lived at Moorshedabad, 30
surrounded by princely magnificence. He was approached
with outward marks of reverence, and his name was used in
public instruments. But in the government of the country
he had less real share than the youngest writer or cadet in
the Company's service.

The English council which represented the Company at

Calcutta was constituted on a very different plan from that
which has since been adopted. At present the Governor is,
as to all executive measures, absolute. He can declare war,
conclude peace, appoint public functionaries or remove them,
in opposition to the unanimous sense of those who sit with
him in council. They are, indeed, entitled to know all that
is done, to discuss all that is done, to advise, to remonstrate,
to send protests to England. But it is with the Governor
that the supreme power resides, and on him that the whole
10 responsibility rests. This system, which was introduced by
Mr. Pitt and Mr. Dundas in spite of the strenuous opposition of Mr. Burke, we conceive to be on the whole the best
that was ever devised for the government of a country where
no materials can be found for a representative constitution.
In the time of Hastings the governor had only one vote in
council, and, in case of an equal division, a casting vote. It
therefore happened not unfrequently that he was overruled
on the gravest questions ; and it was possible that he might
be wholly excluded, for years together, from the real direc-
20 tion of public affairs.

The English functionaries at Fort William had as yet paid
little or no attention to the internal government of Bengal.
The only branch of politics about which they much busied
themselves was negotiation with the native princes. The
police, the administration of justice, the details of the collection of revenue they almost entirely neglected. We may
remark that the phraseology of the Company's servants still
bears the traces of this state of things. To this day they
always use the word " political " as synonymous with
30 " diplomatic." We could name a gentleman still living
who was described by the highest authority as an invalu-
able public servant, eminently fit to be at the head of the
internal administration of a whole presidency, but unfor-
tunately quite ignorant of all political business.

The internal government of Bengal the English rulers
delegated to a great native minister, who was stationed at

Moorshedabad. All military affairs, and, with the exception of what pertains to mere ceremonial, all foreign affairs, were withdrawn from his control ; but the other departments of the administration were entirely confided to him. His own stipend amounted to near a hundred thousand pounds sterling a year. The personal allowance of the nabobs, amounting to more than three hundred thousand pounds a year, passed through the minister's hands, and was, to a great extent, at his disposal. The collection of the revenue, the administration of justice, the maintenance of order, were 10 left to this high functionary ; and for the exercise of his immense power he was responsible to none but the British masters of the country.

A situation so important, lucrative, and splendid, was naturally an object of ambition to the ablest and most powerful natives. Clive had found it difficult to decide between conflicting pretensions. Two candidates stood out prominently from the crowd, each of them the representative of a race and of a religion.

The one was Mahommed Reza Khan, a Mussulman of 20 Persian extraction, able, active, religious after the fashion of his people, and highly esteemed by them. In England he might perhaps have been regarded as a corrupt and greedy politician. But, tried by the lower standard of Indian morality, he might be considered as a man of integrity and honour.

His competitor was a Hindoo Brahmin whose name has, by a terrible and melancholy event, been inseparably associated with that of Warren Hastings, the Maharajah Nuncomar. This man had played an important part in all the 30 revolutions which, since the time of Surajah Dowlah, had taken place in Bengal. To the consideration which in that country belongs to high and pure caste, he added the weight which is derived from wealth, talents, and experience. Of his moral character it is difficult to give a notion to those who are acquainted with human nature only as it appears

in our island. What the Italian is to the Englishman, what
the Hindoo is to the Italian, what the Bengalee is to other
Hindoos, that was Nuncomar to other Bengalees. The
physical organization of the Bengalee is feeble even to
effeminacy. He lives in a constant vapour bath. His pursuits are sedentary, his limbs delicate, his movements
languid. During many ages he has been trampled upon
by men of bolder and more hardy breeds. Courage, independence, veracity, are qualities to which his constitution
10 and his situation are equally unfavourable. His mind bears
a singular analogy to his body. It is weak even to helpless-
ness, for purposes of manly resistance ; but its suppleness
and its tact move the children of sterner climates to admiration not unmingled with contempt. All those arts which
are the natural defence of the weak are more familiar to this
subtle race than to the Ionian of the time of Juvenal, or to
the Jew of the dark ages. What the horns are to the
buffalo, what the paw is to the tiger, what the sting is to
the bee, what beauty, according to the old Greek song,
20 is to woman, deceit is to the Bengalee. Large promises,
smooth excuses, elaborate tissues of circumstantial falsehood, chicanery, perjury, forgery, are the weapons, offensive
and defensive, of the people of the Lower Ganges. All
those millions do not furnish one sepoy to the armies of
the Company. But as usurers, as money-changers, as sharp
legal practitioners, no class of human beings can bear a
comparison with them. With all his softness, the Bengalee
is by no means placable in his enmities or prone to pity.
The pertinacity with which he adheres to his purposes yields
30 only to the immediate pressure of fear. Nor does he lack
a certain kind of courage which is often wanting in his
masters. To inevitable evils he is sometimes found to
oppose a passive fortitude, such as the Stoics attributed to
their ideal sage. An European warrior who rushes on a
battery of cannon with a loud hurrah will sometimes shriek
under the surgeon's knife, and fall into an agony of despair

at the sentence of death. But the Bengalee who would see
his country overrun, his house laid in ashes, his children
murdered or dishonoured, without having the spirit to strike
one blow, has yet been known to endure torture with the
firmness of Mucius, and to mount the scaffold with the
steady step and even pulse of Algernon Sydney.

In Nuncomar, the national character was strongly and
with exaggeration personified. The Company's servants had
repeatedly detected him in the most criminal intrigues. On
one occasion he brought a false charge against another 10
Hindoo, and tried to substantiate it by producing forged
documents. On another occasion it was discovered that
while professing the strongest attachment to the English,
he was engaged in several conspiracies against them, and in
particular that he was the medium of a correspondence
between the court of Delhi and the French authorities in
the Carnatic. For these and similar practices he had been
long detained in confinement. But his talents and influence
had not only procured his liberation, but had obtained for
him a certain degree of consideration even among the British 20
rulers of his country.

Clive was extremely unwilling to place a Mussulman at
the head of the administration of Bengal. On the other
hand, he could not bring himself to confer immense power
on a man to whom every sort of villany had repeatedly been
brought home. Therefore, though the nabob, over whom
Nuncomar had by intrigue acquired great influence, begged
that the artful Hindoo might be intrusted with the government, Clive, after some hesitation, decided honestly and
wisely in favour of Mahommed Reza Khan, who had held 30
his high office seven years when Hastings became Governor.
An infant son of Meer Jaffier was now nabob; and the
guardianship of the young prince's person had been confided
to the minister.

Nuncomar, stimulated at once by cupidity and malice, had
been constantly attempting to undermine his successful

rival. This was not difficult. The revenues of Bengal,
under the administration established by Clive, did not yield
such a surplus as had been anticipated by the Company;
for, at that time, the most absurd notions were entertained
in England respecting the wealth of India. Palaces of
porphyry, hung with the richest brocade, heaps of pearls
and diamonds, vaults from which pagodas and gold mohurs
were measured out by the bushel, filled the imagination
even of men of business. Nobody seemed to be aware of
10 what nevertheless was most undoubtedly the truth, that
India was a poorer country than countries which in Europe
are reckoned poor, than Ireland, for example, or than Portugal. It was confidently believed by lords of the treasury
and members for the city that Bengal would not only defray
its own charges, but would afford an increased dividend to
the proprietors of India stock, and large relief to the
English finances. These absurd expectations were disappointed; and the directors, naturally enough, chose to
attribute the disappointment rather to the mismanagement
20 of Mahommed Reza Khan than to their own ignorance of
the country intrusted to their care. They were confirmed in
their error by the agents of Nuncomar; for Nuncomar had
agents even in Leadenhall Street. Soon after Hastings
reached Calcutta, he received a letter addressed by the Court
of Directors, not to the council generally, but to himself in
particular. He was directed to remove Mahommed Reza
Khan, to arrest him, together with all his family and all his
partisans, and to institute a strict inquiry into the whole
administration of the province. It was added that the
30 Governor would do well to avail himself of the assistance of
Nuncomar in the investigation. The vices of Nuncomar
were acknowledged. But even from his vices, it was said,
much advantage might at such a conjuncture be derived;
and, though he could not safely be trusted, it might still be
proper to encourage him by hopes of reward.
The Governor bore no good will to Nuncomar. Many

years before, they had known each other at Moorshedabad ;
and then a quarrel had risen between them which all the
authority of their superiors could hardly compose. Widely
as they differed in most points, they resembled each other
in this, that both were men of unforgiving natures. To
Mahommed Reza Khan, on the other hand, Hastings had no
feelings of hostility. Nevertheless he proceeded to execute
the instructions of the Company with an alacrity which he
never showed, except when instructions were in perfect conformity with his own views. He had, wisely as we think, 10
determined to get rid of the system of double government in
Bengal. The orders of the directors furnished him with the
means of effecting his purpose, and dispensed him from the
necessity of discussing the matter with his council. He took
his measures with his usual vigour and dexterity. At midnight, the palace of Mahommed Reza Khan at Moorshedabad was surrounded by a battalion of sepoys. The minister
was roused from his slumbers, and informed that he was a
prisoner. With the Mussulman gravity, he bent his head
and submitted himself to the will of God. He fell not 20
alone. A chief named Schitab Roy had been intrusted with
the government of Bahar. His valour and his attachment
to the English had more than once been signally proved.
On that memorable day on which the people of Patna saw
from their walls the whole army of the Mogul scattered by
the little band of Captain Knox, the voice of the British
conquerors assigned the palm of gallantry to the brave
Asiatic. "I never," said Knox, when he introduced Schitab
Roy, covered with blood and dust, to the English functionaries assembled in the factory, "I never saw a native fight 30
so before." Schitab Roy was involved in the ruin of Mahommed Reza Khan, was removed from office, and was
placed under arrest. The members of the council received
no intimation of these measures till the prisoners were on
their road to Calcutta.

35 The inquiry into the conduct of the minister was postponed

on different pretences. He was detained in an easy confinement during many months. In the mean time, the great
revolution which Hastings had planned was carried into
effect. The office of minister was abolished. The internal
administration was transferred to the servants of the Company. A system, a very imperfect system, it is true, of civil
and criminal justice, under English superintendence, was
established. The nabob was no longer to have even an
ostensible share in the government; but he was still to
receive a considerable annual allowance, and to be surrounded
with the state of sovereignty. As he was an infant, it was
necessary to provide guardians for his person and property.
His person was intrusted to a lady of his father's haram,
known by the name of the Munny Begum. The office of
treasurer of the household was bestowed on a son of Nuncomar, named Goordas. Nuncomar's services were wanted,
yet he could not safely be trusted with power; and Hastings
thought it a masterstroke of policy to reward the able and
unprincipled parent by promoting the inoffensive child.

The revolution completed, the double government dissolved, the Company installed in the full sovereignty of
Bengal, Hastings had no motive to treat the late ministers
with rigour. Their trial had been put off on various pleas
till the new organization was complete. They were then
brought before a committee, over which the Governor presided. Schitab Roy was speedily acquitted with honour.
A formal apology was made to him for the restraint to
which he had been subjected. All the Eastern marks of
respect were bestowed on him. He was clothed in a robe of
state, presented with jewels and with a richly harnessed
elephant, and sent back to his government at Patna. But
his health had suffered from confinement; his high spirit
had been cruelly wounded; and soon after his liberation he
died of a broken heart.

The innocence of Mahommed Reza Khan was not so clearly
established. But the Governor was not disposed to deal

harshly. After a long hearing, in which Nuncomar appeared as the accuser, and displayed both the art and the inveterate rancour which distinguished him, Hastings pronounced that the charges had not been made out, and ordered the fallen minister to be set at liberty.

Nuncomar had purposed to **destroy the Mussulman administration**, and to rise on its ruin. Both his malevolence and his cupidity had been disappointed. Hastings had made him a tool, had used him for the purpose of accomplishing the transfer of the government from Moorshedabad to Cal- 10 cutta, from native to European hands. The rival, the enemy, so long envied, so implacably persecuted, had been dismissed unhurt. The situation so long and ardently desired had been abolished. It was natural that the Governor should be from that time an object of the most intense hatred to the vindictive Brahmin. As yet, however, it was necessary to suppress such feelings. The time was coming when that long animosity was to end in a desperate and deadly struggle.

In the mean time, Hastings was compelled to turn his attention to foreign affairs. The object of his diplomacy was at this 20 time simply to get money. The finances of his government were in an embarrassed state ; and this embarrassment he was determined to relieve by some means, fair or foul. The principle which directed all his dealings with his neighbours is fully expressed by the old motto of one of the great predatory families of Teviotdale, "Thou shalt want ere I want." He seems to have laid it down, as a fundamental proposition which could not be disputed, that, when he had not as many lacs of rupees as the public service required, he was to take them from any body who had. One thing, 30 indeed, is to be said in excuse for him. The pressure applied to him by his employers at home, was such as only the highest virtue could have withstood, such as left him no choice except to commit great wrongs, or to resign his high post, and with that post all his hopes of fortune and distinction. The directors, it is true, never enjoined or applauded

any crime. Far from it. Whoever examines their letters
written at that time will find there many just and humane
sentiments, many excellent precepts, in short, an admirable
code of political ethics. But every exhortation is modified
or nullified by a demand for money. "Govern leniently,
and send more money; practise strict justice and moderation towards neighbouring powers, and send more money;"
this is in truth the sum of almost all the instructions that
Hastings ever received from home. Now these instructions,
10 being interpreted, mean simply, "Be the father and the
oppressor of the people; be just and unjust, moderate and
rapacious." The directors dealt with India, as the church, in
the good old times, dealt with a heretic. They delivered the
victim over to the executioners, with an earnest request that
all possible tenderness might be shown. We by no means
accuse or suspect those who framed these despatches of
hypocrisy. It is probable that, writing fifteen thousand
miles from the place where their orders were to be carried
into effect, they never perceived the gross inconsistency of
20 which they were guilty. But the inconsistency was at once
manifest to their lieutenant at Calcutta, who, with an empty
treasury, with an unpaid army, with his own salary often in
arrear, with deficient crops, with government tenants daily
running away, was called upon to remit home another half
million without fail. Hastings saw that it was absolutely
necessary for him to disregard either the moral discourses or
the pecuniary requisitions of his employers. Being forced to
disobey them in something, he had to consider what kind of
disobedience they would most readily pardon; and he cor-
30 rectly judged that the safest course would be to neglect the
sermons and to find the rupees.

A mind so fertile as his, and so little restrained by con-
scientious scruples, speedily discovered several modes of
relieving the financial embarrassments of the government.
The allowance of the Nabob of Bengal was reduced at a
stroke from three hundred and twenty thousand pounds a

year to half that sum. The Company had bound itself to
pay near three hundred thousand pounds a year to the great
Mogul, as a mark of homage for the provinces which he had
intrusted to their care; and they had ceded to him the
districts of Corah and Allahabad. On the plea that the
Mogul was not really independent, but merely a tool in the
hands of others, Hastings determined to retract these concessions. He accordingly declared that the English would
pay no more tribute, and sent troops to occupy Allahabad
and Corah. The situation of these places was such, that 10
there would be little advantage and great expense in retaining them. Hastings, who wanted money and not territory,
determined to sell them. A purchaser was not wanting.
The rich province of Oude had, in the general dissolution of
the Mogul Empire, fallen to the share of the great Mussulman house by which it is still governed. About twenty
years ago, this house, by the permission of the British
government, assumed the royal title; but, in the time of
Warren Hastings, such an assumption would have been
considered by the Mahommedans of India as a monstrous 20
impiety. The Prince of Oude, though he held the power,
did not venture to use the style of sovereignty. To the
appellation of Nabob or Viceroy, he added that of Vizier of
the monarchy of Hindostan, just as in the last century the
Electors of Saxony and Brandenburg, though independent of
the Emperor, and often in arms against him, were proud to
style themselves his Grand Chamberlain and Grand Marshal.
Sujah Dowlah, then Nabob Vizier, was on excellent terms
with the English. He had a large treasure. Allahabad and
Corah were so situated that they might be of use to him and 30
could be of none to the Company. The buyer and seller
soon came to an understanding; and the provinces which
had been torn from the Mogul were made over to the government of Oude for about half a million sterling.

But there was another matter still more important to be
settled by the Vizier and the Governor. The fate of a brave

people was to be decided. It was decided in a manner which has left a lasting stain on the fame of Hastings and of England.

The people of Central Asia had always been to the inhabitants of India what the warriors of the German forests were to the subjects of the decaying monarchy of Rome. The dark, slender, and timid Hindoo shrank from a conflict with the strong muscle and resolute spirit of the fair race, which dwelt beyond the passes. There is reason to believe that, at a period anterior to the dawn of regular history, the people who spoke the rich and flexible Sanscrit came from regions lying far beyond the Hyphasis and the Hystaspes, and imposed their yoke on the children of the soil. It is certain that, during the last ten centuries, a succession of invaders descended from the west on Hindostan : nor was the course of conquest ever turned back towards the setting sun, till that memorable campaign in which the cross of Saint George was planted on the walls of Ghizni.

The Emperors of Hindostan themselves came from the other side of the great mountain ridge ; and it had always been their practice to recruit their army from the hardy and valiant race from which their own illustrious house sprang. Among the military adventurers who were allured to the Mogul standards from the neighbourhood of Cabul and Candahar, were conspicuous several gallant bands, known by the name of the Rohillas. Their services had been rewarded with large tracts of land, fiefs of the spear, if we may use an expression drawn from an analogous state of things, in that fertile plain through which the Ramgunga flows from the snowy heights of Kumaon to join the Ganges. In the general confusion which followed the death of Aurungzebe, the warlike colony became virtually independent. The Rohillas were distinguished from the other inhabitants of India by a peculiarly fair complexion. They were more honourably distinguished by courage in war, and by skill in the arts of peace. While anarchy raged from Lahore to Cape

Comorin, their little territory enjoyed the blessings of repose
under the guardianship of valour. Agriculture and commerce flourished among them; nor were they negligent of
rhetoric and poetry. Many persons now living have heard
aged men talk with regret of the golden days when the
Afghan princes ruled in the vale of Rohilcund.

Sujah Dowlah had set his heart on adding this rich district
to his own principality. Right, or show of right, he had
absolutely none. His claim was in no respect better founded
than that of Catherine to Poland, or that of the Bonaparte
family to Spain. The Rohillas held their country by exactly
the same title by which he held his, and had governed their
country far better than his had ever been governed. Nor
were they a people whom it was perfectly safe to attack.
Their land was indeed an open plain, destitute of natural
defences; but their veins were full of the high blood of
Afghanistan. As soldiers, they had not the steadiness which
is seldom found except in company with strict discipline;
but their impetuous valour had been proved on many fields
of battle. It was said that their chiefs, when united by
common peril, could bring eighty thousand men into the
field. Sujah Dowlah had himself seen them fight, and wisely
shrank from a conflict with them. There was in India one
army, and only one, against which even those proud Caucasian tribes could not stand. It had been abundantly
proved that neither tenfold odds, nor the martial ardour
of the boldest Asiatic nations, could avail aught against
English science and resolution. Was it possible to induce
the Governor of Bengal to let out to hire the irresistible
energies of the imperial people, the skill against which the
ablest chiefs of Hindostan were helpless as infants, the discipline which had so often triumphed over the frantic
struggles of fanaticism and despair, the unconquerable
British courage which is never so sedate and stubborn as
towards the close of a doubtful and murderous day?

This was what the Nabob Vizier asked, and what Hastings

granted. A bargain was soon struck. Each of the negotiators had what the other wanted. Hastings was in need of
funds to carry on the government of Bengal, and to send
remittances to London ; and Sujah Dowlah had an ample
revenue. Sujah Dowlah was bent on subjugating the Rohillas ; and Hastings had at his disposal the only force by
which the Rohillas could be subjugated. It was agreed that
an English army should be lent to the Nabob Vizier, and
that, for the loan, he should pay four hundred thousand
10 pounds sterling, besides defraying all the charge of the troops
while employed in his service.

" I really cannot see," says the Reverend Mr. Gleig, " upon
what grounds, either of political or moral justice, this proposition deserves to be stigmatized as infamous." If we understand the meaning of words, it is infamous to commit a
wicked action for hire, and it is wicked to engage in war
without provocation. In this particular war, scarcely one
aggravating circumstance was wanting. The object of the
Rohilla war was this, to deprive a large population, who had
20 never done us the least harm, of a good government, and to
place them, against their will, under an execrably bad one.
Nay, even this is not all. England now descended far below
the level even of those petty German princes who, about the
same time, sold us troops to fight the Americans. The hussar-
mongers of Hesse and Anspach had at least the assurance
that the expeditions on which their soldiers were to be employed would be conducted in conformity with the humane
rules of civilised warfare. Was the Rohilla war likely to be
so conducted ? Did the Governor stipulate that it should be
30 so conducted ? He well knew what Indian warfare was. He
well knew that the power which he covenanted to put into
Sujah Dowlah's hands would, in all probability, be atrociously
abused ; and he required no guarantee, no promise that it
should not be so abused. He did not even reserve to himself
the right of withdrawing his aid in case of abuse, however
gross. Mr. Gleig repeats Major Scott's absurd plea, that

Hastings was justified in letting out English troops to slaughter the Rohillas, because the Rohillas were not of Indian race, but a colony from a distant country. What were the English themselves? Was it for them to proclaim a crusade for the expulsion of all intruders from the countries watered by the Ganges? Did it lie in their mouths to contend that a foreign settler who establishes an empire in India is a *caput lupinum?* What would they have said if any other power had, on such a ground, attacked Madras or Calcutta, without the slightest provocation? Such a defence 10 was wanting to make the infamy of the transaction complete. The atrocity of the crime, and the hypocrisy of the apology, are worthy of each other.

One of the three brigades of which the Bengal army consisted was sent under Colonel Champion to join Sujah Dowlah's forces. The Rohillas expostulated, entreated, offered a large ransom, but in vain. They then resolved to defend themselves to the last. A bloody battle was fought. "The enemy," says Colonel Champion, "gave proof of a good share of military knowledge ; and it is impossible 20 to describe a more obstinate firmness of resolution than they displayed." The dastardly sovereign of Oude fled from the field. The English were left unsupported ; but their fire and their charge were irresistible. It was not, however, till the most distinguished chiefs had fallen, fighting bravely at the head of their troops, that the Rohilla ranks gave way. Then the Nabob Vizier and his rabble made their appearance, and hastened to plunder the camp of the valiant enemies, whom they had never dared to look in the face. The soldiers of the Company, trained in an exact discipline, 30 kept unbroken order, while the tents were pillaged by these worthless allies. But many voices were heard to exclaim, " We have had all the fighting, and those rogues are to have all the profit."

Then the horrors of Indian war were let loose on the fair valleys and cities of Rohilcund. The whole country was in

a blaze. More than a hundred thousand people fled from
their homes to pestilential jungles, preferring famine, and
fever, and the haunts of tigers, to the tyranny of him, to
whom an English and a Christian government had, for
shameful lucre, sold their substance, and their blood, and
the honour of their wives and daughters. Colonel Champion
remonstrated with the Nabob Vizier, and sent strong representations to Fort William ; but the Governor had made no
conditions as to the mode in which the war was to be carried
10 on. He had troubled himself about nothing but his forty
lacs ; and, though he might disapprove of Sujah Dowlah's
wanton barbarity, he did not think himself entitled to interfere, except by offering advice. This delicacy excites the
admiration of the reverend biographer. "Mr. Hastings,"
he says, "could not himself dictate to the Nabob, nor permit
the commander of the Company's troops to dictate how the
war was to be carried on." No, to be sure. Mr. Hastings
had only to put down by main force the brave struggles of
innocent men fighting for their liberty. Their military
20 resistance crushed, his duties ended ; and he had then only
to fold his arms and look on, while their villages were
burned, their children butchered, and their women violated.
Will Mr. Gleig seriously maintain this opinion ? Is any
rule more plain than this, that whoever voluntarily gives to
another irresistible power over human beings, is bound to
take order that such power shall not be barbarously abused ?
But we beg pardon of our readers for arguing a point so
clear.

We hasten to the end of this sad and disgraceful story.
30 The war ceased. The finest population in India was subjected to a greedy, cowardly, cruel tyrant. Commerce and
agriculture languished. The rich province which had
tempted the cupidity of Sujah Dowlah became the most
miserable part even of his miserable dominions. Yet is the
injured nation not extinct. At long intervals gleams of its
ancient spirit have flashed forth ; and even at this day,

valour, and self-respect, and a chivalrous feeling rare among
Asiatics, and a bitter remembrance of the great crime of
England, distinguish that noble Afghan race. To this day
they are regarded as the best of all sepoys at the cold steel ;
and it was very recently remarked, by one who had enjoyed
great opportunities of observation, that the only natives of
India to whom the word " gentleman " can with perfect propriety be applied are to be found among the Rohillas.

Whatever we may think of the morality of Hastings, it
cannot be denied that the financial results of his policy did
honour to his talents. In less than two years after he
assumed the government, he had, without imposing any
additional burdens on the people subject to his authority,
added about four hundred and fifty thousand pounds to the
annual income of the Company, besides procuring about a
million in ready money. He had also relieved the finances
of Bengal from military expenditure, amounting to near a
quarter of a million a year, and had thrown that charge on
the Nabob of Oude. There can be no doubt that this was a
result which, if it had been obtained by honest means, would
have entitled him to the warmest gratitude of his country,
and which, by whatever means obtained, proved that he
possessed great talents for administration.

In the mean time, Parliament had been engaged in long
and grave discussions on Asiatic affairs. The ministry of
Lord North, in the session of 1773, introduced a measure
which made a considerable change in the constitution of the
Indian government. This law, known by the name of the
Regulating Act, provided that the presidency of Bengal
should exercise a control over the other possessions of the
Company ; that the chief of that presidency should be styled
Governor-General ; that he should be assisted by four Councillors ; and that a supreme court of judicature, consisting of
a chief justice and three inferior judges, should be established at Calcutta. This court was made independent of the
Governor-General and Council, and was intrusted with a

civil and criminal jurisdiction of immense, and, at the same time, of undefined extent.

The Governor-General and Councillors were named in the act, and were to hold their situations for five years. Hastings was to be the first Governor-General. One of the four new Councillors, Mr. Barwell, an experienced servant of the Company, was then in India. The other three, General Clavering, Mr. Monson, and Mr. Francis, were sent out from England.

The ablest of the new Councillors was, beyond all doubt, Philip Francis. His acknowledged compositions prove that he possessed considerable eloquence and information. Several years passed in the public offices had formed him to habits of business. His enemies have never denied that he had a fearless and manly spirit; and his friends, we are afraid, must acknowledge that his estimate of himself was extravagantly high, that his temper was irritable, that his deportment was often rude and petulant, and that his hatred was of intense bitterness and of long duration.

It is scarcely possible to mention this eminent man without adverting for a moment to the question which his name at once suggests to every mind. Was he the author of the Letters of Junius? Our own firm belief is that he was. The evidence is, we think, such as would support a verdict in a civil, nay, in a criminal proceeding. The handwriting of Junius is the very peculiar handwriting of Francis, slightly disguised. As to the position, pursuits, and connections of Junius, the following are the most important facts which can be considered as clearly proved: first, that he was acquainted with the technical forms of the secretary of state's office; secondly, that he was intimately acquainted with the business of the war-office; thirdly, that he, during the year 1770, attended debates in the House of Lords, and took notes of speeches, particularly of the speeches of Lord Chatham; fourthly, that he bitterly resented the appointment of Mr. Chamier to the place of deputy secretary-at-war; fifthly, that he was bound by some strong tie to the first Lord Holland. Now, Francis passed some years in the secretary of state's office. He was subsequently chief clerk of the war-office. He repeatedly mentioned that he had himself, in 1770, heard speeches of Lord Chatham; and some of these speeches were actually printed from his notes. He resigned his clerkship at the war-office from resentment at the appointment of Mr. Chamier. It was by Lord Holland that he was first introduced into the public service. Now, here are five marks, all of which ought to be found in Junius. They are all five found in Francis. We do not believe that more than two of them can be found in any other person whatever. If this argument does not settle the question, there is an end of all reasoning on circumstantial evidence.

The internal evidence seems to us to point the same way. The style of Francis bears a strong resemblance to that of Junius; nor are we disposed to admit, what is generally taken for granted, that the acknowledged compositions of Francis are very decidedly inferior to the anonymous letters. The argument from inferiority, at all events, is one which may be urged with at least equal force against every claimant that has ever been mentioned, with the single exception of Burke; and it would be a waste of time to prove that Burke was not Junius. And what conclusion, after all, can be drawn from mere inferiority? Every writer must produce his best work; and the interval between his best work and his second best work may be very wide indeed. Nobody will say that the best letters of Junius are more decidedly superior to the acknowledged works of Francis than three or four of Corneille's tragedies to the rest, than three or four of Ben Jonson's comedies to the rest, than the Pilgrim's Progress to the other works of Bunyan, than Don Quixote to the other works of Cervantes. Nay, it is certain that the Man in the Mask, whoever he may have been, was a most unequal writer. To go no further than the letters

c

which bear the signature of Junius; the letter to the
king, and the letters to Horne Tooke, have little in common, except the asperity; and asperity was an ingredient
seldom wanting either in the writings or in the speeches of
Francis.

Indeed one of the strongest reasons for believing that
Francis was Junius is the moral resemblance between the
two men. It is not difficult, from the letters which, under
various signatures, are known to have been written by
10 Junius, and from his dealings with Woodfall and others, to
form a tolerably correct notion of his character. He was
clearly a man not destitute of real patriotism and magnanimity, a man whose vices were not of a sordid kind. But
he must also have been a man in the highest degree arrogant
and insolent, a man prone to malevolence, and prone to the
error of mistaking his malevolence for public virtue. "Doest
thou well to be angry?" was the question asked in old time
of the Hebrew prophet. And he answered, "I do well."
This was evidently the temper of Junius; and to this cause
20 we attribute the savage cruelty which disgraces several of
his letters. No man is so merciless as he who, under a
strong self-delusion, confounds his antipathies with his
duties. It may be added that Junius, though allied with
the democratic party by common enmities, was the very
opposite of a democratic politician. While attacking individuals with a ferocity which perpetually violated all the
laws of literary warfare, he regarded the most defective
parts of old institutions with a respect amounting to
pedantry, pleaded the cause of Old Sarum with fervour,
30 and contemptuously told the capitalists of Manchester and
Leeds that, if they wanted votes, they might buy land and
become freeholders of Lancashire and Yorkshire. All this,
we believe, might stand, with scarcely any change, for a
character of Philip Francis.

It is not strange that the great anonymous writer should
have been willing at that time to leave the country which

had been so powerfully stirred by his eloquence. Every thing had gone against him. That party which he clearly preferred to every other, the party of George Grenville, had been scattered by the death of its chief; and Lord Suffolk had led the greater part of it over to the ministerial benches. The ferment produced by the Middlesex election had gone down. Every faction must have been alike an object of aversion to Junius. His opinions on domestic affairs separated him from the ministry; his opinions on colonial affairs from the opposition. Under such circumstances, he had 10 thrown down his pen in misanthropical despair. His farewell letter to Woodfall bears date the nineteenth of January, 1773. In that letter, he declared that he must be an idiot to write again; that he had meant well by the cause and the public; that both were given up; that there were not ten men who would act steadily together on any question. "But it is all alike," he added, "vile and contemptible. You have never flinched that I know of; and I shall always rejoice to hear of your prosperity." These were the last words of Junius. In a year from that time, Philip Francis was on his 20 voyage to Bengal.

With the three new Councillors came out the judges of the Supreme Court. The chief justice was Sir Elijah Impey. He was an old acquaintance of Hastings; and it is probable that the Governor-General, if he had searched through all the inns of court, could not have found an equally serviceable tool. But the members of Council were by no means in an obsequious mood. Hastings greatly disliked the new form of government, and had no very high opinion of his coadjutors. They had heard of this, and were disposed to be 30 suspicious and punctilious. When men are in such a frame of mind, any trifle is sufficient to give occasion for dispute. The members of Council expected a salute of twenty-one guns from the batteries of Fort William. Hastings allowed them only seventeen. They landed in ill-humour. The first civilities were exchanged with cold reserve. On the morrow commenced that long quarrel which, after distracting British India, **was** renewed in England, and in which all the most eminent statesmen and orators of the age took active part on one or the other side.

Hastings was supported by Barwell. **They had not always been friends.** But the arrival of the new members of Council from England naturally had the effect of uniting the old servants of the Company. Clavering, Monson, and Francis formed the majority. They instantly wrested the government out of the hands of Hastings; condemned, certainly not without justice, his late dealings with the Nabob Vizier; recalled the English agent from Oude, and sent thither a creature of their own; ordered the brigade which had conquered the unhappy Rohillas to return to the Company's territories; and instituted a severe inquiry into the conduct of the war. Next, in spite of the Governor-General's remonstrances, they proceeded to exercise, in the most indiscreet manner, their new authority over the subordinate presidencies; threw all the affairs of Bombay into confusion; and interfered, with an incredible union of rashness and feebleness, in the intestine disputes of the Mahratta government. At the same time, they fell on the internal administration of Bengal, and attacked the whole fiscal and judicial system, a system which was undoubtedly defective, but which it was very improbable that gentlemen fresh from England would be competent to amend. The effect of their reforms was that all protection to life and property was withdrawn, and that gangs of robbers plundered and slaughtered with impunity in the very suburbs of Calcutta. Hastings continued to live in the Government-house, and to draw the salary of Governor-General. He continued even to take the lead at the council-board in the transaction of ordinary business; for his opponents could not but feel that he knew much of which they were ignorant, and that he decided, both surely and speedily, many questions which to them would have been hopelessly puzzling. But the higher powers of government and the most valuable patronage had been taken from him.

The natives soon found this out. They considered him as a fallen man; and they acted after their kind. Some of our readers may have seen, in India, a cloud of crows pecking a sick vulture to death, no bad type of what happens in that country, as often as fortune deserts one who has been great and dreaded. In an instant, all the sycophants who had lately been ready to lie for him, to forge for him, to pandar for him, to poison for him, hasten to purchase the favour 10 of his victorious enemies by accusing him. An Indian government has only to let it be understood that it wishes a particular man to be ruined; and, in twenty-four hours, it will be furnished with grave charges, supported by depositions so full and circumstantial that any person unaccustomed to Asiatic mendacity would regard them as decisive. It is well if the signature of the destined victim is not counterfeited at the foot of some illegal compact, and if some treasonable paper is not slipped into a hiding-place in his house. Hastings was now regarded as helpless. The 20 power to make or mar the fortune of every man in Bengal had passed, as it seemed, into the hands of the new Councillors. Immediately charges against the Governor-General began to pour in. They were eagerly welcomed by the majority, who, to do them justice, were men of too much honour knowingly to countenance false accusations, but who were not sufficiently acquainted with the East to be aware that, in that part of the world, a very little encouragement from power will call forth, in a week, more Oateses, and Bedloes, and Dangerfields, than Westminster Hall sees in a 30 century.

It would have been strange indeed if, at such a juncture, Nuncomar had remained quiet. That bad man was stimulated at once by malignity, by avarice, and by ambition. Now was the time to be avenged on his old enemy, to wreak a grudge of seventeen years, to establish himself in the

favour of the majority of the Council, to become the greatest
native in Bengal. From the time of the arrival of the new
Councillors, he had paid the most marked court to them, and
had in consequence been excluded, with all indignity, from
the Government-house. He now put into the hands of
Francis, with great ceremony, a paper containing several
charges of the most serious description. By this document
Hastings was accused of putting offices up to sale, and of
receiving bribes for suffering offenders to escape. In par-
10 ticular, it was alleged that Mahommed Reza Khan had been
dismissed with impunity, in consideration of a great sum
paid to the Governor-General.

Francis read the paper in Council. A violent altercation
followed. Hastings complained in bitter terms of the way
in which he was treated, spoke with contempt of Nuncomar
and of Nuncomar's accusation, and denied the right of the
Council to sit in judgment on the Governor. At the next
meeting of the Board, another communication from Nuncomar was produced. He requested that he might be
20 permitted to attend the Council, and that he might be heard
in support of his assertions. Another tempestuous debate
took place. The Governor-General maintained that the
council-room was not a proper place for such an investigation ; that from persons who were heated by daily conflict
with him he could not expect the fairness of judges ; and
that he could not, without betraying the dignity of his post,
submit to be confronted with such a man as Nuncomar.
The majority, however, resolved to go into the charges.
Hastings rose, declared the sitting at an end, and left the
30 room followed by Barwell. The other members kept their
seats, voted themselves a council, put Clavering in the chair,
and ordered Nuncomar to be called in. Nuncomar not only
adhered to the original charges, but, after the fashion of the
East, produced a large supplement. He stated that Hastings had received a great sum for appointing Rajah Goordas
treasurer of the Nabob's household, and for committing the

care of his Highness's person to the Munny Begum. He put in a letter purporting to bear the seal of the Munny Begum, for the purpose of establishing the truth of his story. The seal, whether forged, as Hastings affirmed, or genuine, as we are rather inclined to believe, proved nothing. Nuncomar, as every body knows who knows India, had only to tell the Munny Begum that such a letter would give pleasure to the majority of the Council, in order to procure her attestation. The majority, however, voted that the charge was made out ; that Hastings had corruptly received 10 between thirty and forty thousand pounds ; and that he ought to be compelled to refund.

The general feeling among the English in Bengal was strongly in favour of the Governor-General. In talents for business, in knowledge of the country, in general courtesy of demeanour, he was decidedly superior to his persecutors. The servants of the Company were naturally disposed to side with the most distinguished member of their own body against a clerk from the war-office, who, profoundly ignorant of the native languages and the native 20 character, took on himself to regulate every department of the administration. Hastings, however, in spite of the general sympathy of his countrymen, was in a most painful situation. There was still an appeal to higher authority in England. If that authority took part with his enemies, nothing was left to him but to throw up his office. He accordingly placed his resignation in the hands of his agent in London, Colonel Macleane. But Macleane was instructed not to produce the resignation, unless it should be fully ascertained that the feeling at the India House was adverse 30 to the Governor-General.

The triumph of Nuncomar seemed to be complete. He held a daily levee, to which his countrymen resorted in crowds, and to which, on one occasion, the majority of the Council condescended to repair. His house was an office for the purpose of receiving charges against the Governor-

General. It was said that, partly by threats, and partly by wheedling, the villanous Brahmin had induced many of the wealthiest men of the province to send in complaints. But he was playing a perilous game. (It was not safe to drive to despair a man of such resources and of such determination as Hastings.) Nuncomar, with all his acuteness, did not understand the nature of the institutions under which he lived. He saw that he had with him the majority of the body which made treaties, gave places, raised taxes.
10 The separation between political and judicial functions was a thing of which he had no conception. It had probably never occurred to him that there was in Bengal an authority perfectly independent of the Council, an authority which could protect one whom the Council wished to destroy, and send to the gibbet one whom the Council wished to protect. Yet such was the fact. The Supreme Court was, within the sphere of its own duties, altogether independent of the Government. Hastings, with his usual sagacity, had seen how much advantage he might derive from possessing
20 himself of this stronghold; and he had acted accordingly. The Judges, especially the Chief Justice, were hostile to the majority of the Council. The time had now come for putting this formidable machinery into action.

On a sudden, Calcutta was astounded by the news that Nuncomar had been taken up on a charge of felony, committed, and thrown into the common gaol. The crime imputed to him was that six years before he had forged a bond. The ostensible prosecutor was a native. But it was then, and still is, the opinion of every body, idiots and biographers
30 excepted, that Hastings was the real mover in the business. The rage of the majority rose to the highest point. They protested against the proceedings of the Supreme Court, and sent several urgent messages to the Judges, demanding that Nuncomar should be admitted to bail. The Judges returned haughty and resolute answers. All that the Council could do was to heap honours and emoluments on the family of

Nuncomar; and this they did. In the mean time the assizes commenced; a true bill was found; and Nuncomar was brought before Sir Elijah Impey and a jury composed of Englishmen. A great quantity of contradictory swearing, and the necessity of having every word of the evidence interpreted, protracted the trial to a most unusual length. At last a verdict of guilty was returned, and the Chief Justice pronounced sentence of death on the prisoner.

Mr. Gleig is so strangely ignorant as to imagine that the judges had no further discretion in the case, and that the 10 power of extending mercy to Nuncomar resided with the Council. He therefore throws on Francis and Francis's party the whole blame of what followed. We should have thought that a gentleman who has published five or six bulky volumes on Indian affairs might have taken the trouble to inform himself as to the fundamental principles of the Indian Government. The Supreme Court had, under the Regulating Act, the power to respite criminals till the pleasure of the Crown should be known. The Council had, at that time, no power to interfere. 20

That Impey ought to have respited Nuncomar we hold to be perfectly clear. Whether the whole proceeding was not illegal, is a question. But it is certain that, whatever may have been, according to technical rules of construction, the effect of the statute under which the trial took place, it was most unjust to hang a Hindoo for forgery. The law which made forgery capital in England was passed without the smallest reference to the state of society in India. It was unknown to the natives of India. It had never been put in execution among them, certainly not for want of delinquents. 30 It was in the highest degree shocking to all their notions. They were not accustomed to the distinction which many circumstances, peculiar to our own state of society, have led us to make between forgery and other kinds of cheating. The counterfeiting of a seal was, in their estimation, a common act of swindling; nor had it ever crossed their minds that it was to be punished as severely as gang-robbery or assassination. A just judge would, beyond all doubt, have reserved the case for the consideration of the sovereign. But Impey would not hear of mercy or delay.

The excitement among all classes was great. Francis and Francis's few English adherents described the Governor-General and the Chief Justice as the worst of murderers. Clavering, it was said, swore that, even at the foot of the gallows, Nuncomar should be rescued. The bulk of the European society, though strongly attached to the Governor-General, could not but feel compassion for a man who, with all his crimes, had so long filled so large a space in their sight, who had been great and powerful before the British empire in India began to exist, and to whom, in the old times, governors and members of council, then mere commercial factors, had paid court for protection. The feeling of the Hindoos was infinitely stronger. They were, indeed, not a people to strike one blow for their countryman. But his sentence filled them with sorrow and dismay. Tried even by their low standard of morality, he was a bad man. But, bad as he was, he was the head of their race and religion, a Brahmin of the Brahmins. He had inherited the purest and highest caste. He had practised with the greatest punctuality all those ceremonies to which the superstitious Bengalees ascribe far more importance than to the correct discharge of the social duties. They felt, therefore, as a devout Catholic in the dark ages would have felt, at seeing a prelate of the highest dignity sent to the gallows by a secular tribunal. According to their old national laws, a Brahmin could not be put to death for any crime whatever. And the crime for which Nuncomar was about to die was regarded by them in much the same light in which the selling of an unsound horse, for a sound price, is regarded by a Yorkshire jockey.

The Mussulmans alone appear to have seen with exultation the fate of the powerful Hindoo, who had attempted to rise by means of the ruin of Mahommed Reza Khan. The

Mahommedan historian of those times takes delight in
aggravating the charge. He assures us that in Nuncomar's
house a casket was found containing counterfeits of the seals
of all the richest men of the province. We have never fallen
in with any other authority for this story, which in itself is
by no means improbable.

The day drew near; and Nuncomar prepared himself to
die with that quiet fortitude with which the Bengalee, so
effeminately timid in personal conflict, often encounters
calamities for which there is no remedy. The sheriff, with 10
the humanity which is seldom wanting in an English gentleman, visited the prisoner on the eve of the execution, and
assured him that no indulgence, consistent with the law,
should be refused to him. Nuncomar expressed his gratitude with great politeness and unaltered composure. Not
a muscle of his face moved. Not a sigh broke from him.
He put his finger to his forehead, and calmly said that fate
would have its way, and that there was no resisting the
pleasure of God. He sent his compliments to Francis,
Clavering, and Monson, and charged them to protect Rajah 20
Goordas, who was about to become the head of the Brahmins
of Bengal. The sheriff withdrew, greatly agitated by what
had passed, and Nuncomar sat composedly down to write
notes and examine accounts.

The next morning, before the sun was in his power, an
immense concourse assembled round the place where the
gallows had been set up. Grief and horror were on every
face; yet to the last the multitude could hardly believe that
the English really purposed to take the life of the great
Brahmin. At length the mournful procession came through 30
the crowd. Nuncomar sat up in his palanquin, and looked
round him with unaltered serenity. He had just parted
from those who were most nearly connected with him.
Their cries and contortions had appalled the European
ministers of justice, but had not produced the smallest
effect on the iron stoicism of the prisoner. The only anxiety

which he expressed was that men of his own priestly caste might be in attendance to take charge of his corpse. He again desired to be remembered to his friends in the Council, mounted the scaffold with firmness, and gave the signal to the executioner. The moment that the drop fell, a howl of sorrow and despair rose from the innumerable spectators. Hundreds turned away their faces from the polluting sight, fled with loud wailings towards the Hoogley, and plunged into its holy waters, as if to purify themselves from the guilt
10 of having looked on such a crime. These feelings were not confined to Calcutta. The whole province was greatly excited; and the population of Dacca, in particular, gave strong signs of grief and dismay.

Of Impey's conduct it is impossible to speak too severely. We have already said that, in our opinion, he acted unjustly in refusing to respite Nuncomar. No rational man can doubt that he took this course in order to gratify the Governor-General. If we had ever had any doubts on that point, they would have been dispelled by a letter which Mr. Gleig has
20 published. Hastings, three or four years later, described Impey as the man "to whose support he was at one time indebted for the safety of his fortune, honour, and reputation." These strong words can refer only to the case of Nuncomar; and they must mean that Impey hanged Nuncomar in order to support Hastings. It is, therefore, our deliberate opinion that Impey, sitting as a judge, put a man unjustly to death in order to serve a political purpose.

But we look on the conduct of Hastings in a somewhat different light. He was struggling for fortune, honour,
30 liberty, all that makes life valuable. He was beset by rancorous and unprincipled enemies. From his colleagues he could expect no justice. He cannot be blamed for wishing to crush his accusers. He was indeed bound to use only legitimate means for that end. But it was not strange that he should have thought any means legitimate which were pronounced legitimate by the sages of the law, by men whose

peculiar duty it was to deal justly between adversaries, and whose education might be supposed to have peculiarly qualified them for the discharge of that duty. Nobody demands from a party the unbending equity of a judge. The reason that judges are appointed is, that even a good man cannot be trusted to decide a cause in which he is himself concerned. Not a day passes on which an honest prosecutor does not ask for what none but a dishonest tribunal would grant. It is too much to expect that any man, when his dearest interests are at stake, and his strongest passions excited, will, as 10 against himself, be more just than the sworn dispensers of justice. To take an analogous case from the history of our own island : suppose that Lord Stafford, when in the Tower on suspicion of being concerned in the Popish plot, had been apprised that Titus Oates had done something which might, by a questionable construction, be brought under the head of felony. Should we severely blame Lord Stafford, in the supposed case, for causing a prosecution to be instituted, for furnishing funds, for using all his influence to intercept the mercy of the Crown? We think not. If a judge, indeed, 20 from favour to the Catholic lords, were to strain the law in order to hang Oates, such a judge would richly deserve impeachment. But it does not appear to us that the Catholic lord, by bringing the case before the judge for decision, would materially overstep the limits of a just self-defence.

While, therefore, we have not the least doubt that this memorable execution is to be attributed to Hastings, we doubt whether it can with justice be reckoned among his crimes. That his conduct was dictated by a profound policy is evident. He was in a minority in Council. It was possible 30 that he might long be in a minority. He knew the native character well. He knew in what abundance accusations are certain to flow in against the most innocent inhabitant of India who is under the frown of power. There was not in the whole black population of Bengal a place-holder, a place-hunter, a government tenant, who did not think that he might better himself by sending up a deposition against the Governor-General. Under these circumstances, the persecuted statesman resolved to teach the whole crew of accusers and witnesses that, though in a minority at the council board, he was still to be feared. The lesson which he gave them was indeed a lesson not to be forgotten. The head of the combination which had been formed against him, the richest, the most powerful, the most artful of the Hindoos, distinguished by the favour of those who then held the government, fenced 10 round by the superstitious reverence of millions, was hanged in broad day before many thousands of people. Every thing that could make the warning impressive, dignity in the sufferer, solemnity in the proceeding, was found in this case. The helpless rage and vain struggles of the Council made the triumph more signal. From that moment the conviction of every native was that it was safer to take the part of Hastings in a minority than that of Francis in a majority, and that he who was so venturous as to join in running down the Governor-General might chance, in the phrase of the 20 Eastern poet, to find a tiger, while beating the jungle for a deer. The voices of a thousand informers were silenced in an instant. From that time, whatever difficulties Hastings might have to encounter, he was never molested by accusations from natives of India.

75 It is a remarkable circumstance that one of the letters of Hastings to Dr. Johnson bears date a very few hours after the death of Nuncomar. While the whole settlement was in commotion, while a mighty and ancient priesthood were weeping over the remains of their chief, the conqueror in 30 that deadly grapple sat down, with characteristic self-possession, to write about the Tour to the Hebrides, Jones's Persian Grammar, and the history, traditions, arts, and natural productions of India.

76 In the mean time, intelligence of the Rohilla war, and of the first disputes between Hastings and his colleagues, had reached London. The directors took part with the majority,

and sent out a letter filled with severe reflections on the conduct of Hastings. They condemned, in strong but just terms,
the iniquity of undertaking offensive wars merely for the
sake of pecuniary advantages. But they utterly forgot that,
if Hastings had by illicit means obtained pecuniary advantages, he had done so, not for his own benefit, but in order to
meet their demands. To enjoin honesty, and to insist on
having what could not be honestly got, was then the constant
practice of the Company. As Lady Macbeth says of her
husband, they "would not play false, and yet would wrongly 10
win."

The Regulating Act, by which Hastings had been appointed Governor-General for five years, empowered the
Crown to remove him on an address from the Company.
Lord North was desirous to procure such an address. The
three members of Council who had been sent out from England were men of his own choice. General Clavering, in
particular, was supported by a large parliamentary connection, such as no cabinet could be inclined to disoblige. The
wish of the Minister was to displace Hastings, and to put 20
Clavering at the head of the government. In the Court of
Directors parties were very nearly balanced. Eleven voted
against Hastings; ten for him. The Court of Proprietors
was then convened. The great sale-room presented a singular
appearance. Letters had been sent by the Secretary of the
Treasury, exhorting all the supporters of government who
held India stock to be in attendance. Lord Sandwich marshalled the friends of the administration with his usual
dexterity and alertness. Fifty peers and privy councillors,
seldom seen so far eastward, were counted in the crowd. 30
The debate lasted till midnight. The opponents of Hastings
had a small superiority on the division; but a ballot was
demanded; and the result was that the Governor-General
triumphed by a majority of above a hundred votes over the
combined efforts of the Directors and the Cabinet. The ministers were greatly exasperated by this defeat. Even Lord

North lost his temper, no ordinary occurrence with him, and threatened to convoke parliament before Christmas, and to bring in a bill for depriving the Company of all political power, and for restricting it to its old business of trading in silks and teas.

Colonel Macleane, who through all this conflict had zealously supported the cause of Hastings, now thought that his employer was in imminent danger of being turned out, branded with parliamentary censure, perhaps prosecuted. The opinion of the crown lawyers had already been taken respecting some parts of the Governor-General's conduct. It seemed to be high time to think of securing an honourable retreat. Under these circumstances, Macleane thought himself justified in producing the resignation with which he had been intrusted. The instrument was not in very accurate form ; but the Directors were too eager to be scrupulous. They accepted the resignation, fixed on Mr. Wheler, one of their own body, to succeed Hastings, and sent out orders that General Clavering, as senior member of Council, should exercise the functions of Governor-General till Mr. Wheler should arrive.

But, while these things were passing in England, a great change had taken place in Bengal. Monson was no more. Only four members of the government were left. Clavering and Francis were on one side, Barwell and the Governor-General on the other ; and the Governor-General had the casting vote. Hastings, who had been during two years destitute of all power and patronage, became at once absolute. He instantly proceeded to retaliate on his adversaries. Their measures were reversed : their creatures were displaced. A new valuation of the lands of Bengal, for the purposes of taxation, was ordered ; and it was provided that the whole inquiry should be conducted by the Governor-General, and that all the letters relating to it should run in his name. He began, at the same time, to revolve vast plans of conquest and dominion, plans which he lived to see realised, though not by himself. His project was to form subsidiary alliances with the native princes, particularly with those of Oude and Berar, and thus to make Britain the paramount power in India. While he was meditating these great designs, arrived the intelligence that he had ceased to be Governor-General, that his resignation had been accepted, that Wheler was coming out immediately, and that, till Wheler arrived, the chair was to be filled by Clavering.

Had Hastings still been in a minority, he would probably have retired without a struggle; but he was now the real 10 master of British India, and he was not disposed to quit his high place. He asserted that he had never given any instructions which could warrant the steps taken at home. What his instructions had been, he owned he had forgotten. If he had kept a copy of them he had mislaid it. But he was certain that he had repeatedly declared to the Directors that he would not resign. He could not see how the court, possessed of that declaration from himself, could receive his resignation from the doubtful hands of an agent. If the resignation were invalid, all the proceedings which were 20 founded on that resignation were null, and Hastings was still Governor-General.

He afterwards affirmed that, though his agents had not acted in conformity with his instructions, he would nevertheless have held himself bound by their acts, if Clavering had not attempted to seize the supreme power by violence. Whether this assertion were or were not true, it cannot be doubted that the imprudence of Clavering gave Hastings an advantage. The General sent for the keys of the fort and of the treasury, took possession of the records, and held a 30 council at which Francis attended. Hastings took the chair in another apartment, and Barwell sat with him. Each of the two parties had a plausible show of right. There was no authority entitled to their obedience within fifteen thousand miles. It seemed that there remained no way of settling the dispute except an appeal to arms; and from such an

D

appeal Hastings, confident of his influence over his countrymen in India, was not inclined to shrink. He directed the
officers of the garrison of Fort William and of all the neighbouring stations to obey no orders but his. At the same
time, with admirable judgment, he offered to submit the
case to the Supreme Court, and to abide by its decision. By
making this proposition he risked nothing; yet it was a
proposition which his opponents could hardly reject. Nobody could be treated as a criminal for obeying what the
10 judges should solemnly pronounce to be the lawful government. The boldest man would shrink from taking arms in
defence of what the judges should pronounce to be usurpation. Clavering and Francis, after some delay, unwillingly
consented to abide by the award of the court. The court
pronounced that the resignation was invalid, and that
therefore Hastings was still Governor-General under the
Regulating Act; and the defeated members of the Council,
finding that the sense of the whole settlement was against
them, acquiesced in the decision.

20 ¶ 2 About this time arrived the news that, after a suit
which had lasted several years, the Franconian courts had
decreed a divorce between Imhoff and his wife. The Baron
left Calcutta, carrying with him the means of buying an
estate in Saxony. The lady became Mrs. Hastings. The
event was celebrated by great festivities; and all the most
conspicuous persons at Calcutta, without distinction of
parties, were invited to the Government-house. Clavering,
as the Mahommedan chronicler tells the story, was sick
in mind and body, and excused himself from joining the
30 splendid assembly. But Hastings, whom, as it should seem,
success in ambition and in love had put into high good-
humour, would take no denial. He went himself to the
General's house, and at length brought his vanquished rival
in triumph to the gay circle which surrounded the bride.
The exertion was too much for a frame broken by mortification as well as by disease. Clavering died a few days later.

82 Wheler, who came out expecting to be Governor-General, and was forced to content himself with a seat at the Council Board, generally voted with Francis. But the Governor-General, with Barwell's help and his own casting vote, was still the master. Some change took place at this time in the feeling both of the Court of Directors and of the Ministers of the Crown. All designs against Hastings were dropped ; and when his original term of five years expired, he was quietly re-appointed. The truth is, that the fearful dangers to which the public interests in every quarter were now 10 exposed, made both Lord North and the Company unwilling to part with a Governor whose talents, experience, and resolution, enmity itself was compelled to acknowledge.

83 The crisis was indeed formidable. That great and victorious empire, on the throne of which George the Third had taken his seat eighteen years before, with brighter hopes than had attended the accession of any of the long line of English sovereigns, had, by the most senseless misgovernment, been brought to the verge of ruin. In America millions of Englishmen were at war with the country from 20 which their blood, their language, their religion, and their institutions were derived, and to which, but a short time before, they had been as strongly attached as the inhabitants of Norfolk and Leicestershire. The great powers of Europe, humbled to the dust by the vigour and genius which had guided the councils of George the Second, now rejoiced in the prospect of a signal revenge. The time was approaching when our island, while struggling to keep down the United States of America, and pressed with a still nearer danger by the too just discontents of Ireland, was to be assailed by 30 France, Spain, and Holland, and to be threatened by the armed neutrality of the Baltic ; when even our maritime supremacy was to be in jeopardy ; when hostile fleets were to command the Straits of Calpe and the Mexican Sea ; when the British flag was to be scarcely able to protect the British Channel. Great as were the faults of Hastings, it

was happy for our country that at that conjuncture, the
most terrible through which she has ever passed, he was
the ruler of her Indian dominions.

¶ 4 An attack by sea on Bengal was little to be apprehended.
The danger was that the European enemies of England
might form an alliance with some native power, might
furnish that power with troops, arms, and ammunition, and
might thus assail our possessions on the side of the land.
It was chiefly from the Mahrattas that Hastings anticipated
10 danger. The original seat of that singular people was the
wild range of hills which runs along the western coast of
India. In the reign of Aurungzebe the inhabitants of those
regions, led by the great Sevajee, began to descend on the
possessions of their wealthier and less warlike neighbours.
The energy, ferocity, and cunning of the Mahrattas, soon
made them the most conspicuous among the new powers
which were generated by the corruption of the decaying
monarchy. At first they were only robbers. They soon rose
to the dignity of conquerors. Half the provinces of the
20 empire were turned into Mahratta principalities. Freebooters, sprung from low castes, and accustomed to menial
employments, became mighty Rajahs. The Bonslas, at the
head of a band of plunderers, occupied the vast region of
Berar. The Guicowar, which is, being interpreted, the
Herdsman, founded that dynasty which still reigns in
Guzerat. The houses of Scindia and Holkar waxed great
in Malwa. One adventurous captain made his nest on the
inpregnable rock of Gooti. Another became the lord of the
thousand villages which are scattered among the green rice-
30 fields of Tanjore.

§ 5 That was the time, throughout India, of double government. The form and the power were every where separated.
The Mussulman nabobs who had become sovereign princes,
the Vizier in Oude, and the Nizam at Hyderabad, still called
themselves the viceroys of the house of Tamerlane. In the
same manner the Mahratta states, though really independent

of each other, pretended to be members of one empire. They all acknowledged, by words and ceremonies, the supremacy of the heir of Sevajee, a *roi fainéant* who chewed bang and toyed with dancing girls in a state prison at Sattara, and of his Peshwa or mayor of the palace, a great hereditary magistrate, who kept a court with kingly state at Poonah, and whose authority was obeyed in the spacious provinces of Aurungabad and Bejapoor.

16 Some months before war was declared in **Europe** the government of Bengal was alarmed by the news that a 10 French adventurer, who passed for a man of quality, had arrived at Poonah. It was said that he had been received there with great distinction, that he had delivered to the Peshwa letters and presents from Louis the Sixteenth, and that a treaty, hostile to England, had been concluded between France and the Mahrattas.

17 Hastings immediately resolved to strike the first blow. The title of the Peshwa was not undisputed. A portion of the Mahratta nation was favourable to a pretender. The Governor-General determined to espouse this pretender's 20 interest, to move an army across the peninsula of India, and to form a close alliance with the chief of the house of Bonsla, who ruled Berar, and who, in power and dignity, was inferior to none of the Mahratta princes.

18 The army had marched, and the negotiations with Berar were in progress, when a letter from the English consul at Cairo brought the news that war had been proclaimed both in London and Paris. All the measures which the crisis required were adopted by Hastings without a moment's delay. The French factories in Bengal were seized. Orders 30 were sent to Madras that Pondicherry should instantly be occupied. Near Calcutta, works were thrown up which were thought to render the approach of a hostile force impossible. A maritime establishment was formed for the defence of the river. Nine new battalions of sepoys were raised, and a corps of native artillery was formed out of the hardy Lascars

of the Bay of Bengal. Having made these arrangements, the Governor-General with calm confidence pronounced his presidency secure from all attack, unless the Mahrattas should march against it in conjunction with the French.

The expedition which Hastings had sent westward was not so speedily or completely successful as most of his undertakings. The commanding officer procrastinated. The authorities at Bombay blundered. But the Governor-General persevered. A new commander repaired the errors of his predecessor. Several brilliant actions spread the military renown of the English through regions where no European flag had ever been seen. It is probable that, if a new and more formidable danger had not compelled Hastings to change his whole policy, his plans respecting the Mahratta empire would have been carried into complete effect.

The authorities in England had wisely sent out to Bengal, as commander of the forces and member of the council, one of the most distinguished soldiers of that time. Sir Eyre Coote had, many years before, been conspicuous among the founders of the British empire in the East. At the council of war which preceded the battle of Plassey, he earnestly recommended, in opposition to the majority, that daring course which, after some hesitation, was adopted, and which was crowned with such splendid success. He subsequently commanded in the south of India against the brave and unfortunate Lally, gained the decisive battle of Wandewash over the French and their native allies, took Pondicherry, and made the English power supreme in the Carnatic. Since those great exploits near twenty years had elapsed. Coote had no longer the bodily activity which he had shown in earlier days ; nor was the vigour of his mind altogether unimpaired. He was capricious and fretful, and required much coaxing to keep him in good humour. It must, we fear, be added that the love of money had grown upon him, and that he thought more about his allowances, and less about his duties, than might have been expected from so eminent a

member of so noble a profession. Still he was perhaps the
ablest officer that was then to be found in the British army.
Among the native soldiers his name was great and his
influence unrivalled. Nor is he yet forgotten by them.
Now and then a white-bearded old sepoy may still be found,
who loves to talk of Porto Novo and Pollilore. It is but a
short time since one of those aged men came to present a
memorial to an English officer, who holds one of the highest
employments in India. A print of Coote hung in the room.
The veteran recognised at once that face and figure which he 10
had not seen for more than half a century, and, forgetting
his salam to the living, halted, drew himself up, lifted his
hand, and with solemn reverence paid his military obeisance
to the dead.

Coote, though he did not, like Barwell, vote constantly
with the Governor-General, was by no means inclined to join
in systematic opposition, and on most questions concurred
with Hastings, who did his best, by assiduous courtship, and
by readily granting the most exorbitant allowances, to
gratify the strongest passions of the old soldier.   20

It seemed likely at this time that a general reconciliation
would put an end to the quarrels which had, during some
years, weakened and disgraced the government of Bengal.
The dangers of the empire might well induce men of
patriotic feeling—and of patriotic feeling neither Hastings
nor Francis was destitute—to forget private enmities, and to
co-operate heartily for the general good. Coote had never
been concerned in faction. Wheler was thoroughly tired of
it. Barwell had made an ample fortune, and, though he had
promised that he would not leave Calcutta while his help was 30
needed in Council, was most desirous to return to England,
and exerted himself to promote an arrangement which would
set him at liberty. A compact was made, by which Francis
agreed to desist from opposition, and Hastings engaged that
the friends of Francis should be admitted to a fair share of
the honours and emoluments of the service. During a few

months after this treaty there was apparent harmony at the council-board.

9 2 Harmony, indeed, was never more necessary ; for at this moment internal calamities, more formidable than war itself, menaced Bengal. The authors of the Regulating Act of 1773 had established two independent powers, the one judicial, the other political ; and, with a carelessness scandalously common in English legislation, had omitted to define the limits of either. The judges took advantage of the indistinct-
10 ness, and attempted to draw to themselves supreme authority, not only within Calcutta, but through the whole of the great territory subject to the presidency of Fort William. There are few Englishmen who will not admit that the English law, in spite of modern improvements, is neither so cheap nor so speedy as might be wished. Still, it is a system which has grown up among us. In some points, it has been fashioned to suit our feelings ; in others, it has gradually fashioned our feelings to suit itself. Even to its worst evils we are accustomed ; and, therefore, though we may complain
20 of them, they do not strike us with the horror and dismay which would be produced by a new grievance of smaller severity. In India the case is widely different. English law, transplanted to that country, has all the vices from which we suffer here ; it has them all in a far higher degree ; and it has other vices, compared with which the worst vices from which we suffer are trifles. Dilatory here, it is far more dilatory in a land where the help of an interpreter is needed by every judge and by every advocate. Costly here, it is far more costly in a land into which the legal practi-
30 tioners must be imported from an immense distance. All English labour in India, from the labour of the Governor-General and the Commander-in-Chief, down to that of a groom or a watchmaker, must be paid for at a higher rate than at home. No man will be banished, and banished to the torrid zone, for nothing. The rule holds good with respect to the legal profession. No English barrister will

work, fifteen thousand miles from all his friends, with the
thermometer at ninety-six in the shade, for the emoluments
which will content him in chambers that overlook the
Thames. Accordingly, the fees at Calcutta are about three
times as great as the fees of Westminster Hall; and this,
though the people of India are, beyond all comparison, poorer
than the people of England. Yet the delay and the expense,
grievous as they are, form the smallest part of the evil which
English law, imported without modifications into India,
could not fail to produce. The strongest feelings of our 10
nature, honour, religion, female modesty, rose up against the
innovation. Arrest on mesne process was the first step in
most civil proceedings; and to a native of rank arrest was
not merely a restraint, but a foul personal indignity. Oaths
were required in every stage of every suit; and the feeling
of a Quaker about an oath is hardly stronger than that of a
respectable native. That the apartments of a woman of
quality should be entered by strange men, or that her face
should be seen by them, are, in the East, intolerable outrages, outrages which are more dreaded than death, and 20
which can be expiated only by the shedding of blood. To
these outrages the most distinguished families of Bengal,
Bahar, and Orissa, were now exposed. Imagine what the
state of our own country would be, if a jurisprudence were
on a sudden introduced among us, which should be to us
what our jurisprudence was to our Asiatic subjects. Imagine
what the state of our country would be, if it were enacted
that any man, by merely swearing that a debt was due to
him, should acquire a right to insult the persons of men of
the most honourable and sacred callings and of women of the 30
most shrinking delicacy, to horsewhip a general officer, to put
a bishop in the stocks, to treat ladies in the way which called
forth the blow of Wat Tyler. Something like this was the
effect of the attempt which the Supreme Court made to
extend its jurisdiction over the whole of the Company's
territory.

A reign of terror began, of terror heightened by mystery; for even that which was endured was less horrible than that which was anticipated. No man knew what was next to be expected from this strange tribunal. It came from beyond the black water, as the people of India, with mysterious horror, call the sea. It consisted of judges not one of whom was familiar with the usages of the millions over whom they claimed boundless authority Its records were kept in unknown characters; its sentences were pronounced in

10 unknown sounds. It had already collected round itself an army of the worst part of the native population, informers, and false witnesses, and common barrators, and agents of chicane, and, above all, a banditti of bailiffs' followers, compared with whom the retainers of the worst English spunging-houses, in the worst times, might be considered as upright and tender-hearted. Many natives, highly considered among their countrymen, were seized, hurried up to Calcutta, flung into the common gaol, not for any crime even imputed, not for any debt that had been proved, but

20 merely as a precaution till their cause should come to trial. There were instances in which men of the most venerable dignity, persecuted without a cause by extortioners, died of rage and shame in the gripe of the vile alguazils of Impey. The harams of noble Mahommedans, sanctuaries respected in the East, by governments which respected nothing else, were burst open by gangs of bailiffs. The Mussulmans, braver and less accustomed to submission than the Hindoos, sometimes stood on their defence; and there were instances in which they shed their blood in the doorway, while

30 defending, sword in hand, the sacred apartments of their women. Nay, it seemed as if even the faint-hearted Bengalee, who had crouched at the feet of Surajah Dowlah, who had been mute during the administration of Vansittart, would at length find courage in despair. No Mahratta invasion had ever spread through the province such dismay as this inroad of English lawyers. All the injustice of

former oppressors, Asiatic and European, appeared as a blessing when compared with the justice of the Supreme Court.

Every class of the population, English and native, with the exception of the ravenous pettifoggers who fattened on the misery and terror of an immense community, cried out loudly against this fearful oppression. But the judges were immovable. If a bailiff was resisted, they ordered the soldiers to be called out. If a servant of the Company, in conformity with the orders of the government, withstood 10 the miserable catchpoles who, with Impey's writs in their hands, exceeded the insolence and rapacity of gang-robbers, he was flung into prison for a contempt. The lapse of sixty years, the virtue and wisdom of many eminent magistrates who have during that time administered justice in the Supreme Court, have not effaced from the minds of the people of Bengal the recollection of those evil days.

The members of the government were, on this subject, united as one man. Hastings had courted the judges; he had found them useful instruments. But he was not dis- 20 posed to make them his own masters, or the masters of India. His mind was large; his knowledge of the native character most accurate. He saw that the system pursued by the Supreme Court was degrading to the government and ruinous to the people; and he resolved to oppose it manfully. The consequence was, that the friendship, if that be the proper word for such a connection, which had existed between him and Impey, was for a time completely dissolved. The government placed itself firmly between the tyrannical tribunal and the people. The Chief Justice pro- 30 ceeded to the wildest excesses. The Governor-General and all the members of Council were served with writs, calling on them to appear before the King's justices, and to answer for their public acts. This was too much. Hastings, with just scorn, refused to obey the call, set at liberty the persons wrongfully detained by the Court, and took measures for

resisting the outrageous proceedings of the sheriffs' officers, if necessary, by the sword. But he had in view another device which might prevent the necessity of an appeal to arms. He was seldom at a loss for an expedient; and he knew Impey well. The expedient, in this case, was a very simple one, neither more nor less than a bribe. Impey was, by act of parliament, a judge, independent of the government of Bengal, and entitled to a salary of eight thousand a year. Hastings proposed to make him also a judge in the
10 Company's service, removable at the pleasure of the government of Bengal; and to give him, in that capacity, about eight thousand a year more. It was understood that, in consideration of this new salary, Impey would desist from urging the high pretensions of his court. If he did urge these pretensions, the government could, at a moment's notice, eject him from the new place which had been created for him. The bargain was struck; Bengal was saved; an appeal to force was averted; and the Chief Justice was rich, quiet, and infamous.

20 Of Impey's conduct it is unnecessary to speak. It was of a piece with almost every part of his conduct that comes under the notice of history. No other such judge has dishonoured the English ermine, since Jefferies drank himself to death in the Tower. But we cannot agree with those who have blamed Hastings for this transaction. The case stood thus. The negligent manner in which the Regulating Act had been framed put it in the power of the Chief Justice to throw a great country into the most dreadful confusion. He was determined to use his power to the
30 utmost, unless he was paid to be still: and Hastings consented to pay him . The necessity was to be deplored. It is also to be deplored that pirates should be able to exact ransom by threatening to make their captives walk the plank. But to ransom a captive from pirates has always been held a humane and Christian act; and it would be absurd to charge the payer of the ransom with corrupting

the virtue of the corsair. This, we seriously think, is a
not unfair illustration of the relative position of Impey,
Hastings, and the people of India. Whether it was right
in Impey to demand or to accept a price for powers which,
if they really belonged to him, he could not abdicate, which,
if they did not belong to him, he ought never to have
usurped, and which in neither case he could honestly sell,
is one question. It is quite another question, whether
Hastings was not right to give any sum, however large, to
any man, however worthless, rather than either surrender 10
millions of human beings to pillage, or rescue them by civil
war.

Francis strongly opposed this arrangement. It may,
indeed, be suspected that personal aversion to Impey was
as strong a motive with Francis as regard for the welfare
of the province. To a mind burning with resentment, it
might seem better to leave Bengal to the oppressors than
to redeem it by enriching them. It is not improbable, on
the other hand, that Hastings may have been the more
willing to resort to an expedient agreeable to the Chief 20
Justice, because that high functionary had already been so
serviceable, and might, when existing dissensions were composed, be serviceable again.

But it was not on this point alone that Francis was now
opposed to Hastings. The peace between them proved to be
only a short and hollow truce, during which their mutual
aversion was constantly becoming stronger. At length an
explosion took place. Hastings publicly charged Francis
with having deceived him, and with having induced Barwell
to quit the service by insincere promises. Then came a dis- 30
pute, such as frequently arises even between honourable men,
when they may make important agreements by mere verbal
communication. An impartial historian will probably be of
opinion that they had misunderstood each other; but their
minds were so much embittered that they imputed to each
other nothing less than deliberate villany. "I do not," said

Hastings, in a minute recorded on the Consultations of the
Government, "I do not trust to Mr. Francis's promises of
candour, convinced that he is incapable of it. I judge of his
public conduct by his private, which I have found to be void
of truth and honour." After the Council had risen, Francis
put a challenge into the Governor-General's hand. It was
instantly accepted. They met, and fired. Francis was shot
through the body. He was carried to a neighbouring house,
where it appeared that the wound, though severe, was not
10 mortal. Hastings inquired repeatedly after his enemy's
health, and proposed to call on him; but Francis coldly
declined the visit. He had a proper sense, he said, of the
Governor-General's politeness, but could not consent to any
private interview. They could meet only at the council-
board.

In a very short time it was made signally manifest to how
great a danger the Governor-General had, on this occasion,
exposed his country. A crisis arrived with which he, and he
alone, was competent to deal. It is not too much to say that,
20 if he had been taken from the head of affairs, the years 1780
and 1781 would have been as fatal to our power in Asia as to
our power in America.

The Mahrattas had been the chief objects of apprehension
to Hastings. The measures which he had adopted for the
purpose of breaking their power, had at first been frustrated
by the errors of those whom he was compelled to employ;
but his perseverance and ability seemed likely to be crowned
with success, when a far more formidable danger showed
itself in a distant quarter.

30 About thirty years before this time, a Mahommedan
soldier had begun to distinguish himself in the wars of
Southern India. His education had been neglected; his
extraction was humble. His father had been a petty officer
of revenue; his grandfather a wandering dervise. But
though thus meanly descended, though ignorant even of
the alphabet, the adventurer had no sooner been placed at

the head of a body of troops than he approved himself a
man born for conquest and command. Among the crowd
of chiefs who were struggling for a share of India, none
could compare with him in the qualities of the captain and
the statesman. He became a general; he became a sovereign. Out of the fragments of old principalities, which
had gone to pieces in the general wreck, he formed for
himself a great, compact, and vigorous empire. That empire
he ruled with the ability, severity, and vigilance of Louis
the Eleventh. Licentious in his pleasures, implacable in 10
his revenge, he had yet enlargement of mind enough to
perceive how much the prosperity of subjects adds to the
strength of governments. He was an oppressor; but he
had at least the merit of protecting his people against all
oppression except his own. He was now in extreme old
age; but his intellect was as clear, and his spirit as high,
as in the prime of manhood. Such was the great Hyder
Ali, the founder of the Mahommedan kingdom of Mysore,
and the most formidable enemy with whom the English
conquerors of India have ever had to contend. 20

102 Had Hastings been governor of Madras, Hyder would
have been either made a friend, or vigorously encountered
as an enemy. Unhappily the English authorities in the
south provoked their powerful neighbour's hostility, without being prepared to repel it. On a sudden, an army of
ninety thousand men, far superior in discipline and effici-
ency to any other native force that could be found in
India, came pouring through those wild passes which, worn
by mountain torrents, and dark with jungle, lead down from
the table-land of Mysore to the plains of the Carnatic. This 30
great army was accompanied by a hundred pieces of cannon;
and its movements were guided by many French officers,
trained in the best military schools of Europe.

103 Hyder was every where triumphant. The sepoys in many
British garrisons flung down their arms. Some forts were
surrendered by treachery, and some by despair. In a few

days the whole open country north of the Coleroon had submitted. The English inhabitants of Madras could already
see by night, from the top of Mount St. Thomas, the eastern
sky reddened by a vast semicircle of blazing villages. The
white villas, to which our countrymen retire after the daily
labours of government and of trade, when the cool evening
breeze springs up from the bay, were now left without
inhabitants ; for bands of the fierce horsemen of Mysore
had already been seen prowling among the tulip-trees, and
10 near the gay verandas. Even the town was not thought
secure, and the British merchants and public functionaries
made haste to crowd themselves behind the cannon of Fort
St. George.

There were the means indeed of assembling an army
which might have defended the presidency, and even driven
the invader back to his mountains. Sir Hector Munro
was at the head of one considerable force ; Baillie was
advancing with another. United, they might have presented a formidable front even to such an enemy as Hyder.
20 But the English commanders, neglecting those fundamental
rules of the military art of which the propriety is obvious
even to men who had never received a military education,
deferred their junction, and were separately attacked.
Baillie's detachment was destroyed. Munro was forced to
abandon his baggage, to fling his guns into the tanks, and
to save himself by a retreat which might be called a
flight. In three weeks from the commencement of the
war, the British empire in Southern India had been
brought to the verge of ruin. Only a few fortified places
30 remained to us. The glory of our arms had departed. It
was known that a great French expedition might soon be
expected on the coast of Coromandel. England, beset by
enemies on every side, was in no condition to protect such
remote dependencies.

Then it was that the fertile genius and serene courage of
Hastings achieved their most signal triumph. A swift ship,

flying before the south-west monsoon, brought the evil
tidings in few days to Calcutta. In twenty-four hours the
Governor-General had framed a complete plan of policy
adapted to the altered state of affairs. The struggle with
Hyder was a struggle for life and death. All minor objects
must be sacrificed to the preservation of the Carnatic.
The disputes with the Mahrattas must be accommodated.
A large military force and a supply of money must be
instantly sent to Madras. But even these measures would
be insufficient, unless the war, hitherto so grossly mis- 10
managed, were placed under the direction of a vigorous
mind. It was no time for trifling. Hastings determined to
resort to an extreme exercise of power, to suspend the
incapable governor of Fort St. George, to send Sir Eyre
Coote to oppose Hyder, and to intrust that distinguished
general with the whole administration of the war.

In spite of the sullen opposition of Francis, who had now
recovered from his wound, and had returned to the Council,
the Governor-General's wise and firm policy was approved
by the majority of the board. The reinforcements were 20
sent off with great expedition, and reached Madras before
the French armament arrived in the Indian seas. Coote,
broken by age and disease, was no longer the Coote of
Wandewash; but he was still a resolute and skilful commander. The progress of Hyder was arrested; and in a
few months the great victory of Porto Novo retrieved the
honour of the English arms.

In the mean time Francis had returned to England, and
Hastings was now left perfectly unfettered. Wheler had
gradually been relaxing in his opposition, and, after the 30
departure of his vehement and implacable colleague, co-
operated heartily with the Governor-General, whose influence over the British in India, always great, had, by the
vigour and success of his recent measures, been considerably
increased.

But, though the difficulties arising from factions within

E

the Council were at an end, another class of difficulties had
become more pressing than ever. The financial embarrassment was extreme. Hastings had to find the means, not
only of carrying on the government of Bengal, but of maintaining a most costly war against both Indian and European
enemies in the Carnatic, and of making remittances to
England. A few years before this time he had obtained
relief by plundering the Mogul and enslaving the Rohillas ;
nor were the resources of his fruitful mind by any means
10 exhausted.

His first design was on Benares, a city which in wealth,
population, dignity, and sanctity, was among the foremost of
Asia. It was commonly believed that half a million of
human beings was crowded into that labyrinth of lofty
alleys, rich with shrines, and minarets, and balconies, and
carved oriels, to which the sacred apes clung by hundreds.
The traveller could scarcely make his way through the press
of holy mendicants and not less holy bulls. The broad and
stately flights of steps which descended from these swarming
20 haunts to the bathing-places along the Ganges were worn
every day by the footsteps of an innumerable multitude of
worshippers. The schools and temples drew crowds of pious
Hindoos from every province where the Brahminical faith
was known. Hundreds of devotees came thither every
month to die : for it was believed that a peculiarly happy
fate awaited the man who should pass from the sacred city
into the sacred river. Nor was superstition the only motive
which allured strangers to that great metropolis. Commerce
had as many pilgrims as religion. All along the shores of
30 the venerable stream lay great fleets of vessels laden with
rich merchandise. From the looms of Benares went forth
the most delicate silks that adorned the balls of St. James's
and of the *Petit Trianon :* and in the bazaars the muslins of
Bengal and the sabres of Oude were mingled with the jewels
of Golconda and the shawls of Cashmere. This rich capital,
and the surrounding tract, had long been under the immedi-

ate rule of a Hindoo prince who rendered homage to the Mogul emperors. During the great anarchy of India the lords of Benares became independent of the court of Delhi, but were compelled to submit to the authority of the Nabob of Oude. Oppressed by this formidable neighbour, they invoked the protection of the English. The English protection was given ; and at length the Nabob Vizier, by a solemn treaty, ceded all his rights over Benares to the Company. From that time the Rajah was the vassal of the government of Bengal, acknowledged its supremacy, and 10 engaged to send an annual tribute to Fort William. This tribute Cheyte Sing, the reigning prince, had paid with strict punctuality.

Respecting the precise nature of the legal relation between the Company and the Rajah of Benares, there has been much warm and acute controversy. On the one side, it has been maintained that Cheyte Sing was merely a great subject on whom the superior power had a right to call for aid in the necessities of the empire. On the other side it has been contended that he was an independent prince, that the only 20 claim which the Company had upon him was for a fixed tribute, and that, while the fixed tribute was regularly paid, as it assuredly was, the English had no more right to exact any further contribution from him than to demand subsidies from Holland or Denmark. Nothing is easier than to find precedents and analogies in favour of either view.

Our own impression is that neither view is correct. It was too much the habit of English politicians to take it for granted that there was in India a known and definite constitution by which questions of this kind were to be decided. 30 The truth is that, during the interval which elapsed between the fall of the House of Tamerlane and the establishment of the British ascendency, there was no such constitution. The old order of things had psssed away : the new order of things was not yet formed. All was transition, confusion, obscurity. Every body kept his head as he best might, and

scrambled for whatever he could get. There have been
similar seasons in Europe. The time of the dissolution of
the Carlovingian empire is an instance. Who would think
of seriously discussing the question, what extent of pecuniary
aid and of obedience Hugh Capet had a constitutional right
to demand from the Duke of Brittany or the Duke of Normandy? The words "constitutional right" had, in that
state of society, no meaning. If Hugh Capet laid hands on
all the possessions of the Duke of Normandy, this might be
10 unjust and immoral; but it would not be illegal, in the
sense in which the ordinances of Charles the Tenth were
illegal. If, on the other hand, the Duke of Normandy made
war on Hugh Capet, this might be unjust and immoral; but
it would not be illegal, in the sense in which the expedition
of Prince Louis Bonaparte was illegal.

Very similar to this was the state of India sixty years ago.
Of the existing governments not a single one could lay claim
to legitimacy, or could plead any other title than recent
occupation. There was scarcely a province in which the real
20 sovereignty and the nominal sovereignty were not disjoined.
Titles and forms were still retained which implied that the
heir of Tamerlane was an absolute ruler, and that the
Nabobs of the provinces were his lieutenants. In reality, he
was a captive. The Nabobs were in some places independent
princes. In other places, as in Bengal and the Carnatic,
they had, like their master, become mere phantoms, and the
Company was supreme. Among the Mahrattas again the
heir of Sevajee still kept the title of Rajah; but he was a
prisoner, and his prime minister, the Peshwa, had become
30 the hereditary chief of the state. The Peshwa, in his turn,
was fast sinking into the same degraded situation to which
he had reduced the Rajah. It was, we believe, impossible to
find, from the Himalayas to Mysore, a single government
which was at once a government *de facto* and a government
de jure, which possessed the physical means of making itself
feared by its neighbours and subjects, and which had at

the same time the authority derived from law and long prescription.

3 Hastings clearly discerned, what was hidden from most of his contemporaries, that such a state of things gave immense advantages to a ruler of great talents and few scruples. In every international question that could arise, he had his option between the *de facto* ground and the *de jure* ground; and the probability was that one of those grounds would sustain any claim that it might be convenient for him to make, and enable him to resist any claim 10 made by others. In every controversy, accordingly, he resorted to the plea which suited his immediate purpose, without troubling himself in the least about consistency; and thus he scarcely ever failed to find what, to persons of short memories and scanty information, seemed to be a justification for what he wanted to do. Sometimes the Nabob of Bengal is a shadow, sometimes a monarch. Sometimes the Vizier is a mere deputy, sometimes an independent potentate. If it is expedient for the Company to show some legal title to the revenues of Bengal, the grant 20 under the seal of the Mogul is brought forward as an instrument of the highest authority. When the Mogul asks for the rents which were reserved to him by that very grant, he is told that he is a mere pageant, that the English power rests on a very different foundation from a charter given by him, that he is welcome to play at royalty as long as he likes, but that he must expect no tribute from the real masters of India.

4 It is true that it was in the power of others, as well as of Hastings, to practise this legerdemain; but in the contro- 30 versies of governments, sophistry is of little use unless it be backed by power. There is a principle which Hastings was fond of asserting in the strongest terms, and on which he acted with undeviating steadiness. It is a principle which, we must own, though it may be grossly abused, can hardly be disputed in the present state of public law. It

is this, that where an ambiguous question arises between two governments, there is, if they cannot agree, no appeal except to force, and that the opinion of the stronger must prevail. Almost every question was ambiguous in India. The English government was the strongest in India. The consequences are obvious. The English government might do exactly what it chose.

The English government now chose to wring money out of Cheyte Sing. It had formerly been convenient to treat 10 him as a sovereign prince; it was now convenient to treat him as a subject. Dexterity inferior to that of Hastings could easily find, in the general chaos of laws and customs, arguments for either course. Hastings wanted a great supply. It was known that Cheyte Sing had a large revenue, and it was suspected that he had accumulated a treasure. Nor was he a favourite at Calcutta. He had, when the Governor-General was in great difficulties, courted the favour of Francis and Clavering. Hastings who, less we believe from evil passions than from policy, seldom left 20 an injury unpunished, was not sorry that the fate of Cheyte Sing should teach neighbouring princes the same lesson which the fate of Nuncomar had already impressed on the inhabitants of Bengal.

In 1778, on the first breaking out of the war with France, Cheyte Sing was called upon to pay, in addition to his fixed tribute, an extraordinary contribution of fifty thousand pounds. In 1779, an equal sum was exacted. In 1780, the demand was renewed. Cheyte Sing, in the hope of obtaining some indulgence, secretly offered the Governor-30 General a bribe of twenty thousand pounds. Hastings took the money, and his enemies have maintained that he took it intending to keep it. He certainly concealed the transaction, for a time, both from the Council in Bengal and from the Directors at home; nor did he ever give any satisfactory reason for the concealment. Public spirit, or the fear of detection, however, determined him to withstand the temptation. He paid over the bribe to the Company's treasury, and insisted that the Rajah should instantly comply with the demands of the English government. The Rajah, after the fashion of his countrymen, shuffled, solicited, and pleaded poverty. The grasp of Hastings was not to be so eluded. He added to the requisition another ten thousand pounds as a fine for delay, and sent troops to exact the money.

The money was paid. But this was not enough. The late events in the south of India had increased the financial 10 embarrassments of the Company. Hastings was determined to plunder Cheyte Sing, and, for that end, to fasten a quarrel on him. Accordingly, the Rajah was now required to keep a body of cavalry for the service of the British government. He objected and evaded. This was exactly what the Governor-General wanted. He had now a pretext for treating the wealthiest of his vassals as a criminal. "I resolved"—these are the words of Hastings himself—"to draw from his guilt the means of relief to the Company's distresses, to make him pay largely for 20 his pardon, or to exact a severe vengeance for past delinquency." The plan was simply this, to demand larger and larger contributions till the Rajah should be driven to remonstrate, then to call his remonstrance a crime, and to punish him by confiscating all his possessions.

Cheyte Sing was in the greatest dismay. He offered two hundred thousand pounds to propitiate the British government. But Hastings replied that nothing less than half a million would be accepted. Nay, he began to think of selling Benares to Oude, as he had formerly sold Allahabad 30 and Rohilcund. The matter was one which could not be well managed at a distance ; and Hastings resolved to visit Benares.

Cheyte Sing received his liege lord with every mark of reverence, came near sixty miles, with his guards, to meet and escort the illustrious visitor, and expressed his deep

concern at the displeasure of the English. He even took
off his turban, and laid it in the lap of Hastings, a gesture
which in India marks the most profound submission and
devotion. Hastings behaved with cold and repulsive severity. Having arrived at Benares, he sent to the Rajah a
paper containing the demands of the government of Bengal.
The Rajah, in reply, attempted to clear himself from the
accusations brought against him. Hastings, who wanted
money and not excuses, was not to be put off by the ordi-
10 nary artifices of Eastern negotiation. He instantly ordered
the Rajah to be arrested and placed under the custody of
two companies of sepoys.

In taking these strong measures, Hastings scarcely showed
his usual judgment. It is probable that, having had little
opportunity of personally observing any part of the population of India, except the Bengalees, he was not fully aware
of the difference between their character and that of the
tribes which inhabit the upper provinces. He was now
in a land far more favourable to the vigour of the human
20 frame than the Delta of the Ganges; in a land fruitful of
soldiers, who have been found worthy to follow English
battalions to the charge and into the breach. The Rajah
was popular among his subjects. His administration had
been mild; and the prosperity of the district which he
governed presented a striking contrast to the depressed
state of Bahar under our rule, and a still more striking
contrast to the misery of the provinces which were cursed
by the tyranny of the Nabob Vizier. The national and
religious prejudices with which the English were regarded
30 throughout India were peculiarly intense in the metropolis
of the Brahminical superstition. It can therefore scarcely
be doubted that the Governor-General, before he outraged
the dignity of Cheyte Sing by an arrest, ought to have
assembled a force capable of bearing down all opposition.
This had not been done. The handful of sepoys who
attended Hastings would probably have been sufficient to

overawe Moorshedabad, or the Black Town of Calcutta.
But they were unequal to a conflict with the hardy rabble
of Benares. The streets surrounding the palace were filled
by an immense multitude, of whom a large proportion,
as is usual in Upper India, wore arms. The tumult became
a fight, and the fight a massacre. The English officers
defended themselves with desperate courage against over-
whelming numbers, and fell, as became them, sword in
hand. The sepoys were butchered. The gates were forced.
The captive prince, neglected by his jailers during the 10
confusion, discovered an outlet which opened on the preci-
pitous bank of the Ganges, let himself down to the water
by a string made of the turbans of his attendants, found a
boat, and escaped to the opposite shore.

If Hastings had, by indiscreet violence, brought himself
into a difficult and perilous situation, it is only just to
acknowledge that he extricated himself with even more than
his usual ability and presence of mind. He had only fifty
men with him. The building in which he had taken up his
residence was on every side blockaded by the insurgents. 20
But his fortitude remained unshaken. The Rajah from the
other side of the river sent apologies and liberal offers.
They were not even answered. Some subtle and enterpris-
ing men were found who undertook to pass through the
throng of enemies, and to convey the intelligence of the
late events to the English cantonments. It is the fashion of
the natives of India to wear large earrings of gold. When
they travel, the rings are laid aside, lest the precious metal
should tempt some gang of robbers, and, in place of the ring,
a quill or a roll of paper is inserted in the orifice to prevent 30
it from closing. Hastings placed in the ears of his messengers
letters rolled up in the smallest compass. Some of these
letters were addressed to the commanders of the English
troops. One was written to assure his wife of his safety.
One was to the envoy whom he had sent to negotiate with
the Mahrattas. Instructions for the negotiation were needed;

and the Governor-General framed them in that situation of extreme danger, with as much composure as if he had been writing in his palace at Calcutta.

Things, however, were not yet at the worst. An English officer of more spirit than judgment, eager to distinguish himself, made a premature attack on the insurgents beyond the river. His troops were entangled in narrow streets, and assailed by a furious population. He fell, with many of his men ; and the survivors were forced to retire.

This event produced the effect which has never failed to follow every check, however slight, sustained in India by the English arms. For hundreds of miles round, the whole country was in commotion. The entire population of the district of Benares took arms. The fields were abandoned by the husbandmen, who thronged to defend their prince. The infection spread to Oude. The oppressed people of that province rose up against the Nabob Vizier, refused to pay their imposts, and put the revenue officers to flight. Even Bahar was ripe for revolt. The hopes of Cheyte Sing began to rise. Instead of imploring mercy in the humble style of a vassal, he began to talk the language of a conqueror, and threatened, it was said, to sweep the white usurpers out of the land. But the English troops were now assembling fast. The officers, and even the private men, regarded the Governor-General with enthusiastic attachment, and flew to his aid with an alacrity which, as he boasted, had never been shown on any other occasion. Major Popham, a brave and skilful soldier, who had highly distinguished himself in the Mahratta war, and in whom the Governor-General reposed the greatest confidence, took the command. The tumultuary army of the Rajah was put to rout. His fastnesses were stormed. In a few hours, above thirty thousand men left his standard, and returned to their ordinary avocations. The unhappy prince fled from his country for ever. His fair domain was added to the British dominions. One of his relations indeed was appointed rajah ; but the Rajah of Benares was henceforth to be, like the Nabob of Bengal, a mere pensioner.

By this revolution, an addition of two hundred thousand pounds a year was made to the revenues of the Company. But the immediate relief was not as great as had been expected. The treasure laid up by Cheyte Sing had been popularly estimated at a million sterling. It turned out to be about a fourth part of that sum; and, such as it was, it was seized by the army, and divided as prize-money.

10

Disappointed in his expectations from Benares, Hastings was more violent than he would otherwise have been, in his dealings with Oude. Sujah Dowlah had long been dead. His son and successor, Asaph-ul-Dowlah, was one of the weakest and most vicious even of Eastern princes. His life was divided between torpid repose and the most odious forms of sensuality. In his court there was boundless waste, throughout his dominions wretchedness and disorder. He had been, under the skilful management of the English government, gradually sinking from the rank 20 of an independent prince to that of a vassal of the Company. It was only by the help of a British brigade that he could be secure from the aggressions of neighbours who despised his weakness, and from the vengeance of subjects who detested his tyranny. A brigade was furnished; and he engaged to defray the charge of paying and maintaining it. From that time his independence was at an end. Hastings was not a man to lose the advantage which he had thus gained. The Nabob soon began to complain of the burden which he had undertaken to bear. His revenues, 30 he said, were falling off; his servants were unpaid; he could no longer support the expense of the arrangement which he had sanctioned. Hastings would not listen to these representations. The Vizier, he said, had invited the Government of Bengal to send him troops, and had promised to pay for them. The troops had been sent. How

long the troops were to remain in Oude was a matter not
settled by the treaty. It remained, therefore, to be
settled between the contracting parties. But the contracting parties differed. Who then must decide? The stronger.
Hastings also argued that, if the English force was
withdrawn, Oude would certainly become a prey to anarchy,
and would probably be overrun by a Mahratta army.
That the finances of Oude were embarrassed he admitted.
But he contended, not without reason, that the embarrass-
10 ment was to be attributed to the incapacity and vices of
Asaph-ul-Dowlah himself, and that, if less were spent on
the troops, the only effect would be that more would be
squandered on worthless favourites.

Hastings had intended, after settling the affairs of
Benares, to visit Lucknow, and there to confer with
Asaph-ul-Dowlah. But the obsequious courtesy of the
Nabob Vizier prevented this visit. With a small train he
hastened to meet the Governor-General. An interview
took place in the fortress which, from the crest of the pre-
20 cipitous rock of Chunar, looks down on the waters of the
Ganges.

At first sight it might appear impossible that the negotiation should come to an amicable close. Hastings
wanted an extraordinary supply of money. Asaph-ul-
Dowlah wanted to obtain a remission of what he already
owed. Such a difference seemed to admit of no compromise. There was, however, one course satisfactory to
both sides, one course by which it was possible to relieve
the finances both of Oude and of Bengal; and that course
30 was adopted. It was simply this, that the Governor-
General and the Nabob Vizier should join to rob a third
party; and the third party whom they determined to rob
was the parent of one of the robbers.

The mother of the late Nabob, and his wife, who was the
mother of the present Nabob, were known as the Begums or
Princesses of Oude. They had possessed great influence over

Sujah Dowlah, and had, at his death, been left in possession
of a splendid dotation. The domains of which they received
the rents and administered the government were of wide
extent. The treasure hoarded by the late Nabob, a treasure
which was popularly estimated at near three millions sterling,
was in their hands. They continued to occupy his favourite
palace at Fyzabad, the Beautiful Dwelling; while Asaph-ul-
Dowlah held his court in the stately Lucknow, which he
had built for himself on the shores of the Goomti, and had
adorned with noble mosques and colleges.   10

Asaph-ul-Dowlah had already extorted considerable sums
from his mother. She had at length appealed to the English;
and the English had interfered. A solemn compact had been
made, by which she consented to give her son some pecuniary
assistance, and he in his turn promised never to commit any
further invasion of her rights. This compact was formally
guaranteed by the government of Bengal. But times had
changed; money was wanted; and the power which had
given the guarantee was not ashamed to instigate the spoiler
to excesses such that even he shrank from them.   20

It was necessary to find some pretext for a confiscation
inconsistent, not merely with plighted faith, not merely with
the ordinary rules of humanity and justice, but also with
that great law of filial piety which, even in the wildest tribes
of savages, even in those more degraded communities which
wither under the influence of a corrupt half-civilization, retains a certain authority over the human mind. A pretext
was the last thing that Hastings was likely to want. The
insurrection at Benares had produced disturbances in Oude.
These disturbances it was convenient to impute to the Prin- 30
cesses. Evidence for the imputation there was scarcely any;
unless reports wandering from one mouth to another, and
gaining something by every transmission, may be called
evidence. The accused were furnished with no charge; they
were permitted to make no defence; for the Governor-General
wisely considered that, if he tried them, he might not be able

to find a ground for plundering them. It was agreed between him and the Nabob Vizier that the noble ladies should, by a sweeping measure of confiscation, be stripped of their domains and treasures for the benefit of the Company, and that the sums thus obtained should be accepted by the government of Bengal in satisfaction of its claims on the government of Oude.

31 While Asaph-ul-Dowlah was at Chunar, he was completely subjugated by the clear and commanding intellect of the
10 English statesman. But when they had separated, the Vizier began to reflect with uneasiness on the engagement into which he had entered. His mother and grandmother protested and implored. His heart, deeply corrupted by absolute power and licentious pleasures, yet not naturally unfeeling, failed him in this crisis. Even the English resident at Lucknow, though hitherto devoted to Hastings, shrank from extreme measures. But the Governor-General was inexorable. He wrote to the resident in terms of the greatest severity, and declared that, if the spoliation which had been
20 agreed upon were not instantly carried into effect, he would himself go to Lucknow, and do that from which feebler minds recoil with dismay. The resident, thus menaced, waited on his Highness, and insisted that the treaty of Chunar should be carried into full and immediate effect. Asaph-ul-Dowlah yielded, making at the same time a solemn protestation that he yielded to compulsion. The lands were resumed; but the treasure was not so easily obtained. It was necessary to use violence. A body of the Company's troops marched to Fyzabad, and forced the gates of the
30 palace. The Princesses were confined to their own apartments. But still they refused to submit. Some more stringent mode of coercion was to be found. A mode was found of which, even at this distance of time, we cannot speak without shame and sorrow.

32 There were at Fyzabab two ancient men, belonging to that unhappy class which a practice, of immemorial antiquity in

the East, has excluded from the pleasures of love and from the hope of posterity. It has always been held in Asiatic courts that beings thus estranged from sympathy with their kind are those whom princes may most safely trust. Sujah Dowlah had been of this opinion. He had given his entire confidence to the two eunuchs; and after his death they remained at the head of the household of his widow.

These two men were, by the orders of the British government, seized, imprisoned, ironed, starved almost to death, in order to extort money from the Princesses. After they had 10 been two months in confinement, their health gave way. They implored permission to take a little exercise in the garden of their prison. The officer who was in charge of them stated that, if they were allowed this indulgence, there was not the smallest chance of their escaping, and that their irons really added nothing to the security of the custody in which they were kept. He did not understand the plan of his superiors. Their object in these inflictions was not security but torture; and all mitigation was refused. Yet this was not the worst. It was resolved by an English 20 government that these two infirm old men should be delivered to the tormentors. For that purpose they were removed to Lucknow. What horrors their dungeon there witnessed can only be guessed. But there remains on the records of Parliament, this letter, written by a British resident to a British soldier.

"Sir, the Nabob having determined to inflict corporal punishment upon the prisoners under your guard, this is to desire that his officers, when they shall come, may have free access to the prisoners, and be permitted to do with them as 30 they shall see proper."

While these barbarities were perpetrated at Lucknow, the Princesses were still under duresse at Fyzabad. Food was allowed to enter their apartments only in such scanty quantities that their female attendants were in danger of perishing with hunger. Month after month this cruelty

continued, till at length, after twelve hundred thousand
pounds had been wrung out of the Princesses, Hastings
began to think that he had really got to the bottom of their
revenue, and that no rigour could extort more. Then at
length the wretched men who were detained at Lucknow
regained their liberty. When their irons were knocked off,
and the doors of their prison opened, their quivering lips, the
tears which ran down their cheeks, and the thanksgivings
which they poured forth to the common Father of Mussul-
10 mans and Christians, melted even the stout hearts of the
English warriors who stood by.

There is a man to whom the conduct of Hastings, through
the whole of these proceedings, appears not only excusable
but laudable. There is a man who tells us that he "must
really be pardoned if he ventures to characterize as something preeminently ridiculous and wicked, the sensibility
which would balance against the preservation of British
India a little personal suffering, which was applied only so
long as the sufferers refused to deliver up a portion of that
20 wealth, the whole of which their own and their mistresses'
treason had forfeited." We cannot, we must own, envy the
reverend biographer, either his singular notion of what con-
stitutes preeminent wickedness, or his equally singular per-
ception of the preeminently ridiculous. Is this the generosity
of an English soldier? Is this the charity of a Christian
priest? Could neither of Mr. Gleig's professions teach him
the first rudiments of morality? Or is morality a thing
which may be well enough in sermons, but which has nothing
to do with biography?

30 But we must not forget to do justice to Sir Elijah Impey's
conduct on this occasion. It was not indeed easy for him
to intrude himself into a business so entirely alien from all
his official duties. But there was something inexpressibly
alluring, we must suppose, in the peculiar rankness of the
infamy which was then to be got at Lucknow. He hurried
thither as fast as relays of palanquin-bearers could carry

him. A crowd of people came before him with affidavits against the Begums, ready drawn in their hands. Those affidavits he did not read. Some of them, indeed, he could not read; for they were in the dialects of Northern India, and no interpreter was employed.* He administered the oath to the deponents, with all possible expedition, and asked not a single question, not even whether they had perused the statements to which they swore. This work performed, he got again into his palanquin, and posted back to Calcutta, to be in time for the opening of term. The 10 cause was one which, by his own confession, lay altogether out of his jurisdiction. Under the charter of justice, he had no more right to inquire into crimes committed by natives in Oude than the Lord President of the Court of Session of Scotland to hold an assize at Exeter. He had no right to try the Begums, nor did he pretend to try them. With what object, then, did he undertake so long a journey? Evidently in order that he might give, in an irregular manner, that sanction which in a regular manner he could not give, to the crimes of those who had recently hired him; 20 and in order that a confused mass of testimony which he did not sift, which he did not even read, might acquire an authority not properly belonging to it, from the signature of the highest judicial functionary in India.

The time was approaching, however, when he was to be stripped of that robe which has never, since the Revolution,

* This passage has been slightly altered. As it originally stood, Sir Elijah Impey was described as ignorant of all the native languages in which the depositions were drawn. A writer who apparently has had access to some private source of information has contradicted this statement, and has asserted that Sir Elijah knew Persian and Bengalee. Some of the depositions were certainly in Persian. Those therefore Sir Elijah might have read if he had chosen to do so. But others were in the vernacular dialects of Upper India, with which it is not alleged that he had any acquaintance. Why the Bengalee is mentioned it is not easy to guess. Bengalee at Lucknow would have been as useless as Portuguese in Switzerland.

been disgraced so foully as by him. The state of India had for some time occupied much of the attention of the British Parliament. Towards the close of the American war, two committees of the Commons sat on Eastern affairs. In one Edmund Burke took the lead. The other was under the presidency of the able and versatile Henry Dundas, then Lord Advocate of Scotland. Great as are the changes which, during the last sixty years, have taken place in our Asiatic dominions, the reports which those committees laid

10 on the table of the House will still be found most interesting and instructive.

There was as yet no connection between the Company and either of the great parties in the state. The ministers had no motive to defend Indian abuses. On the contrary, it was for their interest to show, if possible, that the government and patronage of our Oriental empire might, with advantage, be transferred to themselves. The votes therefore, which, in consequence of the reports made by the two committees, were passed by the Commons, breathed the

20 spirit of stern and indignant justice. The severest epithets were applied to several of the measures of Hastings, especially to the Rohilla war; and it was resolved, on the motion of Mr. Dundas, that the Company ought to recall a Governor-General who had brought such calamities on the Indian people, and such dishonour on the British name. An act was passed for limiting the jurisdiction of the Supreme Court. The bargain which Hastings had made with the Chief Justice was condemned in the strongest terms; and an address was presented to the King, praying that Impey might

30 be ordered home to answer for his misdeeds.

Impey was recalled by a letter from the Secretary of State. But the proprietors of India Stock resolutely refused to dismiss Hastings from their service, and passed a resolution affirming, what was undeniably true, that they were intrusted by law with the right of naming and removing their Governor-General, and that they were not bound to obey the directions of a single branch of the legislature with respect to such nomination or removal.

Thus supported by his employers, Hastings remained at the head of the government of Bengal till the spring of 1785. His administration, so eventful and stormy, closed in almost perfect quiet. In the Council there was no regular opposition to his measures. Peace was restored to India. The Mahratta war had ceased. Hyder was no more. A treaty had been concluded with his son, Tippoo; and the Carnatic had been evacuated by the armies of Mysore. 10 Since the termination of the American war, England had no European enemy or rival in the Eastern seas.

On a general review of the long administration of Hastings, it is impossible to deny that, against the great crimes by which it is blemished, we have to set off great public services. England had passed through a perilous crisis. She still, indeed, maintained her place in the foremost rank of European powers; and the manner in which she had defended herself against fearful odds had inspired surrounding nations with a high opinion both of her spirit 20 and of her strength. Nevertheless, in every part of the world, except one, she had been a loser. Not only had she been compelled to acknowledge the independence of thirteen colonies peopled by her children, and to conciliate the Irish by giving up the right of legislating for them; but, in the Mediterranean, in the Gulf of Mexico, on the coast of Africa, on the continent of America, she had been compelled to cede the fruits of her victories in former wars. Spain regained Minorca and Florida; France regained Senegal, Goree, and several West Indian Islands. The only quarter 30 of the world in which Britain had lost nothing was the quarter in which her interests had been committed to the care of Hastings. In spite of the utmost exertions both of European and Asiatic enemies, the power of our country in the East had been greatly augmented. Benares was subjected; the Nabob Vizier reduced to vassalage. That our

influence had been thus extended, nay, that Fort William
and Fort St. George had not been occupied by hostile armies,
was owing, if we may trust the general voice of the English
in India, to the skill and resolution of Hastings.

His internal administration, with all its blemishes, gives
him a title to be considered as one of the most remarkable
men in our history. He dissolved the double government.
He transferred the direction of affairs to English hands.
Out of a frightful anarchy, he educed at least a rude and
10 imperfect order. The whole organization by which justice
was dispensed, revenue collected, peace maintained throughout a territory not inferior in population to the dominions of
Louis the Sixteenth or of the Emperor Joseph, was formed
and superintended by him. He boasted that every public
office, without exception, which existed when he left Bengal,
was his creation. It is quite true that this system, after all
the improvements suggested by the experience of sixty
years, still needs improvement, and that it was at first far
more defective than it now is. But whoever seriously con-
20 siders what it is to construct from the beginning the whole
of a machine so vast and complex as a government will allow
that what Hastings effected deserves high admiration. To
compare the most celebrated European ministers to him
seems to us as unjust as it would be to compare the best
baker in London with Robinson Crusoe, who, before he
could bake a single loaf, had to make his plough and his
harrow, his fences and his scarecrows, his sickle and his flail,
his mill and his oven.

The just fame of Hastings rises still higher, when we
30 reflect that he was not bred a statesman ; that he was sent
from school to a counting-house ; and that he was employed
during the prime of his manhood as a commercial agent, far
from all intellectual society.

Nor must we forget that all, or almost all, to whom, when
placed at the head of affairs, he could apply for assistance,
were persons who owed as little as himself, or less than him-

self, to education. A minister in Europe finds himself, on
the first day on which he commences his functions, surrounded by experienced public servants, the depositaries of
official traditions. Hastings had no such help. His own
reflection, his own energy, were to supply the place of all
Downing Street and Somerset House. Having had no
facilities for learning, he was forced to teach. He had
first to form himself, and then to form his instruments ;
and this not in a single department, but in all the departments of the administration. 10

146 It must be added that, while engaged in this most arduous
task, he was constantly trammelled by orders from home,
and frequently borne down by a majority in council. The
preservation of an Empire from a formidable combination of
foreign enemies, the construction of a government in all its
parts, were accomplished by him, while every ship brought
out bales of censure from his employers, and while the
records of every consultation were filled with acrimonious
minutes by his colleagues. We believe that there never
was a public man whose temper was so severely tried ; not 20
Marlborough, when thwarted by the Dutch Deputies ; not
Wellington, when he had to deal at once with the Portuguese Regency, the Spanish Juntas, and Mr. Percival. But
the temper of Hastings was equal to almost any trial. It
was not sweet ; but it was calm. Quick and vigorous as his
intellect was, the patience with which he endured the most
cruel vexations, till a remedy could be found, resembled the
patience of stupidity. He seems to have been capable of
resentment, bitter and long-enduring ; yet his resentment
so seldom hurried him into any blunder that it may be 30
doubted whether what appeared to be revenge was any
thing but policy.

147 The effect of this singular equanimity was that he always
had the full command of all the resources of one of the most
fertile minds that ever existed. Accordingly no complica-
tion of perils and embarrassments could perplex him. For

every difficulty he had a contrivance ready; and, whatever may be thought of the justice and humanity of some of his contrivances, it is certain that they seldom failed to serve the purpose for which they were designed.

Together with this extraordinary talent for devising expedients, Hastings possessed, in a very high degree, another talent scarcely less necessary to a man in his situation; we mean the talent for conducting political controversy. It is as necessary to an English statesman in the East that he should be able to write, as it is to a minister in this country that he should be able to speak. It is chiefly by the oratory of a public man here that the nation judges of his powers. It is from the letters and reports of a public man in India that the dispensers of patronage form their estimate of him. In each case, the talent which receives peculiar encouragement is developed, perhaps at the expense of the other powers. In this country, we sometimes hear men speak above their abilities. It is not very unusual to find gentlemen in the Indian service who write above their abilities. The English politician is a little too much of a debater; the Indian politician a little too much of an essayist.

Of the numerous servants of the Company who have distinguished themselves as framers of minutes and despatches, Hastings stands at the head. He was indeed the person who gave to the official writing of the Indian governments the character which it still retains. He was matched against no common antagonist. But even Francis was forced to acknowledge, with sullen and resentful candour, that there was no contending against the pen of Hastings. And, in truth, the Governor-General's power of making out a case, of perplexing what it was inconvenient that people should understand, and of setting in the clearest point of view whatever would bear the light, was incomparable. His style must be praised with some reservation. It was in general forcible, pure, and polished; but it was sometimes, though not often, turgid, and, on one or two occasions, even bombastic. Perhaps the fondness of Hastings for Persian literature may have tended to corrupt his taste.

And, since we have referred to his literary tastes, it would be most unjust not to praise the judicious encouragement which, as a ruler, he gave to liberal studies and curious researches. His patronage was extended, with prudent generosity, to voyages, travels, experiments, publications. He did little, it is true, towards introducing into India the learning of the West. To make the young natives of Bengal familiar with Milton and Adam Smith, to substitute 10 the geography, astronomy, and surgery of Europe for the dotages of the Brahminical superstition, or for the imperfect science of ancient Greece transfused through Arabian expositions, this was a scheme reserved to crown the beneficent administration of a far more virtuous ruler. Still, it is impossible to refuse high commendation to a man who, taken from a ledger to govern an empire, overwhelmed by public business, surrounded by people as busy as himself, and separated by thousands of leagues from almost all literary society, gave, both by his example and by his 20 munificence, a great impulse to learning. In Persian and Arabic literature he was deeply skilled. With the Sanscrit he was not himself acquainted ; but those who first brought that language to the knowledge of European students owed much to his encouragement. It was under his protection that the Asiatic Society commenced its honourable career. That distinguished body selected him to be its first president ; but, with excellent taste and feeling, he declined the honour in favour of Sir William Jones. But the chief advantage which the students of Oriental letters derived from 30 his patronage remains to be mentioned. The Pundits of Bengal had always looked with great jealousy on the attempts of foreigners to pry into those mysteries which were locked up in the sacred dialect. Their religion had been persecuted by the Mahommedans. What they knew of the spirit of the Portuguese government might warrant them in apprehending persecution from Christians. That apprehension, the wisdom and moderation of Hastings removed. He was the first foreign ruler who succeeded in gaining the confidence of the hereditary priests of India, and who induced them to lay open to English scholars the secrets of the old Brahminical theology and jurisprudence.

It is indeed impossible to deny that, in the great art of inspiring large masses of human beings with confidence and attachment, no ruler ever surpassed Hastings. If he had made himself popular with the English by giving up the Bengalese to extortion and oppression, or if, on the other hand, he had conciliated the Bengalese and alienated the English, there would have been no cause for wonder. What is peculiar to him is that, being the chief of a small band of strangers who exercised boundless power over a great indigenous population, he made himself beloved both by the subject many and by the dominant few. The affection felt for him by the civil service was singularly ardent and constant. Through all his disasters and perils, his brethren stood by him with steadfast loyalty. The army, at the same time, loved him as armies have seldom loved any but the greatest chiefs who have led them to victory. Even in his disputes with distinguished military men, he could always count on the support of the military profession. While such was his empire over the hearts of his countrymen, he enjoyed among the natives a popularity, such as other governors have perhaps better merited, but such as no other governor has been able to attain. He spoke their vernacular dialects with facility and precision. He was intimately acquainted with their feelings and usages. On one or two occasions, for great ends, he deliberately acted in defiance of their opinion; but on such occasions he gained more in their respect than he lost in their love. In general, he carefully avoided all that could shock their national or religious prejudices. His administration was indeed in many respects faulty; but the Bengalee standard of good government was not high. Under the Nabobs, the hurricane of Mahratta cavalry had passed annually over the rich alluvial plain. But even the Mahratta shrank from a conflict with the mighty children of the sea; and the immense rice-harvests of the Lower Ganges were safely gathered in, under the protection of the English sword. The first English conquerors had been more rapacious and merciless even than the Mahrattas; but that generation had passed away. Defective as was the police, heavy as were the public burdens, it is probable that the oldest man in Bengal could 10 not recollect a season of equal security and prosperity. For the first time within living memory, the province was placed under a government strong enough to prevent others from robbing, and not inclined to play the robber itself. These things inspired good-will. At the same time, the constant success of Hastings and the manner in which he extricated himself from every difficulty made him an object of superstitious admiration; and the more than regal splendour which he sometimes displayed dazzled a people who have much in common with children. Even now, after the lapse 20 of more than fifty years, the natives of India still talk of him as the greatest of the English; and nurses sing children to sleep with a jingling ballad about the fleet horses and richly caparisoned elephants of Sahib Warren Hostein.

The gravest offences of which Hastings was guilty did not affect his popularity with the people of Bengal; for those offences were committed against neighbouring states. Those offences, as our readers must have perceived, we are not disposed to vindicate; yet, in order that the censure may be justly apportioned to the transgresson, it is fit that the 30 motive of the criminal should be taken into consideration. The motive which prompted the worst acts of Hastings was misdirected and ill-regulated public spirit. The rules of justice, the sentiments of humanity, the plighted faith of treaties, were in his view as nothing, when opposed to the immediate interest of the state. This is no justification,

according to the principles either of morality, or of what we believe to be identical with morality, namely, far-sighted policy. Nevertheless the common sense of mankind, which in questions of this sort seldom goes far wrong, will always recognise a distinction between crimes which originate in an inordinate zeal for the commonwealth, and crimes which originate in selfish cupidity. To the benefit of this distinction Hastings is fairly entitled. There is, we conceive, no reason to suspect that the Rohilla war, the revolution of
10 Benares, or the spoliation of the Princesses of Oude, added a rupee to his fortune. We will not affirm that, in all pecuniary dealings, he showed that punctilious integrity, that dread of the faintest appearance of evil, which is now the glory of the Indian civil service. But when the school in which he had been trained and the temptations to which he was exposed are considered, we are more inclined to praise him for his general uprightness with respect to money, than rigidly to blame him for a few transactions which would now be called indelicate and irregular, but which even now
20 would hardly be designated as corrupt. A rapacious man he certainly was not. Had he been so, he would infallibly have returned to his country the richest subject in Europe. We speak within compass, when we say that, without applying any extraordinary pressure, he might easily have obtained from the zemindars of the Company's provinces and from neighbouring princes, in the course of thirteen years, more than three millions sterling, and might have outshone the splendour of Carlton House and of the *Palais Royal.* He brought home a fortune such as a Governor-General, fond of
30 state, and careless of thrift, might easily, during so long a tenure of office, save out of his legal salary. Mrs. Hastings, we are afraid, was less scrupulous. It was generally believed that she accepted presents with great alacrity, and that she thus formed, without the connivance of her husband, a private hoard amounting to several lacs of rupees. We are the more inclined to give credit to this story, because

Mr. Gleig, who cannot but have heard it, does not, as far as we have observed, notice or contradict it.

154 The influence of Mrs. Hastings over her husband was indeed such that she might easily have obtained much larger sums than she was ever accused of receiving. At length her health began to give way; and the Governor-General, much against his will, was compelled to send her to England. He seems to have loved her with that love which is peculiar to men of strong minds, to men whose affection is not easily won or widely diffused. The talk of Calcutta ran for some 10 time on the luxurious manner in which he fitted up the round-house of an Indiaman for her accommodation, on the profusion of sandal-wood and carved ivory which adorned her cabin, and on the thousands of rupees which had been expended in order to procure for her the society of an agreeable female companion during the voyage. We may remark here that the letters of Hastings to his wife are exceedingly characteristic. They are tender, and full of indications of esteem and confidence; but, at the same time, a little more ceremonious than is usual in so intimate a relation. The 20 solemn courtesy with which he compliments "his elegant Marian" reminds us now and then of the dignified air with which Sir Charles Grandison bowed over Miss Byron's hand in the cedar parlour.

155 After some months Hastings prepared to follow his wife to England. When it was announced that he was about to quit his office, the feeling of the society which he had so long governed manifested itself by many signs. Addresses poured in from Europeans and Asiatics, from civil functionaries, soldiers, and traders. On the day on which he delivered up 30 the keys of office, a crowd of friends and admirers formed a lane to the quay where he embarked. Several barges escorted him far down the river; and some attached friends refused to quit him till the low coast of Bengal was fading from the view, and till the pilot was leaving the ship.

156 Of his voyage little is known, except that he amused him-

self with books and with his pen ; and that, among the compositions by which he beguiled the tediousness of that long
leisure, was a pleasing imitation of Horace's *Otium Divos
rogat*. This little poem was inscribed to Mr. Shore, afterwards Lord Teignmouth, a man of whose integrity, humanity,
and honour, it is impossible to speak too highly ; but who,
like some other excellent members of the civil service, extended to the conduct of his friend Hastings an indulgence
of which his own conduct never stood in need.

10 The voyage was, for those times, very speedy. Hastings
was little more than four months on the sea. In June, 1785,
he landed at Plymouth, posted to London, appeared at Court,
paid his respects in Leadenhall Street, and then retired with
his wife to Cheltenham.

He was greatly pleased with his reception. The King
treated him with marked distinction. The Queen, who had
already incurred much censure on account of the favour
which, in spite of the ordinary severity of her virtue, she
had shown to the "elegant Marian," was not less gracious
20 to Hastings. The Directors received him in a solemn sitting ;
and their chairman read to him a vote of thanks which they
had passed without one dissentient voice. "I find myself,"
said Hastings, in a letter written about a quarter of a year
after his arrival in England, "I find myself every where, and
universally, treated with evidences, apparent even to my own
observation, that I possess the good opinion of my country."

The confident and exulting tone of his correspondence
about this time is the more remarkable, because he had
already received ample notice of the attack which was in
30 preparation. Within a week after he landed at Plymouth,
Burke gave notice in the House of Commons of a motion
seriously affecting a gentleman lately returned from India.
The session, however, was then so far advanced, that it was
impossible to enter on so extensive and important a subject.

Hastings, it is clear, was not sensible of the danger of his
position. Indeed that sagacity, that judgment, that readi-

ness in devising expedients, which had distinguished him
in the East, seemed now to have forsaken him ; not that
his abilities were at all impaired ; not that he was not
still the same man who had triumphed over Francis and
Nuncomar, who had made the Chief Justice and the Nabob
Vizier his tools, who had deposed Cheyte Sing, and repelled
Hyder Ali. But an oak, as Mr. Grattan finely said, should
not be transplanted at fifty. A man who, having left England when a boy, returns to it after thirty or forty years
passed in India, will find, be his talents what they may, 10
that he has much both to learn and to unlearn before he
can take a place among English statesmen. (The working
of a representative system, the war of parties, the arts of
debate, the influence of the press, are startling novelties to
him.) Surrounded on every side by new machines and new
tactics, he is as much bewildered as Hannibal would have
been at Waterloo, or Themistocles at Trafalgar. His very
acuteness deludes him. His very vigour causes him to
stumble. The more correct his maxims, when applied to
the state of society to which he is accustomed, the more 20
certain they are to lead him astray. This was strikingly
the case with Hastings. In India he had a bad hand ;
but he was master of the game, and he won every stake.
In England he held excellent cards, if he had known how
to play them ; and it was chiefly by his own errors that
he was brought to the verge of ruin.

Of all his errors the most serious was perhaps the choice
of a champion. Clive, in similar circumstances, had made a
singularly happy selection. He put himself into the hands
of Wedderburn, afterwards Lord Loughborough, one of the 30
few great advocates who have also been great in the House
of Commons. To the defence of Clive, therefore, nothing
was wanting, neither learning nor knowledge of the world,
neither forensic acuteness nor that eloquence which charms
political assemblies. Hastings intrusted his interests to a
very different person, a major in the Bengal army, named

Scott. This gentleman had been sent over from India some time before as the agent of the Governor-General. It was rumoured that his services were rewarded with Oriental munificence ; and we believe that he received much more than Hastings could conveniently spare. The major obtained a seat in Parliament, and was there regarded as the organ of his employer. It was evidently impossible that a gentleman so situated could speak with the authority which belongs to an independent position.

10 Nor had the agent of Hastings the talents necessary for obtaining the ear of an assembly which, accustomed to listen to great orators, had naturally become fastidious. He was always on his legs ; he was very tedious ; and he had only one topic, the merits and wrongs of Hastings. Every body who knows the House of Commons will easily guess what followed. The Major was soon considered as the greatest bore of his time. His exertions were not confined to Parliament. There was hardly a day on which the newspapers did not contain some puff upon Hastings

20 signed *Asiaticus* or *Bengalensis*, but known to be written by the indefatigable Scott ; and hardly a month in which some bulky pamphlet on the same subject, and from the same pen, did not pass to the trunk-makers and the pastry-cooks. As to this gentleman's capacity for conducting a delicate question through Parliament, our readers will want no evidence beyond that which they will find in letters preserved in these volumes. We will give a single specimen of his temper and judgment. He designated the greatest man then living as "that reptile Mr. Burke."

30 In spite, however, of this unfortunate choice, the general aspect of affairs was favourable to Hastings. The King was on his side. The Company and its servants were zealous in his cause. Among public men he had many ardent friends. Such were Lord Mansfield, who had outlived the vigour of his body, but not that of his mind ; and Lord Lansdowne, who, though unconnected with any

party, retained the importance which belongs to great
talents and knowledge. The ministers were generally
believed to be favourable to the late Governor-General.
They owed their power to the clamour which had been
raised against Mr. Fox's East India Bill. The authors of
that bill, when accused of invading vested rights, and of
setting up powers unknown to the constitution, had defended themselves by pointing to the crimes of Hastings,
and by arguing that abuses so extraordinary justified
extraordinary measures. Those who, by opposing that 10
bill, had raised themselves to the head of affairs, would
naturally be inclined to extenuate the evils which had
been made the plea for administering so violent a remedy;
and such, in fact, was their general disposition. The Lord
Chancellor Thurlow, in particular, whose great place and
force of intellect gave him a weight in the government
inferior only to that of Mr. Pitt, espoused the cause of
Hastings with indecorous violence. Mr. Pitt, though he
had censured many parts of the Indian system, had
studiously abstained from saying a word against the late 20
chief of the Indian government. To Major Scott, indeed,
the young minister had in private extolled Hastings as a
great, a wonderful man, who had the highest claims on
the government. There was only one objection to granting
all that so eminent a servant of the public could ask.
The resolution of censure still remained on the Journals
of the House of Commons. That resolution was, indeed,
unjust; but, till it was rescinded, could the minister
advise the King to bestow any mark of approbation on
the person censured? If Major Scott is to be trusted, Mr. 30
Pitt declared that this was the only reason which prevented the government from conferring a peerage on the
late Governor-General. Mr. Dundas was the only inportant
member of the administration who was deeply committed
to a different view of the subject. He had moved the
resolutions which created the difficulty; but even from him

little was to be apprehended. Since he presided over the committee on Eastern affairs, great changes had taken place. He was surrounded by new allies; he had fixed his hopes on new objects; and whatever may have been his good qualities,—and he had many,—flattery itself never reckoned rigid consistency in the number.

From the ministry, therefore, Hastings had every reason to expect support; and the ministry was very powerful. The Opposition was loud and vehement against him. But the Opposition, though formidable from the wealth and influence of some of its members, and from the admirable talents and eloquence of others, was outnumbered in parliament, and odious throughout the country. Nor, as far as we can judge, was the Opposition generally desirous to engage in so serious an undertaking as the impeachment of an Indian Governor. Such an impeachment must last for years. It must impose on the chiefs of the party an immense load of labour. Yet it could scarcely, in any manner, affect the event of the great political game. The followers of the coalition were therefore more inclined to revile Hastings than to prosecute him. They lost no opportunity of coupling his name with the names of the most hateful tyrants of whom history makes mention. The wits of Brooks's aimed their keenest sarcasms both at his public and at his domestic life. Some fine diamonds which he had presented, as it was rumoured, to the royal family, and a certain richly carved ivory bed which the Queen had done him the honour to accept from him, were favourite subjects of ridicule. One lively poet proposed that the great acts of the fair Marian's present husband should be immortalized by the pencil of his predecessor; and that Imhoff should be employed to embellish the House of Commons with paintings of the bleeding Rohillas, of Nuncomar swinging, of Cheyte Sing letting himself down to the Ganges. Another, in an exquisitely humorous parody of Virgil's third eclogue, propounded the question

what that mineral could be of which the rays had power
to make the most austere of princesses the friend of a
wanton. A third described, with gay malevolence, the
gorgeous appearance of Mrs. Hastings at St. James's, the
galaxy of jewels, torn from Indian Begums, which adorned
her head-dress, her necklace gleaming with future votes,
and the depending questions that shone upon her ears.
Satirical attacks of this description, and perhaps a motion
for a vote of censure, would have satisfied the great body
of the Opposition. But there were two men whose indig- 10
nation was not to be so appeased, Philip Francis and
Edmund Burke.

Francis had recently entered the House of Commons, and
had already established a character there for industry and
talent. He laboured indeed under one most unfortunate
defect, want of fluency. But he occasionally expressed himself with a dignity and energy worthy of the greatest orators.
Before he had been many days in parliament, he incurred the
bitter dislike of Pitt, who constantly treated him with as
much asperity as the laws of debate would allow. Neither 20
lapse of years nor change of scene had mitigated the enmities
which Francis had brought back from the East. After his
usual fashion, he mistook his malevolence for virtue, nursed
it, as preachers tell us that we ought to nurse our good dis-
positions, and paraded it, on all occasions, with Pharisaical
ostentation.

The zeal of Burke was still fiercer; but it was far purer.
Men unable to understand the elevation of his mind have
tried to find out some discreditable motive for the vehemence
and pertinacity which he showed on this occasion. But they 30
have altogether failed. The idle story that he had some
private slight to revenge has long been given up, even by
the advocates of Hastings. Mr. Gleig supposes that Burke
was actuated by party spirit, that he retained a bitter
remembrance of the fall of the coalition, that he attributed
that fall to the exertions of the East India interest, and that

he considered Hastings as the head and the representative of
that interest. This explanation seems to be sufficiently
refuted by a reference to dates. The hostility of Burke to
Hastings commenced long before the coalition; and lasted
long after Burke had become a strenuous supporter of those
by whom the coalition had been defeated. It began when
Burke and Fox, closely allied together, were attacking the
influence of the crown, and calling for peace with the
American republic. It continued till Burke, alienated from
10 Fox, and loaded with the favours of the crown, died, preaching a crusade against the French republic. It seems absurd
to attribute to the events of 1784 an enmity which began in
1781, and which retained undiminished force long after
persons far more deeply implicated than Hastings in the
events of 1784 had been cordially forgiven. And why should
we look for any other explanation of Burke's conduct than
that which we find on the surface? The plain truth is that
Hastings had committed some great crimes, and that the
thought of those crimes made the blood of Burke boil in his
20 veins. For Burke was a man in whom compassion for suffering, and hatred of injustice and tyranny, were as strong as in
Las Casas or Clarkson. And although in him, as in Las
Casas and in Clarkson, these noble feelings were alloyed with
the infirmity which belongs to human nature, he is, like
them, entitled to this great praise, that he devoted years of
intense labour to the service of a people with whom he had
neither blood nor language, neither religion nor manners in
common, and from whom no requital, no thanks, no applause
could be expected.
30 His knowledge of India was such as few even of those
Europeans who have passed many years in that country have
attained, and such as certainly was never attained by any
public man who had not quitted Europe. He had studied
the history, the laws, and the usages of the East with an
industry such as is seldom found united to so much genius
and so much sensibility. Others have perhaps been equally

laborious, and have collected an equal mass of materials.
But the manner in which Burke brought his higher powers
of intellect to work on statements of facts, and on tables of
figures, was peculiar to himself. In every part of those huge
bales of Indian information which repelled almost all other
readers, his mind, at once philosophical and poetical, found
something to instruct or to delight. His reason analysed
and digested those vast and shapeless masses; his imagination animated and coloured them. Out of darkness, and
dulness, and confusion, he formed a multitude of ingenious 10
theories and vivid pictures. He had, in the highest degree,
that noble faculty whereby man is able to live in the past
and in the future, in the distant and in the unreal. India
and its inhabitants were not to him, as to most Englishmen,
mere names and abstractions, but a real country and a real
people. The burning sun, the strange vegetation of the
palm and the cocoa tree, the rice-field, the tank, the huge
trees, older than the Mogul empire, under which the village
crowds assemble, the thatched roof of the peasant's hut, the
rich tracery of the mosque where the imaum prays with his 20
face to Mecca, the drums, and banners, and gaudy idols, the
devotees swinging in the air, the graceful maiden, with the
pitcher on her head, descending the steps to the river-side,
the black faces, the long beards, the yellow streaks of sect,
the turbans and the flowing robes, the spears and the silver
maces, the elephants with their canopies of state, the gorgeous palanquin of the prince, and the close litter of the
noble lady, all those things were to him as the objects amidst
which his own life had been passed, as the objects which lay
on the road between Beaconsfield and St. James's Street. 30
All India was present to the eye of his mind, from the halls
where suitors laid gold and perfumes at the feet of sovereigns
to the wild moor where the gipsy camp was pitched, from
the bazars, humming like bee-hives with the crowd of
buyers and sellers, to the jungle where the lonely courier
shakes his bunch of iron rings to scare away the hyænas.

He had just as lively an idea of the insurrection at Benares
as of Lord George Gordon's riots, and of the execution of
Nuncomar as of the execution of Dr. Dodd. Oppression in
Bengal was to him the same thing as oppression in the streets
of London.

He saw that Hastings had been guilty of some most
unjustifiable acts. All that followed was natural and necessary in a mind like Burke's. His imagination and his
passions, once excited, hurried him beyond the bounds of
10 justice and good sense. His reason, powerful as it was,
became the slave of feelings which it should have controlled.
His indignation, virtuous in its origin, acquired too much of
the character of personal aversion. He could see no miti-
gating circumstance, no redeeming merit. His temper,
which, though generous and affectionate, had always been
irritable, had now been made almost savage by bodily
infirmities and mental vexations. Conscious of great powers
and great virtues, he found himself, in age and poverty, a
mark for the hatred of a perfidious court and a deluded
20 people. In Parliament his eloquence was out of date. A
young generation, which knew him not, had filled the House.
Whenever he rose to speak, his voice was drowned by the
unseemly interruptions of lads who were in their cradles
when his orations on the Stamp Act called forth the applause
of the great Earl of Chatham. These things had produced
on his proud and sensitive spirit an effect at which we cannot
wonder. He could no longer discuss any question with
calmness, or make allowance for honest differences of opinion.
Those who think that he was more violent and acrimonious
30 in debates about India than on other occasions are ill
informed respecting the last years of his life. In the
discussions on the Commercial Treaty with the Court of
Versailles, on the Regency, on the French Revolution, he
showed even more virulence than in conducting the impeachment. Indeed it may be remarked that the very persons
who called him a mischievous maniac, for condemning in

burning words the Rohilla war and the spoliation of the Begums, exalted him into a prophet as soon as he began to declaim, with greater vehemence, and not with greater reason, against the taking of the Bastile and the insults offered to Marie Antoinette. To us he appears to have been neither a maniac in the former case, nor a prophet in the latter, but in both cases a great and good man, led into extravagance by a tempestuous sensibility which domineered over all his faculties.

It may be doubted whether the personal antipathy of 10 Francis, or the nobler indignation of Burke, would have led their party to adopt extreme measures against Hastings, if his own conduct had been judicious. He should have felt that, great as his public services had been, he was not faultless; and should have been content to make his escape, without aspiring to the honours of a triumph. He and his agent took a different view. They were impatient for the rewards which, as they conceived, were deferred only till Burke's attack should be over. They accordingly resolved to force on a decisive action, with an enemy for whom, if 20 they had been wise, they would have made a bridge of gold. On the first day of the session of 1786, Major Scott reminded Burke of the notice given in the preceding year, and asked whether it was seriously intended to bring any charge against the late Governor-General. This challenge left no course open to the Opposition, except to come forward as accusers, or to acknowledge themselves calumniators. The administration of Hastings had not been so blameless, nor was the great party of Fox and North so feeble, that it could be prudent to venture on so bold 30 a defiance. The leaders of the Opposition instantly returned the only answer which they could with honour return; and the whole party was irrevocably pledged to a prosecution.

Burke began his operations by applying for papers. Some of the documents for which he asked were refused by the ministers, who, in the debate, held language such as strongly confirmed the prevailing opinion, that they intended to support Hastings. In April the charges were laid on the table. They had been drawn by Burke with great ability, though in a form too much resembling that of a pamphlet. Hastings was furnished with a copy of the accusation ; and it was intimated to him that he might, if he thought fit, be heard in his own defence at the bar of the Commons.

Here again Hastings was pursued by the same fatality which had attended him ever since the day when he set foot on English ground. It seemed to be decreed that this man, so politic and so successful in the East, should commit nothing but blunders in Europe. Any judicious adviser would have told him that the best thing which he could do would be to make an eloquent, forcible, and affecting oration at the bar of the House ; but that, if he could not trust himself to speak, and found it necessary to read, he ought to be as concise as possible. Audiences accustomed to extemporaneous debating of the highest excellence are always impatient of long written compositions. Hastings, however, sat down as he would have done at the Government-house in Bengal, and prepared a paper of immense length. That paper, if recorded on the consultations of an Indian administration, would have been justly praised as a very able minute. But it was now out of place. It fell flat, as the best written defence must have fallen flat, on an assembly accustomed to the animated and strenuous conflicts of Pitt and Fox. The members, as soon as their curiosity about the face and demeanour of so eminent a stranger was satisfied, walked away to dinner, and left Hastings to tell his story till midnight to the clerks and the Sergeant-at-arms.

All preliminary steps having been duly taken, Burke, in the beginning of June, brought forward the charge relating to the Rohilla war. He acted discreetly in placing this accusation in the van ; for Dundas had formerly moved, and the House had adopted, a resolution condemning, in the most severe terms, the policy followed by Hastings with regard to Rohilcund. Dundas had little, or rather nothing, to say in defence of his own consistency ; but he put a bold face on the matter, and opposed the motion. Among other things, he declared that, though he still thought the Rohilla war unjustifiable, he considered the services which Hastings had subsequently rendered to the state as sufficient to atone even for so great an offence. Pitt did not speak, but voted with Dundas ; and Hastings 10 was absolved by a hundred and nineteen votes against sixty-seven.

Hastings was now confident of victory. It seemed, indeed, that he had reason to be so. The Rohilla war was, of all his measures, that which his accusers might with greatest advantage assail. It had been condemned by the Court of Directors. It had been condemned by the House of Commons. It had been condemned by Mr. Dundas, who had since become the chief minister of the Crown for Indian affairs. Yet Burke, having chosen this strong ground, had 20 been completely defeated on it. That, having failed here, he should succeed on any point, was generally thought impossible. It was rumoured at the clubs and coffee-houses that one or perhaps two more charges would be brought forward, that if, on those charges, the sense of the House of Commons should be against impeachment, the Opposition would let the matter drop, that Hastings would be immediately raised to the peerage, decorated with the star of the Bath, sworn of the privy council, and invited to lend the assistance of his talents and experience to the India board. 30 Lord Thurlow, indeed, some months before, had spoken with contempt of the scruples which prevented Pitt from calling Hastings to the House of Lords ; and had even said, that if the Chancellor of the Exchequer was afraid of the Commons, there was nothing to prevent the Keeper of the Great Seal from taking the royal pleasure about a patent of peerage.

The very title was chosen. Hastings was to be Lord Daylesford. For, through all changes of scene and changes of
fortune, remained unchanged his attachment to the spot
which had witnessed the greatness and the fall of his family,
and which had borne so great a part in the first dreams of
his young ambition.

But in a very few days these fair prospects were overcast.
On the thirteenth of June, Mr. Fox brought forward, with
great ability and eloquence, the charge respecting the treat-
10 ment of Cheyte Sing. Francis followed on the same side.
The friends of Hastings were in high spirits when Pitt rose.
With his usual abundance and felicity of language, the
Minister gave his opinion on the case. He maintained that
the Governor-General was justified in calling on the Rajah
of Benares for pecuniary assistance, and in imposing a fine
when that assistance was contumaciously withheld. He
also thought that the conduct of the Governor-General during the insurrection had been distinguished by ability and
presence of mind. He censured, with great bitterness, the
20 conduct of Francis, both in India and in Parliament, as
most dishonest and malignant. The necessary inference
from Pitt's arguments seemed to be that Hastings ought
to be honourably acquitted; and both the friends and the
opponents of the Minister expected from him a declaration
to that effect. To the astonishment of all parties, he concluded by saying that, though he thought it right in
Hastings to fine Cheyte Sing for contumacy, yet the amount
of the fine was too great for the occasion. On this ground,
and on this ground alone, did Mr. Pitt, applauding every
30 other part of the conduct of Hastings with regard to
Benares, declare that he should vote in favour of Mr. Fox's
motion.

The House was thunderstruck; and it well might be so.
For the wrong done to Cheyte Sing, even had it been as
flagitious as Fox and Francis contended, was a trifle when
compared with the horrors which had been inflicted on

Rohilcund. But if Mr. Pitt's view of the case of Cheyte
Sing were correct, there was no ground for an impeachment,
or even for a vote of censure. If the offence of Hastings
was really no more than this, that, having a right to impose
a mulct, the amount of which mulct was not defined, but
was left to be settled by his discretion, he had, not for his
own advantage, but for that of the state, demanded too
much, was this an offence which required a criminal proceeding of the highest solemnity, a criminal proceeding, to
which, during sixty years, no public functionary had been 10
subjected? We can see, we think, in what way a man
of sense and integrity might have been induced to take any
course respecting Hastings, except the course which Mr. Pitt
took. Such a man might have thought a great example
necessary, for the preventing of injustice, and for the .
vindicating of the national honour, and might, on that
ground, have voted for impeachment both on the Rohilla
charge, and on the Benares charge. Such a man might have
thought that the offences of Hastings had been atoned for
by great services, and might, on that ground, have voted 20
against the impeachment, on both charges. With great
diffidence, we give it as our opinion that the most correct
course would, on the whole, have been to impeach on the
Rohilla charge, and to acquit on the Benares charge. Had
the Benares charge appeared to us in the same light in
which it appeared to Mr. Pitt, we should, without hesitation,
have voted for acquittal on that charge. The one course
which it is inconceivable that any man of a tenth part of
Mr. Pitt's abilities can have honestly taken was the course
which he took. He acquitted Hastings on the Rohilla 30
charge. He softened down the Benares charge till it became
no charge at all ; and then he pronounced that it contained
matter for impeachment.

115 Nor must it be forgotten that the principal reason assigned
by the ministry for not impeaching Hastings on account of
the Rohilla war was this, that the delinquencies of the early

part of his administration had been atoned for by the excellence of the later part. Was it not most extraordinary
that men who had held this language could afterwards vote
that the later part of his administration furnished matter
for no less than twenty articles of impeachment? They first
represented the conduct of Hastings in 1780 and 1781 as so
highly meritorious that, like works of supererogation in the
Catholic theology, it ought to be efficacious for the cancelling
of former offences; and they then prosecuted him for his
10 conduct in 1780 and 1781.

The general astonishment was the greater, because, only
twenty-four hours before, the members on whom the minister could depend had received the usual notes from the
Treasury, begging them to be in their places and to vote
against Mr. Fox's motion. It was asserted by Mr. Hastings
that, early on the morning of the very day on which the
debate took place, Dundas called on Pitt, woke him, and was
closeted with him many hours. The result of this conference
was a determination to give up the late Governor-General to
20 the vengeance of the Opposition. It was impossible even for
the most powerful minister to carry all his followers with
him in so strange a course. Several persons high in office,
the Attorney-General, Mr. Glenville, and Lord Mulgrave,
divided against Mr. Pitt. But the devoted adherents who
stood by the head of the government without asking questions, were sufficiently numerous to turn the scale. A
hundred and nineteen members voted for Mr. Fox's motion;
seventy-nine against it. Dundas silently followed Pitt.

That good and great man, the late William Wilberforce,
30 often related the events of this remarkable night. He
described the amazement of the House, and the bitter reflections which were muttered against the Prime Minister
by some of the habitual supporters of government. Pitt
himself appeared to feel that his conduct required some
explanation. He left the treasury bench, sat for some time
next to Mr. Wilberforce, and very earnestly declared that he

had found it impossible, as a man of conscience, to stand any longer by Hastings. The business, he said, was too bad. Mr. Wilberforce, we are bound to add, fully believed that his friend was sincere, and that the suspicions to which this mysterious affair gave rise were altogether unfounded.

Those suspicions, indeed, were such as it is painful to mention. The friends of Hastings, most of whom, it is to be observed, generally supported the administration, affirmed that the motive of Pitt and Dundas was jealousy. Hastings was personally a favourite with the king. He was 10 the idol of the East India Company and of its servants. If he were absolved by the Commons, seated among the Lords, admitted to the Board of Control, closely allied with the strong-minded and imperious Thurlow, was it not almost certain that he would soon draw to himself the entire management of Eastern affairs? Was it not possible that he might become a formidable rival in the cabinet? It had probably got abroad that very singular communications had taken place between Thurlow and Major Scott, and that, if the First Lord of the Treasury was afraid to recommend 20 Hastings for a peerage, the Chancellor was ready to take the responsibility of that step on himself. Of all ministers, Pitt was the least likely to submit with patience to such an encroachment on his functions. If the Commons impeached Hastings, all danger was at an end. The proceeding, however it might terminate, would probably last some years. In the mean time, the accused person would be excluded from honours and public employments, and could scarcely venture even to pay his duty at court. Such were the motives attributed by a great part of the public to the 30 young minister, whose ruling passion was generally believed to be avarice of power.

The prorogation soon interrupted the discussions respecting Hastings. In the following year, those discussions were resumed. The charge touching the spoliation of the Begums was brought forward by Sheridan, in a speech which was so

imperfectly reported that it may be said to be wholly lost, but which was, without doubt, the most elaborately brilliant of all the productions of his ingenious mind. The impression which it produced was such as has never been equalled. He sat down, not merely amidst cheering, but amidst the loud clapping of hands, in which the Lords below the bar and the strangers in the gallery joined. The excitement of the House was such that no other speaker could obtain a hearing ; and the debate was adjourned. The ferment spread
10 fast through the town. Within four and twenty hours, Sheridan was offered a thousand pounds for the copyright of the speech, if he would himself correct it for the press. The impression made by this remarkable display of eloquence on severe and experienced critics, whose discernment may be supposed to have been quickened by emulation, was deep and permanent. Mr. Windham, twenty years later, said that the speech deserved all its fame, and was, in spite of some faults of taste, such as were seldom wanting either in the literary or in the parliamentary performances of
20 Sheridan, the finest that had been delivered within the memory of man. Mr. Fox, about the same time, being asked by the late Lord Holland what was the best speech ever made in the House of Commons, assigned the first place, without hesitation, to the great oration of Sheridan on the Oude charge.

When the debate was resumed, the tide ran so strongly against the accused that his friends were coughed and scraped down. Pitt declared himself for Sheridan's motion ; and the question was carried by a hundred and seventy-
30 five votes against sixty-eight.

The Opposition, flushed with victory and strongly supported by the public sympathy, proceeded to bring forward a succession of charges relating chiefly to pecuniary transactions. The friends of Hastings were discouraged, and, having now no hope of being able to avert an impeachment, were not very strenuous in their exertions. At length the House, having agreed to twenty articles of charge, directed Burke to go before the Lords, and to impeach the late Governor-General of High Crimes and Misdemeanours. Hastings was at the same time arrested by the Sergeant-at-arms, and carried to the bar of the Peers.

The session was now within ten days of its close. It was, therefore, impossible that any progress could be made in the trial till the next year. Hastings was admitted to bail; and further proceedings were postponed till the Houses should re-assemble.   10

When Parliament met in the following winter, the Commons proceeded to elect a committee for managing the impeachment. Burke stood at the head; and with him were associated most of the leading members of the Opposition. But when the name of Francis was read a fierce contention arose. It was said that Francis and Hastings were notoriously on bad terms, that they had been at feud during many years, that on one occasion their mutual aversion had impelled them to seek each other's lives, and that it would be improper and indelicate 20 to select a private enemy to be a public accuser. It was urged on the other side with great force, particularly by Mr. Windham, that impartiality, though the first duty of a judge, had never been reckoned among the qualities of an advocate; that in the ordinary administration of criminal justice among the English, the aggrieved party, the very last person who ought to be admitted into the jury-box, is the prosecutor; that what was wanted in a manager was, not that he should be free from bias, but that he should be able, well informed, energetic, and active. 30 The ability and information of Francis were admitted; and the very animosity with which he was reproached, whether a virtue or a vice, was at least a pledge for his energy and activity. It seems difficult to refute these arguments. But the inveterate hatred borne by Francis to Hastings had excited general disgust. The House

decided that Francis should not be a manager. Pitt voted
with the majority, Dundas with the minority.

173 In the mean time, the preparations for the trial had proceeded rapidly ; and on the thirteenth of February, 1788,
the sittings of the Court commenced. There have been
spectacles more dazzling to the eye, more gorgeous with
jewellery and cloth of gold, more attractive to grown-up
children, than that which was then exhibited at Westminster ; but, perhaps, there never was a spectacle so well
10 calculated to strike a highly cultivated, a reflecting, an
imaginative mind. All the various kinds of interest which
belong to the near and to the distant, to the present and
to the past, were collected on one spot, and in one hour.
All the talents and all the accomplishments which are
developed by liberty and civilisation were now displayed,
with every advantage that could be derived both from co-
operation and from contrast. Every step in the proceedings carried the mind either backward, through many
troubled centuries, to the days when the foundations of our
20 constitution were laid ; or far away, over boundless seas
and deserts, to dusky nations living under strange stars,
worshipping strange gods, and writing strange characters from right to left. The High Court of Parliament
was to sit, according to forms handed down from the
days of the Plantagenets, on an Englishman accused of
exercising tyranny over the lord of the holy city of
Benares, and over the ladies of the princely house of
Oude.

174 The place was worthy of such a trial. It was the great
30 hall of William Rufus, the hall which had resounded with
acclamations at the inauguration of thirty kings, the hall
which had witnessed the just sentence of Bacon and the
just absolution of Somers, the hall where the eloquence
of Strafford had for a moment awed and melted a
victorious party inflamed with just resentment, the hall
where Charles had confronted the High Court of Justice

with the placid courage which has half redeemed his
fame. Neither military nor civil pomp was wanting. The
avenues were lined with grenadiers. The streets were
kept clear by cavalry. The peers, robed in gold and
ermine, were marshalled by the heralds under Garter King-
at-arms. The judges in their vestments of state attended
to give advice on points of law. Near a hundred and
seventy lords, three fourths of the Upper House as the
Upper House then was, walked in solemn order from their
usual place of assembling to the tribunal. The junior 10
baron present led the way, George Eliott, Lord Heath-
field, recently ennobled for his memorable defence of
Gibraltar against the fleets and armies of France and
Spain. The long procession was closed by the Duke of
Norfolk, Earl Marshal of the realm, by the great digni-
taries, and by the brothers and sons of the King. Last
of all came the Prince of Wales, conspicuous by his fine
person and noble bearing. The grey old walls were hung
with scarlet. The long galleries were crowded by an
audience such as has rarely excited the fears or the 20
emulation of an orator. There were gathered together,
from all parts of a great, free, enlightened, and prosperous
empire, grace and female loveliness, wit and learning, the
representatives of every science and of every art. There
were seated round the Queen the fair-haired young daughters
of the house of Brunswick. There the Ambassadors of
great Kings and Commonwealths gazed with admiration
on a spectacle which no other country in the world could
present. There Siddons, in the prime of her majestic
beauty, looked with emotion on a scene surpassing all the 30
imitations of the stage. There the historian of the Roman
Empire thought of the days when Cicero pleaded the
cause of Sicily against Verres, and when, before a senate
which still retained some show of freedom, Tacitus thun-
dered against the oppressor of Africa. There were seen,
side by side, the greatest painter and the greatest scholar of

the age. The spectacle had allured Reynolds from that easel which has preserved to us the thoughtful foreheads of so many writers and statesmen, and the sweet smiles of so many noble matrons. It had induced Parr to suspend his labours in that dark and profound mine from which he had extracted a vast treasure of erudition, a treasure too often buried in the earth, too often paraded with injudicious and inelegant ostentation, but still precious, massive, and splendid. There appeared the voluptuous

10 charms of her to whom the heir of the throne had in secret plighted his faith. There too was she, the beautiful mother of a beautiful race, the Saint Cecilia whose delicate features, lighted up by love and music, art has rescued from the common decay. There were the members of that brilliant society which quoted, criticized, and exchanged repartees, under the rich peacock-hangings of Mrs. Montague. And there the ladies whose lips, more persuasive than those of Fox himself, had carried the Westminster election against palace and treasury, shone round Georgiana

20 Duchess of Devonshire.

The Sergeants made proclamation. Hastings advanced to the bar and bent his knee. The culprit was indeed not unworthy of that great presence. He had ruled an extensive and populous country, and made laws and treaties, had sent forth armies, had set up and pulled down princes. And in his high place he had so borne himself, that all had feared him, that most had loved him, and that hatred itself could deny him no title to glory, except virtue. He looked like a great man, and not like a bad man. A

30 person small and emaciated, yet deriving dignity from a carriage which, while it indicated deference to the court, indicated also habitual self-possession and self-respect, a high and intellectual forehead, a brow pensive, but not gloomy, a mouth of inflexible decision, a face pale and worn, but serene, on which was written, as legibly as under the picture in the council-chamber at Calcutta, *Mens*

æqua in arduis; such was the aspect with which the great proconsul presented himself to his judges.

His counsel accompanied him, men all of whom were afterwards raised by their talents and learning to the highest posts in their profession, the bold and strong-minded Law, afterwards Chief Justice of the King's Bench; the more humane and eloquent Dallas, afterwards Chief Justice of the Common Pleas; and Plomer who, near twenty years later, successfully conducted in the same high court the defence of Lord Melville, and subsequently 10 became Vice-chancellor and Master of the Rolls.

But neither the culprit nor his advocates attracted so much notice as the accusers. In the midst of the blaze of red drapery, a space had been fitted up with green benches, and tables for the Commons. The managers, with Burke at their head, appeared in full dress. The collectors of gossip did not fail to remark that even Fox, generally so regardless of his appearance, had paid to the illustrious tribunal the compliment of wearing a bag and sword. Pitt had refused to be one of the conductors of the im- 20 peachment; and his commanding, copious, and sonorous eloquence was wanting to that great muster of various talents. Age and blindness had unfitted Lord North for the duties of a public prosecutor; and his friends were left without the help of his excellent sense, his tact, and his urbanity. But, in spite of the absence of these two distinguished members of the Lower House, the box in which the managers stood contained an array of speakers such as perhaps had not appeared together since the great age of Athenian eloquence. There were Fox and Sheridan, 30 the English Demosthenes and the English Hyperides. There was Burke, ignorant, indeed, or negligent of the art of adapting his reasonings and his style to the capacity and taste of his hearers, but in amplitude of comprehension and richness of imagination superior to every orator, ancient or modern. There, with eyes reverentially fixed

H

on Burke, appeared the finest gentleman of the age, his form developed by every manly exercise, his face beaming with intelligence and spirit, the ingenious, the chivalrous, the high-souled Windham. Nor, though surrounded by such men, did the youngest manager pass unnoticed. At an age when most of those who distinguished themselves in life are still contending for prizes and fellowships at college, he had won for himself a conspicuous place in parliament. No advantage of fortune or connection was
10 wanting that could set off to the height his splendid talents and his unblemished honour. At twenty-three he had been thought worthy to be ranked with the veteran statesmen who appeared as the delegates of the British Commons, at the bar of the British nobility. All who stood at that bar, save him alone, are gone, culprit, advocates, accusers. To the generation which is now in the vigour of life, he is the sole representative of a great age which has passed away. But those who, within the last ten years, have listened with delight, till the morning sun
20 shone on the tapestries of the House of Lords, to the lofty and animated eloquence of Charles Earl Grey, are able to form some estimate of the powers of a race of men among whom he was not the foremost.

The charges and the answers of Hastings were first read. The ceremony occupied two whole days, and was rendered less tedious than it would otherwise have been by the silver voice and just emphasis of Cowper, the clerk of the court, a near relation of the amiable poet. On the third day Burke rose. Four sittings were occupied by his
30 opening speech, which was intended to be a general introduction to all the charges. With an exuberance of thought and a splendour of diction which more than satisfied the highly-raised expectation of the audience, he described the character and institutions of the natives of India, recounted the circumstances in which the Asiatic empire of Britain had originated, and set forth the constitution of

the Company and of the English Presidencies. Having
thus attempted to communicate to his hearers an idea of
Eastern society, as vivid as that which existed in his own
mind, he proceeded to arraign the administration of Hastings as systematically conducted in defiance of morality
and public law. The energy and pathos of the great
orator extorted expressions of unwonted admiration from
the stern and hostile Chancellor, and, for a moment,
seemed to pierce even the resolute heart of the defendant.
The ladies in the galleries, unaccustomed to such displays 10
of eloquence, excited by the solemnity of the occasion, and
perhaps not unwilling to display their taste and sensibility, were in a state of uncontrollable emotion. Hand-
kerchiefs were pulled out ; smelling-bottles were handed
round ; hysterical sobs and screams were heard ; and Mrs.
Sheridan was carried out in a fit. At length the orator
concluded. Raising his voice till the old arches of Irish
oak resounded, "Therefore," said he, "hath it with all
confidence been ordered by the Commons of Great Britain,
that I impeach Warren Hastings of high crimes and mis- 20
demeanours. I impeach him in the name of the Commons'
House of Parliament, whose trust he has betrayed. I
impeach him in the name of the English nation, whose
ancient honour he has sullied. I impeach him in the
name of the people of India, whose rights he has trodden
under foot, and whose country he has turned into a desert.
Lastly, in the name of human nature itself, in the name
of both sexes, in the name of every age, in the name of
every rank, I impeach the common enemy and oppressor
of all !"   30
When the deep murmur of various emotions had sub-
sided, Mr. Fox rose to address the Lords respecting the
course of proceeding to be followed. The wish of the
accusers was that the Court would bring to a close the
investigation of the first charge before the second was
opened. The wish of Hastings and of his counsel was

that the managers should open all the charges, and produce all the evidence for the prosecution, before the defence began. The Lords retired to their own House to consider the question. The Chancellor took the side of Hastings. Lord Loughborough, who was now in opposition, supported the demand of the managers. The division showed which way the inclination of the tribunal leaned. A majority of near three to one decided in favour of the course for which Hastings contended.

When the Court sat again, Mr. Fox, assisted by Mr. Grey, opened the charge respecting Cheyte Sing, and several days were spent in reading papers and hearing witnesses. The next article was that relating to the Princesses of Oude. The conduct of this part of the case was intrusted to Sheridan. The curiosity of the public to hear him was unbounded. His sparkling and highly finished declamation lasted two days ; but the Hall was crowded to suffocation during the whole time. It was said that fifty guineas had been paid for a single ticket. Sheridan, when he concluded, contrived, with a knowledge of stage-effect which his father might have envied, to sink back, as if exhausted, into the arms of Burke, who hugged him with the energy of generous admiration.

June was now far advanced. The session could not last much longer ; and the progress which had been made in the impeachment was not very satisfactory. There were twenty charges. On two only of these had even the case for the prosecution been heard ; and it was now a year since Hastings had been admitted to bail.

The interest taken by the public in the trial was great when the Court began to sit, and rose to the height when Sheridan spoke on the charge relating to the Begums. From that time the excitement went down fast. The spectacle had lost the attraction of novelty. The great displays of rhetoric were over. What was behind was not of a nature to entice men of letters from their books in the morning, or

to tempt ladies who had left the masquerade at two to be
out of bed before eight. There remained examinations and
cross-examinations. There remained statements of accounts.
There remained the reading of papers, filled with words un-
intelligible to English ears, with lacs and crores, zemindars
and aumils, sunnuds and perwannahs, jaghires and nuzzurs.
There remained bickerings, not always carried on with the
best taste or with the best temper, between the managers of
the impeachment and the counsel for the defence, particularly
between Mr. Burke and Mr. Law. There remained the end- 10
less marches and counter-marches of the Peers between their
House and the Hall : for as often as a point of law was to be
discussed, their Lordships retired to discuss it apart; and the
consequence was, as a peer wittily said, that the Judges
walked and the trial stood still.

It is to be added that, in the spring of 1788 when the trial
commenced, no important question, either of domestic or
foreign policy, excited the public mind. The proceeding in
Westminster Hall, therefore, naturally attracted most of the
attention of Parliament and of the public. It was the one 20
great event of that season. But in the following year the
King's illness, the debates on the Regency, the expectation
of a change of Ministry, completely diverted public attention
from Indian affairs ; and within a fortnight after George the
Third had returned thanks in St. Paul's for his recovery, the
States-General of France met at Versailles. In the midst of
the agitation produced by these events, the impeachment was
for a time almost forgotten.

The trial in the Hall went on languidly. In the session of
1788, when the proceedings had the interest of novelty, and 30
when the Peers had little other business before them, only
thirty-five days were given to the impeachment. In 1789,
the Regency Bill occupied the Upper House till the session
was far advanced. When the King recovered the circuits
were beginning. The judges left town ; the Lords waited
for the return of the oracles of jurisprudence ; and the con-

sequence was that during the whole year only seventeen days
were given to the case of Hastings. It was clear that the
matter would be protracted to a length unprecedented in the
annals of criminal law.

In truth, it is impossible to deny that impeachment, though
it is a fine ceremony, and though it may have been useful in
the seventeenth century, is not a proceeding from which
much good can now be expected. Whatever confidence may
be placed in the decisions of the Peers on an appeal arising
10 out of ordinary litigation, it is certain that no man has the
least confidence in their impartiality, when a great public
functionary, charged with a great state crime, is brought to
their bar. They are all politicians. There is hardly one
among them whose vote on an impeachment may not be
confidently predicted before a witness has been examined;
and, even if it were possible to rely on their justice, they
would still be quite unfit to try such a cause as that of
Hastings. They sit only during half the year. They have
to transact much legislative and much judicial business. The
20 law-lords, whose advice is required to guide the unlearned
majority, are employed daily in administering justice elsewhere. It is impossible, therefore, that during a busy session,
the Upper House should give more than a few days to an
impeachment. To expect that their Lordships would give up
partridge-shooting, in order to bring the greatest delinquent
to speedy justice, or to relieve accused innocence by speedy
acquittal, would be unreasonable indeed. A well-constituted
tribunal, sitting regularly six days in the week, and nine
hours in the day, would have brought the trial of Hastings
30 to a close in less than three months. The Lords had not
finished their work in seven years.

The result ceased to be matter of doubt, from the time
when the Lords resolved that they would be guided by the
rules of evidence which are received in the inferior courts of
the realm. Those rules, it is well known, exclude much
information which would be quite sufficient to determine the

conduct of any reasonable man, in the most important transactions of private life. Those rules, at every assizes, save
scores of culprits whom judges, jury, and spectators, firmly
believe to be guilty. But when those rules were rigidly
applied to offences committed many years before, at the
distance of many thousand miles, conviction was, of course,
out of the question. We do not blame the accused and his
counsel for availing themselves of every legal advantage in
order to obtain an acquittal. But it is clear that an acquittal
so obtained cannot be pleaded in bar of the judgment of 10
history.

Several attempts were made by the friends of Hastings to
put a stop to the trial. In 1789 they proposed a vote of
censure upon Burke, for some violent language which he had
used respecting the death of Nuncomar and the connection
between Hastings and Impey. Burke was then unpopular
in the last degree both with the House and with the country.
The asperity and indecency of some expressions which he
had used during the debates on the Regency had annoyed
even his warmest friends. The vote of censure was carried ; 20
and those who had moved it hoped that the managers would
resign in disgust. Burke was deeply hurt. But his zeal for
what he considered as the cause of justice and mercy triumphed over his personal feelings. He received the censure
of the House with dignity and meekness, and declared that
no personal mortification or humiliation should induce him
to flinch from the sacred duty which he had undertaken.

In the following year the Parliament was dissolved, and
the friends of Hastings entertained a hope that the new
House of Commons might not be disposed to go on with the 30
impeachment. They began by maintaining that the whole
proceeding was terminated by the dissolution. Defeated on
this point, they made a direct motion that the impeachment
should be dropped ; but they were defeated by the combined
forces of the Government and the Opposition. It was, however, resolved that, for the sake of expedition, many of the

articles should be withdrawn. In truth, had not some such measure been adopted, the trial would have lasted till the defendant was in his grave.

At length, in the spring of 1795, the decision was pronounced, near eight years after Hastings had been brought by the Sergeant-at-arms of the Commons to the bar of the Lords. On the last day of this great procedure the public curiosity, long suspended, seemed to be revived. Anxiety about the judgment there could be none ; for it had been
10 fully ascertained that there was a great majority for the defendant. Nevertheless many wished to see the pageant, and the Hall was as much crowded as on the first day. But those who, having been present on the first day, now bore a part in the proceedings of the last, were few ; and most of those few were altered men.

As Hastings himself said, the arraignment had taken place before one generation, and the judgment was pronounced by another. The spectator could not look at the woolsack, or at the red benches of the Peers, or at the green benches of the
20 Commons, without seeing something that reminded him of the instability of all human things, of the instability of power and fame and life, of the more lamentable instability of friendship. The great seal was borne before Lord Loughborough who, when the trial commenced, was a fierce opponent of Mr. Pitt's government, and who was now a member of that government, while Thurlow, who presided in the court when it first sat, estranged from all his old allies, sat scowling among the junior barons. Of about a hundred and sixty nobles who walked in the procession on
30 the first day, sixty had been laid in their family vaults. Still more affecting must have been the sight of the managers' box. What had become of that fair fellowship, so closely bound together by public and private ties, so resplendent with every talent and accomplishment ? It had been scattered by calamities more bitter than the bitterness of death. The great chiefs were still living, and still in the full vigour

of their genius. But their friendship was at an end. It had
been violently and publicly dissolved, with tears and stormy
reproaches. If those men, once so dear to each other, were
now compelled to meet for the purpose of managing the
impeachment, they met as strangers whom public business
had brought together, and behaved to each other with cold
and distant civility. Burke had in his vortex whirled
away Windham. Fox had been followed by Sheridan and
Grey.

Only twenty-nine Peers voted. Of these only six found 10
Hastings guilty on the charges relating to Cheyte Sing and
to the Begums. On other charges, the majority in his
favour was still greater. On some, he was unanimously
absolved. He was then called to the bar, was informed
from the woolsack that the Lords had acquitted him,
and was solemnly discharged. He bowed respectfully and
retired.

We have said that the decision had been fully expected.
It was also generally approved. At the commencement of
the trial there had been a strong and indeed unreasonable 20
feeling against Hastings. At the close of the trial there was
a feeling equally strong and equally unreasonable in his
favour. One cause of the change was, no doubt, what is
commonly called the fickleness of the multitude, but what
seems to us to be merely the general law of human nature.
Both in individuals and in masses violent excitement is
always followed by remission, and often by reaction. We
are all inclined to depreciate whatever we have overpraised,
and, on the other hand, to show undue indulgence where we
have shown undue rigour. It was thus in the case of 30
Hastings. The length of his trial, moreover, made him an
object of compassion. It was thought, and not without
reason, that, even if he was guilty, he was still an ill-used
man, and that an impeachment of eight years was more than
a sufficient punishment. It was also felt that, though, in the
ordinary course of criminal law, a defendant is not allowed to

set off his good actions against his crimes, a great political
cause should be tried on different principles, and that a man
who had governed an empire during thirteen years might
have done some very reprehensible things, and yet might be
on the whole deserving of rewards and honours rather than
of fine and imprisonment. The press, an instrument
neglected by the prosecutors, was used by Hastings and his
friends with great effect. Every ship, too, that arrived from
Madras or Bengal, brought a cuddy full of his admirers.
10 Every gentleman from India spoke of the late Governor-
General as having deserved better, and having been treated
worse, than any man living. The effect of this testimony
unanimously given by all persons who knew the East, was
naturally very great. Retired members of the Indian services, civil and military, were settled in all corners of the
kingdom. Each of them was, of course, in his own little
circle, regarded as an oracle on an Indian question ; and they
were, with scarcely one exception, the zealous advocates of
Hastings. It is to be added, that the numerous addresses to
20 the late Governor-General, which his friends in Bengal
obtained from the natives and transmitted to England, made
a considerable impression. To these addresses we attach
little or no importance. (That Hastings was beloved by the
people whom he governed is true ; but the eulogies of
pundits, zemindars, Mahommedan doctors, do not prove it to
be true.) For an English collector or judge would have found
it easy to induce any native who could write to sign a
panegyric on the most odious ruler that ever was in India.
It was said that at Benares, the very place at which the acts
30 set forth in the first article of impeachment had been committed, the natives had erected a temple to Hastings ; and
this story excited a strong sensation in England. (Burke's
observations on the apotheosis were admirable. He saw no
reason for astonishment, he said, in the incident which had
been represented as so striking. He knew something of the
mythology of the Brahmins. He knew that as they wor-

shipped some gods from love, so they worshipped others from fear. He knew that they erected shrines, not only to the benignant deities of light and plenty, but also to the fiends who preside over small-pox and murder. Nor did he at all dispute the claim of Mr. Hastings to be admitted into such a Pantheon. This reply has always struck us as one of the finest that ever was made in Parliament. It is a grave and forcible argument, decorated by the most brilliant wit and fancy.

Hastings was, however, safe. But in every thing except 10 character, he would have been far better off if, when first impeached, he had at once pleaded guilty, and paid a fine of fifty thousand pounds. He was a ruined man. The legal expenses of his defence had been enormous. The expenses which did not appear in his attorney's bill were perhaps larger still. Great sums had been paid to Major Scott. Great sums had been laid out in bribing newspapers, rewarding pamphleteers, and circulating tracts. Burke, so early as 1790, declared in the House of Commons that twenty thousand pounds had been employed in corrupting the press. It 20 is certain that no controversial weapon, from the gravest reasoning to the coarsest ribaldry, was left unemployed. Logan defended the accused governor with great ability in prose. For the lovers of verse, the speeches of the managers were burlesqued in Simpkin's letters. It is, we are afraid, indisputable that Hastings stooped so low as to court the aid of that malignant and filthy baboon John Williams, who called himself Anthony Pasquin. It was necessary to subsidise such allies largely. The private hoards of Mrs. Hastings had disappeared. It is said that the banker to whom they 30 had been entrusted had failed. Still if Hastings had practised strict economy, he would, after all his losses, have had a moderate competence ; but in the management of his private affairs he was imprudent. The dearest wish of his heart had always been to regain Daylesford. At length, in the very year in which his trial commenced, the wish was

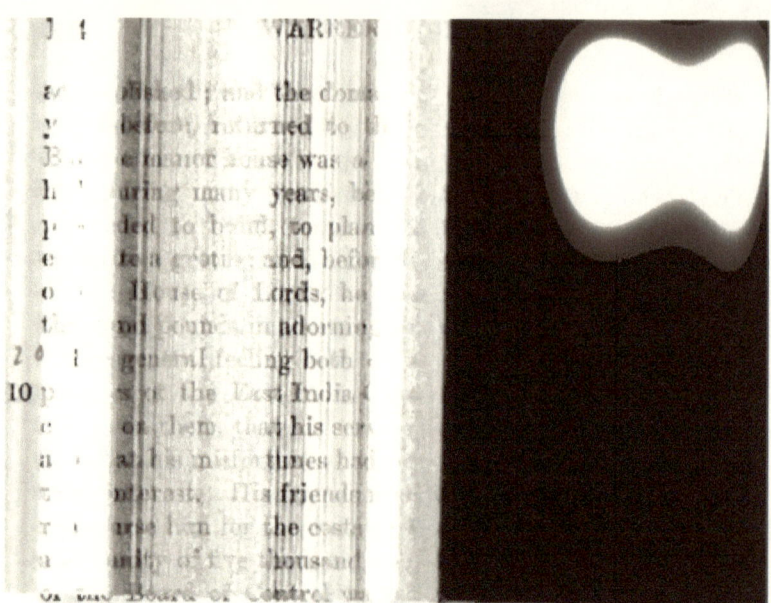

the Board of Control was Mr. Dundas, who had himself been
a party to the impeachment, who had, on that account, been
reviled with great bitterness by the adherents of Hastings,
20 and who, therefore, was not in a very complying mood. He
refused to consent to what the Directors suggested. The
Directors remonstrated. A long controversy followed.
Hastings, in the mean time, was reduced to such distress,
that he could hardly pay his weekly bills. At length a
compromise was made. An annuity of four thousand a year
was settled on Hastings; and in order to enable him to meet
pressing demands, he was to receive ten years' annuity in
advance. The Company was also permitted to lend him
fifty thousand pounds, to be repaid by instalments without
30 interest. This relief, though given in the most absurd
manner, was sufficient to enable the retired governor to live
in comfort, and even in luxury, if he had been a skilful
manager. But he was careless and profuse, and was more
than once under the necessity of applying to the Company
for assistance, which was liberally given.

He had security and affluence, but not the power and dignity which, when he landed from India, he had reason to expect. He had then looked forward to a coronet, a red riband, a seat at the Council Board, an office at Whitehall. He was then only fifty-two, and might hope for many years of bodily and mental vigour. The case was widely different when he left the bar of the Lords. He was now too old a man to turn his mind to a new class of studies and duties. He had no chance of receiving any mark of royal favour while Mr. Pitt remained in power; and, when Mr. Pitt retired, Hastings was approaching his seventieth year. 10

Once, and only once, after his acquittal, he interfered in politics; and that interference was not much to his honour. In 1804 he exerted himself strenuously to prevent Mr. Addington, against whom Fox and Pitt had combined, from resigning the Treasury. It is difficult to believe that a man so able and energetic as Hastings can have thought that, when Bonaparte was at Boulogne with a great army, the defence of our island could safely be intrusted to a ministry which did not contain a single person whom flattery could describe as a great statesman. It is also certain that, on the 20 important question which had raised Mr. Addington to power, and on which he differed from both Fox and Pitt, Hastings, as might have been expected, agreed with Fox and Pitt, and was decidedly opposed to Addington. Religious intolerance has never been the vice of the Indian service, and certainly was not the vice of Hastings. But Mr. Addington had treated him with marked favour. Fox had been a principal manager of the impeachment. To Pitt it was owing that there had been an impeachment; and Hastings, we fear, was on this occasion guided by personal considerations, rather 30 than by a regard to the public interest.

The last twenty-four years of his life were chiefly passed at Daylesford. He amused himself with embellishing his grounds, riding fine Arab horses, fattening prize-cattle, and trying to rear Indian animals and vegetables in England. He sent for seeds of a very fine custard-apple, from the

garden of what had once been his own villa, among the
green hedgerows of Allipore. He tried also to naturalise
in Worcestershire the delicious leechee, almost the only fruit
of Bengal which deserves to be regretted even amidst the
plenty of Covent Garden. The Mogul emperors, in the time
of their greatness, had in vain attempted to introduce into
Hindostan the goat of the table-land of Thibet, whose down
supplies the looms of Cashmere with the materials of the
finest shawls. Hastings tried, with no better fortune, to
10 rear a breed at Daylesford; nor does he seem to have
succeeded better with the cattle of Bootan, whose tails are
in high esteem as the best fans for brushing away the
mosquitoes.

Literature divided his attention with his conservatories
and his menagerie. He had always loved books, and they
were now necessary to him. Though not a poet, in any
high sense of the word, he wrote neat and polished lines
with great facility, and was fond of exercising this talent.
Indeed, if we must speak out, he seems to have been more of
20 a Trissotin than was to be expected from the powers of his
mind, and from the great part which he had played in life.
We are assured in these Memoirs that the first thing which
he did in the morning was to compose a copy of verses.
When the family and guests assembled, the poem made its
appearance as regularly as the eggs and rolls; and Mr. Gleig
requires us to believe that, if from any accident Hastings
came to the breakfast-table without one of his charming
performances in his hand, the omission was felt by all as
a grievous disappointment. Tastes differ widely. For our-
30 selves we must say that, however good the breakfasts at
Daylesford may have been,—and we are assured that the tea
was of the most aromatic flavour, and that neither tongue
nor venison-pasty was wanting,—we should have thought
the reckoning high if we had been forced to earn our repast
by listening every day to a new madrigal or sonnet composed by our host. We are glad, however, that Mr. Gleig

has preserved this little feature of character, though we
think it by no means a beauty. It is good to be often
reminded of the inconsistency of human nature, and to learn
to look without wonder or disgust on the weaknesses which
are found in the strongest minds. Dionysius in old times,
Frederic in the last century, with capacity and vigour equal
to the conduct of the greatest affairs, united all the little
vanities and affectations of provincial blue-stockings. These
great examples may console the admirers of Hastings for the
affliction of seeing him reduced to the level of the Hayleys 10
and Sewards.

When Hastings had passed many years in retirement, and
had long outlived the common age of men, he again became
for a short time an object of general attention. In 1813 the
charter of the East India Company was renewed; and much
discussion about Indian affairs took place in Parliament.
It was determined to examine witnesses at the bar of the
Commons; and Hastings was ordered to attend. He had
appeared at that bar once before. It was when he read his
answer to the charges which Burke had laid on the table. 20
Since that time twenty-seven years had elapsed; public
feeling had undergone a complete change; the nation had
now forgotten his faults, and remembered only his services.
The reappearance, too, of a man who had been among the
most distinguished of a generation that had passed away,
who now belonged to history, and who seemed to have risen
from the dead, could not but produce a solemn and pathetic
effect. The Commons received him with acclamations, ordered
a chair to be set for him, and when he retired, rose and uncovered. There were, indeed, a few who did not sympathise 30
with the general feeling. One or two of the managers of the
impeachment were present. They sate in the same seats
which they had occupied when they had been thanked for
the services which they had rendered in Westminster Hall:
for, by the courtesy of the House, a member who has been
thanked in his place is considered as having a right always

to occupy that place. These gentlemen were not disposed to
admit that they had employed several of the best years of
their lives in persecuting an innocent man. They accordingly
kept their seats, and pulled their hats over their brows ; but
the exceptions only made the prevailing enthusiasm more
remarkable. The Lords received the old man with similar
tokens of respect. The University of Oxford conferred on
him the degree of Doctor of Laws ; and, in the Sheldonian
Theatre, the under-graduates welcomed him with tumultuous
10 cheering.

These marks of public esteem were soon followed by marks
of royal favour. Hastings was sworn of the Privy Council,
and was admitted to a long private audience of the Prince
Regent, who treated him very graciously. When the Emperor of Russia and the King of Prussia visited England,
Hastings appeared in their train both at Oxford and in the
Guildhall of London, and, though surrounded by a crowd of
princes and great warriors, was every where received by the
public with marks of respect and admiration. He was
20 presented by the Prince Regent both to Alexander and
to Frederic William ; and his Royal Highness went so
far as to declare in public that honours far higher than
a seat in the Privy Council were due, and would soon
be paid, to the man who had saved the British dominions
in Asia. Hastings now confidently expected a peerage ;
but, from some unexplained cause, he was again disappointed.

He lived about four years longer, in the enjoyment of
good spirits, of faculties not impaired to any painful or
30 degrading extent, and of health such as is rarely enjoyed
by those who attain such an age. At length, on the twenty-
second of August, 1818, in the eighty-sixth year of his age,
he met death with the same tranquil and decorous fortitude
which he had opposed to all the trials of his various and
eventful life.

With all his faults,—and they were neither few nor small,

—only one cemetery was worthy to contain his remains. In that temple of silence and reconciliation where the enmities of twenty generations lie buried, in the Great Abbey which has during many ages afforded a quiet resting-place to those whose minds and bodies have been shattered by the contentions of the Great Hall, the dust of the illustrious accused should have mingled with the dust of the illustrious accusers. This was not to be. Yet the place of interment was not ill chosen. Behind the chancel of the parish church of Daylesford, in earth which already held the bones of many chiefs of the house of Hastings, was laid the coffin of the greatest man who has ever borne that ancient and widely extended name. On that very spot probably, fourscore years before, the little Warren, meanly clad and scantily fed, had played with the children of ploughmen. Even then his young mind had revolved plans which might be called romantic. Yet, however romantic, it is not likely that they had been so strange as the truth. Not only had the poor orphan retrieved the fallen fortunes of his line. Not only had he repurchased the old lands, and rebuilt the old dwelling. He had preserved and extended an empire. He had founded a polity. He had administered government and war with more than the capacity of Richelieu. He had patronised learning with the judicious liberality of Cosmo. He had been attacked by the most formidable combination of enemies that ever sought the destruction of a single victim; and over that combination, after a struggle of ten years, he had triumphed. He had at length gone down to his grave in the fulness of age, in peace, after so many troubles, in honour, after so much obloquy. Those who look on his character without favour or malevolence will pronounce that, in the two great elements of all social virtue, in respect for the rights of others, and in sympathy for the sufferings of others, he was deficient. His principles were somewhat lax. His heart was somewhat hard. But while we cannot with truth describe him either

I

as a righteous or as a merciful ruler, we cannot regard without admiration the amplitude and fertility of his intellect, his rare talents for command, for administration, and for controversy, his dauntless courage, his honourable poverty, his fervent zeal for the interests of the state, his noble equanimity, tried by both extremes of fortune, and never disturbed by either.

i think his talent rather than
is interest prompted him to
id so well the interests of
he Company, of England, and
i India.

NOTES.

P. 1. l. 1. **This book,** Gleig's *Life of Warren Hastings*, 3 vols., 1841 : Gleig, George Robert, 1796-1888, entered at Oxford in 1811, but left before taking his degree to join the 85th Regiment with which he served in the Peninsular and American Wars ; in 1816 he went on half-pay, and returned to Oxford. Later on he was ordained a clergyman, and ultimately became Chaplain-General of the Forces. Besides the *Life of Warren Hastings*, he was author of *Campaigns of the British Army at Washington and New Orleans, Life of Sir Thomas Munro, History of India, Lives of Military Commanders*, various Novels, Essays, etc. **manufactured,** a scornful expression, as though the book were merely the work of manual labour and owed nothing to intelligence or literary skill.

l. 8. **undigested correspondence,** a mass of letters printed without any such arrangement as would guide the reader in following the narrative.

l. 13. **a bookmaker,** one who cannot be said to *write* books, but only to *make* books by putting together material supplied to him, a sort of scissors and paste operation : cp. " manufactured," l. 1.

ll. 19, 20. **is neither ... Scott,** is very far from having the literary power possessed by either Goldsmith or Scott. Goldsmith's school *History of Greece* was a very poor piece of work, undertaken not because he had deeply studied the subject or as a scholar was well fitted for the task, but because his poverty obliged him to accept any employment for his pen that was offered him. Scott's *Life of Napoleon* was likewise a piece of mere drudgery for which his genius was but poorly adapted.

ll. 25-P. 2. l. 2. **which bear...Man,** which in point of moral doctrine are as much below the standard of Machiavelli's "Prince" as that work is below the "Whole Duty of Man." **The Prince,** *Del Principe*, was a treatise on King-craft written by Nicolo Machiavelli, the celebrated Florentine statesman and historian, in 1542, for the instruction of the young Lorenzo de Medici. Of

131

its character Macaulay, *Essay on Machiavelli*, writes, "It is
indeed scarcely possible for any person not well acquainted with
the history and literature of Italy to read, without horror and
amazement, the celebrated treatise which has brought so much
obloquy on the name of Machiavelli. Such a display of wickedness, naked, yet not ashamed, such cool, judicious, scientific
atrocity seem rather to belong to a fiend than to the most
depraved of men. Principles which the most hardened ruffian
would scarcely hint to his most trusted accomplice, or avow,
without the disguise of palliating sophism, even to his own mind,
are professed without the slightest circumlocution, and assumed
as the fundamental axioms of all political science." Later on in
the same Essay, Macaulay attributes the immorality of the book
rather to the spirit of the times, the state of moral feeling among
the Italians of the period, than to any peculiar depravity of
character and intellect on the part of its author. **the Whole
Duty of Man,** a well-known treatise on the subject, which has
been ascribed on strong grounds to Richard Allestre, D.D.,
Regius Professor of Divinity, Oxford, and Provost of Eton.
Cowper spoke of it as " that repository of self-righteousness and
pharisaical lumber"; an opinion with which Southey wholly
disagreed.

l. 6. **Furor Biographicus,** the mania which causes biographers
to see nothing but perfection in the characters of those whose
lives they have undertaken to write : what Macaulay elsewhere
calls the *lues Boswelliana*, because in Boswell's Life of Johnson
the disease was exhibited in its most prominent form.

l. 7. **the goitre,** a swelling of the throat prevalent more especially in mountainous districts, but supposed to be due rather to
some mineral impregnation of the drinking water than to the
climate ; F. *goître*, a swelled neck, Lat. *guttur*, throat.

ll. 15, 6. **neither is it that** ... 1813, see below, pp. 127, 8.

ll. 17-9. **to represent ... ridiculous,** *i.e.* because according to
Macaulay's belief, great crimes were proved against him. Yet,
though high-handed acts and mistakes of policy are to be set down
to the account of Hastings, the dark spots on his fame, which Macaulay has laboured to make still darker, have on fuller inquiry
been shown to be set upon it by calumny and ignorance of facts,
and his private character may be said to have been almost stainless. For a full consideration of the more important charges
brought against him, see Appendixes.

ll. 25, 6. **the splendour ... spots,** his fame was so bright that
even many spots could not obscure it. The image is from spots
on the sun.

l. 27. **Mr. Mill,** the value of Mill's *History of India*, though
in some respects great, is much marred by his unfairness, which

in respect to Hastings is most pronounced. Sir J. Stephen and Sir J. Strachey convict him of bad faith, inaccuracy, and misrepresentation.

l. 30. **a daub ... unnatural, a mere** mass of colour that blurred instead of revealing the characteristics of the real man : to **daub** is to smear over, to plaster : **insipid**, tasteless, without flavour, here = giving no taste of what the man was.

l. 32. **young Lely,** Sir Peter Lely, a celebrated portrait painter, 1617-1680, born in Westphalia. The name of his father, a native of Holland, was Van der Waes, and Le Lys or Lely, a nickname given to him, was adopted by his son. In 1641 he came to England where he was patronized successively by Charles I., Cromwell, and Charles II., the last of whom appointed him state-painter, and conferred knighthood upon him. Originally a painter of historical subjects and landscapes, he afterwards became famous as a portrait painter of the school of Vandyck. His most famous work is a collection of portraits of the ladies of Charles the Second's Court. Cromwell was painted by him about 1650.

P. 3. l. 1. **regular features,** here used contemptuously of commonplace features that showed no distinctive traits of character, though want of individuality is not necessarily involved in regularity of feature.

l. 2. **curl-pated minions,** effeminate courtiers who wore their hair long and paid great attention to the curling of their locks, as contrasted with the " Roundheads," the Puritan followers of Cromwell, who in their austerity cut their hair close. The love-locks, afterwards so fashionable and so often the subject of ridicule and satire, were introduced from France by Charles the First. **minion,** a favourite flatterer ; F. *mignon,* adjective, dainty, neat, spruce.

l. 3. **should go forth,** *sc.* to the world.

l. 6. **policy,** statesmanship.

ll. 10, 1. **Warren Hastings ... race,** Hastings derived his Christian name from his mother, Hester Warren, daughter of a gentleman who owned a small estate in Gloucestershire. The taunt which Burke at the impeachment of Hastings flung at him of his being of "low, obscure, and vulgar origin," is supposed to have been due to the scandalous malignity of Francis. But, says Trotter, *Warren Hastings,* p. 9, "Had the charge been never so well founded, it could have taken nothing from the honour due to one whose public record needed no blazonry from the College of Heralds."

l. 12. **the great Danish sea-king,** Hasting, the Danish leader who invaded England in 893. See Green, *A Short History of the English People,* p. 53.

ll. 17, 8. **One branch ... Pembroke,** this was Laurence Hastings, son of John, third Baron Hastings. He served with Edward the Third in Flanders, and was, in 1339, created Earl Palatine of Pembroke, as representative of his great-uncle, Aymer de Valence, who died in 1324.

ll. 18-21. **From another ... historians,** William, Lord Hastings, 1430-1483, was for his services in the Civil Wars rewarded by Edward the Fourth, on his accession to the throne, with various valuable posts, among them that of lord chamberlain of the royal household. Sir Thomas More gives an account of the charge of treason brought against him by Gloucester, and of his execution at the Tower, and this account has been dramatized by Shakespeare in his *Richard the Third*.

ll. 22-4. **which, after long ... romance.** When, by the death of Francis, tenth Earl of Huntingdon, in 1789, the Earldom of Huntingdon became dormant, an eccentric clergyman, Theophilus Henry Hastings, assumed the title of Earl of Huntingdon, to which he was entitled by his descent from Francis, the second Earl, but took no steps to prove his right. On his death, in 1804, his nephew, Hans Francis Hastings, made some attempt to investigate his claim to the Earldom, but was soon compelled to abandon it for want of money. In 1817 his friend, Henry Nugent Bell, a legal antiquary, took the case up, and it was mainly owing to his exertions that Hans Francis established his claim. Bell "published a detailed account of the proceedings in the 'Huntingdon Peerage,' and the narrative of his various adventures ... displays a suspicious luxuriance of imagination not altogether in keeping with what professed to be a grave genealogical treatise" ... (*Dict. of Nat. Biog.*).

l. 25. **The lords of the manor.** "The lord [of a manor] was usually a baron, or other person of power and consequence, to whom had been granted an estate in fee simple in a tract of land. Of this land he retained as much as was necessary for his own use, as his own demesne, and usually built upon it a mansion or manor house" (Williams, *Law of Real Property*, p. 107, 6th ed.).

l. 29. **not ennobled,** not, like some of its branches, numbering among its members barons or earls: **highly considered,** held in esteem as of great local importance.

ll. 32, 3. **sent his plate ... Oxford,** sent the silver utensils of his household to be coined into money for the benefit of the King, who at that time had set up his Court at Oxford: **plate,** originally meaning a thin piece of metal, flat dish (F. *plat*, flat, from Greek πλατύς, broad), was later used especially of silver plates, dishes, candlesticks, etc., in domestic use.

ll. 35, 6. **was glad ... Lenthal,** this member of the family was John Hastings, who "was fain at last to make over all his

Yelford lands to Speaker Lenthall [who presided at the trial of Charles the First], and bury himself in the old decayed manor-house at Daylesford" (Trotter, p. 8).

P. 4, l. 3. **a merchant of London,** Mr. Jacob Knight.

ll. 5, 6. **had presented ... parish.** "An advowson is a perpetual right of presentation to an ecclesiastical benefice. The owner of the advowson is termed the patron of the benefice ... As patron he simply enjoys a right of nomination from time to time, as the living becomes vacant. And this right he exercises by a *presentation* to the bishop of some duly qualified clerk or clergyman, whom the bishop is accordingly bound to institute to the benefice and to cause him to be inducted into it" (Williams, *The Law of Real Property*, p. 307, 6th ed.). A **rectory** differs from a *vicarage* in that the rector receives the greater and the vicar only the lesser tithes. The origin of this difference is that when the advowsons of rectories were in the hands of spiritual patrons, they considered themselves to be the most fit persons to be rectors of the parish, so far as the receipt of tithes and other profits of the rectory were concerned, and left the duties of the cure to be performed by some poor priest as their vicar or deputy.

l. 10. **tithes,** a tithe (A.S. *teoða*, tenth) was the tenth part of the produce of the land offered to the clergy. Originally the payment was made in kind, but this has since been commuted for a payment in money made according to a periodical valuation of the land.

l. 12. **a place in the Customs,** a situation as clerk in the Customs' Office in London.

l. 13. **Pynaston,** or "Penyston," as it was more correctly spelt. Macaulay's words "an idle worthless boy" are based on Gleig's assertions; but when Penyston married he was six and twenty years of age.

ll. 14, 5. **died ... Indies,** that he went abroad after his wife's death is probably true, though even this is not certain; that he went to the West Indies is mere hearsay.

ll. 18, 9. **Warren ... 1732,** according to Keene (*Dict. of Nat. Biog.*) and Trotter, at Churchill in Oxfordshire, a few miles from Daylesford in Worcestershire; according to Lyall, at Daylesford itself. Penyston Hastings lived at Churchill, and on the front of his house there, which was by no means the house of one so poor as Gleig represents him, Earl Ducie erected a tablet stating that Warrren was born there, but even this is not certain.

l. 20. **his distressed grandfather,** his paternal grandfather, the rector above-mentioned.

l. 28. **how kindly ... book,** with what interest and eagerness he learnt his lessons.

l. 33. **their splendid housekeeping,** the profuse hospitality for which they were celebrated.

P. 5, ll. 4, 5. **He would ... Daylesford,** he was determined by recovering the property of his ancestors to recover also the right to be known as Hastings of Daylesford.

l. 12. **chequered,** varied: "the term *checky* in heraldry," says Skeat, "means that the shield is marked out into squares like a chess-board. To *checker* in like manner is 'to mark out like a chess-board'; hence to mark with cross-lines; and generally to variegate ... — O. F. *eschequier*, a chess-board; also an exchequer —O. F. *eschec*, check (at chess) !"

l. 18. **Newington,** a small town in Kent about forty miles from London.

l. 20. **seminary,** place of education: originally a seed garden, hence a place in which learning was sown. In former days Oxford and Cambridge were frequently spoken of as "seminaries of sound learning."

l. 21. **Westminster School,** founded by Henry VIII., and richly endowed by Elizabeth in 1560.

l. 22. **Vinny Bourne,** Vincent Bourne, chiefly renowned for the elegance of his Latin poems, a fellow of Trinity College, Cambridge, who on leaving college became a Master in Westminster School, where he remained till his death. His Latin poems were greatly admired by Lamb.

l. 23. **Churchill,** Charles, 1731-64, chiefly famous for his vigorous satires, chief among which were *The Rosciad, The Prophecy of Famine, The Duellist, The Conference, The Author, The Candidate;* a friend of Garrick's and a great admirer of Wilkes. **Colman,** George, 1732-1794, author of odes, prologues, epilogues, introductions, essays, and especially dramatic works, among which were *Polly Honeycombe, The Jealous Wife, The Deuce is in him,* as well as adaptations of Shakespeare and of Beaumont and Fletcher.

l. 24. **Lloyd,** Robert, an inferior poet; **Cumberland,** Richard, 1732-1811, a voluminous dramatist, author of *The Brothers, The Fashionable Lover, The Jew, The Wheel of Fortune, The West Indian,* etc., etc. Also of novels, memoirs, odes, translations, and controversial works; **Cowper,** William, the well-known poet.

l. 30. **the shy and secluded poet.** Macaulay in his Essay on *Moore's Life of Byron* speaks of Cowper as "the gentle, shy, melancholy Calvinist, whose spirit had been broken by fagging at school—who had not courage to earn a livelihood by reading the titles of bills in the House of Lords—and whose favourite associates were a blind lady and an evangelical clergyman."

l. 33. played in the cloister, the celebrated Cloisters of Westminster Abbey, adjoining the school, are of different dates, from the time of the Confessor to that of Edward the Third.

ll. 33-5. refused to believe ... wrong, Cowper's lines on the occasion were as follows :—

> " Hastings ! I knew thee young, and of a mind,
> While young, humane, conversable, and kind ;
> Nor can I well believe thee—gentle *then*—
> Now grown a villain, and the *worst* of men ;
> But rather some suspect, who have oppress'd
> And worried thee, as not themselves the *best*."

l. 36. among ... Ouse, in 1767 Cowper removed from Huntingdon to Olney, a village on the Ouse, in the north of Buckinghamshire, where he remained till his death in 1800. Macaulay is here referring to Cowper's poem entitled " The Dog and the Lily " ; in which are the lines, " It was the time when Ouse displayed His lilies newly blown ; Their beauties I intent survey'd, And one I wished my own."

P. 6, l. 2. His spirit ... tried, by the religious doubts and perplexities by which he was assailed during the greater portion of his life and which frequently impelled him with the desire to take his own life. The temptations which Macaulay goes on to mention are such as had assailed Hastings.

ll. 7, 8. Firmly ... depravity, though in theory he firmly held the Calvinistic doctrine that all men are desperately wicked.

ll. 8-11. his habits ... dominion, his own peaceful and innocent manner of life made it impossible to conceive that anyone of a nature so noble as Hastings could become capable of such crimes as were imputed to him.

ll. 14-8. But, we think ... prank, this guess of Macaulay's has no justification in anything we know of Impey's later life. He may have joined Hastings in schoolboy pranks, and perhaps then as afterwards have yielded to the stronger will of his schoolfellow, but that he had to be bribed to take his share in them is a purely gratuitous assumption. Macaulay, following Burke and Mill, had made up his mind that bribery induced Impey to serve Hastings in India, and he here prepares the way for his account of the transaction by making an ungenerous insinuation : **fag is here** used as an equivalent to ' tool,' instrument ; the fag, in ordinary school language, is a younger boy employed by his elders in semi-menial duties, such as running on errands, brushing clothes, cooking food, etc.; and as Hastings and Impey were of the same age and in the same form, there could have been no such relation between the two.

l. 20. boatman, ' oar,' as we should now say.

l. 21. **the foundation,** in an endowed school those boys are said to be 'on the foundation,' or to be 'foundationers,' who during their school and college days are supported wholly or partly from the revenues by which the school was founded, and the expression here is equivalent to a foundation scholarship, *i.e.* a scholarship paid to a student while at school.

l. 22. **the dormitory,** famous nowadays as the room in which the Westminster Play, generally one of Terence or Plautus, is performed at the end of each year.

l. 24. **a studentship,** a term peculiar to Christ Church College, Oxford, and answering to a scholarship at other colleges.

ll. 33, 4. **He even ... Oxford,** this statement is made by Hastings himself in an autobiography which he began when an old man, but wearied of after writing four pages.

ll. 35, 6. **He thought ... sufficient,** by **hexameters and pentameters** Macaulay means composition in Latin verse generally, the two more ordinary forms of such composition being the heroic verse of six feet and the elegiac couplet of six and five feet alternately. In using the word **wasted,** Mr. Chiswick's opinion, not Macaulay's, is expressed.

P. 7, l. 1. **a writership,** the older term for a civil servant of the company was 'writer,' such servants being in its earlier days clerks in the factories, with none of the revenue or magisterial duties which they were so soon to acquire.

ll. 8-10. **he sailed ... following,** the voyage even for those days was unusually long, but it often lasted many months. Sir C. Lawson, in his monograph on Hastings in the *Journal of Indian Art,* etc., says he *arrived* in January, 1750.

l. 12. **Fort William,** the new fort which Clive began to build in 1757. The phrase is still retained as the official designation of the Government of Calcutta, as is Fort St. George of Madras.

l. 14. **Dupleix,** Joseph, the celebrated Frenchman, who so distinguished himself in the service of the French East India Company that he was in 1742 appointed governor of Pondicherry. Had his ambitious designs of conquest been supported by his government at home, the struggle between the French and the English for empire in India would have been greatly prolonged, and by some it is thought might have terminated differently. He died in disgrace and poverty.

ll. 14-6. **had transformed ... generals,** by compelling them to play those parts in resisting the French designs.

l. 16. **The war of the succession,** in 1748, on the death of the Nizám ul Mulk, Viceroy of the Dakhan, Chanda Sáhib, son-in-law of a former Nawáb of the Karnátak, disputed the title of Anwár ud din, then in possession of that province. Joining with Mirzafar Jang, a grandson of the Nizám, who had set up a claim to the Viceroyalty, and applying to the French for assistance, he attacked, routed, and killed Anwár ud din, and made himself master of nearly the whole of the Karnátak. Clive, who had come out as a 'writer,' but had turned himself into a soldier, was deputed by the Madras Government to resist the combination by an attack upon Arcot, the capital of the Karnátak, and the result was that after various sieges and engagements Chanda Sáhib lost all his possessions, fell into the hands of the Maráthas, by whom he was put to death; while the French power in Southern India was effectually broken.

ll. 27-30. the prince ... Bahar, this was Ali Vardi Khán, the Nawáb of Bengal, whose "firm government had maintained a barrier against invasion, and had kept peace within his borders" (Lyall).

P. 8, l. 4. declared ... English, on war breaking out in Europe between the French and English, an attempt was made by the Company to fortify Calcutta. The Nawáb ordered the work to be stopped, but his orders were disregarded, and he at once marched on Kásimbázár.

l. 8. the Dutch Company, which first turned their attention to the Eastern trade about 1580, and at one time had settlements in India at Chinsurah, Negapatanam, Sadras, Pulicat, and Bimlipatanam.

l. 11. the Black Hole, this tragedy took place on the night of the 20th of June, 1756, a hundred and forty-six English men and women being shut up in a small guard-room about twenty feet long by fourteen wide, and having only two small windows strongly barred. In the morning twenty-two men and one woman came out alive. For a graphic account of the terrible sufferings undergone, see Macaulay's Essay on *Clive*, or Trotter's *Warren Hastings*, pp. 19, 20.

l. 15. Fulda, more properly 'Falta,' a village and Dutch station near the confluence of the Húgli with the Damodar.

l. 19. at large, not in actual confinement, but allowed freedom of exercise within certain limits.

ll. 21-3. The treason ... progress, the reference is to a conspiracy formed against him by Rae Dalab, his minister of finance; Mir Jáfar, his commander-in-chief; and Jagat Seth, the richest banker in India. The object of the confederates was to place Mir Jafár on the throne. Clive, on reaching Calcutta, determined to give support to the project, and sent letters of the most soothing character to Surája Daula to put him off his guard. When all was ready for the attack, Clive wrote to the Nawáb in a very different tone, setting forth all the wrongs which the British had suffered at his hands, declaring his intention

to submit the points in dispute between them to Mir Jáfar and
the Hindu grandees at his court, and announcing that he and his
troops would do themselves the honour of waiting on his Highness.
Surája Daula instantly assembled his whole force and marched
to encounter the English.   The result was the battle of Plassey,
in which, with a force of three thousand men (one thousand of
whom were English), Clive utterly routed the Nawáb's army of
sixty thousand of all arms.

P. 9, l. 5. a member of Council, as a member of Council in
these early times was something very different from such an
official at the present day, it may be as well to give some account
of his status when Hastings received the appointment; and, as
collateral to the matter, a statement of the salaries paid to the
different ranks of the Company's servants.   "In 1750 the Company's settlements," says Trotter, p. 13, "in Bengal, Bombay,
and Madras, were governed each by a President and a Council of
senior merchants.   The President's salary was then but £300 a
year, while those of his Councillors ranged from £40 to £100.
The senior merchants received £40, junior merchants £30, factors
£15, and writers only £5 a year. ... But the Company's servants
were permitted to eke out their pay with the profits of private
trade."

ll. 7-10. an interval ... government, for this period "the only
excuse to be made is that it is very short, and so crowded with
strange incidents, perilous adventures, and precipitate changes,
that one cannot wonder if the actors in such a drama lost their
heads.   In June, 1756, the Company had been turned out of
Fort William and all their up-country factories in Bengal; part
of their establishment was in the Black Hole; the rest, half-
starved, upon an island in the Hooghly river.   Within twelve
months the Company were virtually lords of Bengal, and all the
treasures of the state and resources of the provinces were at
their absolute disposal; the French had lost all their settlements;
their trade, up to that time considerable, was annihilated, and the
export business of the country had become an English monopoly.
A few years later the Company found themselves de facto rulers
of Behar, the great province that extends from Bengal proper
westward up to the Ganges at Benares, four hundred miles from
Calcutta.   They had come for commerce and had found conquest; they had been compelled to choose between their own
expulsion and the overthrow of the native government; they
fought for their own hand, and won so easily that they found
the whole power and responsibility of administration thrust
upon them without warning, experience, or time for preparation" (Lyall, pp. 19, 20).

l. 18. The master caste, the English, the dominant class, as
Macaulay terms them just below.

l. 35. **the enlarged policy,** the larger and more statesmanlike idea of government.

P. 10, l. 10. **rotten boroughs,** a term used of boroughs where the number of voters was very small, in some of them because they had decayed in size since members were first given them, in others because they had been allowed members in order that they might be under the influence of the Crown. The power of nominating these members was usually in the hands of the Crown or of some neighbouring landlord, or was sold to the highest bidder. At one period it is asserted that two hundred members of Parliament were returned by places with less than a hundred electors, and that three hundred and fifty-seven members were nominated by one hundred and fifty-four patrons. Macaulay is probably alluding to Clive's candidature in 1754 at the borough of St. Michael, "one of those wretched Cornish boroughs," as he says in his Essay on *Clive*, "which were swept away by the Reform Act in 1832."

l. 11. **St. James's Square,** at that time a locality even more fashionable than at present.

ll. 17, 8. **It is certain ... poor,** so poor, indeed, that "Raymond, the French translator of the *Sair Matákharin*, says he was obliged to borrow money from an Armenian merchant for his expenses in going home" (Lyall, p. 19).

l. 29. **many lamentable blemishes,** it must be remembered that this is said under the wholly untenable belief that his conduct as regards Nand Kumár, the Rohilla War, Chait Sing, and the Begams, was as bad as the malice of his enemies represented it.

l. 35. **squeamish,** over-particular, unnecessarily delicate.

P. 11, l. 2. **buccaneer,** "originally one who dries and smokes flesh on a *boucan* after the manner of the Indians. The name was first given to the French hunters of St. Domingo, who prepared the flesh of the wild oxen and boars in this way. 2. (From the habits which these subsequently assumed:) A name given to piratical rovers who formerly infested the Spanish coasts in America. 3. By extension: A sea-rover who makes hostile attacks upon the coast, a filibuster. F. *boucaner*, to dry meat on a barbecue" (Murray, *Eng. Dict.*). **a galleon,** originally a Spanish word for an armed ship of large burden, then especially a large vessel containing **treasure, such** as ingots of silver, or rich merchandise.

l. 18. **liberal studies,** the study of such subjects as language, literature, art, etc., which enlarge and elevate a man's mind.

ll. 27, 8. **which lie ... track,** which are not to be met with in the beaten path along which men ordinarily walk.

l. 34. **the revival of letters,** a phrase in common use for the

revival of learned studies, about 1450, after their eclipse during
the 'Dark Ages'; also sometimes called the 'Renaissance.'

P. 12, l. 2. **Hafiz and Ferdusi,** two famous Persian poets, who
flourished in the eleventh and thirteenth centuries respectively.

ll. 8-12. **Long after, ... intercourse,** "In a letter to him at
Calcutta, dated 30th March, 1774, Dr. Johnson remarked,
'Though I have had but little personal knowledge of you, I have
had enough to make me wish for more, and though it is now a
long time since I was honoured by your visit, I had too much
pleasure from it to forget it.' He then alluded to Hastings's
efforts 'to increase the learning of your country by the introduction of the Persian language,' and requested his acceptance of
an accompanying copy of Sir William Jones's 'Persian Grammar.'
Later in the same year Dr. Johnson forwarded to the Governor-
General a copy of his own 'Journey to the Western Isles of
Scotland'; and said, 'I wish you a prosperous government, a
safe return, and a long enjoyment of plenty and tranquillity'"
(Sir C. Lawson).

l. 27. **Imhoff,** a baron, "who had been an officer in the army
of a minor German state, had obtained the recommendation of
Queen Charlotte, and was proceeding to Madras, ostensibly to
seek employment in the local army, but with some view to
portrait-painting" (*Dict. Nat. Biog.*). Macaulay's sneer, in the
words "He called himself a baron," is undeserved. Sir C.
Lawson shows that he was the third son of Baron Christopher
Imhoff, and "seventeenth in direct descent from a crusader of
the name of Hoff, upon whom a German emperor bestowed a coat
of arms, and conferred the prefix of 'Im,' in recognition of an act
of great gallantry in the field."

l. 30. **pagodas,** a gold coin, worth about nine shillings.

ll. 32, 3. **a native ... Archangel,** "He read it no doubt in the
Siyyar Mutaqherin, vol. ii. p. 476, translator's note, 'Born at
Archangel,' etc." (Stephen, *The Story of Nuncomar,* i. 266).

P. 13, l. 9. **a sail,** the meeting with another vessel.

P. 14, l. 8. **Franconia,** in Saxony.

l. 11. **they should ... together,** *i.e.* the Imhoffs as man and wife.

l. 13. **complaisant,** ready to condone an intimacy which, if he
had been a man of honour, he would have looked upon as the
last disgrace to be endured.

l. 19. **The Reverend,** notice the sarcasm. A clergyman of the
Church of England condoning the baseness of a husband!

ll. 21, 2. **conduct ... lovers,** the best excuse that could be made
for the behaviour of Hastings and the Baroness was that her
husband showed so little love for her and so little regard for her
honour that he was willing to be bribed into a divorce.

l. 34. **In a very ... reform,** he repressed the extortions of the
native middle-men upon the cotton and silk weavers, so that
before he left Madras a steady improvement had taken place in
the bales of silk and cotton prepared for the English markets;
and he drew up a well-considered scheme for placing the Company's investments on a better footing.

P. 15, ll. 28-30. **in the same relation ..** Pepin, Odoacer, usually
called King of the Heruli, was the leader of the barbarians who
overthrew the Western Empire in A.D. 476, and drove Romulus
Augustulus into exile. Odoacer took the title of King of Italy,
but was shortly afterwards overthrown by Theodoric, King of
the Goths, when he took refuge in Ravenna. There he was
besieged by Theodoric for three years, and at last capitulated on
condition that he and Theodoric should share the kingdom of
Italy. Theodoric, however, put him to death in 493. Chilperic
II., King of Neustria, was overthrown by Charles Martel, a
descendant of the Pepins. Pepin the Short, as he was called,
was *major domus* to the Merovingian Emperor of Austrasia,
Childeric III., on whose deposition by the Pope in 752 he founded
the Karling dynasty.

l. 33. **public instruments,** documents, proclamations, writs,
etc.

l. 34. **cadet,** here a subaltern in the army; a word more commonly used of a young military student, but also for a younger
member of a family, as the ' cadet of an ancient and noble family ';
from "F. *cadet* ... a Poitou word ... The Prov. form is *capdet*,
formed from a Low Lat. *capitettum,* a neuter form not found ...
[which] would mean literally ' a little head.' The eldest son was
called *caput,* the ' head ' of the family, the second the *capitettum,*
or lesser head " (Skeat, *Ety. Dict.*).

P. 16, l. 3. **all executive measures,** as contrasted with **legis-**
lative and judicial measures.

ll. 10, 1. **This** system ... Dundas, Pitt's East India Bill was
carried in 1784; it "preserved in appearance the political and
commercial powers of the Directors, while establishing a Board
of Control, formed from members of the Privy Council, for the
approval or annulling of their acts. Practically, however, the
powers of the Board of Directors were absorbed by a secret
committee of three elected members of that body, to whom all
the more important administrative functions had been reserved
by the bill, while those of the Board of Control were virtually
exercised by its President. As the President was in effect a new
Secretary of State for the Indian Department, and became an
important member of each Ministry, responsible, like his fellow-
members, for his action to Parliament, the administration of
India was thus made a part of the general system of the English

Government; while the secret committee supplied the experience of Indian affairs in which the Minister might be deficient" (Green, *Short History*, etc., p. 795).

l. 16. **a casting vote**, a vote which decided the issue when the numbers were equal in any discussion.

ll. 28-30. **To this day ...** "diplomatic," properly speaking, **political** is that which has to do with civil government; **diplomatic** that which has to do with negotiations with foreign powers; the derivation of the latter word is from Lat. *diploma*, a document conferring a privilege, from Gk. δίπλωμα, literally anything folded double, diplomas apparently having originally been so folded. Even now 'political officers' in India are those who reside at native courts as agents of the British Government for the purpose of conducting negotiations, conveying the wishes of that Government on any matter, etc.

P. 17, l. 2. **mere ceremonial**, the formal ceremonies to be observed in dealing with foreign courts and their representatives.

l. 5. **stipend**, salary.

l. 6. **sterling**, genuine, of true weight; probably a contraction of 'Easterling,' the Easterlings or North Germans being the first moneyers in England.

ll. 8, 9. **and was ... disposal**, the position of the minister as agent of the company being such that the Nawáb would be afraid to resist any proposition that minister might make as to the use to which the Nawáb's personal allowance should be put.

l. 17. **conflicting pretensions**, the claims which the two candidates could urge to the appointment, there being much to be said in favour of each of the rivals.

l. 29. **Maharajah, the title** was not hereditary from his ancestors, but was conferred by one of the Nawábs when such titles were cheap. Nand Kumár was not indeed a man of any family, or even a high-caste Brahman.

l. 32. **consideration**, respect, deference.

P. 18, l. 3. **that was ... Bengalees**, this may have been true as regards Nand Kumár's moral nature, but physically he was, according to Sir Gilbert Elliot's description, "in person tall and majestic, robust yet graceful," and according to Boswell of "an excessively strong constitution."

l. 16. **the Ionian ... Juvenal**, the reference is to Juvenal's Third Satire, in which the Ionian is described as made up of subtle versatility; see *Satire*, iii. 60-78.

l. 17. **the Jew ... ages**, when being the aversion of every European nation they were obliged to resort to cunning to escape that tyranny and spoliation which in their case was considered as perfectly justifiable.

ll. 10, 20. **what beauty ... woman,** a reference to the pseudo-Anacreon, who after saying that nature gives horns to bulls, hoofs to horses, swiftness to hares, etc., adds that to women she gives "beauty in place of shield and sword, and she who possesses that is victorious over arms and fire."

l. 21. **elaborate ... falsehood,** webs of falsehood woven with elaborate skill and strengthened by details, giving to the whole an appearance of genuine consistency ; **tissue** is that which is woven, from *tissu,* the old past participle of F. *tistre,* modern F. *tisser,* to weave.

l. 22. **chicanery,** mean deception, sharp practice.

l. 32. **his masters,** those who are his superiors in active courage and physical prowess ; not here the English who were his masters in another sense.

l. 33. **the Stoics,** the disciples and followers of Zeno who, about B.C. 320, when he had developed his philosophical system, opened his school in the porch adorned with the paintings of Polygnotus, *Stoa Poecile ;* the main doctrine of his philosophy was a contempt of all outward circumstances, especially of pain, distress, etc.

l. 34. **their ideal** sage, the man who realized their loftiest conception of a perfectly wise man ; here meaning Zeno.

P. 19, l. 5. **Mucius,** Scævola, when taken prisoner in his attempt to kill Porsena, the Etruscan King, who was then blockading Rome, with the object of restoring Tarquinius Superbus, was by that king condemned to be burnt alive. Hereupon Mucius thrust his right hand into a fire lighted for a sacrifice, and held it there without flinching. Porsena, in admiration of his firmness, spared his life. From this exploit he acquired the name of Scævola, *i.e.* left-handed.

l. 6. **Algernon Sydney,** who was to be beheaded for his imputed share in the Rye-house plot, and met his death with unmoved constancy in 1682 ; see Green, *Short History,* etc., p. 661.

P. 20, ll. 1-3. **The revenues ... Company,** "Whoever gained by it [the land revenue], the Company were defrauded of their rightful share. The bulk of it was drained off by a few native officers, a number of Zamíndárs, or revenue farmers, and a swarm of greedy underlings, at the cost not only of the Company, but of millions of helpless rack-rented husbandmen. After the famine of 1770 the collecting of revenue in many districts seemed like trying to squeeze water out of a dry sponge" (Trotter, pp. 59, 60).

l. 4. **for, at that time,** the anticipations of the Company were based on these false notions, and so were disappointed.

l. 6. **porphyry,** a hard, variegated rock, of purple and white colour ; Gk. πορφύρεος, purple.

K

l. 7. **gold mohurs**, a coin at that time worth sixteen rupees, but now of greater relative value.

l. 23. **Leadenhall Street**, where was the head office of the Company.

P. 21, ll. 1-3. **Many years ... compose**, their quarrel was regarding their respective functions and jurisdiction, and was ultimately adjusted by Clive.

l. 11. **the system of double government**, by which the administration of the finances of the country, though really in the hands of the Company, was nominally under the jurisdiction of the Nawáb.

l. 24. **On that memorable day**, in April, 1760, the Emperor Sháh Álam was attacking Jáfar, whom the English had made Nawáb of Bengal, and had reached Murshidábád : about the 22nd he marched back and laid siege to Patna, aided by Chevalier Law with some guns. The garrison had repelled two assaults when Knox appeared with 200 Europeans, a battalion of sepoys, and a small detail of artillery. After the failure of the second assault he got into Patna, and the next day sallied forth and fell upon the besiegers who were speedily routed and fled precipitately a distance of fifty miles.

P. 22, l. 10. **a considerable annual allowance, viz.** sixteen lakhs of rupees, half his former allowance.

l. 14. **Munny Begum**, the widow of Mir Jáfar.

l. 19. **the inoffensive child**, Gurdás, who had had no share in Nand Kumár's villanies, was an adult.

l. 30. **harnessed**, decked with handsome trappings; so we speak of "harness" for armour, even in the case of men.

l. 31. **sent back ... Patna**, as deputy-governor of Bahár.

l. 34. **of a broken heart.** This is merely a conjecture of Mill's adopted by Macaulay.

l. 35-P. 23, l. 5. **The innocence ... liberty.** "The trial of Muhammad Raza Khán," says Trotter, pp. 66-7, "lingered on for a whole year. The charges against him were investigated day by day with unflagging patience; Hastings himself filling the twofold part of examiner and interpreter. The result of examining scores of witnesses and hundreds of documents deepened his old distrust of Nanda-Kumár, and convinced him that, even if the accused were in any way guilty, the time for proving him so had gone by. Nanda-Kumár's evidence broke down egregiously. The evil old Bráhman could only produce accounts that proved nothing, and reiterate charges which he always failed to make good. At last the long enquiry ended in an acquittal, which the Court of Directors subsequently confirmed. The victim of their rashness and Nanda-Kumár's hate was restored ere long to much of his former eminence. More fortunate than his fellow-sufferer, he lived to hold high office under the government of Bengal, and to see his old traducer doomed to a felon's death."

ll. 20, 1. **The object ... money**, this is Macaulay's way of preparing the ground for his charge that the Rohilla War was undertaken without any regard to the dangers which threatened the British power in India. For an examination of the whole subject, see Appendix I.

ll. 25, 6. **the old motto ... Teviotdale**, this is, or was, the motto of the Cranstouns, who appear to have been great lords of Teviotdale in the old Border days, but now live at Corehouse, close to the Falls of the Clyde. Henry of Cranstoun is mentioned in Scott's *Lay of the Last Minstrel*.

P. 24, ll. 8, 9. **this is in truth ... home.** "This," says Strachey, *Hastings and the Rohilla War*, p. 264, "is a somewhat exaggerated statement, but it is substantially true."

P. 25, ll. 5-8. **On the plea ... concessions**, Sháh Álam had flung himself into the hands of the Maráthas, the worst enemies of the British power, who treated him as a mere puppet, and he had given into their keeping the provinces of Kora and Allahábád, which Clive had restored to him in 1765. To pay tribute to him was therefore in reality to pay tribute to the Maráthas, and the Court of Directors had some years before suggested the very step that Hastings now took in case "he should fling himself into the hands of the Maráthas, or any other power."

ll. 15, 6. **the great Mussulman ... governed**, this was written in 1841 ; in 1856 Dalhousie annexed the province of Oudh.

ll. 19, 21. **such an assumption ... impiety**, as being an assertion of independence of the Great Mughal, the head of the Musalmáns in India.

l. 23. **Vizier**, minister ; more correctly transliterated 'Wazír.'

l. 25. **Elector**, a title given to those German princes who formerly had the right to take part in the election of the Emperor.

l. 29. **Allahabad**, a province whose capital is on the Jamna, about five hundred miles north-west of Calcutta.

l. 30. **Corah**, "the town of Kora, now much decayed, is about a hundred miles to the north-west of Allahabad. It was a place of great importance, and the capital of a province of the Mughal empire. The provinces given to the Emperor by Clive were often called Kora and Karra, the latter being the name of a considerable town about forty miles to the north-west of Allahabad" (Strachey, p. 37).

P. 26, l. 9. **the passes,** *sc.* of the Caucasus; the passes, from 10,000 to 13,000 feet high, are a spur of the Pámír separating the Kábul country from the valley of the Oxus.

l. 12. **Hyphasis,** the modern Beás, one of the five rivers from which the Panjáb, the country of five rivers, gets its name: **Hystaspes,** or rather Hydaspes, the modern Jhelam, another of the same network of rivers.

l. 18. **Ghizni,** a fortress captured by **Sir J. Keane** in 1839. It had been seized by the Ghuri Sultán in 1152, after which it became deserted. In 1758 it was occupied by Nádir Sháh on his invasion of India, and at his death was incorporated in the Dauráni empire by Ahmad the Abdáli.

l. 24. **Cabul,** on a river of the same name, the capital of Afghánistán: **Candahar,** another large town and fortress in Afghánistán, about 300 miles south-west of Kábul.

l. 26. **Rohillas,** for an account of this Afghán tribe, see Appendix I.

l. 27. **fiefs of the spear,** lands held on the tenure of military service.

l. 28. **analogous ... things,** the feudal system in Europe.

l. 29. **Ramgunga,** the principal river of Rohilkhand.

l. 30. **Kumaon,** a mountainous district to the north of Rohilkhand in which are many of the loftier peaks of the Himalayas, and whose chief town is 'bleak Almora.'

l. 31. **Aurungzebe,** one of the four sons of Sháhjáhán, who reigned from 1659 to 1707.

l. 36. **Lahore,** now the capital of the Panjáb, on the river Rávi: **Cape Comorin,** the southernmost point of India.

P. 27, ll. 3, 4. **nor were they ... poetry,** see Appendix I.

ll. 10, 1. **that of Catherine ... Spain,** in 1773 Catherine, Empress of Russia, in conjunction with the sovereigns of Austria and Prussia, seized on Poland, which they divided among themselves, though having no claim to it but that of might: in 1808 Napoleon, with no better claim, conquered Spain, and placed his brother Joseph on the throne. On this Sir J. Strachey remarks, pp. 25, 6, "When Macaulay compares the actions of Shuja-ud-Daula in Rohilkhand to those of Catherine in Poland and those of the Bonapartes in Spain, the reader assumes that the position of the Rohillas was similar to that of the Poles and Spaniards, that of an injured people violently oppressed by foreign invaders ... It would be less inaccurate to compare the position of the Rohillas in Rohilkhand with that of the Russians in Poland, or with that of the French in Spain in the time of Napoleon. The three cases had at least this in common, that in each of them a body of foreign soldiers was more or less successful in imposing, by violence and bloodshed, its rule over a large and unwilling population. The Rohillas were as much foreigners in Rohilkhand as Frenchmen in Spain or Russians in Poland."

l. 21. **eighty thousand men,** this is an exaggeration, if Macaulay means that they could bring this number of their own people into the field. The Rohillas in Rohilkhand probably never numbered more than forty thousand. Macaulay's estimate is taken from Mill, who took it from Verelst, but Verelst was referring to the probable number of Afghans that could be brought together not in Rohilkhand alone but in the whole of Northern India, if the various chiefs were united.

l. 22. **Sujah Dowlah ... fight,** as for instance when Major Munro with a force of seven thousand men, mostly sepoys, won the splendid victory of Baksár over fifty thousand of Shuja's own troops in October, 1764.

ll. 24, 5. **Caucasian tribes,** Macaulay means the Afgháns, who were supposed to have come from Mount Caucasus.

l. 30. **the imperial people,** people formed for empire, the English.

P. 28, l. 1. **A bargain ... struck,** see Appendix I.

ll. 24, 5. **The hussar-mongers ... Anspach,** the princes of Hesse and Anspach, two German duchies, who virtually sold their subjects to serve as mercenaries with the British.

P. 29, l. 6. **Did it lie in their mouths,** could they with any propriety say?

l. 8. **a caput lupinum,** a wolf's head, *i.e.* what might well be cut off.

l. 17. **offered a large ransom,** this is not the case; Háfiz Rahmat would make no promise of payment of the sum due to the Wazír according to the treaty made between them; see Appendix I.

ll. 22, 3. **The dastardly ... field,** see Appendix I.

P. 30, ll. 1-6. **More than ... daughters,** those who fled to "pestilential jungles,"—by which Macaulay means the Tarái, a belt of forest land at the foot of the hills,—were not Rohillas, but the Hindu cultivators, who very soon returned to their homes, and neither they nor the Rohillas suffered anything as regards "the honour of their wives and daughters."

l. 26. **to take order,** to take measures, act in such a way as to ensure that, etc.

l. 35. **the injured nation,** on the term nation as applied to the Rohillas, see Appendix I.

P. 31, l. 4. **at the cold steel,** in a bayonet charge or a hand to hand combat with swords.

l. 26. **Lord North**, Prime Minister from 1770 to 1782.

P. 32, l. 2. **undefined extent**, the evils resulting from this want of strict definition are noticed further on, pp. 56-60.

l. 8. **Clavering**, says Trotter, p. 96, "was an honest, hot-headed soldier, who had led the attack on Guadeloupe in 1759, and whose Parliamentary influence had raised him into favour with the King and Lord North": Monson "appears to have been a man of small intellect, arrogant, rash, self-willed, but easily led by those who paid him the needful deference."

l. 15. **manly spirit**, if manly is here nothing more than a synonym of 'fearless,' 'bold,' it is applicable enough to Francis, but his behaviour to Hastings was full of misrepresentation and underhand malice.

l. 23. **Letters of Junius**, published in 1769-72 in the *Public Advertiser*, and addressed to a variety of public men.

l. 35. **Lord Chatham**, the elder Pitt, several times Prime Minister.

P. 33, ll. 1, 2. **the first Lord Holland**, Henry Fox, father of his greater son, Charles James Fox.

ll. 13-5. **If this argument ... evidence**, strong as Macaulay's arguments are, the controversy still rages, though most people believe that Francis was Junius.

l. 31. **Corneille**, 1606-84, the creator of the French drama, pro-duced thirty-three plays besides several volumes of poetry.

l. 33. **Bunyan**, John, a Baptist minister, 1628-88, who wrote the famous allegory of the *Pilgrim's Progress*, the *Holy War*, *Grace Abounding*, etc.

l. 34. **Cervantes**, the great Spanish novelist; 1547-1616.

l. 35. **the Man in the Mask**, here meaning of course Junius, but in allusion to the 'Man in the Iron Mask,' the name given to a French state prisoner whose face was always concealed in an iron mask, and who has not been identified.

P. 34, l. 1. **letter to the king**, one of the most famous and most violent of the series, published 19th December, 1779.

l. 2. **Horne Tooke**, a clergyman and politician, best known as the author of the *Diversions of Purley*, a work on philology of which most of the conclusions have been proved unsound by more recent investigations.

l. 10. **Woodfall**, the printer who was prosecuted for publishing the letters.

l. 18. **the Hebrew prophet**, Jonah; see ch. iv., ver. 9.

ll. 28, 9. **a respect ... pedantry**, a veneration similar to that of bookworms for works that have no better claim to honour than the fact of their being antiquated.

l. 29. **Old Sarum**, a village in Wiltshire which, till the Reform Bill of 1832, returned a member of Parliament by the vote of a single householder.

ll. 30, 1. **Manchester and Leeds**, which, though large and populous towns, returned no member of Parliament till the same Reform Bill.

P. 35, l. 3. **George Grenville**, Prime Minister from 1763-5.

l. 6. **the Middlesex election**, John Wilkes, notorious for his profane and licentious life, was three times elected for Middlesex, but being prosecuted for libellous, seditious, and immoral works, was refused admission to the House of Commons, though in the end he took his seat in 1774. A graphic account of all the circumstances will be found in Macaulay's Essay on *The Earl of Chatham*.

l. 7. **faction**, party ; not here used in its more unfavourable sense.

ll. 13, 4. **he must be ... again**, it would be utter folly in him to continue his letters when he saw how useless was the hope of stirring up any party to support the views he advocated.

ll. 22, 3. **With the three ... Court**, but in a different vessel.

l. 27. **tool**, Impey may sometimes have been too ready to help Hastings, as in the matter of the affidavits, but he was no tool. When he felt he had just cause, he vigorously opposed Hastings.

l. 31. **punctilious**, unduly sensitive in regard to the marks of honour to which they thought themselves entitled. Their grievance on this matter they at once made the subject of minutes and correspondence, and even thought them of sufficient importance to be recorded in their first Despatch to the Court of Directors.

P. 36, ll. 10-2. **condemned ... Vizier**, and yet they were eager enough to enforce payment of the money due from the Wazír on account of the Rohilla War.

l. 13. **creature**, nominee ; apparently not used here in its more offensive sense.

ll. 19-22. **threw all ... government**, in 1774 Raghunáth Rao, commonly called Raghuba, who on the death of his nephew, the Peshwa, in 1773, had got himself installed as his successor in that office, was opposed by Nána Farnavís, posthumous son of the late Peshwa. Defeated in the field, he entered into an alliance with the Bombay Government, agreeing in return for a body of troops to cede to that Government the island of Salsette, and the port of Bassein. The majority in Council condemned these negotiations, and ordered Keating's column to return to Bombay. The consequence was that the Bombay Government, by the treaty of Purandhar, engaged to give up Salsette, as well as other conquests, in exchange for a district near Broach, and a promise of twelve lakhs of rupees towards the expenses of the war. "Hastings' opponents had the spirit indeed to join with him in refusing on any terms to give up Salsette. But when the Directors announced their approval of the treaty with Raghuba, and condemned the policy which issued in the treaty of Purandhar, Francis and Clavering threw all the blame of failure on the Governor-General himself" (Trotter, p. 126).

ll. 22, 3. **fell on ... Bengal,** they abolished the provincial courts that Hastings had set up, restored the jurisdiction of the Nawáb, and re-appointed Muhammad Raza Khán to his old post.

P. 37, l. 4. **after their kind,** according to their nature.

l. 17. **It is well,** *i.e.* fortunate for the person accused.

ll. 29, 30. **Oateses ... Dangerfields.** Oates, Bedloe, and Dangerfield in 1678 pretended to have discovered a Popish plot aiming at the subversion of Protestantism and the death of the king. See Green, *Short History,* etc., pp. 650, 1.

ll. 35, 6. **to wreak ... years,** to satisfy the malice he had cherished since he first quarrelled with Hastings in 1758.

P. 38, l. 3. **paid ... them,** sought their favour by every kind of servility.

l. 4. **with all indignity,** with every mark of disgrace.

ll. 26, 7. **that he could not ... Nuncomar,** see Appendix II.

l. 34. **produced a ... supplement,** rather he gave details of his charges.

P. 39, l. 9. **attestation,** *sc.* by means of her seal.

l. 24. **higher authority,** the Court of Directors.

ll. 29-31. **unless it should ... Governor-General,** Hastings' words were, "if the first advices from England contain a disapprobation of the treaty of Benares or of the Rohilla war, and mark an evident disinclination towards me."

P. 40, l. 2. **wheedling,** coaxing, cajoling; the word is supposed by Skeat to be from G. *wedeln,* to wag the tail, to fan.

l. 5. **resources,** *sc.* of his mind.

ll. 19, 20. **possessing ... stronghold,** getting the Supreme Court on his side.

l. 25. **committed,** for trial.

ll. 28-30. **But it was then ... business,** see Appendix II.

P. 41, l. 1. **assizes,** a session of a court of justice; O.F. *assis,* an assembly of judges.

l. 2. **a true bill was found,** *i.e.* the Grand Jury gave as their decision that there was sufficient *prima facie* evidence for the matter to be tried before a common jury.

l. 3. **before Sir Elijah Impey,** this is disingenuous. Macaulay, in order to strengthen his case against Impey, conceals the fact that the trial was before the four judges who comprised the Supreme Court—all of whom agreed with Impey's summing up— and an English jury, the members of which the prisoner was at liberty to challenge in case he objected to their choice, and several of whom he did challenge.

ll. 19, 20. **The Council ... interfere,** but a recommendation from them to the effect that a reprieve should be granted until the case was referred home would have been one that could not be disregarded. The Council declined to make such a recommendation, Clavering assigning as a reason that it was a private transaction of Nand Kumár's own, that it had no relation whatever to the public concerns of the country, and that he would not make any application in favour of a man who had been guilty of forgery. In this view Monson concurred. Impey declared, in his defence, that if such an application had been made to the Court it would have been granted at once.

ll. 21, 2. **That Impey ... clear,** see a statement of Sir J. Stephen's views on this point in Appendix II.

ll. 29, 30. **It had never ... delinquents,** see Appendix II.

P. 42, l. 4. **But Impey ... delay,** another piece of injustice to Impey. He did not hurry on the execution, nor was it in his single power to show mercy.

ll. 8, 9. **Clavering ... rescued,** there is no authority whatever for this statement.

l. 22. **a Brahmin of the Brahmins,** nothing more than a rhetorical expansion of the previous words.

ll. 29, 30. **According to ... whatever,** yet many Brahmans had suffered death since the introduction of English law, and a Brahman had even been sentenced capitally on a forgery indictment, though the sentence was commuted on petition. Macaulay's insinuation, therefore, that such a fate was unprecedented has no force.

ll. 31-3. **was regarded ... jockey,** "that is," says Sir J. Stephen, "in the sight of a mere breach of warranty."

P. 43, l. 1. **The Mahommedan historian,** this was Sayyid Ghulám Husen Khán; his history was entitled Siyyár-ul-Mutákharín, or the "Review of Modern Times," and was translated by a French refugee named Raymond, who called himself Mustapha. In confirmation of his story as regards Nand Kumár, Barwell, in one of his letters to his sister, says that "fourteen blank covers of letters sealed with many English gentlemen's and Hindostanee names were found in the Maha Rajah Nuncomar's house, and delivered into Council, as may be fully proved by reference to the Records of Council."

P. 44, l. 12. **Dacca**, a large and populous town about 150 miles north-east of Calcutta, and once the capital of Bengal. It was formerly famous for the beauty of its muslins, and its rice is still the finest in India.

ll. 16-8. **No rational man ... Governor-General**, see Appendix II.

ll. 23-5. **These strong ... Hastings**, see Sir J. Stephen's explanation in the same Appendix.

P. 45, l. 13. **Lord Stafford**, a Catholic nobleman beheaded in 1680 for his share in the Popish plot invented by Oates : see above, p. 37, l. 29.

P. 46, l. 31. **Tour to the Hebrides**, by Johnson, in 1773 ; a narrative of a journey he made with Boswell to Scotland and the adjacent islands on the west coast: **Jones's Persian Grammar**, in 1771 Sir William Jones, a famous Oriental scholar, published this work.

P. 47, ll. 9-11. **As Lady Macbeth ... win**," *Macb.* i. 5. 22, 3.

l. 14. **on an address ... Company**, in case the Company should address the Crown with a petition for his removal.

ll. 21, 2. **Court of Directors**, the governing body elected by the votes of the proprietors of India stock.

l. 24. **The great sale-room**, in which were held auctions of the goods received from India.

l. 27. **held India stock**, had shares in the Company, and therefore were entitled to votes: **Lord Sandwich**, John Montagu, fourth Earl of Sandwich, 1718-1792, First Lord of the Admiralty in 1763 and 1771, and Secretary of State in the former year.

l. 28. **the friends of the administration**, those of the proprietors of India stock who were supporters of Lord North's government, and therefore wished to get rid of Hastings.

l. 30. **seldom ... eastward**, the India Office being in Leadenhall Street, at the extreme east of London, while the residences of these peers were in the west end, the fashionable quarter.

l. 32. **a ballot**, in which the voting was secret, and in which, though the number of voters might be against Hastings, the number of votes would not necessarily be so, since the amount of stock held by each proprietor regulated the number of votes he could give.

P. 48, l. 10. **the crown lawyers**, the legal advisers of the government, more especially the Lord Chancellor, the Attorney-General, and the Solicitor-General.

ll. 12, 3. **an honourable retreat**, by a voluntary resignation without waiting for dismissal.

ll. 15, 6. **The instrument ... form**, it being merely part of a private letter from Hastings to Macleane, instead of a formal document addressed to the Court of Directors.

ll. 29-32. **He instantly ... ordered**, by the death of Monson his hands were "strengthened at a timely moment for the work of revising the land settlements of 1772. In order to collect full materials for the new settlement he appointed a special commission of enquiry, headed by Anderson and Bogle, two of the ablest civil officers in Bengal. A few weeks later, Middleton resumed his old post of Resident at Lucknow in the room of Francis' favourite, Bristow. The younger Fowke was speedily recalled from Benares" (Trotter, p. 128).

P. 49, l. 1. **subsidiary alliances**, alliances in which the native powers were to maintain a British force at their own expense, and so virtually come under the control of the Company's Government.

l. 3. **Berar**, a province of Central India belonging to the Nizám of Haidarábád : paramount, supreme, chief.

P. 50, ll. 2-4. **He directed ... his**, "By virtue of his office the Governor-General would also act as Commander-in-Chief. His counter-orders to the troops were cheerfully obeyed. Colonel Morgan closed the gates of Fort William against General Clavering, and a like answer came from Barrackpur and Baj-Baj" (Trotter, pp. 136, 7).

ll. 35, 6. **The exertion ... later**, there seems no warrant for connecting his death with his presence at the wedding. He was taken ill on his way home from a visit to Impey, and died within the fortnight.

P. 51, ll. 9-13. **The truth is ... acknowledge**, "the East India proprietors stood by Hastings, discerning him to be the best man for their interests in a stormy time. Burgoyne had surrendered at Saratoga : the French had just declared war ; and on the whole the Ministers could not venture to send out a new and untried Governor-General to India" (Lyall, p. 90).

ll. 25, 6. **humbled ... Second**, the reference is to the elder Pitt and the series of victories obtained by the British forces throughout the world during his administration.

l. 30. **the too just .. Ireland**, these had reference to commercial and religious restrictions. In 1779 the Sheriffs of Dublin stated to the Lord-Lieutenant that the poor were on the brink of starvation, and nothing but freedom of trade would save them. The Catholics were furious about their religious disabilities, and something was done to ameliorate their position by the first Catholic Relief Bill passed in July of the same year.

l. 32. **the armed ... Baltic**, the combination of Russia, Sweden, and Denmark to resist the claim which England had hitherto maintained to search their ships if suspected of carrying arms or men to be used against it.

l. 33. **jeopardy**, imminent danger ; from "O.F. *jeu parti*, a divided game … a game in which the chances are exactly even " … (Skeat, *Ety. Dict.*).

l. 34. **Calpe**, the classical name for the modern Gibraltar.

P. 52, l. 11. **wild range of hills**, otherwise called the ' Sáhyádri range.'

l. 13. **Sevajee**, Madho Rao Siváji, founder of the Marátha power in the reign of Aurangzeb. See Appendix IV.

ll. 17, 8. **generated … monarchy**, who owed their origin to the gradual breaking up of the Mughal empire, which followed upon the reign of Aurangzeb ; the metaphor is that of insect life generated in decomposing bodies.

l. 20. **Freebooters**, plunderers, those who unscrupulously made a booty or spoil of the possessions of others.

l. 22. **The Bonslas**, one of the Marátha families, who were finally subdued in 1817.

l. 24. **The Guicowar**, or more properly Gaekwár, a title given to a prince who still reigns at Baroda, about 300 miles almost direct north of Bombay.

l. 26. **Scindia**, whose descendant, the chief representative of the Maráthas in India, reigns at Gwáliár, about eighty miles south-east of Agra. **Holkar**, another Marátha chief, whose descendant reigns at Indor in Málwa, about a hundred miles east of Baroda.

l. 28. **Gooti**, in the Bellári district, north of Maisúr.

l. 30. **Tanjore**, about 200 miles almost direct south of Pondicherry.

l. 35. **Tamerlane**, or Timúr-lang, *i.e.* the lame Timúr, the great Tátar shepherd who descended upon India in 1398 and laid the foundations of the Mughal empire, which Bábar and Akbar afterwards consolidated.

P. 53, l. 3. **a roi fainéant**, an idle, slothful sovereign ; a king in name, who leaves all his functions to be discharged by subordinates, and gives himself up to dissolute enjoyment : **bang**, or *bhang*, an intoxicating drug made from wild hemp, and taken generally in smoking.

l. 4. **Sattara**, a fortified town about 100 miles south-east of Bombay.

l. 5. **Peshwa**, literally ' president,' ' chief minister.'

l. 6. **Poonah**, about 80 miles south-east of Bombay ; now the residence of the Bombay government for part of the hot weather.

l. 8. **Aurungabad**, a city about 250 miles north-east of Bombay : **Bejapoor**, rather more than 250 miles south-east of Sattára.

ll. 10, 1. **a French adventurer,** "the Chevalier St. Lubin who had induced the French minister to entrust him with a commission to visit India, reconnoitre the situation, and to report on the practicability of landing a force upon the coast from the Isle of France" (Lyall, p..94).

l. 19. **a pretender, this was Raghunáth Rao, or Raghuba,** already mentioned.

ll. 28-30. **All the measures ... delay,** Francis, as usual, condemned the proceedings taken by Hastings, and Wheler joined with him.

l. 30. **The French ... Bengal,** the principal of these was Chandranagar, a few miles west of Calcutta.

l. 31. **Pondicherry,** the chief French settlement in southern India, about 90 miles direct south of Madras; now one of the few French possessions left.

l. 36. **Lascars,** native sailors; the word is from the Persian *lashkar,* army.

P. 54, l. 3. **his presidency,** sc. Bengal: so called from being governed by the President of the Council. The three Presidencies of Bengal, Madras, and Bombay, are now subdivided into ten provinces.

ll. 9, 10. **A new commander ... predecessor,** this was Goddard, who took the field in January, 1780, quickly captured the important city of Ahmadábád, and twice defeated the combined armies of Holkar and Sindhia.

l. 13. **a new ... danger,** that arising from collision with Haidar Ali and the French in southern India.

l. 18. **Sir Eyre Coote,** it was in 1761 that this general first distinguished himself when he compelled the French commander, the daring Lally, to surrender himself and the capital, Pondicherry.

ll. 25, 6. **the brave ... Lally,** "Thomas Arthur, Count Lally and Baron Tollendal, son of Sir Gerard O'Lally, who, after the capture of Limerick in 1691, had migrated to France and had entered the service of Louis XIV. Nine years after there was born to Sir Gerard the son who, trained from his earliest youth in the French armies, had merited at Fontenoy the commendations of Marshal Saxe; who had taken part in the '45, and had fought at Laffeldt.".... On his return to France, after captivity in England, "he was condemned on the most casual evidence, and after three years of lingering agony was condemned to be beheaded. On May 8, 1766, he was transferred from prison to a dung-cart, and with a gag thrust into his mouth, was taken through the streets of Paris to the scaffold" (Malleson, *Dupleix,* pp. 168, 175). "The wretched government," says Macaulay,

Essay on *Clive*, "of Lewis the Fifteenth had murdered, directly
or indirectly, almost every Frenchman who had served his
country with distinction in the East. Labourdonnais was flung
into the Bastile, and, after years of suffering, left only to die.
Dupleix, stripped of his immense fortune and broken-hearted by
humiliating attendance in ante-chambers, sank into an obscure
grave. Lally was dragged to the common place of execution
with a gag between his lips." **Wandewash**, a fortified town
between Madras and Pondicherry.

l. 35. **allowances**, personal and local additions to pay.

P. 55, l. 6. **Porto Novo and Pollilore**, at the former place Coote
finished his long campaign in the Karnátak by a decisive victory
in July, 1781, defeating Haidar Ali's army of 80,000 men by a
force of only one-tenth of those numbers ; the victory at Polilur
in August was less decisive.

l. 8. **a memorial**, a petition for the redress of some grievance,
or the concession of some favour.

l. 19. **the most ... allowances**, allowances for travelling expenses, table-money, etc., paid on a scale which he had no right
to claim.

l. 20. **the strongest passions**, avarice and self-indulgence.

ll. 27, 8. **Coote ... faction**, Coote had never espoused the cause
of either party in the Council with factious warmth.

ll. 32, 3. **to promote ... liberty**, to bring about a reconciliation
which would enable him to quit the Council without having to
leave Hastings to face a hostile majority.

l. 35. **the friends of Francis**, those of the Company's service to
whom Francis had shown favour.

P. 56, l. 1. **apparent harmony**, for Francis had never abandoned
his rancour towards Hastings.

l. 4. **internal calamities**, on this quarrel between the Council
and the Supreme Court, see Appendix III.

l. 25. **vices**, imperfections and drawbacks.

ll. 34, 5. **No man ... zone**, exile, in any case painful enough,
becomes doubly painful when it is to a climate utterly different
from that of one's own country.

P. 57, ll. 3, 4. **in chambers ... Thames**, an allusion to the
Temple Inns of Court on the banks of the Thames.

l. 5. **Westminster Hall**, where the chief law courts were held.

l. 9. **modifications**, alterations adapting it to the manners and
customs of the country.

l. 12. **Arrest on mesne process**, the introduction of this law
"into India was," says Sir J. Stephen, "indefensible. The effect

of it was that on an affidavit sworn behind his back a man might
be arrested at Dacca, for instance, or Patna, and brought to Calcutta, there to be imprisoned at a distance of many hundred miles
from his home, unless he could give bail for an action perhaps
unjustly brought against him. Even if he pleaded to the jurisdiction, and his plea was allowed, he was put to much inconvenience, and, at all events, he had to employ at a great expense
English attorneys and counsel" (ii. p. 145): **mesne**, middle,
intermediate between accusation and trial.

ll. 15-7. **the feeling ... native**, Macaulay has no authority for
this statement; native witnesses perhaps object to oaths when
they do not intend to tell the truth.

l. 18. **quality**, rank; the term 'a person of quality' was, not
very long ago, commonly used for a 'nobleman.

l. 21. **can be expiated ... blood**, nothing less than the death of
those who had committed the outrage could suffice to blot out
its disgrace.

l. 30. **callings**, professions; here the clerical profession.

ll. 32, 3, **to treat ... Tyler**, in 1380 Wat Tyler, who afterwards
headed an insurrection, slew a tax-collector for a gross insult to
one of his daughters.

P. 58, ll. 1-10. **A reign ... sounds**, see Sir J. Stephen's criticism
of this passage in Appendix III.

l. 12. **barrators**, as a law term this word means one who
vexatiously raises, or incites, to litigation; one who from malicious-
ness, or for the sake of gain, raises discord among neighbours;
but it is also used in a variety of other senses, especially of those
given to fraudulent transactions or quarrelsome behaviour:
agents of chicane, men employed in every kind of shifty and
subtle intrigue.

l. 15. **spunging-houses**, the houses of sheriffs' officers in which
debtors were formerly confined before trial, and where the
charges were so extortionate that the inmates were squeezed dry
like a spunge.

l. 21-P. 59, l. 17. **There were instances ... days**, see Appendix
III. for Sir J. Stephen's criticism of this passage.

l. 23. **alguazils**, a Spanish adaptation of Arabic *al-wazir*, the
minister, and used in Spanish both for a justiciary and a bailiff.
Here of course Macaulay employs the word in its lowest sense,
and with the intention of implying extortionate and cruel
treatment.

l. 33. **Vansittart**, Governor of Bengal in the interval between
Clive's first and second administrations, who vainly endeavoured
to check the excesses of the Company's servants.

P. 59, l. 5. **pettifoggers**, instruments of petty extortion.

l. 11. **catchpoles, bailiffs**; literally the word means one who hunts or chases fowls ; though not in earlier times used in a contemptuous sense, it has long had that sense.

l. 12. **gang-robbers**, the *dakaits* who, till late years, infested India.

l. 26-9. **The consequence ... dissolved**, this sneer is ungenerous, and there is no reason to suppose that the friendship between Hastings and Impey was less disinterested than ordinary friendships. For the rest of the paragraph, see Appendix III.

ll. 35, 6. **Hastings ... call**, Sir J. Stephen remarks, " The passage as to Hastings's ' just scorn ' at being sued for his public acts is remarkable. Surely it is one of the fundamental principles of English law that a man who holds a public office is liable to an action for abusing its powers. That Macaulay of all men should deny this is wonderful " (ii. 253).

P. 60, l. 12. **eight thousand ... more**, this is an **exaggeration** ; the salary was R5000 a month or £6000 a year.

ll. 23, 4. **since Jefferies ... Tower**, the infamous judge whose cruelty in the ' bloody assize,' after Monmouth's rebellion, is unparalleled in history. The name is properly ' Jeffreys,' not ' Jefferies.' On James's flight he was thrown into the Tower by the supporters of William the Third.

ll. 33, 4. **walk the plank**, a mode of punishment common among pirates, who obliged their captives to walk up a plank of wood balanced on the vessel's bulwarks which tilted downwards with their weight and launched them into the sea.

P. 61, l. 1. **corsair, pirate**; F. *corsaire*, literally one who makes the course or cruise.

ll. 5-7. **if they ... usurped**, these powers of course did not belong to him as Chief Justice of the Supreme Court, and they were not in any sense usurped, but were legally conferred upon him by Hastings.

l. 13. **Francis ... arrangement**, Francis " protested that the government were conceding to their enemy all that they had been fighting for " ; ... and " departed for England with a fresh store of accusations against both Hastings and Impey, which he so used as to procure Impey's recall by Lord Shelburne's Ministry on this very charge, and to increase the growing distrust and uneasiness in Parliament regarding the Governor-General's proceedings " (Lyall, p. 115).

ll. 32, 3. **verbal communication**, strictly speaking this should be ' *oral* communication,' for a communication by means of words may be made in writing as well as in speaking.

P. 62, l. 7. **They met, and fired**, " they met at a spot still well remembered in Calcutta tradition [near the present Cathedral].

taking ground at a distance of fourteen paces, measured out by Colonel Watson, one of the seconds, who said that Charles Fox and Adams had fought (1779) at that distance; although Hastings observed that it was a great distance for pistols. The seconds had baked the powder for their respective friends [the duel took place in the rainy season], nevertheless Francis' pistol missed fire. Hastings waited till he had primed again and missed, when he returned the shot so effectively that Francis was carried home with a ball in his right side. The remarkable coolness of Hastings was noticed; he objected to the spot first proposed as being overshadowed by trees; and probably those were right who inferred from his behaviour that he intended to hit his man" (Lyall, pp. 111, 2).

l. 30. **a Mahommedan soldier,** Haidar Ali.

l. 33. **extraction,** origin, family.

l. 34. **dervise,** or 'darwesh,' a wandering mendicant.

P. 63, ll. 4, 5. **the qualities ... statesman,** the qualities that go to the making up of a great general or a great statesman.

ll. 6, 7. **the fragments ... wreck,** the various principalities subordinate to the emperor, which, when the empire broke up, fell into a state of anarchy and confusion.

ll. 9, 10. **Louis the Eleventh,** who reigned from 1461 to 1483, was one of the greatest French kings, whether in matters of war or those of peaceful administration. When he died, he had assured the unity of France and her preponderance in Europe.

ll. 23-5. **Unhappily ... repel it,** his hostility was provoked first by the capture in 1779 of Mahé, the only settlement remaining to the French, in whose defence Haidar's troops had taken part, and still more so by the march of a British force through a strip of his own country.

ll. 28-30. **those wild passes ... Carnatic,** the passes of the Western Gháts.

P. 64, l. 1. **the Coleroon,** or Kolrún, the lower branch of the Káveri, rising in Maisúr and flowing into the Bay of Bengal.

l. 3. **Mount St. Thomas,** about six miles from the city of Madras.

l. 9. **tulip-trees,** a species of Magnolia introduced from the valley of the Mississippi.

l. 16. **Sir Hector Munro,** see note, p. 27, l. 22.

l. 25. **tanks,** open reservoirs of water common in India.

l. 32. **coast of Coromandel,** running along the Bay of Bengal.

P. 65, l. 1. **the south-west monsoon,** the periodical wind blowing in the Indian Ocean; on the two monsoons, that from the south-west in the summer and that from the north-east in winter, India is dependent for its rain; the word **monsoon** is from the Arabic *mansim*, season.

l. 7. **accommodated,** settled by some compromise. The arrangements were made through the medium of the Rája of Berár, and two thousand Marátha horse were lent to Pearse's column, despatched from Bengal to join Coote. The Marátha chief, Mudaji, was himself converted, in Hastings' words, "from an ostensible enemy to a declared friend."

l. 14. **the incapable ... St. George,** Whitehill.

P. 66, ll. 14, 5. **that labyrinth...alleys,** narrow streets through which it is difficult to find one's way, and in which the buildings are so lofty.

l. 16. **oriels,** the word is generally used for a recess [with a window] in a room, but also for a portico or for a small room. It is in the first of these senses apparently that Macaulay uses the word, as he does in his Essay on *Bacon*, where he speaks of "the fair pupils of Ascham and Aylmer ... who, while the horns were sounding and the dogs in full cry, sat in the lonely *oriel*, with eyes rivetted to that immortal page which tells how meekly and bravely the first great martyr of intellectual liberty took the cup from his weeping gaoler." Skeat says the word is derived from the Lat. *aureolum,* gilded or ornamented with gold, from the custom of gilding certain apartments : **the sacred apes,** in India apes are considered sacred on account of their monkey-god, Hanumán.

l. 18. **holy mendicants,** the *faqírs* with whom India abounds: **holy bulls,** the Brahmanical bulls ; they are turned out as a sacrifice to Siva, and thus become a sort of special consecration.

l. 33. **Petit Trianon,** there were two Trianons, the grand Trianon, an elegant little château, in the form of a horse-shoe, of one storey, built by Louis XIV. for Madame de Maintenon ; and the Petit Trianon built by Louis XV. for Madame du Barry, and afterwards the favourite resort of Marie Antoinette, Queen of Louis XVI. ; in a later edition Macaulay substitutes "Versailles" for **Petit Trianon : muslins of Bengal,** especially from Dacca.

l. 34. **sabres of Oude,** for the inlaying of which the Lucknow artizans were famous.

l. 35. **Golconda,** in Haidarábád, formerly famous for its diamond mines : **shawls of Cashmere,** these shawls, still so famous, are made from the wool of the Thibet goat.

P. 67, l. 1. **Hindoo prince,** Chait Sing was nothing more than a large *zamíndár*, or landholder, whose father, the first Rája, became a vassal of the Nawáb Wazír of Oudh. Like all other large *zamíndárs*, he was bound by long custom and written agreement to aid the English, to whom his fief had been made over by the Nawáb, with men and money in times of extraordinary need. The turn of Macaulay's sentence would make it appear that there had been a long line of princes of this family, whereas in reality Chait Sing was only third in descent from an adventurer who had ousted his own patron from the lands he held as *zamindár* under the Mughal rule.

l. 36. **kept his head ... might,** maintained his position by any means that lay in his power.

P. 68, ll. 2, 3. **The time ... empire,** at the deposition of Charles the Fat in 887.

l. 5. **Hugh Capet,** Duke of Francia, was crowned king at Rheims in 987, and took the title of *Rex Francorum*, king of the Franks.

l. 6. **Duke ... Normandy,** the Duke of Normandy was one of the vassals of Hugh Capet, and he in his turn claimed homage of the Duke of Brittany.

l. 11. **ordinances ... Tenth,** his three ordinances of 1830 destroyed the liberty of the press, dissolved the Chamber of Deputies, and restricted the franchise.

l. 15. **Prince Louis Bonaparte,** afterwards Emperor Napoleon III., who twice made an attempt to seize the kingdom of France, first at Strasburg, and afterwards at Boulogne.

l. 24. **he was a captive,** in the hands of the Maráthas.

ll. 34, 5. **de facto,** in reality : **de jure,** by right.

P. 69, l. 2. **prescription,** that title which long possession of anything gives to its continued enjoyment. This tenure is the modern equivalent of the Roman 'usucapion,' according to which "commodities which had been uninterruptedly possessed for a certain period became the property of the possessor" (Maine, *Ancient Law*, p. 284).

l. 24. **a mere pageant,** a mere show, mere appearance with no reality behind it. Originally the word **pageant** meant a moveable scaffold such as was used in the representation of the old mystery or miracle plays, plays embodying some of the events and truths of the Christian religion.

l. 26. **play at royalty,** play at being a sovereign by keeping up kingly ceremonial and show, but exercising no power.

l. 30. **legerdemain,** literally, sleight of hand, hence dexterity in handling a subject.

l. 31. **sophistry,** disingenuous reasoning.

P. 70, ll. 2, 3. **no appeal ... force,** no power to which application can be made to decide the question, no possible solution except a resort to physical force.

ll. 9-11. **It had formerly ... subject**, this is not a fact. Chait Sing had always been a vassal, and the terms of his vassalage had been enforced.

ll. 16-8. **He had ... Clavering**, especially he had sent a messenger to congratulate Clavering on his temporary accession to the Governor-Generalship.

ll. 30-5. **Hastings took ... concealment**, the money was twice offered to Hastings. At first he refused it. When the offer was repeated, he accepted the money, directing it to be received by the sub-Treasurer of the Council and deposited in his name, intending to convert it to a public use. In November he communicated the fact to the Court of Directors, and as soon as Francis, whose interference in the matter he was desirous of preventing, had left India, he at once carried the money to the public accounts. That he had no intention of keeping it for himself is shown by his openly avowing its receipt to his friend Sullivan in August of the same year.

P. 71, l. 5. **pleaded poverty**, besides the rich treasure stored up in his coffers, he had a revenue of half a million sterling.

ll. 11-5. **Hastings ... government**, there is no evidence that Hastings wished to fasten a quarrel on the Rája. It was on the advice of Sir Eyre Coote, and with the concurrence of the Council, that Hastings in 1780 called upon him to furnish two thousand horse for the public service. The Rája offered to furnish five hundred and as many match-lock men, but even these were not forthcoming, though his body-guard alone was larger than the force which Hastings required of him.

ll. 22-5. **The plan ... possessions**, there is nothing whatever to show that Hastings would not have been satisfied if his original demands had been complied with.

ll. 29, 30. **he began ... Oude**, this statement again is made without any evidence to confirm it.

l. 35. **sixty miles**, to Baxár on the Ganges.

P. 72, l. 11. **to be arrested**, he was not, as the words would seem to imply, placed in confinement, but was simply told to consider himself under arrest in his own house, a guard of sepoys being sent to prevent his escaping.

l. 20. **the Delta of the Ganges**, that portion of eastern Bengal in which Calcutta is situated, the home of the Bengalis whom Macaulay speaks of as living "in a constant vapour bath."

P. 73, l. 1. **the Black ... Calcutta**, the native quarter of Calcutta.

l. 9. **The sepoys were butchered**, the sepoy guard had nothing but unloaded muskets and no ammunition.

l. 26. **the English cantonments**, at Cawnpore, Chunár, and Lucknow.

l. 35. **the envoy**, Colonel Muir, who was then negotiating with Sindhia.

P. 74, ll. 4, 5. **An English ... judgment**, Mayaffre, who made a rush upon the Rája's fortified palace at Rámnagar without waiting for Popham, and with Captain Doxatt, thirty-three "rangers," and almost all the sepoys of Blair's battalion, perished in the attempt.

ll. 13, 4. **The entire ... arms**, in a few days Chait Sing had mustered an army of 40,000 men within ten miles of Chunár, to which Hastings had retreated.

l. 18. **imposts**, taxes, but here used as = to unjust taxes.

ll. 31, 2. **His fastnesses ... stormed**, the capture of the fortress of Bijaigarh put an end to the brief campaign.

l. 35-P. 75, l. 2. **One of his ... pensioner**, "his zemindari estates were declared to be forfeited, and were bestowed on a grandson of Bulwunt Singh ; from whom they have descended to the present Maharajah of Benares, a very loyal and distinguished nobleman" (Lyall, p. 126).

ll. 19, 20. **under the skilful ... government**, so far as this is true, it was due to "the hard conditions imposed by the Francis faction in 1775" whereby he "was sinking deeper and deeper into the Company's debt. In six years that debt had risen to a million and a half, chiefly on account of the British garrisons which alone stood between the Wazír and general anarchy" (Trotter, p. 181). To Francis and his colleagues, moreover, it was due that Asaf-ud-daula was compelled to surrender the two millions sterling, which Shuja had stored up, to the Queen-mother, who claimed them under a will that was never produced. Hastings had at the time steadily refused his sanction to these proceedings, and was therefore not disinclined by a reversal of the policy he had condemned to assist Asaf-ud-daula to recover what had been unjustly taken from him.

P. 76, l. 3. **the contracting parties**, the Nawáb and the British government who had made the contract.

ll. 26, 7. **Such a difference ... compromise**, it seemed impossible that when the wants of each party were so diametrically opposed, any arrangement could be come to by which each would be satisfied.

l. 33. **robbers.** If the term is to be used it applies more justly to the Queen-mother than to Asaf-ud-daula.

P. 77, ll. 1, 2. **been left ... dotation**, this was a landed estate which yielded the Queen-mother fifty thousand pounds a year.

l. 7. **Fyzabad**, a city in Oudh, about 60 miles east of Lucknow.

l. 9. **the Goomti**, a tributary of the Ganges.

ll. 11, 2. **Asaph-ul-Dowlah ... mother**, the Nawáb had not " extorted" any sums from the Begam. He obtained one loan from her of twenty-six lakhs of rupees for which he gave her an estate of four times the value, and another loan of thirty lakhs on account of his patrimony, for which he gave her a full acquittal as to the rest, and secured her estates to her without interference for life.

ll. 15, 6. **he in his turn ... rights**, he had never committed any invasion of her rights.

ll. 18-20. **the power ... them**, Hastings, as already stated, had always opposed the arrangement made so much to the advantage of the Begams at the expense of the Nawáb, and having now proof that they had helped Chait Sing with men and money, and fomented insurrection against their own sovereign, he felt that they deserved small mercy at the Nawáb's hands. He therefore gave his assent to the resumption of the estates held by them, but pledged the Nawáb to grant his kinswomen liberal pensions in exchange for the military fiefs which they had no right to hold. The Nawáb was a weak creature; his mother a woman of strong mind and violent temper, and on his return to Lucknow, his courage began to fail him. He had gained time, and probably thought that Hastings's demand for payment of his debt to the Company might be evaded for the present.

ll. 25, 6. **which wither ... civilization**, which, though partially civilized, instead of finding in such civilization the strength which goes with its purer forms, are only enfeebled by it when accompanied by corruption. A savage state of life may still be strong and healthy, a corrupt half-civilization has all the elements of weakness and none of the elements of strength. Macaulay refers to the conditions of life in which the Nawáb was living.

ll. 28, 9. **The insurrection ... Onde**, this is ingeniously put and would make it appear that Hastings, having caused the insurrection in Benares, was indirectly answerable for the disturbances in Oudh; but Macaulay is reversing cause and effect, for Hastings had proof from Hannay, Middleton, and other officers, that the Begams' troops had aided Chait Sing, and that numbers of people, horse and foot, were daily sent to him from Faizábád. This, as regards the Company, was his "pretext" for punishing the Begams; while, as regards the Nawáb, he saw in the disturbances fomented by them, a justification for their being made to disgorge that which they had unjustly withheld from him.

P. 78, ll. 12, 3. **His mother ... implored**, rather they were stubborn and indignant, and the Nawáb was daunted by their resistance.

ll. 15-7. **Even ... measures**, yet in his letters he wrote in the strongest terms of the Bhao Begam, declaring that she had "forfeited every claim she had to the protection of the British government," and Burke afterwards argued that his charges against her were brought by him to justify spoliation. I cannot find in Forrest's Records any mention of the letter from Hastings which Macaulay says was "in terms of greatest severity," and according to Impey's account, he was directed to convey to the Resident Hastings's views on the subject, Hastings saying to Impey that "he was apprehensive the mildness of Mr. Middleton's temper would prevent him from urging the Nabob effectually to carry it [the treaty of Chunár] into execution."

l. 27. **resumed**, taken back by the Nawáb.

P. 79, ll. 20, 1. **an English government**, for this at all events Hastings was not answerable, though Macaulay's wording of the sentence seems intended to imply it. The eunuchs were not two "infirm old men"; one of them was seen by Lord Valentia twenty years later, and was then "well, fat, and enormously rich."

l. 33. **under duresse, in** strict confinement. On the whole subject of the eunuchs and the Begams, Mr. Forrest remarks, "In order to recover the treasure the Nawab and his Ministers had to adopt severe measures towards the two eunuchs who had the chief influence over the Begums. The cruelty practised by the Nawab and his servants has been greatly exaggerated, but it was sufficient to have justified the interference of the Resident. To have countenanced it by transmitting the orders of the Vizier was a grave offence. But for what took place Hastings at Calcutta cannot be held responsible. He ordered the Resident not to permit any negotiation or forbearance, but there is a wide gulf between legitimate severity and cruelty." Nevertheless it can hardly be maintained that Hastings took sufficient precautions against the excesses which, knowing the Wazír's character, he might have anticipated.

P. 80, ll. 12-29. **There is a man ... biography?** in his revised edition of the Essay, Macaulay omits the whole of this passage.

l. 30-P. 81, l. 24. **But we must not ... India**, on the whole of this paragraph see Appendix III.

l. 1. **affidavits**, properly the third person singular, perfect tense, of the Low Lat. *affidare*, to make oath.

ll. 18, 9. **in an irregular manner**, he not being able to give it in a regular manner as he might have done in a judicial proceeding.

l. 20. **the crimes ... him**, Macaulay assumes that Hastings had bribed Impey by the judgeship in the Sadr Diwáni Adálat, and also that Impey was conscious that Hastings had been guilty of crimes in deposing Chait Sing, and entering into the Chunár treaty.

P. 82, l. 7. **Lord Advocate**, the highest judicial functionary in Scotland.

ll. 17-20. **The votes ... justice**, it does not necessarily follow that the votes they helped to swell were dictated by stern justice, if it was to the interest of ministers "to show ... themselves."

l. 31. **the Secretary of State**, Lord Shelburne. Impey, however, though recalled, was not dismissed from his office. He continued to hold it five years longer, when he resigned. It was not till the impeachment of Hastings was coming on that any charge was brought against Impey.

P. 83, ll. 23, 4. **thirteen colonies**, afterwards the United States of America.

l. 29. **Minorca**, an island in the Mediterranean: **Florida**, in the south-east of North America: **Senegal**, in Western Africa: **Goree**, a small island on the western coast of Africa.

P. 84, ll. 3, 4. **if we may ... India**, Macaulay can hardly mean to express doubt as to these results being due to Hastings.

l. 13. **Louis the Sixteenth**, king of France: **the Emperor Joseph**, of Austria.

ll. 14-6. **He boasted ... creation**, his words were in his defence before the House of Lords, "Every division of official business, and every department of government which now exists in Bengal, ... are of my formation. The establishment formed for the administration of the revenue, the institution of the courts of civil and criminal justice in the province of Bengal and its immediate dependencies, the form of government established for the province of Benares ... were created by me. Two great sources of revenue, opium and salt, were of my creation ... To sum up all, I maintained the provinces of my immediate administration in a state of peace, plenty, and security, when every other member of the British empire was involved in external war or civil tumult."

P. 85, ll. 3, 4. **the depositaries ... traditions**, those who from long familiarity with the modes of procedure in their respective offices are able to guide the Minister in all technical details.

l. 6. **Downing Street ... House**, the former containing the chief political offices; the latter, the Admiralty, Inland Revenue, etc., offices.

l. 12. **trammelled**, hampered; a 'trammel' is a net, shackle, anything that confines or restrains.

l. 17. **bales of censure**, with an allusion to the freight of vessels with bales of cotton, silk, etc., such as were exported from India.

l. 21. **thwarted ... Deputies**, the Deputies, as the representatives of our Dutch allies in the war, having a voice in the operations to be undertaken, and constantly using it to check Marlborough's daring designs against the common foe.

ll. 22, 3. **the Portuguese ... Percival,** Wellington in his efforts to expel the French from Spain and Portugal being similarly subject to interference from, and inadequate support by, the Spanish and Portuguese Councils, and having at the same time to put up with the dilatory measures of Mr. Percival, then Prime Minister, in supplying him with reinforcements, etc., and the restrictions put upon that freedom of action which was necessary to success.

ll. 27, 8. **resembled ... stupidity,** looked like that dull patience which is the outcome not of determination but of inability to see that there is anything to rebel against.

l. 34. **had the full ... resources,** the resources of his mind, his quickness in discovering the best way out of a difficulty, were not paralysed by outbursts of passion or impetuosity of desire.

P. 86, ll. 16, 7. **at the expense ... powers,** the other powers losing strength in proportion as one single power is developed.

ll. 17, 8. **speak ... abilities,** convey by their excellence in speaking an impression of greater ability than is really possessed.

l. 20. **a little ... debater,** a little too much given to thinking that statesmanship is best shown in meeting the arguments of opponents.

ll. 31, 2. **of perplexing ... understand,** of wrapping up in ambiguous and intricate language that which he did not wish to be seen in all its naked plainness.

l. 34. **with some reservation,** in qualified terms, in terms not wholly eulogistic.

P. 87, ll. 1, 2. **Perhaps ... taste,** Persian literature abounding in flowery and ornate language.

ll. 5, 6. **curious researches,** inquiries into out-of-the way subjects.

ll. 6, 7. **His patronage ... publications,** he encouraged with a far-seeing, and in the best sense remunerative, outlay of money, voyages, etc.

l. 12. **dotages,** drivelling teachings.

ll. 13, 4. **transfused ... expositions,** not coming directly from its Greek sources, but modified by the interpretations put upon it by Arabian commentators.

l. 15. **a far ... ruler,** Lord William Bentinck, so largely aided by Macaulay himself.

l. 17. **taken from a ledger,** his early occupation being merely that of a clerk in a commercial concern.

l. 26. **the Asiatic Society**, the well-known Society in Calcutta for the encouragement of all branches of Oriental learning.

l. 28. **with excellent ... feeling**, in recognising Sir W. Jones as so much his superior in Oriental learning.

l. 31. **Pundits**, men learned in the Sanskrit language and literature; the literal meaning of the word is merely 'learned.'

l. 34. **the sacred dialect**, Sanskrit.

P. 88, l. 4. **hereditary priests**, the Brahman pandits.

l. 18. **the civil service**, the Company's civil administrators as contrasted with the Company's army, equally its servants.

l. 28. **their vernacular dialects**, the spoken language of the people as contrasted with the classical language of their literature; **vernacular**, literally 'belonging to home-born slaves,' then 'native,' 'indigenous.'

l. 31. **for great ends**, with important objects in view.

P. 89, ll. 1, 2. **the hurricane ... cavalry**, the Marátha cavalry that swept everything before it as effectually as a hurricane; a metaphor instead of a simile.

l. 2. **rich alluvial plain**, the plain fertilized by the matter washed down by the great river running through it.

l. 20. **much ... children**, much the same love of outward pomp and show as that of children.

ll. 22-4. **and nurses ... Hostein**, this is an amusing mistake. The jingle in question *háthí par hauda, ghore par zín, jaldi jao, jaldi jao, Warren Hastín, i.e.* with *hauda* on elephant, saddle on horse, quickly go, quickly go, Warren Hastings, was in ridicule of his flight from Benares.

P. 90, l. 19. **indelicate and irregular**, such as a man with a delicate sense of integrity and a lofty code of honour would avoid.

l. 28. **Carlton House**, the residence of the Prince of Wales, afterwards George the Fourth, notorious for the splendour and extravagance of its decorations and festivities: **Palais Royal**, formerly a palace of great magnificence in Paris.

ll. 28-31. **He brought ... salary**, his salary for thirteen years was £25,000 a year, and he brought home about £120,000, including that settled on his wife, amounting to £40,000, which apparently is what Macaulay calls her "private hoard."

P. 91, l. 12. **the round-house**, the stern cabin: **Indiaman**, the name formerly given to vessels trading to the East Indies.

l. 13. **sandal-wood**, a sweet-scented wood found more especially in the south of India; a French corruption of the Persian *chandal.*

ll. 21, 2. **his elegant Marian,** her Christian name was Anna Maria Apollonia.

l. 23. **Sir Charles Grandison,** the dignified hero of Richardson's novel of that title : **Miss Byron,** the lady of his love.

l. 24. **the cedar parlour,** the room wainscotted with cedar in Sir Charles Grandison's home.

P. 92, ll. 3, 4. **Horace's .. rogat,** the opening words of the sixteenth ode of the second book of Odes by Q. Horatius Flaccus, the Roman poet. The following is the first stanza :—

> "For ease the harassed seaman prays,
> When equinoctial tempests raise
>   The Cape's surrounding wave ;
> When hanging o'er the reef he hears
> The cracking mast, and sees, or fears,
>   Beneath, his wat'ry grave."

l. 4. **Mr. Shore,** Governor-General of India from 1793 to 1798.

l. 13. **paid ... street,** called upon the Board of Directors.

l. 14. **Cheltenham,** in Gloucestershire, a favourite retreat of Anglo-Indians on account of its mild climate.

l. 17. **incurred much censure,** for receiving at Court one who had been divorced from her husband. A fortnight after the landing of Mrs. Hastings, "she was presented by Lady Weymouth to King George the Third and Queen Charlotte. Two more weeks passed, and she was again received by their Majesties ; and according to a letter that was written to Hastings by his agent, Major Scott, ... she 'met with still greater marks of attention if possible' ... The friendliness of the Queen to a *divorcée* was regretted by Colonel Fairly and Captain Price, two of the King's equerries, and defended by Mrs. Schwellengberg, the Chief Keeper, and Miss Fanny Burney, the Assistant Keeper of the Queen's Robes." The latter "represented to the equerries that in England 'a divorce could only take place upon misconduct,' whereas in Germany 'a divorce from misconduct prohibited a second marriage, which could only be permitted where the divorce was the mere effect of disagreement from dissimilar tempers.' The equerries said that they had never heard this before ; and Colonel Fairly added, that 'it ought to be made known, both for the sake of Mrs. Hastings, and because she had been received at Court, which gave everybody the greatest surprise, and me, in my ignorance, the greatest concern on account of the Queen '" (Sir C. Lawson).

P. 93, l. 16. **Hannibal,** the great Carthaginian general who so nearly succeeded in breaking the power of Rome in the Punic wars.

l. 17. **Themistocles,** the Athenian commander, famous for his victory over the Persians at Salamis, B.C. 480.

ll. 17-9. **His very ... stumble,** he reasons on wrong premisses, and therefore the greater his acuteness the further it carries him from a just conclusion. The fact that he is so vigorous causes him to proceed at a pace that will bring him to the ground, whereas had he been feeble, he would have taken care to avoid the obstacles in his path.

l. 22. **In India .. hand,** a metaphor from cards, at which a hand is the number of cards dealt to a player ; in his case those were bad cards, cards not likely to win the game.

l. 23. **master of the game,** thoroughly skilled in all the diffi-culties of the game, a player of the first rank.

ll. 30-2. **one of the few ... Commons,** the eloquence and power of argument which make a great advocate being of a different character from those which make a great debater in the House of Commons.

l. 34. **forensic acuteness,** that acuteness which is most useful in a law-court ; the Roman *forum* was at once a market place, a place for the discussion of public affairs, and the site of the law-courts.

P. 94, l. 13. **He was ... legs,** he was ever getting up to speak.

ll. 18-21. **There was hardly ... Scott,** Sir A. Lyall quotes the *Rolliad*, "Reams and reams of tracts that without pain Incessant spring from Scott's prolific brain."

ll. 23, 4. **pass ... pastry-cooks,** the former using this waste-paper to line the trunks they made, the latter for baking their cakes upon.

l. 28. **temper,** frame of mind.

P. 95, l. 5. **Mr. Fox's ... Bill,** introduced in 1783 ; Fox's pro-posal was to transfer the political government from the Directors of the Company to a board of seven Commissioners, whose office was to be held for five years. Its rejection brought about the fate of the Shelburne Ministry.

l. 15. **great place,** office of Lord Chancellor.

l. 26. **The resolution of censure,** that carried by Dundas ; see above, p. 82.

ll. 34, 5. **who was deeply ... subject,** who by his action in bringing on the vote of censure was bound to oppose any honour being done to Hastings.

P. 96, ll. 1, 2. **the committee ... affairs,** the Board of Control.

l. 3. **new allies,** new party allies ; at the former date he was in alliance with Burke and his supporters.

ll. 5, 6. **flattery ... number,** not even those most inclined to flatter him could pay him the compliment of saying that he was consistent.

l. 19. **affect .. game,** help to secure the political results they desired.

l. 20. **The followers of the coalition,** the Whig supporters of Fox coalesced with the Tories who still clung to Lord North, with the object of overturning the Shelburne Ministry,—"the most unscrupulous coalition," says Green, "known in our history."

ll. 23, 4. **The wits of Brooks's,** Brooks's Club in St. James's Street, the great Whig Club which numbered amongst its members Sheridan, Burke, Fox, Garrick, and many other men of great wit and humour.

l. 27. **a certain ... bed,** it appears that the present was one of two ivory chairs, quaintly carved and gilded, each with five legs, not an ivory bed, though Hastings in his letters speaks of an "ivory cot" which he had in India.

l. 34. **swinging,** from the gallows.

l. 36. **Virgil's third eclogue,** the eclogues of P. Vergilius Maro, the author of the *Aeneid*, are bucolic poems in imitation of the Sicilian poet, Theocritus. The third eclogue is a rustic singing-match between two shepherds.

P. 97, l. 5. **galaxy of jewels,** jewels which in their number and brilliancy resembled the Milky Way in the heavens; galaxy, from Gk. γάλα, milk.

l. 6. **her necklace ... votes,** her necklace, the bright gems in which were to be used in bribing voters in the House of Commons to support Pitt, and so her husband's cause.

l. 7. **and the depending ... ears,** the ear-rings she wore, which were to be turned to the same use; **depending** is used in a double sense, literally, hanging as the ear-rings hung from her ears, figuratively, of questions yet to be decided. Sir A. Lyall quotes the *Probationary Ode* to which Macaulay refers—

> "Oh Pitt, with awe behold that precious throat
> Whose necklace teems with many a future vote!
> Pregnant with Burgage gems each hand she wears,
> And lo! depending questions gleam upon her ears."

"Burgage" is a freehold property in a borough; also, a house or other property held by burgage tenure, *i.e.* tenure held of the king or other lord for a certain yearly rent, and "Burgage gems" means gems which by their value would give a right to a vote for a borough equally with the possession of freehold property.

ll. 19, 20. **with as much ... allow,** using against him the bitterest terms that parliamentary courtesy would permit.

l. 35. **fall of the coalition,** see note, p. 96, l. 20.

P. 98, l. 9. **alienated from Fox**, with whom Burke quarrelled on the subject of the French Revolution.

ll. 10, 1. **preaching ... republic**, endeavouring to stir up in others the same bitter hatred that he himself felt towards the French republic.

l. 22. **Las Casas or Clarkson**, the former a Catholic bishop, who spent many years among the South American Indians, and made every effort to save them from the cruelty of the Spanish; the latter a Quaker, to whom, with Wilberforce, the abolition of the slave trade was due.

l. 24. **the infirmity ... nature**, if Macaulay refers to any particular infirmity, he probably means the intolerance of such men towards those less enthusiastic than themselves.

l. 36. **sensibility**, quickness of feeling, which enabled him to throw himself into the position and manner of life of others.

P. 99, l. 9. **coloured them**, gave them a vividness which did not belong to them in the state in which they came to him; lighted them up with the colour that a painter gives to a pencil sketch.

l. 15. **abstractions**, things which exist only in idea, abstracted from all material embodiment.

ll. 17, 8. **the huge trees**, Macaulay is referring especially to the *pipal* trees to be found in every village of Upper India, and which are to the villagers what the oaks are in England.

l. 20. **tracery**, delicate carved outline: **mosque**, or *masjid*, the temple of Musalmáns: **imaum**, or *imám*, the Muslim priest.

l. 21. **face to Mecca**, the masjid always faces east towards Mecca, the sacred city in Arabia in which Muhammad was born: **gaudy idols**, painted and gaily decked; the idols are those of the Hindus, the Musalmáns abjuring anything of the kind, so much so that they object even to the statues of men.

l. 22. **devotees ... air**, a reference to the *charak-puja*, in honour of the goddess Káli, in which the devotee is suspended in the air by an iron hook through the fleshy part of the back.

l. 24. **the yellow ... sect**, worn in the centre of the forehead.

ll. 25, 6. **silver maces**, the *chobs* borne before princes and great men: **the elephants ... state**, the *haudas* of elephants belonging to princes are often plated with silver, and have gorgeous canopies over them.

l. 27. **the close litter**, this is the same as the *palki* or palanquin, but its doors are always kept close to prevent the inmates from being seen.

l. 30. **Beaconsfield**, Burke's country residence in Buckinghamshire.

l. 32. **laid gold**, the *nazar*, or customary offering of gold coins made at a public *darbár* or at private interviews.

l. 33. **gipsy camp**, though the gipsies originally came from India, Macaulay here means nothing more than wandering tribes generally. ·

ll. 35, 6. **where the lonely ... hyænas**, in those parts in which the mails are carried by runners, the bag is still slung on a pole with bells or iron rings to frighten away wild animals.

P. 100, l. 2. **Lord ... riots**, the 'No Popery' riots in London, in 1780, headed by Lord George Gordon, a fanatical Protestant. They lasted for many days; gaols were broken open, and many houses belonging to Catholics burnt to the ground.

l. 3. **Dr. Dodd**, hanged in June, 1777, for forging a bond of Lord Chesterfield's.

ll. 20, 1. **A young ... House**, Burke first entered Parliament in 1765.

l. 24. **the Stamp Act**, the Act which, in 1765, obliged the American colonists to affix a stamp on all legal documents issued within the Colonies, the value of the stamp being paid to the British revenue.

ll. 32, 3. **the Commercial Treaty ... Versailles**, concluded by Pitt in 1787: **the Regency**, rendered necessary by the King's becoming insane : **the French Revolution**, in 1789.

P. 101, l. 4. **the Bastile**, the prison in Paris used especially for political offenders ; burnt down at the outbreak of the Revolution.

l. 5. **Marie Antoinette**, the queen of Louis the Sixteenth, executed during the Revolution, 1793. Burke's impassioned language regarding the Revolution never rose to a greater height than in his famous passage on the wrongs of this unfortunate woman.

ll. 21, 2. **they would ... gold**, would have given every facility for retreating from their engagement to impeach. The phrase "to build a bridge of gold" is said to have been first used by Philip of Macedon in his war with the Athenians.

ll. 22, 3. **Major Scott ... year**, it was believed by many at the time that if Scott had never written or spoken in the House of Commons in behalf of Hastings, there would have been no impeachment.

L. 34. **papers**, the necessary documents on which to found and support his charges.

P. 102, ll. 3-5. **They had been ... pamphlet**, Sir J. Stephen's opinion on this matter differs widely from Macaulay's, "It is impossible," he says, "to imagine anything worse of their kind than the articles which he preferred against Hastings. ... An accusation ought to state directly, unequivocally, and without going into either argument or evidence, that at such a time and place the person accused has done such and such things, thereby committing an offence against such and such a law. The articles of impeachment against both Hastings and Impey violated every one of these obvious rules. Instead of being short, full, pointed, and precise, they are bulky pamphlets sprinkled over with imitations of legal phraseology. They are full of invective, oratorical matter, needless recitals, arguments, statements of evidence—everything in fact that can possibly serve to make an accusation difficult to understand and to meet ... they are as shuffling and disingenuous in substance, as they are clumsy, awkward, and intricate in form.".

ll. 22, 3. **a paper ... length,** Hastings had only five days in which to write this paper.

l. 26. **It fell flat,** it did not produce that effect for which Hastings hoped ; though Hastings himself mistook the deference with which it was heard for approval, and wrote to a friend in India, " It instantly turned all minds to my own way."

ll. 31, 2. **the clerks and the Sergeant-at-arms,** *i.e.* the officers of the House who could not leave till the sitting was over.

l. 36-P. 103, l. 3. **for Dundas ... Rohilcund,** and therefore the members of the Ministry to which Dundas belonged could not well oppose the charge.

l. 23. **coffee-houses,** the forerunners of the modern clubs.

l. 28, 9. **the star of the Bath,** except the order of the Garter, the highest of English orders of knighthood.

l. 29. **sworn ... council,** sworn in as a member of the council which gives advice to the sovereign, and which is bound to keep its proceedings secret.

l. 36. **from taking ... peerage,** from inquiring the king's wishes as to the signing of a patent conferring a peerage.

P. 104, l. 12. **felicity of language,** skilful choice of words ; so we say ' in happy terms'; ' felicity ' and ' happy' suggesting that the result attained was in a measure due to good fortune.

l. 16. **contumaciously,** out of mere obstinacy and without any good reason.

P. 105, l. 10. **during sixty years,** the last impeachment being that of Harley in 1716.

l. 16. **vindicating ... honour,** asserting the national honour by the punishment of those who had cast a stain upon it.

l. 19. **atoned for,** the literal sense of ' atone' is to make *at one,* to reconcile ; here the meaning is ' compensated.'

P. 106, l. 7. **works of supererogation,** works over and above those that a man is called upon to perform.

l. 13. **the usual notes,** circulars sent out by the party 'whip' in the case of a division in the House on a matter of importance.

l. 18. **closeted with him,** shut up with him in private consultation.

P. 107, l. 1. **as a man of conscience,** with any regard for conscientiousness.

l. 2. **The business ... bad,** Hastings's behaviour, he said, was such as could not be passed over without censure.

ll. 23, 4. **to submit ... functions,** to endure that any of his subordinates should take upon himself a duty that belonged to the Prime Minister alone. "On the whole," says Sir A. Lyall, "it is a reasonable conclusion that Pitt and Dundas ... did resolve, after private consultation, not to stand between Hastings and his powerful accusers at the risk of some loss of political character and some strain upon their ascendency in the House and the country."

l. 33. **The prorogation,** of Parliament till the next session.

P. 108, l. 6. **below the bar,** below the barrier within which sit the Members of the House. Nowadays there is a gallery in the House called 'The Peers' Gallery,' in which the Peers gather on the occasion of any important debate.

l. 16. **Mr. Windham,** see Macaulay's description of this statesman, p. 114, ll. 1-4.

ll. 27, 8. **his friends .. down,** by coughing and scraping their feet on the floor the House prevented Hastings's friends from being heard.

P. 109, l. 5. **carried,** brought; not literally carried.

ll. 25-8. **that in the ordinary ... prosecutor,** Macaulay, in assenting to this argument, overlooks the fact that "the aggrieved party" is seeking a remedy for a personal wrong, for which no one but himself will seek redress, while the managers appointed by the House were supposed to be actuated by no personal considerations but merely to have the interests of justice at heart and to seek the maintenance of the honour of the country as vested in its hands.

P. 110, l. 7. **cloth of gold,** cloth embroidered and interwoven with gold threads.

ll. 16, 7. **with every ... contrast,** these talents and accomplishments were enhanced on the one hand by the way in which those of each of the managers were supplemented by those of the rest, and on the other hand by the prominence which contrast gave to individuality.

M

l. 23. **from right to left,** this of course applies only to Persian and Hindustáni, not to Sanskrit and its derivatives, such as Hindi and Bengali.

l. 32. **just sentence of Bacon,** passed upon him in 1621 for taking bribes when Lord Chancellor.

l. 33. **just absolution of Somers,** Somers was impeached in 1701, with Russell and Montague, for his share in the Partition Treaties by which it was sought to avoid the difficulties of the Spanish succession on the death of Philip III. of Spain. The House of Commons, however, would not appear to prosecute, and the House of Lords declared him acquitted.

l. 34. **Strafford,** Earl, impeached and beheaded in 1641 for counselling Charles I. to adopt illegal measures.

P. 111, ll. 4, 5. **robed ... ermine,** with their robes of ermine fur and their coronets on their heads.

ll. 5, 6. **Garter King-at-arms,** the head of the College of Heralds ; see note on page 103, l. 28.

ll. 8, 9. **three fourths ... then was,** their numbers are much greater now.

l. 15. **Earl ... realm,** this dignity has been hereditary in the family since the time of Thomas, Earl of Norfolk, younger son of Edward I.

l. 17. **Prince of Wales,** afterwards King George the Fourth.

l. 29. **Siddons,** Mrs. Sarah, the celebrated tragic actress of the period.

ll. 31, 2. **the historian ... Empire,** Gibbon, Edward, author of *The Decline and Fall of the Roman Empire.*

ll. 32, 3. **when Cicero ... Verres,** among the more famous of Cicero's orations are those against Verres, who as propraetor of Sicily had been guilty of great extortion and cruelty.

ll. 34-6. **Tacitus...Africa,** Tacitus, whose fame is greater as a historian than as an orator, was in the reign of Nerva, A.D. 99, appointed together with the younger Pliny, to prosecute Marius, proconsul of Africa.

P. 112, l. 1. **Reynolds,** Sir Joshua, a famous portrait-painter of the time, and intimate friend of Johnson and Burke.

l. 4. **Parr,** Samuel, a learned classical scholar.

l. 5. **that dark ... mine,** ancient classical literature

ll. 9-11. **the voluptuous ... faith,** Mrs. Fitzherbert, who was privately married to the Prince of Wales.

l. 12. **the Saint Cecilia,** Mrs. Sheridan for her skill in, and love of, music, was painted by Reynolds in the character of St. Cecilia, according to the legend, a Roman virgin of rank, who embraced

Christianity in the reign of Antoninus. She is said to have invented the organ, and she was canonized as the guardian saint of
music. See Dryden's two odes in honour of St. Cecilia's day.

ll. 14-7. **There were ... Montague,** Mrs. Montague, with Mrs.
Vesey and Mrs. Ord, held re-unions at which in place of the
usual card-playing they endeavoured to encourage intellectual
and literary conversation. One of the habitués of these gather-
ings always wore blue worsted, instead of black silk, stockings,
and in reference to this Admiral Boscawen is said to have dubbed
the coterie the ' Blue Stocking Society.'

ll. 17-20. **And there ... Devonshire,** the Duchess of Devonshire
with a band of lady friends canvassed for Fox when he stood for
Westminster, and the Duchess gained the vote of an obstinate
opponent, a butcher, by allowing him to kiss her ; the persuasive-
ness of Fox's lips was of course in his eloquence : **against ...
treasury,** the king and the ministry being opposed to Fox.

l. 21. **made proclamation,** citing Hastings before the Commons.

l. 22. **culprit,** the word is more generally used of a convicted
person.

l. 36. **Mens ... arduis,** a mind serene amidst difficulties.

P. 113, l. 2. **proconsul,** properly one who acted for a consul,
but in later times one who at the close of his consulship in Rome
became governor of a province, or military commander under a
governor.

l. 11. **Vice-chancellor ... Rolls,** judges of the Court of Chancery
subordinate to the Lord-Chancellor ; **Rolls,** literally of parchment,
hence public records.

l. 16. **in full dress,** in the dress worn at court, black velvet
coat, knee-breeches, silk stockings and bag-wig.

l. 19. **a bag,** a small silken pouch to contain the back hair of a
wig.

l. 22. **muster,** array.

l. 31. **the English ... Hyperides,** two great orators of Athens, the
former the greatest orator the world has known, contemporaries
and friends.

P. 114, l. 1. **the finest ... age,** the most accomplished and highly-
bred man of his time.

l. 9. **connection,** relationship to high-born families.

l. 13. **delegates,** persons deputed to represent.

l. 20. **the tapestries ... Lords,** destroyed in the fire by which
the old House of Lords was burnt down, October 16, 1834.

l. 27. **silver voice,** liquid and sweet-toned, like that of a silver
bell.

P. 115, l. 8. **the stern ... Chancellor,** Lord Thurlow, a warm admirer and friend of Hastings.

ll. 12, 3. **perhaps ... sensibility,** perhaps glad of an opportunity of showing how capable they were of justly appreciating real eloquence, and how full they were of delicate feeling for injured persons.

ll. 17, 8. **the old arches ... oak,** "Westminster Hall, first built by William Rufus, was almost rebuilt by Richard II., who added the noble roof of cobwebless beams of Irish oak 'in which spiders cannot live,' which we now see" (Hare, *Walks in London*, ii. 411).

P. 116, l. 10. **Mr. Grey,** Charles Grey, afterwards Lord Grey, a distinguished Whig politician, Prime Minister, 1830-4.

ll. 19-21. **Sheridan ... envied,** his father having been an actor. Of Sheridan's speech Sir A. Lyall remarks, "It would be most presumptuous to suppose that Sheridan did not know how best to persuade and please the House of Lords; but if the summary of this oration has been fairly given in Debrett's history of the trial, the modern reader will probably be **startled** at the quantity of declamation, invocation, metaphor, humorous illustration, and caricature, that is employed to throw a glaring light upon a sufficiently ill-favoured business, and to over-drive the true arguments for condemning the Governor-General's part in it. No one in these days uses irony and bitter sarcasm against a prisoner on his trial, nor is it thought fair or judicious to introduce grotesque figures of speech or degrading comparisons." ...

P. 117, l. 1. **masquerade,** here meaning a masked ball, or a ball generally.

l. 5. **lacs,** a sum of ten thousand pounds : **crores,** the sum of a million pounds : **zemindars,** land-holders.

l. 6. **aumils,** governors of a district : **sunnuds,** certificates granting a title to something or other : **perwannahs,** documents under the hand of a magistrate conveying orders or instructions : **jaghires,** landed estates : **nuzzurs,** presents to persons in authority. These words would now be written *lákh, karor, zamíndár, ámil, sanad, parwána, jáegír, nazar.*

l. 7. **bickerings,** ill-tempered, contentious, arguments.

l. 10. **Mr. Law,** Edward, afterwards first Lord Ellenborough.

l. 22. **the King's illness,** his insanity.

l. 26. **States-General,** the representative assembly of the French people summoned during the Revolution, and afterwards called the National Assembly : **Versailles,** about 11 miles from Paris, where the Court formerly resided.

ll. 34, 5. **the circuits were beginning,** the judges were setting out on their tours throughout the country, and therefore could not attend to give their decisions on points of law.

P. 118, l. 20. **law-lords,** judges raised to the peerage and so having a seat in the House of Lords.

ll. 24-7. **To expect ... indeed, partridge-shooting** begins on the 1st of September, and it is usual for Parliament to rise for its holidays before that date. Macaulay's remark is of course ironical.

P. 119, ll. 2-4. **Those rules ... guilty,** Macaulay, however, does not mean to deny that in ordinary trials the nett result of these rules is a gain.

ll. 10-11. **cannot be pleaded ... history,** cannot be used as an argument to upset that verdict which history records, a verdict which Macaulay means to imply was in the main condemnatory of Hastings: **in bar of,** in law a bar is a plea or objection of force sufficient to arrest entirely an action or claim, and hence **in bar of** is used of an objection sufficient to prevent or counteract something.

l. 14. **some violent language,** Burke had said that Hastings had murdered Nand Kumár by the hands of Impey, and on the petition of Hastings to the House of Commons complaining of such language, that House resolved that Burke's words ought not to have been used.

P. 120, l. 18. **the woolsack,** the Lord Chancellor's seat in the House of Lords, originally consisting of a large bag of wool covered with red cloth, but, though fashioned like a seat, having neither back nor arms. It is said to have had its origin in the circumstance of wool being anciently a staple article of produce in England.

l. 23. **The great seal,** of the Lord Chancellor, which on state occasions is borne before that official.

ll. 27, 8. **estranged ... barons,** having quarrelled with his party and no longer having an official seat as Lord Chancellor, he was obliged to sit with the rest of the law-lords.

P. 121, ll. 1-3. **It had been ... reproaches,** on the 6th May, 1791, Burke rose in the House to explain himself on the Revolution in France. "He had no sooner risen, than interruptions broke out from his own side, and a scene of great disorder followed. Burke was incensed beyond endurance by this treatment, for even Fox and Windham had taken part in the tumult against him. With much bitterness he commented on Fox's previous eulogies of the Revolution, and finally there came the fatal words of severance. 'It is indiscreet,' he said, 'at any period, but especially at my time of life, to provoke enemies, or to give my friends occasion to desert me. Yet if my firm and steady adherence to the British Constitution place me in such a dilemma, I am ready to risk it, and with my last words to exclaim, "Fly from the French Constitution."' Fox at this point eagerly called to him that there was no loss of friends. 'Yes, yes,' cried Burke, 'there is a loss of friends. I know the price of my conduct. I have done my duty at the price of my friend. Our friendship is at an end'... Fox, as might have been expected from his warm and generous nature, was deeply moved, and is described as weeping, even to sobbing. He repeated his former acknowledgment of his debt to Burke, and he repeated his former expression of faith in the blessings which the abolition of royal despotism would bring to France. With unabated vehemence Burke again rose to denounce the French Constitution, ... After a short rejoinder from Fox, the scene came to a close, and the once friendly intercourse between the two heroes was at an end" (Morley, *Burke, English Men of Letters*, pp. 181, 2).

ll. 7, 8. **Burke ... Windham**, Burke's alarm about the Revolution communicated itself to Windham, and by its impetuosity swept him away as helpless against it as anything floating on the waters is helpless against the furious eddy of a whirlpool. Windham's nature was, or had become, irresolute in the extreme ; and, like all irresolute men, when once he had made his choice, between the doctrines of Fox and those of Burke, the impulse to which he had yielded carried him headlong to the utmost depths, and his alarm was greater than even that of Burke. Sheridan and Grey followed Fox, but without violence or precipitation.

l. 27. **remission**, abatement of violence : **reaction**, an impulse in a direction opposite to that towards which the excitement had before been directed.

P. 122, l. 9. **cuddy**, an old term for the general cabin in a merchant vessel.

l. 19. **numerous addresses**, among these were letters 'of friendship and commiseration' from the Begams he was accused of maltreating.

l. 25. **Mahommedan doctors**, *i.e. maulavis*, men learned in law and theology.

l. 26. **collector**, the chief revenue officer of a district.

l. 33. **apotheosis**, deification.

P. 123, l. 4. **fiends ... murder**, the goddess Káli, or Durga, wife of Siva, who presided over smallpox, and also was worshipped by the murderous Thags.

l. 6. **Pantheon**, temple dedicated to all the gods.

ll. 13, 4. **The legal expenses**, "His defence had cost him, or rendered him liable for £100,000, and his own means were exhausted, and his wife's accumulations out of her marriage settlement had been greatly reduced by the failure of a Dutch firm" (Sir C. Lawson).

l. 23. **Logan,** a Scotch minister who wrote a pamphlet in defence of Hastings, and was prosecuted in consequence by the House of Commons.

l. 25. **Simpkin's letters,** entitled "Letters of Simkin on the trial of Hastings," 1791. The author was **Captain R. Broome,** who called himself, "Simkin the Second."

l. 28. **Anthony Pasquin,** "in the 16th century, at the stall of a cobbler named *Pasquin* [Pasquino], at Rome, a number of idle persons used to assemble to listen to his pleasant sallies ... and indulge in raillery at the expense of the passers-by. After the cobbler's death the statue of a gladiator was found near his stall, to which the people gave his name, and on which the wits of the time, secretly at night, affixed their lampoons" (Haydn, *Dict. of Dates,* quoted by Skeat). Hence the word *pasquinade,* a lampoon, satire.

l. 29. **The private hoards,** see above, p. 90, l. 28-31.

P. 124, l. 1. **alienated,** which had passed into the hands of others.

l. 5. **to form ... water,** to lay out an ornamental lake.

l. 16. **the Board of Control,** the government board which exercised a supervision over the acts of the Court of Directors.

P. 125, l. 2. **a red riband,** a broad sash worn by knights of the order of the Bath.

l. 3. **an office at Whitehall,** an official appointment from Government, the chief offices of which are in Whitehall.

l. 7. **a new class.. duties,** such as an appointment of a political character in England would entail.

l. 17. **was at Boulogne,** mustering his troops with the intention of invading England.

l. 21. **important ... power,** his opposition to the removal of the disabilities which lay upon Catholics.

ll. 24-6. **Religious ... Hastings,** such want of toleration on religious matters as Addington showed in regard to Catholics was not one of Hastings's failings, and his support of Addington could not consequently have been due to that cause.

l. 36. **custard-apple,** a fruit about the size of a ribstone pippin, formed in the inside of seeds embedded in a creamy, or custard-like, pulp.

P. 126, l. 2. **Allipore,** an outskirt of Calcutta.

l. 3. **leechee**, a fruit about the size of a walnut, with a rough shell covering an opaque white pulp, somewhat like the white of a boiled egg, and very delicious in taste; originally brought from China.

l. 5. **Covent Garden**, the great fruit and flower market of London.

l. 11. **Bootan**, an independent territory on the north-eastern frontier of Bengal: **whose tails**, these fans, called *châoris*, mounted in the horns of deer, are used by table-servants at meals, or by grooms at the back of carriages.

l. 20. **Trissotin**, the name of a character in Molière's comedy of *Les Femmes Savantes*, half man of fashion, half man of letters.

l. 34. **the reckoning**, the price to be paid.

l. 35. **madrigal**, properly a pastoral song, Ital. *mandra*, a flock, with suffix -*gale*, pertaining to.

P. 127, l. 5. **Dionysius**, the younger, tyrant of Syracuse, B.C. 367-343, whose court was the resort of philosophers and men of letters.

l. 6. **Frederic**, second of the name, King of Prussia, and commonly entitled "the Great," who spent much of his time in literary pursuits and aimed at being thought a poet; 1712-97.

l. 8. **provincial blue-stockings**, see note on p. 112, ll. 14-7; provincial is used to mark the inferiority in intelligence of these blue-stockings in comparison with those enjoying the more refined and intellectual society of the capital.

ll. 10, 1. **the Hayleys and Sewards**, people like Hayley and Seward, very third-rate authors who once enjoyed considerable reputation.

l. 30. **uncovered**, took off their hats, which many members wear when seated.

P. 128, ll. 8, 9. **the Sheldonian Theatre**, the Senate House at Oxford.

l. 17. **the Guildhall**, answering to the Town Hall in other towns and cities, the hall where the different guilds or companies of the city meet for the election of mayors, sheriffs, and burgesses, and further used as a court for the administration of justice in petty cases, and as a banqueting hall for civic festivities. The present building was begun in 1411, but little of the original structure now remains.

ll. 21-5. **his Royal ... Asia**, the Prince Regent in presenting Hastings to these monarchs spoke of him as "the most deserving and one of the worst-used men in the Empire."

P. 129, ll. 3-6. **the Great Abbey ... Hall**, Westminster Abbey, the burial place of so many of England's greatest men ; **the Great Hall**, Westminster Hall, *i.e.* the Houses of Parliament.

ll. 8-13. **Yet the place ... name**, "He was buried near his mother, and among his ancestors for many generations, in a new vault, close behind the chancel, which is marked by a pillar bearing an urn with his two names carved upon it, and surrounded by iron railings. The following inscription appears on a plain tablet within the church: 'In a vault just beyond the eastern extremity of this church lies the body of the Right Honourable Warren Hastings, of Daylesford House, in this parish, the first Governor-General of the British Territories in India, a member of His Majesty's Most Honourable Privy Council, L.L.D., F.R.S., the last public effort of whose eminently virtuous and lengthened life was the re-erection of the second edifice [*i.e.* the rebuilding of Daylesford Church], which he superintended with singular energy and interest to its completion, and in which, alas! the holy rites of sepulture were very shortly afterwards performed over his mortal remains. He died 22nd August, 1818, aged 85 years and 8 months. 'Lord, now lettest Thou Thy servant depart in peace'" (Sir C. Lawson). His widow also erected a tablet to his memory in Westminster Abbey.

l. 22. **He had founded a polity,** the whole administrative system of India up to that time was due to him.

l. 23. **Richelieu,** 1585-1642, Cardinal and Duke, the great French minister of state during the reign of Louis XIII.

l. 24. **Cosmo,** de' Medici, 1389-1464, a native of Florence, famous as a munificent patron of literature and art.

l. 29. **in the fulness of age,** at a ripe old age, in his eighty-sixth year.

APPENDIX I.

THE ROHILLA WAR.

Of the twenty charges presented by the managers of the impeachment of Hastings, that of the Rohilla War was the strongest. It was intrinsically strong because the proceedings of Hastings had undoubtedly resulted in bloodshed and hardship. It was, for the purpose of the impeachment, adventitiously strong because, as Macaulay says, "It had been condemned by the Court of Directors. It had been condemned by the House of Commons. It had been condemned by Mr. Dundas, who had since become the chief minister of the Crown for Indian affairs." The three points on which it was endeavoured to prove Hastings guilty were (1) that for such a war there was no justification, (2) that had there been justification, the war was attended with unnecessary cruelty, (3) that for such cruelty Hastings was answerable, if not in authorizing it, at all events in not taking sufficient precautions against its committal and in not checking it when brought to his notice.

In discussing these points my endeavour will merely be to summarize as clearly and as briefly as possible the facts, arguments, and conclusions of the exhaustive work recently published by Sir John Strachey under the title of *Hastings and the Rohilla War.* Sir John Strachey speaks with perhaps unrivalled authority not merely because he has studied with minute care every narrative of the events and every official paper that bears upon them, but because during a long period of service in Rohilkhand he was brought into close contact with the people of the country and with the descendants of those who were supposed to be so cruelly treated. That the two were not identical will be immediately shown. "Rohilkhand," says Sir John Strachey, "has an area of 12,000 square miles, and extends from Hardwar, where the Ganges enters the plains from the mountains, along the foot of the Garwhal and Kumáon Himalaya, to the frontiers of Oudh, a distance of nearly 200 miles. It is now one of the richest and most highly cultivated parts of the North-Western Provinces; it includes six

186

British districts and many large towns, and in the middle of the province lies the small native state of Rampur, with about half a million people, ruled by a Mahommedan prince, the descendant and representative of one of the Rohilla chiefs of whose history I am about to write. We shall not find in the plains of Rohilkhand the 'fair valleys' of Macaulay's description; his 'snowy heights' at the sources of the Ramganga, the chief river of central Rohilkhand, are not quite so imaginary, but the beautiful hills from which it comes are hardly more snowy than those at the sources of the Thames."* Whoever the aborigines of this tract, the earliest inhabitants known to history were Hindus. When, with the rest of northern India, it became a province of the Mughal empire, many grants of lands were given to Musalmáns, and during their occupation a considerable proportion of the people embraced the Muslim religion. The country, in the main fertile and well-wooded, naturally attracted the notice of the hardy races beyond the north-western frontier, and the Hindu chiefs were too much occupied with their own quarrels to present a united front against interlopers. Thus, about the middle of the eighteenth century, the Rohillas, for the most part Yusufzai Afgháns, had made themselves masters of the whole of Katehr, as it was formally called, and given it the name it still bears. The word "Rohilla" means merely "mountaineer" or "highlander," though it presently came to be synonymous with Pathán or Afghán. It is important to bear in mind the facts of this occupation, because Burke, Mill, and Macaulay have all insisted in giving the title of "nation" to a band of foreigners who had no better claim to the country than that of conquest, very recent conquest, their rule having lasted only some thirty-five years. It is also important to understand the character of these invaders, and their relation to the older inhabitants of the country. Of their character Sir J. Strachey remarks,† that "when they have been settled for several generations among a comparatively civilized people [they] lose in a great measure, but by no means entirely their barbarous characteristics, but the Pathan when he first entered India was, as he still is in his native mountains, a ruthless and treacherous savage. The character which these people bore in the last century was so precisely that which they bear now, that a description of them at the present day is as applicable as it would have been in the time of Ali Mohammad or of Hastings." He then quotes from Mr. D. Ibbetson's Report on the Census of the Punjab (1881), and from the Hayát-i-Afghán, a work descriptive of the people of this tribe on the Punjab frontier. Though these authorities give the Pathán credit for courage, open-handed hospitality, an air of masculine independ-

* *Hastings and the Rohilla War*, p. 9.
† *Hastings and the Rohilla War*, pp. 22-7.

ence, a high sense of honour, and a jealous regard for the honour
of their women, they also speak of him as being bloodthirsty,
cruel, vindictive, desperately treacherous, scornful of peaceful
occupations, invincibly ignorant, arrogant to a degree, boastful,
avaricious, devoid of all notion of gratitude, etc., etc. "I am
far," continues Sir John, "from wishing it to be supposed that
all the Rohillas were savages of this type. Some of them had
been settled in India long enough to give them a tinge of civilization, **and** some of their chiefs were undoubtedly deserving of
respect, but it is a matter of historical certainty that the descrip-
tions which I have quoted would have been generally applicable to
them...'Agriculture and commerce,' Macaulay writes, 'flourished
among them, nor were they negligent of rhetoric and poetry.'
The connection of the Rohillas with agriculture was this, that
they collected the rents and revenue of the land as zemindars or
superior landlords, the land itself being left in the occupation of
the Hindu cultivators...Middleton, who was British resident
with the Vizier during the whole of the Rohilla war, speaking of
what he had himself seen and learned by personal observation in
Rohilkhand, stated in his evidence before the House of Commons,
'the Rohillas never applied themselves to any profession but
arms, never to husbandry, manufactures, or mechanic arts.'"
As to the "rhetoric and poetry" of Macaulay's idyllic romance,
there appears to be no other foundation for their ascription to
the Rohillas in general than the fact that their chief, Háfiz
Rahmat, was something of a poet, and that the members of his
family were men of education. Of the relative numbers of the
Rohillas to the Hindus whom they conquered, it is probable that
when they were ejected from Rohilkhand the former were to the
latter as some forty thousand to a million. The chain of events
which ultimately led to British intervention was as follows. In
1759 the Maráthas invaded Rohilkhand, and the Rohilla chiefs
asked **for** help from Shuja-ud-daula, who, rapidly marching
from Lucknow, drove the invaders with heavy loss across the
Ganges. Twelve years later the Maráthas again invaded Rohilkhand. The Wazír's assistance was asked as before; and having
good reason to believe that as soon as Rohilkhand had been
conquered, his own territories would be the object of these
insatiable freebooters, he was willing enough to support those who
by their geographical position formed a buffer to his territory.
He was, indeed, so greatly alarmed for his own safety that he
sought to engage the Company in some concerted defence against
a danger which, not without reason, he represented as threatening them in the event of his own overthrow. The Calcutta
authorities, though anxious that other powers should resist the
Maráthas, were unwilling to give their co-operation. However,
at the Wazír's urgent entreaty they sent the Commander-in-Chief,
Sir Robert Barker, to report on the circumstances, and ultimately,

by that officer's active intervention and persuasion, a treaty of
alliance, offensive and defensive, was concluded between the
Wazír and the Rohillas. The attestation of the treaty by the
English General was looked upon by both parties as a guarantee
of its fulfilment, and as such Hastings later on felt bound to
regard it. Before long this obligation was to be tested. Internal
dissensions among the Rohillas, and particularly the defection of
one of their principal nobles, Zábita Khán, who before the end of
1772 openly joined the Maráthas, so alarmed the Wazír that he
urgently sought the protection of an English force. Hastings
consented to defend Oudh, but refused to allow the English
troops to go beyond the Wazír's frontiers, or to engage in an
offensive war against the Maráthas. The following year, therefore, Sir R. Barker, with a brigade consisting of two battalions
of European infantry, six battalions of sepoys, and a company of
artillery, marched to join the Wazír, who then wrote assuring
Háfiz Rahmat, the Rohilla chief, that the joint force would soon
arrive to assist him against the now threatening Maráthas, and
urging him to be ready to co-operate actively in the common
cause. The Rohilla shilly-shallied, entered into negotiations
with the Maráthas, and seemed on the point of joining them
against the Wazír. Angered by the apparent treachery of his
allies, the Wazír sounded Sir R. Barker on the subject of [seizing
upon the Rohilla territory, offering large concessions to the
Company if it would lend him aid to his project. Before, however, such a proposal could be considered, Háfiz Rahmat, finding
that the Maráthas would not risk an encounter with the English,
declared to the Wazír that he was ready to carry out his former
engagements, and promised to lose no time in paying the instalments of forty lacs of rupees due under the treaty of the preceding
year on account of the Wazír's help. For some time the
Maráthas lingered in the neighbourhood, and Shuja-ud-daula was
dissuaded by Sir R. Barker from pressing for payment lest
Háfiz Rahmat should throw himself into the arms of the invaders.
On their final disappearance, the Wazír returned to the subject,
only to meet with evasions from the Rohilla. Before long it
became quite evident that nothing was to be got from him; and
Hastings, who had never doubted that safety to Oudh and to the
British possessions was possible only "by giving to the dominions
of the Vizier their natural boundaries, and including within one
ring-fence the whole of Rohilkhand and Oudh," now felt that the
time had come for seriously considering Shuja-ud-daula's pro-
posal. He therefore offered an interview, and, the Wazír
eagerly agreeing, this took place at Benares on the 19th of
August, 1773. The result was a treaty concluded on the 7th of
September. Of this treaty the first portion had reference only
to the cession of Kora and Allahábád to the Vizier on payment
of fifty lakhs of rupees, and with this matter we are not here

concerned. As regards Rohilkhand, the following are the terms agreed upon subject to confirmation by the Council in Calcutta :

"Whereas the Rohilla chiefs, in the month of June 1772, entered into a treaty with the Vizier, in the presence and with the concurrence of General Sir Robert Barker, by which they engaged to pay him forty lakhs of rupees for his assistance against the Marathas, and which treaty they have treacherously broken ; it is therefore agreed that a Brigade of the Company's forces shall join the Vizier, and assist to punish them, and that he shall pay the whole of its expense. By a Brigade is meant : two battalions of Europeans, one company of Artillery, and six battalions of Sepoys, and the expense is settled at Sonaut Rupees 210,000 per month. The Company's troops shall not cross the Ganges, nor march beyond the foot of the hills. The Vizier shall retain as his own that part of the Rohilla country which lies on the north-east side of the Ganges, but in consideration of the Company's relinquishing all claim to share in the said country, although it is to be conquered by their joint forces, the Vizier engages to make them an acknowledgment of forty lakhs of rupees, and in future to defray the whole expense of the Company's troops, agreeable to the data above-mentioned, whenever he has occasion for their assistance, notwithstanding it is stipulated in the second article of the treaty of Allahabad, concluded by the Vizier and the Company on the 16th August, 1765, that he shall pay only their extraordinary charges."...

The remainder of the draft is not material, its two other clauses dealing only with the time for which the brigade shall be at the Vizier's disposal, and the details of payment. Everything seemed now to be settled. Shuja-ud-daula, however, on a further consideration of the liabilities he had undertaken, felt doubtful as to the prudence of an immediate invasion of Rohilkhand, and Hastings readily assented to a postponement of operations. Further, as no final conclusion had been arrived at, Hastings, on his return to Calcutta, though recording the wish of the Wazír for assistance in subjugating Rohilkhand, thought it more prudent not to state to the Council how far the negotiations had gone. A few weeks later the Wazír reopened the subject in two letters to Hastings, the latter letter definitely asking for a fulfilment of the agreement entered into at Benares, and being accompanied by a separate paper summarizing his proposals in the following terms :—"On condition of the entire expulsion of the Rohillas, I will pay to the Company the sum of forty lakhs of rupees in ready money whenever I shall discharge the English troops, and until the expulsion of the Rohillas shall be effected I will pay the expenses of the English troops,—that is to say I will pay the sum of Rs. 210,000 monthly." On the day after this letter was received, Hastings and the Select Committee of the Council recorded a resolution in assent to the Wazír's proposals, and Hastings was empowered to answer his letters, setting forth in full and explicit terms the conditions on which the required assistance would be granted. Before, however, sending this answer, it was decided that in a matter so important the whole of the proceedings should be considered by the Council at large. For three successive days the matter was debated by nine out of the ten members. Much diversity of opinion was shown, no two members agreeing on all points. At last Hastings was authorized to draw up a resolution expressing, as well as he was able, the general view. The resolution thus prepared, and accepted by the whole Council, approved of Hastings's answer already mentioned, but at the same time recorded a hearty wish " to avoid the expedition proposed," great doubt as to its present expediency, and a hope that the stringency of the conditions imposed would drive the Wazír into a refusal of them. At the same time the Council confirmed the resolution of the Committee drawn up on the 19th of October, "that the 2nd Brigade now quartered at Dinapore be ordered to march on the Vizier's requisition, ... and that every preparation be made for putting the 2nd Brigade in readiness to take the field on the shortest notice." On the 10th of January, 1774, an answer was received from the Wazír declining to undertake the expedition under the terms offered. Less than a month later he again changed his mind, agreed to all the conditions upon which the co-operation of a British force was to be obtained, and asked that a brigade might be at once ordered to join him and take part in the proposed expedition. It now became impossible for the Bengal Government to refuse consent. Colonel Champion, who on Sir R. Barker's retirement from the service had been appointed provisional Commander-in-Chief, was directed to assume command of the troops, already on their way to join the Wazír, and was informed that the object of the expedition was the reduction of the Rohilla country lying between the Ganges and the mountains. Colonel Champion's powers were strictly confined to the military conduct of the expedition, the management of all political relations with the Wazír being entrusted to Middleton, then the Company's Agent at the Court of Lucknow. The British force consisted of one company of artillery, the 2nd European regiment, the select picket, consisting of about a hundred cadets waiting for their commissions, and the 2nd Brigade composed of six battalions of native infantry under the command of Colonel Galliez. The Wazír's army is said to have numbered 100,000 men. On the near approach of these forces to the Rohilla frontier, the chief, Háfiz Rahmat, became anxious to enter into negotiations with Shuja-ud-daula. The latter demanded a large sum—according to Champion two karors of rupees—for the aid he had given the Rohillas against the Maráthas. Háfiz Rahmat wrote more letters, but does not appear to have made any endeavour to meet the Wazír's demands even in part, or to have offered any basis for negotiation, even if there had been a desire on the Wazír's part for an amicable arrangement. But no such desire existed. The time for negotiation had passed, and Shuja-ud-daula was determined upon having vengeance. The two armies met on the 23rd of April, 1774, at Miránpur Katra in the Sháhjáhánpur district with the result narrated by Macaulay. One point in that narrative needs a passing notice. "The dastardly sovereign of Oude," we are told, "fled from the field." This statement is based upon Champion's charge of "shameful pusillanimity" against the Wazír. But Champion seems to have borne no good will towards that prince, of whom Sir Henry Lawrence writes that "whatever were his faults," he "was never before accused of cowardice"; and, says Sir J. Strachey, "The official returns of killed and wounded seem to make it probable that the Vizier's infantry took a larger share in the action than might be supposed from Colonel Champion's despatch, for while the loss of the Company's English and native troops was 132, that of the troops of the Vizier, not including his cavalry for which there is no return, was 254."

We now come to the results of the victory, to Macaulay's picture of the cruelties to which the Rohillas were subjected, and to the share imputed to Hastings in those cruelties. On the death of Háfiz Rahmat, Faizullah Khán, the eldest surviving son of Ali Muhammad became the acknowledged head of the Rohillas. "Faizullah Khan," says Sir John Strachey, "lost no time in endeavouring to open negotiations with the commander of the English forces and the Vizier, and towards the end of May he sent an envoy to Colonel Champion with definite proposals." In these proposals large sums of money were offered to the English and to the Wazír on condition that the whole of Rohilkhand should be given up by them to him. The Wazír and Hastings scornfully rejected these offers; and as Faizullah Khán still remained in arms, it was decided to attack him in order to bring the war to an end. When, however, the advanced hosts of the English were within a mile of those of the Rohillas, Faizullah again opened negotiations. The result was a treaty concluded on the 7th October, 1774, between the Wazír and Faizullah, and attested by Colonel Champion. "It provided," says Sir J. Strachey, "that Faizullah Khan should retain possession of the territory formerly allotted to him in Rohilkhand by his father Ali Mohammad, with the city and district of Rampur. ... It was stipulated that Faizullah Khan should retain in his service a force of not more than 5,000 men, that he should, if called on to do so, render certain military services to the Vizier, and enter into no correspondence with any powers excepting the Vizier and the English. Faizullah Khan, it was further provided, 'shall send the remainder of the Rohillas to the other side of the river' ... Immediately after the signature of the treaty, the Vizier and the English withdrew their forces; Faizullah Khan went with his 5,000 men to Rampur, and assumed quiet possession of the country assigned to him; the rest of the Rohilla troops marched, under the command of some of their chiefs, across the Ganges into the district of Zábita Khan, their countryman. The number of Rohillas who thus left Rohilkhand is said by Hamilton to have been 17,000 or 18,000. According to Colonel Champion it was about 20,000, including camp followers. Many of the Rohilla soldiers entered the service of Zábita Khan, and many soon returned to Rohilkhand, and obtained employment with Faizullah Khan or in the army of the Vizier. No Rohillas except those under arms with Faizullah Khan were compelled to cross the Ganges; the rest were unmolested, and either remained in their former homes or settled in the Rampur State. Whatever may have been the misgovernment or absence of government in Rohilkhand after the fall of the Rohilla dominion, there is no reason to suppose that either at this or any subsequent time the Rohillas suffered any special persecution or oppression from the Oudh authorities." Such is a succinct account of the results of the war. It will presently be necessary to examine in some detail the atrocities said to have attended it. But before doing so, it will be well to clear up one point; the nature of the "extermination" of which Burke and Mill make so much capital.

The First Article of Charge presented by Burke to the House of Commons on the 4th of April, 1786, opens with the words "That the said Warren Hastings ... did, in September 1773, enter into a private engagement with the said Nabob of Oudh ... to furnish him for a stipulated sum of money, to be paid to the East India Company, with a body of troops, *for the declared purpose of thoroughly extirpating the nation of the Rohillas.*"... Mill, in his *History*, confirms Burke in the following words:— "Not only was the ferocity of Indian depredation let loose upon the wretched inhabitants, but as the intention of the Vizier, according to what he had previously and repeatedly declared to the British government, was to *exterminate the Rohillas*, every one who bore the name of Rohilla was either butchered, or found his safety in flight and exile." Mill in a note quotes in confirmation of his assertion two passages from letters which passed between Hastings and the Wazír in 1773. The former letter, from Hastings to the Wazír, says, "I have received your Excellency's letter, mentioning ... that, should the Rohillas be guilty of a breach of their agreement [viz.: about the forty lakhs], we will *thoroughly exterminate* them, and settle your Excellency in the country";...The Wazír's letter says, "During an interview at Benares, it was agreed that I should pay, etc., ... and that I should, with the assistance of the

N

English forces, endeavour to punish and *exterminate the Rohillas out of their country.*" The correspondence between Hastings and the Wazír was carried on in Persian. The original letters cannot now be discovered, but the words "exterminate" and "extirpate" are those of the official Interpreter who translated the Persian letters into English. In regard to the former term we have that officer's assertion that the Persian word employed was *istisál,* and that in rendering it by "extermination" he had no idea of conveying the meaning affixed to it in the Charge, that of massacring the whole body of the Rohillas, but merely that of destroying their power and expelling them as a body from the country—a sense justified, as he points out, by the authority of Dr. Johnson, who explains it in one sense "to remove," and also by its literal use. For "extirpate," occurring in the translation of a letter from Hastings to the Wazír in November, 1774, it appears that the Persian term was *ikhráj;* for in a letter from Hastings to the Court of Directors, in which he says that the real sense of the term rendered "extirpate" was "expel or remove," that Persian word is written in the margin, with the obvious intention of showing that it was the expression used by the Wazír. Challenged on the subject, Hastings declared that not only was this the meaning in which he used the word, but that the "extirpation" which actually took place "consisted in nothing more than in removing from their offices the Rohillas who had the official management of the country, and from the country the soldiers who had opposed us in the conquest." That the two Persian or, more strictly speaking, Arabic, words may well bear the meaning which Hastings gives them, is the decision of scholars whose authority is beyond all question : that the "extermination" or "extirpation" was such as Hastings asserts it to have been, is shown by the testimony before the House of Commons of Colonel Champion, by no means a friendly witness. His evidence is explicit on the following points and is corroborated by that of Major Balfour, who served under him, and of Mr. Middleton, the Resident at the Court of Lucknow : that "the military portion of the nation" were only required to cross the Ganges, and were not put to death ; that probably some 45,000 men, including camp followers, remained in the country under Faizullah Khán : that perhaps 20,000 men in arms were required to pass the Ganges : that, excepting those who fell in battle, he knew nothing of any being put to death ; that many and many thousands of the inhabitants of the country remained in it ; that none but those in arms, with the camp followers and their families, were driven across the Ganges. As to the expulsion of those in arms,—which is what the "extermination" or "extirpation" amounts to,—Sir J. Strachey remarks, "The stipulation of the treaty, that men actually under arms should leave Rohilkhand, was perfectly reasonable.

It was necessary for the peace of the country, and it involved little hardship, for all that happened to the Rohilla soldiers whom it affected was that after a march of a few miles they crossed the Ganges into the territory of Zabita Khan, their own countryman. The facts cannot be summed up more accurately than in the words of Hastings, ... ' We conquered the country from the conquerors of it, and substituted another rule in the place of theirs, upon the same principle of right and usage (the right of the war being pre-supposed), as a British commander in Europe would expel the soldiers of a conquered town, and garrison it with his own, which by the same figure of speech, and with equal propriety, might be called an "extirpation." ' "

We may now return to the "atrocities." Such as they were, they are to be imputed solely to the Wazír and his agents; the only charge against Hastings being that he, in part at least, admitted and defended them. The evidence on the subject is to be found (1) in the letters of Champion during the occupation of Rohilkhand, (2) in the evidence given by Champion and others before the Council and before the House of Commons, (3) in the records of contemporaneous histories. "The first reference," says Sir J. Strachey,* "to any excesses of the troops of the Vizier is contained in a private letter from Hastings, sent in reply to one written by Colonel Champion when the army entered Rohilkhand, and before the defeat of the Rohillas. Colonel Champion's letter is not forthcoming, but it is clear from the reply of Hastings, from the instructions of the Government, and from other papers, that the Vizier had given orders for the devastation of the country, but that the English Commander protested against them and succeeded, after a short time, in stopping their execution." In his answer, Hastings emphatically supports Champion's protest. On the news being received of the defeat of the Rohillas, Hastings, writing in the name of the Government, repeats the commendation given to Champion, although nothing further has been reported of any atrocities. When, a little later, Champion refers to the maltreatment of Háfiz Rahmat's family and of the inhabitants of the country, but gives no specific instance, Hastings, as the mouthpiece of the Council, writes, "We desire, therefore, to be immediately advised of the particulars of the treatment which you allude to, that we may judge of the measures proper to be adopted. In the interim, we recommend you to urge, in your own behalf, and in the name of the Board, such remonstrances to the Vizier, against any rigorous treatment of the Rohilla chiefs and their families, as you may think the occasion to require. From the readiness which the Vizier testified in a former instance to

* *Hastings and the Rohilla War*, pp. 188, 9.

be influenced by your advice and persuasion, we flatter ourselves we may expect the same good fruits from your interposition now." A few days later came a private letter from
Champion, enclosing an official request that he might be allowed
to return to Calcutta. "Not only do I wish," he wrote, "to
get down as soon as possible to put my little affairs in the best
order for my return to Europe, but I must be candid enough to
unbosom myself to you freely, and confess that the nature of the
service, and the terms on which I have been employed, [? in]
this campaign have been inexpressibly disagreeable. The
authority given to the Vizier over your army has totally absorbed that degree of consequence due to my station. My hands
have been tied up from giving protection or asylum to the
miserable. I have been obliged to give a deaf ear to the
lamentable cries of the widow and fatherless, and to shut my
eyes against a wanton display of violence and oppression, of
inhumanity and cruelty."... He then goes on to recommend that
the family of Háfiz Rahmat should be taken under the Company's
protection, and to instance some of the hardships to which they
had been subjected. Hastings's reply is too long to be quoted in
full. He points out that "it never could have been suspected
by the Board that their orders to you should have tied up your
hands from protecting the miserable, stopped your ears to the
cries of the widows and fatherless, or shut your eyes against the
wanton display of oppression and cruelty" : that his advice and
remonstrance ought, if used, to have had the same effect that
they had when the ravages of the country were stopped at his
intercession on the occupation of the country : that if any other
more effectual remedy, or any addition which could be given to
his authority, not liable to the objection of establishing a divided
power or an unjust usurpation of the Wazír's authority, would
be gladly agreed to by the Board ; that he had instructed the
Resident at the Wazír's Court to make the strongest representations on the subject : but that in the relations the Board stood
to the Wazír it was impossible to take the family of Háfiz
Rahmat immediately under its protection. The instructions to
the Resident were most stringent. "Tell him," [the Wazír] says
Hastings among other things, "that the English manners are
abhorrent of every species of inhumanity and oppression, and
enjoin the gentlest treatment of a vanquished enemy. Require
and entreat his observance of this principle towards the family
of Háfiz. Tell him my instructions to you ; generally, but
urgently, enforce the same maxims ; and that no part of his
conduct will operate so powerfully in winning the affections of
the English as instances of benevolence and feeling for others.
If these arguments do not prevail, you may inform him directly
that you have my orders to insist upon a proper treatment of
the family of Háfiz Rahmat, since in our alliance with him

our national character is involved in every act which subjects
his own to reproach ; that I shall publicly exculpate this
Government from the imputation of assenting to such a procedure, and shall reserve it as an objection to any future engagements with him when the present service shall have been
accomplished." How Hastings's instructions to the resident were
carried out will be seen further on.   Omitting two letters of
Champion's which have no great bearing on the controversy,
we come to his reply to the letter of the 23rd May, in which he
had been ordered by Hastings to furnish full particulars of the
maltreatment to which Háfiz Rahmat's family had been subjected.
This reply, while complaining of the Wazir's disregard of his
remonstrances and repeating the charge of cruelty to the family
of Háfiz, contains no specific instances of which Champion had
proof, and says nothing of cruelty to the Rohillas generally.   It,
however, again urged that he should "be invested with full
authority to effectually prevent the Vizier from perpetrating any
enormity, under the shield of our force, that could in any degree
redound to the discredit of our reputation."   Such extended
powers the Board in their answer decline to give, and, after re-
capitulating their relations to the Wazir, they thus continue,
" The intemperate and tyrannical conduct of the Vizier after his
conquest, as you have represented, cannot fail to prove highly
dissatisfactory to us, and although we do not regard ourselves
either as answerable for his actions, or obliged absolutely to
interfere for restraining them, yet we should have been glad to
have been furnished with such materials as would enable us,
upon good grounds, to expostulate with him on the injustice and
impropriety of such a conduct.   It was in this view that we
requested you to acquaint us with instances of his cruelties, but we
confess ourselves exceedingly disappointed in receiving, instead of
a precise account of facts, only three letters of loose declamation,
which however pathetically written, contain not one single
instance of the Vizier's particular cruelty towards the family
of Hafiz, and indeed express only such sentiments as we can
easily conceive to exist in the breasts of that unfortunate family,
... For this reason we repeat our desire to be furnished with a
particular account of the treatment which the family of Hafiz
has received, and we shall then take such steps for their relief
as the circumstances shall require.   In the meantime, we hope
that the remonstrances which the President informs us he has
directed the Resident to make to the Vizier on this subject, will
be sufficient to render any more direct interposition needless."...
The "particular account" thus demanded was never furnished,
though Colonel Champion remained in Rohilkhand several months
after he received these orders.   When questioned on the point
before the House of Commons, he replied, "In answer to that question, I must observe that repeatedly, before the date of that letter

and afterwards, I thought the remonstrances I made were sufficient, and therefore did not comply with the orders I received."
The Board's letter was sent on July 1st, and the only notice
it received was a reply dated September 3rd, in which Colonel
Champion speaks of having already "attested the truth of the
complaints, which I will venture to say bear more than one or
two instances of cruelty; I might add others, such as these unhappy captives being driven to the necessity of supplicating and
receiving alms from myself and gentlemen of my family to purchase
sustenance; their even begging for water to drink, their struggling
who should first be served with it, etc. In short, the gross
maltreatment of these families amounts to an axiom in the minds
of the English army, and even in the Vizier's own troops."
Hopeless, apparently, of getting any more distinct statement
from Colonel Champion, Hastings wrote to the Resident on the
subject. "The enormities he [Colonel Champion] insists upon
are of a nature that I think could not have escaped your observation ... I wish the truth to appear, neither glossed by favour
nor blackened by prejudice; let me therefore beg of you to
furnish me with the fullest information you can obtain of the
Vizier's treatment of the family of Hafiz, etc., and to support
your accounts with the strongest proofs that can be produced."...
Middleton's reply will be noticed later on. But in the meanwhile it will be as well to make an end of Champion's statements
subsequent to his leaving Rohilkhand. That, so far, Hastings
had in no wise defended the atrocities attributed to Wazir is
plain enough; nor can any such defence be alleged against him
in the future. Champion's accusations, however, against the
Wazir now become definite enough. For in November, 1774,
Shuja-ud-daula sent to Hastings a letter filled with complaints
against the Commander-in-Chief and his troops. To this Champion found it necessary to reply, and he was able to do this at a
favourable moment, the new Government having come into
power, and Hastings being in a minority at the Board. Among
the charges now made we are told that, on the march from
Pilibhit to Bisauli, the wife and children of Háfiz, the widow
of his eldest son, the wife of his eldest surviving son, and some
hundreds of miserable captive women were dragged in triumph
on carts; that at Bareli and Aonla the inhabitants were indis-
criminately plundered; that at Bisauli the whole army were
witnesses of scenes that cannot be described; that when on the
march the sepoys were withdrawn from the villages they were
sent to protect, those villages were set in flames by way of
bonfire for his Excellency; that the Wazir's conduct to the
families of Mohibullah Khán and Fattehullah Khán were both
treacherous and dastardly, they being robbed of their property
and dishonoured in the persons of their women; that the family
of Dundi Khán was robbed of their throne, despoiled of their

honour, and subjected to bondage of the greatest severity. Such are the chief statements in his long and rambling letter. When examined a month later before the Council—a Council known to be hostile to Hastings—these statements shrank in a most wonderful manner. As to the worst charges, his answers generally were prefixed by such words as "It appeared so to me"; "I did hear such report, but as to the grounds I have none sufficient to prove the accusation"; "It was reported to me that they [the families of the chiefs] were in want of everything that could make their situation tolerably comfortable"; "It was reported to me that they were in want"; "I cannot charge my memory, but beg leave to refer to the correspondence." They were, in fact, as Sir J. Strachey remarks, "meagre and evasive, couched in such general terms, and so extremely short, that they add little to our knowledge." Those given on the same subject before the House of Commons in 1786 failed to elicit anything of value as to the authority on which his statements had been made, except that his information was obtained through spies set to furnish it. On the same points the evidence of Colonel Leslie and Major Hannay, both in Rohilkhand during its conquest and occupation, were taken before the Council, and by neither was any atrocity, except that of burning villages, deposed to on their own knowledge, though vague reports had reached their ears. A third officer, Major Balfour, who likewise had been through the campaign, was examined before the House of Commons. His evidence, both as to the facts and the consequences of the war, were still less to the discredit of the Wazír. The whole of the recorded evidence of the English military officers who took part in the war, in regard to the cruelties said to have been committed by the Wazír, has now been examined, and we may go back to the correspondence between Hastings and Middleton. In the latter's first letter, written on the 17th June, 1774, he says that though he cannot by any means acquit the Wazír of the charge made against him on the score of his treatment of Háfiz Rahmat's family, and his wanton ravages of the country, he believes that those charges had been exaggerated. The story of his having dishonoured Mohibullah Khán's daughter he shows to be unfounded; the severity with which Dundi Khán's family had been treated was, in his opinion, in some measure justified by their treachery; Háfiz Rahmat's family, he admits, had "suffered much distress and inconvenience for want of proper accommodation in camp, but my own knowledge does not furnish me with any instances of cruelty or violence wantonly exercised upon them." The Wazír had promised to allot a handsome provision for the maintenance of that family, while their removal, and that of Dundi Khán's family, to Faizábád had been carried out under due precautions for their proper treatment. On the 5th July, Middleton again wrote to Hastings. Reports as to the Wazír's behaviour towards his prisoners were constantly reaching his ears, and their persistence made him lend some credit to them. He therefore earnestly remonstrated with the Wazír, threatening him with the displeasure of Hastings, in case the rumours should be true, and the forfeiture of "every claim to that support and protection which the English have on all occasions manifested such readiness to yield him." All the charges urged were positively denied by the Wazír, and Middleton, when examined before the House of Commons, admitted that after sending his letter to Hastings "he had reason to think more favourably of the character of the Vizier," and that he "found that many of the reports that had been propagated to his prejudice, from the best information he could obtain, were without foundation." In the same evidence he said that "he knew of no instance of cruelty, in the course of the war upon the Rohillas, either by Shuja-ud-daula or by his orders"; that he understood the article in the treaty with Faizullah Khán, requiring the Rohillas to leave the country, to apply only to the troops under arms and their chiefs; that they crossed the Ganges into the territory of their countrymen, Zábita Khán; that many of them, although not publicly permitted, returned to Rohilkhand, and either went to Faizullah Khán or enlisted in the Wazír's army; and that for the peace of the country he could suggest no better plan than that of compelling the Rohillas to cross the Ganges. Of contemporaneous histories, Sir J. Strachey quotes from the Gulistán-i-Rahmat, by the son of Háfiz Rahmat, from Hamilton's History, and from the Siyár-ul-Mutákhárín, by Syad Ghulám Husen Khán, in none of which is there any mention of excesses or atrocities. He then goes on to prove beyond all possible doubt that Mill in his account of the Rohilla War deliberately falsified history. With the greater part of the correspondence between Hastings, Champion, and Middleton, and the evidence taken before the House of Commons, that historian "deliberately omitted all mention of the fact that Hastings, in language as strong as it was possible to find, had repeatedly expressed his detestation of the cruelties attributed to the Vizier, and had issued the instructions which seemed to him most likely to stop them. Not content with this suppression of the truth, Mill, ... has stated that Hastings defended the atrocities of the Vizier, and in proof of his assertion he has professed to quote the very words of Hastings himself. I do not use language too strong for the occasion when I say that a more baseless calumny was never recorded by one calling himself an historian. The words which Mill has cited are to be found, not in any reply to the representations of Colonel Champion while the war was in progress, but in a Minute written by Hastings on the 10th January, 1775, in answer to a letter, attacking him in unmeasured terms, which had been sent to the

Court of Directors by Clavering, Monson, and Francis, who then
formed the Majority in Council. According to a custom very
usual with him, Mill has separated from the context the particular words that suited his purpose, and suppressing the rest,
he gives his garbled extract as the proof of a false and atrocious
charge." Summing up the whole question of the atrocities, Sir
J. Strachey continues,*

"The statement that atrocities were defended or excused by
Hastings had its origin in a baseless falsehood. He did all in his
power to cause the war to be conducted with humanity, and, considering all the circumstances of the case, his efforts were successful.
From the time when the army of the Vizier entered Rohilkhand to
the conclusion of the treaty of peace with Faizullah Khan, nearly six
months elapsed. In the first week of this period, while hostilities
were in progress, and in the three or four days which followed the
defeat of the Rohillas, many villages were burned, and whatever
property could be carried off was plundered. This occurred in a small
tract of country between the Oudh frontier and Pilibhit. There was
no serious loss of life or personal suffering, because the villages had
been, for the most part, entirely deserted by their inhabitants, who,
according to their established custom on the approach of danger, had
fled to the Tarái and forest, taking with them their cattle and such
valuables as they could easily remove. The rest of Rohilkhand, a
country nearly as large as Belgium, was rapidly occupied without
opposition, after the defeat of the Rohillas, and there is no reason to
suppose that in any part of it, or at any time, any serious excesses
were committed by the troops of the Vizier. Long before the submission of Faizullah Khan, the Hindu inhabitants, who constituted nearly
the whole population, were, for the most part, following their usual
occupations. There is nothing to show that they were anywhere
exposed to any extraordinary hardship or ill-treatment beyond that
inevitable in a time of war. In regard to the Rohillas, whose numbers
were comparatively small, the story of their cruel extermination is
absolutely false, nor is there a particle of evidence that any atrocities
were committed upon them at any time during the war. Excepting
the men who fell in battle, there is no evidence that any Rohilla was
put to death, or was treated with any inhumanity. The only Rohillas
who were compelled to leave Rohilkhand, other than the principal
chiefs, were the soldiers actually under arms with Faizullah Khan.
Under one of the conditions of the final treaty of peace, they crossed
the Ganges into the friendly territory of Zabita Khan, their countryman. The rest of the Rohillas were unmolested, or went into Rampur,
the Rohilla State assigned by treaty to Faizullah Khan, their recognised chief. The Rohilla chiefs were generally treated with consideration and lenity. Two of them only, the sons of Dundi Khan,
who had broken engagements which they had entered into with the
Vizier, were, not unjustly, punished with temporary confinement and
confiscation of their property ; but they suffered no serious ill-treatment and they were soon released. The ladies of the families of
Hafiz Rahmat and Dundi Khan, with their dependents, suffered much

* Pp. 231-3.

distress and inconvenience from their removal into camp, and from
the absence of proper arrangements for their comfort and for their
maintenance, and their jewels and personal ornaments were taken
from them. The stories that they were, in any case, subjected to
personal outrage or gross insult are absolutely false, without any
vestige of foundation. ... I do not doubt that this, like every other
war, brought with it an amount of misery far worse than that of
which any direct evidence is now before us, but at the same time it
seems to me clear that Shuja-ud-daula would have been justified in
saying that the campaign in Rohilkhand had been carried on with an
absence of violence and bloodshed and generally with a degree of
humanity altogether unusual in Indian warfare. Nor can I doubt
that this result was mainly due to the remonstrances of Hastings.
'History,' writes Mr. Forrest, 'furnishes no more striking example of
the growth and vitality of a slander. The Rohilla atrocities owe their
birth to the malignity of Champion and Francis; their growth to the
rhetoric of Burke; and their wide diffusion to the brilliancy and
pellucid clearness of Macaulay's style.' The only defect I can find in
this perfectly just judgment is that in pronouncing it Mr. Forrest has
forgotten the History of James Mill."

One point remains for consideration, viz., the objects with
which the Rohilla war was undertaken. Macaulay, as will be
seen in his Essay, held that the acquisition of money was the
sole object that Hastings had in view. "That he, [Macaulay],"
says Sir J. Strachey, "never investigated the facts for himself
is clear. With the exception of a few erroneous statements taken
from the speeches or charges of Burke, everything that he has
written on the subject is traceable to Mill, nor can I blame him
for believing that Mill's authority might be accepted as con-
clusive. His version of the story of the Rohilla war is not history
but rhetoric, and I do not propose to criticize it. The grave and
deliberate allegations of Mill stand on a different footing from the
rhetoric of Macaulay and the passionate invective of Burke ... The
sole authority quoted is that of Hastings himself; he is judged
and condemned by his own words; there is nothing to lead the
reader to suppose that Hastings ever gave any other explanation
of his motives."* Now, at no time did Hastings conceal that an
improvement of the Company's finances was *one* of the objects he
had in view. He stated it in various of his official Minutes, he
openly avowed it in his answer to Burke's charges before the
House of Commons. But this improvement was "an accessory
argument" in favour of the war, not a principal argument. And
as his avowals were so pertinaciously urged against him, it might
be supposed that in common justice the principal arguments so
repeatedly set forth by him would receive some credit. These
arguments were, (1) "Justice to the Vizier, for the aggravated
breach of treaty by the Rohilla chiefs: (2) The honour of the
Company, pledged implicitly by General Barker's attestation for

* P. 236.

the accomplishment of this treaty, and which, added to their alliance with the Vizier, engaged us to see redress obtained for the perfidy of the Rohillas : (3) The completion of the line of defence of the Vizier's dominions by extending his boundary to the natural barrier formed by the northern chain of hills and the Ganges, and their junction." Over and over again in his Minutes and Despatches does Hastings asseverate such to have been his principal reasons for engaging in the war. Over and over again does he justify those reasons and set forward the arguments by which they were supported in his understanding. Yet his traducers have combined either to ignore them altogether or to treat them as mere flimsy pretexts. Space does not allow of my making extracts of sufficient length to show the importance which Hastings attached to the principles on which he acted or the weight which his defence might be supposed to have with candid judges. I must content myself with one more quotation from Sir J. Strachey and one from Sir A. Lyall's *Warren Hastings*.

"Whatever view," says Sir J. Strachey,[*] "be taken of the propriety of engaging in the Rohilla war, enough has, I think, been said to show that the story of Hastings letting out the English troops for hire to slaughter an unoffending people, without cause or provocation, for the sole and infamous purpose of putting money into the pockets of his masters, is not true. It was invented by the malignity of Francis, it was adopted by Burke with an indignation of which the motives were honourable but which were blind and unreasoning, it was written down as history by Mill when the evidence of its falsehood was in his hands, and it was then thrown by Macaulay into the rhetorical shape in which it has ever since compelled acceptance from the majority of Englishmen. Before the war was undertaken, while it was in progress, after it had been successfully completed, but when no hostile imputations connected with it had been made, and afterwards when Hastings had to defend himself against the attacks of his enemies, he never varied in the explanation of his policy. That policy was based on the necessity of guarding against the risk of ruin to ourselves and to our ally. The primary object of the war was to obtain security against the danger which at that time overshadowed all other considerations, that of invasion by the Marathas, who were not far from achieving that universal dominion over India which they openly declared to be their aim. To guard against this danger, Hastings, like Clive, his great predecessor, believed that no measure of precaution could be so efficacious as the maintenance of the territories of the Nawab Vizier of Oudh as a barrier between Bengal and the constantly troubled countries of Northern India. He believed that to secure this object it was necessary that the only road by which Oudh was easily accessible to the inroads of the Maratha armies should be closed. The only means by which this could be done was by the union of Rohilkhand with Oudh, and by the expulsion of the band of turbulent and faithless Afghans who, not many years before, had established themselves in the very quarter from which danger

* Pp. 257-264.

threatened. It had been proved by experience that to obtain the
desired security by an alliance with the Rohillas was impossible. A
treaty had been entered into between the Rohilla chiefs and the
Vizier, by which the Vizier bound himself to protect Rohilkhand
against the Marathas, and the Rohillas, on their part, engaged to pay
to him, in consideration of that protection, the sum of £500,000.
Although the treaty was one to which we were not avowedly a party,
it had been concluded with the strenuous co-operation and advice of
our Commander-in-Chief, it had been attested by his signature, and it
had been approved by our Government. We had given to the Vizier the
active and effectual assistance of our army in enabling him to carry out
his obligations, and had expelled the Marathas from Rohilkhand. The
Rohillas, on their side, refused to fulfil their engagements, and paid
nothing to the Vizier. All this afforded in the belief of Hastings
ample **justification to** the Vizier for undertaking the war, and ample
justification to us for giving him the help without which he might
probably have been unsuccessful. ... The question of morality, if it is to
be argued, can only be stated thus :—Is a British governor justified in
making war upon a confederacy of barbarous chiefs, who, not long
before, had imposed their rule on a population foreign to themselves
in race and religion ; through whose country the only road lies open
for attacks by savage invaders upon a British ally, whose security is
essential to the security of British possessions ; who are too weak and
too treacherous to be relied on to close this road ; and who have
injured that ally by breaking a treaty with him negotiated and
attested by a British General, and approved by the British Government ? Upon such a question there can hardly be much difference of
opinion. The only reasonable answer is that, in such a case, the
supreme duty of a governor is to make the dominions under his care
secure from foreign attack ; that if Hastings believed **that the**
security of the British provinces depended on that of Oudh, he was
bound to take measures of precaution against a common danger ;
and that if he found it impossible to reconcile the protection of
Oudh and of British territory with the maintenance of the dominion
of the Rohilla chiefs, he was right in the conclusion that their do-
minion must cease. It may doubtless be contended that Hastings
overrated some of the elements of danger, or committed other errors
of judgment, but at all events there is no room for moral reprobation.
By ignoring the difficulties and complexities of the situation, it is
easy to argue broadly that it is wrong to engage in war without provocation, that the Rohillas had not provoked us, and that the attack
upon them was therefore unjustifiable. In the opinion of Hastings
the conduct of the Rohillas in breaking their treaty with our ally,
and in carrying on negotiations with the common enemy, constituted
provocation, and that term can hardly be limited to the case of actual
aggression. However this may be, maxims of this sort could afford
no assistance to a governor dealing with the question whether Oudh
and the British provinces should be allowed to remain exposed to
invasion, or how invasion might best be averted. Financial advantage
was, as Hastings wrote to Colonel Champion, ... 'an accessory argument.' Having satisfied himself that the establishment of the Vizier's
government in Rohilkhand was necessary, he had to settle the terms
on which **our** co-operation should be afforded. Without that co-

operation there was obviously no certainty of success. .... Assuming
with Hastings that the resolution to establish the Vizier's government
in Rohilkhand was politically wise, there was nothing unreasonable
in the stipulation that in addition to the actual charges of the English
brigade, the Vizier, 'in consideration of the Company relinquishing
all claim to share in the Rohilla country, although it is to be conquered
by their joint forces,' should pay forty lakhs of rupees on the successful completion of the war ... If the English Government had itself
borne the whole expense of its operations, and had received nothing
from the Vizier, the motives with which the war was undertaken
would have been less open to misrepresentation, but they would not,
as Hastings himself said, have thereby become more or less just or
honourable. If the war was made the opportunity of bringing profit
to the stronger power, it did not differ in this respect from many more
serious contests. It is true that we might sometimes have been better
pleased if Hastings in his despatches and minutes had said less regarding the financial advantages of his agreement with the Vizier, ... But
the circumstances under which he was placed ought not to be forgotten.
He had frequently to justify to the Directors at home measures of
policy opposed to their orders, or of which their approval was doubtful, and it was natural that he should, when it was possible to do so,
lay stress on those conditions which would be most likely to reconcile
them to his proceedings. The East India Company of those days was
essentially mercantile, and the Directors were ready to pardon much
that they thought politically inexpedient if it could be shown to be
pecuniarily profitable. ... Judged by its results, the policy of Hastings
was eminently successful. Many a 'wild Mahratta battle' had still
to be fought. Nearly thirty years after the Rohilla war, Maratha
armies were still contending with the English for empire in India, and
Wellesley and Lake were winning their victories of Assaye and Argaum
and Laswari. More than forty years elapsed before the power of the
Marathas was finally swept away, but during the whole of this time
they never attacked or seriously threatened Rohilkhand. The occupation of that province gave to Oudh and to Bengal that permanent protection against the most dangerous of our Indian enemies which it had
been the aim of Hastings to secure."

Sir Alfred Lyall's view of the case is far less favourable to
Hastings.

"It is true," * he says, "that his barrier-policy may be said to have
been so far successful that the Vizier retained undisturbed possession
of his acquisitions until the end of the century, when Rohilcund was
ceded to the English. Nevertheless nothing but the urgent necessity
of self-preservation can warrant an unprovoked invasion of a neighbour's country ; and it must be confessed that the war has left a stain
upon the reputation of the Company in India, where a shifty line of
policy is far more unsafe than a weak frontier ; while it has been the
last occasion upon which English troops have joined in a campaign
with Indian allies, without retaining control of the operations. ... Mr.
Gleig dilates upon the absurdity of holding Hastings responsible for

* *Warren Hastings*, pp. 48-50.

'details of military operations' which he never sanctioned or approved; and totally fails to perceive that all men, especially men in command, are directly answerable for the indirect but probable consequences of their acts and orders. The expedition against the Rohillas was wrong in principle, for they had not provoked us, and the Vizier could only be relied upon to abuse his advantages. ... On the other hand, Macaulay's splendid and glittering phrases have thrown a false air of romance over the real origin and character of the Rohilla chiefships, which merely represented the fortuitous partition of an imperial province among military adventurers. In their origin, political constitution, and their relation to the bulk of people, they might be likened to the Mamelukes of Egypt, who also were a military confederacy under a chief of their own, paying a nominal allegiance to the Sultan for a province which they had seized. And they were in reality suppressed for reasons not unlike those which led to the political destruction of Poland, because their constitution was weak and turbulent, and because, therefore, they could not be trusted to hold an important position on the frontiers of more powerful states."...

If, after citing such high authorities, it is at all worth while to give my own opinion on the subject, I should say that while it seems to me that the position in which Hastings found himself justified his helping the Wazir to expel the Rohillas from Rohil-khand, it did not justify him in leaving that prince so far un-fettered as regards the manner in which the country was to be occupied and its inhabitants to be treated. Experience must have taught Hastings that the Wazir was not likely to be too scrupulous, and it was incumbent upon him to take precautions which would make impossible any abuse of conquest. Exagger-ated as are the accounts of the "atrocities," there can, I think, be no doubt that there was an amount of licence which would have been avoided had more exact conditions of the alliance been made beforehand. Further, it seems to me that Hastings himself soon became conscious of having given the Wazir too free a hand. That the remonstrances conveyed through Champion and Middle-ton were genuine enough, may be readily admitted. That they were effectual in preventing, or at all events in arresting, any grave excesses, has, I think, been shown. But all through the correspondence there seems to run an uneasy feeling that the opportunity had been let slip for placing a sufficient curb upon the Wazir's actions while yet it was in the power of Hastings to dictate.

APPENDIX II.

HASTINGS, IMPEY, AND NAND KUMAR.

IF, in trusting to Mill for his account of the Rohilla War, Macaulay has been singularly unfortunate, he has fared even worse as regards the evidence upon which he built up his declamatory periods against Hastings and Impey in the story of Nand Kumár. For it may be said at the outset that absolutely no stain now rests upon the fame of either in the matter of Macaulay's "judicial murder." That this is so is due almost entirely to Sir James Stephen. His unwearied patience has gone minutely into every document that bears upon the subject, his skill and legal learning have disentangled every knot and sifted from the vast mass of fabrication and prejudice the residue of wholesome truth. It will be necessary to follow the great jurist at considerable length, though I trust that to dispassionate minds whatever may seem tedious will be forgiven for the interest of the result. Of the position in which Hastings stood to the rest of his Council nothing need be added to Macaulay's vivid account. Nor will it be worth while to say anything as to the feelings with which Hastings and Nand Kumár entered upon their memorable duel, except that their mutual animosity was of long standing and that Nand Kumár skilfully chose the moment when he might hope to have Hastings at a disadvantage. My narrative, following Sir J. Stephen's scheme, will deal with (1) the accusation of corruption brought by Nand Kumár against Hastings, (2) the accusation of conspiracy brought by Hastings, and the accusation of forgery brought by Mohan Parshád against Nand Kumár, (3) the trial of Nand Kumár and the subsequent events down to the time of his execution.

Macaulay's summary of Nand Kumár's accusation, and of the Council's proceedings on receiving it, is short, but accurate as far as it goes. The matter, however, is important only as regards the suspicion that Hastings in order to escape conviction determined upon destroying his accuser. Briefly stated, the accusation was that Hastings had accepted in bribes and gifts something between three and four hundred thousand rupees. Of this sum Nand Kumár alleged that he himself had sent Hastings eight bags of gold *mohrs* of the value of about a hundred thousand rupees as a thank-offering for the appointment of his son to the treasurership of the titular subahdár's household, the remainder being a present from the Manni

Begam, widow of Mir Jáfir, who had been made guardian of
the Subahdár in the place of Muhammad Raza Khán. As to
his own present, Nand Kumár produced no corroborative
evidence, while his account was discredited by his vin-
dictiveness, his inconsistency of statement, his avowed com-
plicity in the alleged corrupt acts, as agent for the Begam,
and his often-proved rascality. In support of his story regarding the Begam, Nand Kumár delivered a translation, and
showed what he declared to be the original, of a letter from
the Begam. Of the genuineness of the letter no proof was
adduced except that it bore upon it a stamp with the Begam's
name. This, however, was no proof, for Nand Kumár was
shown in the case of other persons to have in his possession
seals belonging to them, or counterfeiting the origins. The
story told in the letter does not on its face agree with the
charge made by Nand Kumár. His story was that the Begam
had given Hastings at Murshidábád a lakh of rupees, and had
caused one Nur Sing to pay him at Kásimbázár a further lakh
and a half. The letter stated that she was to pay Hastings
two lakhs, and that she was raising one lakh to be paid at
Murshidábád, and it begs Nand Kumár to pay the other lakh
to Hastings at Calcutta, and promises to repay him. Had the
Board compared Nand Kumár's statement with the Begam's
letter they would have seen that there was urgent need of
inquiry. The only questions they asked of Nand Kumár were
such as would serve to strengthen his case. "They took no
steps," says Sir James Stephen,* " to ascertain the authenticity
of the letter attributed to the Munny Begum, beyond comparing
the inscriptions on two seals. They did not even impound the
alleged original, but returned it to Nuncomar. They did not
even send for the persons alleged by Nuncomar to have delivered
and received the bags of gold, nor did they ask a single question
as to the time when, and the place where the gold was delivered,
the person from whom he got so large a sum, the books in which
he had made entries about it, the place and time of his alleged conversation with Hastings on the subject, or any of the other obvious
matters by which his truthfulness might be tested." The only
point in which Nand Kumár's story received any corroboration
was as to a lakh and a half of rupees said to have been presented
to Hastings by the Begam. From an inquiry into her books
it appeared that this sum was paid to Hastings at Murshidábád in 1772, as a customary allowance on the visit of the
Governor to the Nawáb and made at the same rate and for the
same purpose with which it had been made to Clive and Verelst,
former governors. To none of the charges would Hastings give a
denial at the time. This may have been unwise, but it is easily

* *The Story of Nuncomar*, etc., i. 60-2.

intelligible. Francis, Clavering, and Monson, were his bitter
enemies, and by them a denial would have been received with
scorn. A denial would, moreover, have looked like an admission
that he was bound to answer before his enemies. They from the
first had by their acts adjudged him guilty, and a man of so
haughty a spirit and a nature so cautious would not unnaturally
say, 'Except before a Committee to whose impartiality I can
trust, I will give no answer of any kind to such a charge.' It
may also be, as Sir J. Stephen supposes, that his silence
"arose from the fact that he had received from the Begam the
lakh and a half for entertainment, ... and that as he could not
absolutely deny every part of Nand Kumár's story he thought it
better not to make a qualified partial denial of it, and to leave
his enemies to prove what they could." At his impeachment he
denied to his counsel that he had received any money whatever
from Nand Kumár, or from the Begam, except the lakh and a
half already mentioned. "That a consciousness of guilt should
have prevented Hastings," says Sir J. Stephen, "from making
these statements in 1775, when he was in great danger of losing
his office, and that it should not have prevented him from making
them to his own counsel when nothing was to be gained by falsehood and nothing to be feared from sincerity, appears to me incredible." The next point for consideration in Nand Kumár's
accusation is this. Had that accusation, as was suggested,
brought Hastings into such straits that no escape was left him
but by murdering Nand Kumár by the help of Impey? "Upon
this question," says Sir J. Stephen,* "the following matters are
to be considered. First, Hastings, upon the supposition of his
guilt, would not be saved by Nuncomar's death from the only
danger to which Nuncomar's charges exposed him, the danger,
namely, of being recalled in disgrace by the Directors, and being
saddled with a chancery suit for the payment of about £40,000
on his return home. ... The evidence of Nuncomar was already
given. The persons he had named might be interrogated. If
the Court of Directors attached weight to Nuncomar's evidence
it was not likely that his judicial murder, supposing it to be
successfully carried out, would lessen its weight. If they did not
attach weight to it there was no occasion to perform, or try to
perform, that most critical and difficult operation. Some confirmation is given to this by the circumstance that on the 27th
March, a fortnight after Nuncomar's accusation, Hastings wrote
to his agents in England, giving them (in a most irregular,
unbusiness-like form) authority to resign his office 'if the first
advices from England contain a disapprobation of the treaty of
Benares or of the Rohilla war, and mark an evident disinclination
towards me.' A man was hardly likely to plan a judicial murder

* Pp. 74, 5.

O

in order to avoid the possible loss of an office which he had
authorised his agent to resign upon a contingency unconnected
with the person to be murdered.   On the other hand, it is to be
noticed that his authority was withdrawn, and that Hastings
announced his intention of staying where he was, on the 18th
May, Nuncomar having been committed for trial in the interval,
and being, as Hastings observes in his letter, 'in a fair way to be
hanged.'"   Of this letter Sir J. Stephen adds in a footnote, "It
certainly shows that Hastings was pleased at Nuncomar's being
'in a fair way to be hanged'; but if he had been actually engaged
at the time in a conspiracy to murder him, he would hardly have
chuckled over the matter to his agents.   I should have expected
him to avoid the topic.   The tone of the letter is rather that of
a man who has met with a piece of unexpected good luck than
that of a murderer who has taken the first step towards the
execution of his design and sees its consummation—a doubtful
and dangerous process, drawing unpleasantly near."   Burke and
Mill severely censured Hastings for stifling inquiry into Nand
Kumár's accusation, by refusing to allow his accuser to appear
before himself in Council in support of his charges.   Hastings
naturally resented such an indignity, and to myself there scarcely
seems need for any serious argument.   Sir J. Stephen, however,
and Mr. Forrest have thought it worth while to take up the point,
and I quote from the latter's admirable Introduction to his *Administration of Warren Hastings*, published last year.   "Even if
Nundcoomar had borne an unblemished character, Hastings would
have been justified in refusing to submit to the disgrace and
mortification of the head of a Government being accused in person
during the sitting of the Council over which he presided.   Such
a procedure must have brought his office into contempt and injured
the dignity of station which a man has interest to preserve.   It
moreover was unnecessary for the purpose either of eliciting
truth or of promoting justice.   A Committee of inquiry, consisting
of the Council without Hastings, would have been equally
efficacious for these purposes.   Hastings did not dispute the right
of his colleagues to make an inquiry into the charges of corruption
brought against him, nor did he, as Mill states, 'raise any
pretences for stifling inquiry.'   He only pointed out the mode of
conducting it which would be least injurious to the dignity and
authority of the Government.   As Hastings wrote to the Directors
—'Had the majority been disposed to accept of my proposition
of appointing a Committee for prosecuting their inquiries either
into these or the Ranny's allegations, they might have obtained
the same knowledge and all the satisfaction in this way that they
could have expected from an inquisition taken by the Board at
large, their proceedings would have had the appearance at least
of regularity, and my credit would have been less affected by
them.   The only point which they could possibly gain by per-

sisting in bringing such a subject before the Board was to gain a public triumph over me, and expose my place and person to insult.' "

Of the two accusations brought against Nand Kumár the first was a charge of conspiring with other persons to make false accusations against Hastings and Barwell. It had its origin in certain representations made to Hastings by one Kamál-ud-dín who complained that two Europeans, father and son, named Fowke, Nand Kumár, and Rádha Charan had compelled him by threats to sign a document stating that he had bribed Hastings and Barwell, and also had forced him to testify to the correctness of a certain account. Hastings referred Kamál-ud-dín to the Chief Justice, and he with the other members of the Supreme Court, acting as Justices of the Peace, investigated the complaint, summoning Hastings and Barwell to be present. The younger Fowke was discharged, and Hastings and Barwell were called upon to say whether they would prosecute the others. This they bound themselves over to do, and at the assizes all the defendants were acquitted of the charge of conspiracy against Hastings ; Rádha Charan was acquitted, and Nand Kumár and the elder Fowke were convicted, of conspiracy against Barwell. At this prosecution of their favourite and tool the majority in the Council were fiercely indignant. They regarded it as a counterstroke to Nand Kumár's attack on Hastings, as no doubt it was ; and, it may be said, a perfectly fair counterstroke if Hastings believed Kamál-ud-dín's complaint to be true, as in all appearance it certainly was. But their indignation would have been far less intense if it had not been that a few days later a much more dangerous prosecution followed. This second attack was by them at once put down to the instigation of Hastings, while others were persuaded that the ostensible prosecutor would not have dared to resort to it but for the encouragement afforded by the success which Hastings had scored. The charge now brought forward was one of forgery, the accuser an attorney named Mohan Prasád. For more than two years Mohan Prasád had been trying to get hold of certain documents necessary to his case, which originally was a civil suit against Nand Kumár for upwards of a lakh of rupees said to be due to the estate of Mohan Prasád's principal, a banker named Buláqi Dás. During the litigation, an imputation of forgery had been cast upon Nand Kumár, and Mohan Prasád now determined upon a criminal prosecution. But the long-desired documents were still wanting, and it was not till many months later that, on the establishment of the Supreme Court, they came into his possession. He at once carried out his intention ; Nand Kumár was brought before the magistrates and committed for trial in the ordinary course. The indictment consisted of twenty counts, all of which had reference to the forging of a bond with intent to defraud or to the publishing of a forged bond with the same intent. "The question in the case," says Sir J. Stephen, "was whether the deed was really forged. There could be no question that it was published, or that if it was a forgery Nuncomar knew of it." The trial was held before the full bench of the Supreme Court, consisting of the Chief Justice and three Puisne Judges, not, as Macaulay unfairly states, before "Sir Elijah Impey." It lasted for seven days, and the Judges were unanimous. The prisoner was defended by the best talent then to be had in Calcutta, the examination and cross-examination of witnesses were minute and protracted, the attitude of the Court seems to have inclined to leniency, and the verdict was that of an English jury. Sir J. Stephen gives a full analysis of all the evidence, and Sir E. Impey's summing-up *in extenso*. In regard to any collusion between Hastings and the prosecutor, he points out that the counsel for the defence from first to last "never suggested, either directly or by a single question in cross-examination, that the accusation against Nuncomar was a malicious prosecution got up to silence the accuser of Hastings. Nothing could have been more urgently to the purpose, nothing, if the fact were so, could be more easy to prove. Mohun Persaud was not only the prosecutor, but one of the principal witnesses for the prosecution. He was recalled eight or nine times in the course of the trial. Nuncomar (as I have already said) stated as the principal occasion of his accusation of Hastings, the favour which he had shown to Mohun Persaud. Questions asked with common skill might have brought out Mohun Persaud's intimacy with Hastings, his knowledge of Nuncomar's having accused Hastings of corruption, the fact (if it was a fact), that he had held communication with Hastings on the subject—in a word, anything which was known or suspected as to the origin of the prosecution. Not a question of the sort was asked, and surely this proves that Nuncomar and his attorney had no definite knowledge or distinct suspicion on the subject ... Putting all these matters * together," he concludes, "my own opinion is that no man ever had, or could have, a fairer trial than Nuncomar, and that Impey in particular behaved with absolute fairness and as much indulgence as was compatible with his duty ... There is not a word in his summing-up of which I should have been ashamed had I said it myself, and all my study of the case has not suggested to me a single observation in Nuncomar's favour which is not noticed by Impey. As to the verdict, I think that there was ample evidence to support it. Whether it was in fact correct is a point on which it is impossible for me to give an unqualified opinion, as it is of course impossible now to judge decidedly of the credit of witnesses, and as I do not understand some part of the exhibits." ... In agreement with Sir J. Stephen's verdict is the opinion of Sir A. Lyall, of whose candid impartiality

---

* Much to which Sir J. Stephen here refers has been necessarily omitted.

I have already spoken. "It may be accepted," he says, "upon Sir James Stephen's authority, that no evidence can be produced to justify conclusions adverse to the innocence of Hastings upon a charge that has from its nature affected the popular tradition regarding him far more deeply than the accusations of high-handed oppressive political transactions, which are little understood and leniently condemned by the English at large. There is really nothing to prove that he had anything to do with the prosecution, or that he influenced the sentence; for the circumstances which have been strung together to support the belief in his guilt are all reconcilable with a theory of his innocence." ... So, too, with reference to Sir J. Stephen's work, Sir J. Strachey remarks, "One at least of the imaginary crimes to which I have referred—the judicial murder of Nandkumar by Impey and Hastings—will hardly again appear in sober history." To the same effect write Captain Trotter and Mr. Forrest—all of whom have had occasion to study the subject with care, and all of whom have a wide and intimate knowledge of Indian character and Indian life.

APPENDIX III.

THE IMPEACHMENT OF IMPEY.

CLOSELY connected with the trial of Nand Kumár was the impeachment of Impey. Stripped of all verbiage, the charges on which this impeachment was based are, in Sir J. Stephen's words, "first, that he acted illegally in trying Nand Kumár at all: secondly, that he misconducted himself at the trial: thirdly, that he conspired with Hastings to cause Nand Kumár to be prosecuted on a capital charge: fourthly, that from a corrupt wish to screen Hastings he refused to give Nand Kumár leave to appeal, and refused to respite Nand Kumár." Five other charges were stated against Impey. They will be noticed hereafter; but as not one of them was ever proceeded with, it will be convenient to keep them separate. In Impey's behalf it is especially important that every fact should be cleared up, because Macaulay, while bitterly inveighing against Hastings, has shown himself capable of fully appreciating his many great qualities, and has, so to speak, allowed his statesmanlike government as a set-off against his crimes; whereas in regard to Impey the bitterness, even intensified, stands out at every point without being relieved by any admiration of services

which, though less brilliant than those of Hastings, were
certainly meritorious.   Macaulay never loses an opportunity
for sneers, imputations of unworthy motive, suggestions of
innate meanness.   He goes out of the way, indeed, to imagine
to himself and to paint for his readers a portrait that has no
resemblance to what is really known of its original; and in any
other writer but one of such genuine kindliness of heart the
animation and minuteness with which he fills in his damnatory
details might reasonably be ascribed to a personal animosity.
In justice therefore to a man whose memory has long suffered
undeserved obloquy, it will probably be forgiven if my review
of the case, founded on Sir J. Stephen's book, shall seem
somewhat tedious.   The first charge against Impey is that he
acted illegally in trying Nand Kumár at all.   Two preliminary
points half alleged, half insinuated, by Impey's prosecutors,
may be passed over with slight notice.   The former is that
Impey ought to have quashed the indictment because "it was
considered" by some unknown and unmentioned persons "as
a political measure," and because circumstances existed which
"could leave no doubt in the mind and opinion of any person
acquainted therewith" (which Impey was not alleged to be),
"that the said prosecution was set on foot with the view of
defeating the said accusation" (against Hastings).   The latter
is that even if the law of England justified Impey's course, it
was so opposed to natural justice that he was a criminal for
putting it in force.   In regard to the former objection "it is
enough to say that it assumes first—that judges ought to take
judicial notice of rumours imputing malicious motives to prosecutors; secondly, that the fact (proved by such rumours) that
a prosecutor is actuated by a malicious motive establishes the
innocence of the person accused; and thirdly, that if the judge
is convinced of the innocence of the accused by a rumour that
the prosecutor is malicious, it becomes the judge's duty to
'quash the indictment,' by which I suppose the author of the
charge meant to prevent the case from being tried, for the
quashing of one indictment does not interfere with the pre-
sentment of another for the same offence."   In regard to the
latter, "To punish a judge for enforcing a bad law implies a
right and duty on the part of the judge to decide whether the
law is good or not; and this puts the judge above the legislature."*   The second charge was that the criminal law of
England as regards forgery was not in force as part of the
law administered by the Supreme Court, or not in force at the
time when the forgery in question was supposed to be committed.   Impey's contention in his defence was that as regards
Calcutta it was in force at the date on which the bond was

* *The Story of Nuncomar*, ii. 16, 7.

uttered. The question is too technical, and too much encumbered with legal rulings, for any discussion here. Sir J. Stephen, who sets forth the arguments on both sides, says, "Upon fully considering all these matters, I think that as a matter of legal theory Impey's view was, to say the least, defensible. It was certainly inconsistent with later decisions, but if it is regarded as being on that account wrong, I think that the mistake into which the Court fell was innocent and in good faith." "It must, however," he adds, "be said that in a doubtful and novel matter of this sort the Court would have acted wisely in saying that an indictment for the forgery as a misdemeanour at common law would be the proper course to take. A conviction upon such an indictment would have been followed by fine and imprisonment to any extent which the Court thought proper, and this would, I think, have been under all the circumstances a punishment sufficient for the ends of justice." ... It should, however, be pointed out that if Impey's opinion was wrong, his brother judges were equally to blame, and that neither they nor the counsel for the defence raised the question as to the date at which English law was introduced into Calcutta, the only point mooted being that of Chambers as to the suitability of the English law of forgery for Calcutta. The next charge against Impey was that he summed up with "scandalous partiality" and manifested great anxiety to secure Nand Kumár's conviction. This question has already been dealt with and Sir J. Stephen's view of the case given. The third charge was that of a conspiracy between Hastings and Impey to cause Nand Kumár to be tried and convicted on a capital charge. As regards Hastings. It was not pretended that there was any distinct proof of this conspiracy, nor even directly alleged in the articles of charge that such a conspiracy ever existed. The allegation made was that there was ground for a suspicion of conspiracy in the interest of Hastings in getting rid of Nand Kumár, and in the coincidence in point of time between the accusation of Hastings by Nand Kumár and that of Nand Kumár by Mohan Prásad. So vague a suspicion would probably have long since passed from the minds of all dispassionate persons if it had not been for one circumstance of which Macaulay has made so much. "Hastings," he says, "three or four years later described Impey as the man to whose support he was at one time indebted for the safety of his 'fortune, honour, and reputation.' These strong words can refer only to the case of Nuncomar, and they must mean that Impey hanged Nuncomar in order to support Hastings." On this Sir J. Stephen remarks,* "The argument founded on this letter appears to

* ii. pp. 44, 5.

me to be worthless. The exact date of the letter is not given
by Mr. Gleig, but it must have been written in 1780, at the
height of the contest between the Governor-General and
Council and the Supreme Court to which it relates. ... It is
remarkable that a passage to the same effect appears in a
letter from Impey to Dunning in March, 1780. Impey says,
'The power which is exerted against me would not have
existed in the hands in which it is if I had not helped to keep
it there, and it was used against me at the time when I was
living, in all appearance, in the utmost confidence of familiarity
with the possessor of it.' ... Is this the language of two murderers about each other? Would one such wretch look back
with affectionate regret to the happy time when by the hand
of the other he assassinated their common victim? ... If there
was such a bond of infamy between two men, each would shun
all reference to it, especially to a third person, as he would
shun the avowal even to himself of any other abominable and
horrible crime. Macaulay's supposition is not only revolting
and improbable, but also quite unnecessary. Each of these
passages, to my mind, obviously refers to the support
given to Hastings by Impey and the rest of the judges,
when Clavering tried to dispossess Hastings from the office of
Governor-General, in the summer of 1777, in the manner related
by Macaulay himself, and when Hastings was secured in his
office entirely by the view taken of the case by the judges to
whom the rival claims of the parties were referred." Admitting
the probability of this explanation, Sir A. Lyall observes,* "But
the words certainly read more like a reference to some confidential
transaction than to such a public and formal proceeding as the
Court's finding upon a case submitted for opinion." I do not
myself see why the reference should be to a "*confidential* transaction." At the same time, there lurks something suspicious in
the words "honour and reputation." Hastings would no doubt
have been ruined in "fortune" had the judges decided against
him. But in what way would his "honour and reputation"
have suffered? Possibly—an alternative suggested by Sir A.
Lyall—Hastings might have alluded to Impey's support in the
matter of Nand Kumár if it had been given without any collusion
or private understanding. To return to Impey. If the evidence
of conspiracy is, as regards Hastings, without any solid foundation, as regards Impey the facts are all against it. For "the
argument assumes that Impey had something to do with the
early steps in the case, and so with the time when the case was
brought before him. This is contrary to the fact. Whatever
wickedness is imputed to Impey, he could not interfere with the
time when the prosecution began. His opportunity of miscon-

* *Warren Hastings*, p, 59.

ducting himself would not arise till the prisoner was brought before him by others. He was not even the committing magistrate. Nuncomar was committed by Hyde and Lemaistre, who could not, when Mohun Persaud swore an information before them, refuse to proceed, or, if they thought it a case for committal, to commit. When Nuncomar was committed, his trial at the next session was a matter of course, over which none of the judges had any influence whatever. ...These considerations are enough to show that even if the coincidence in time between the two accusations were unexplained it would prove nothing against either Hastings or Impey, but it was explained by the evidence of Boughton Rose and Farrer already referred to... In particular Farrer proved that the prosecution of Nuncomar for forgery had been determined on long before Nuncomar accused Hastings of corruption, and explained the circumstances which led to the warrant not being issued till May, 1775. It must have been issued within a very few days after the forged deed was procured by the solicitor of the prosecutor, and it could not have been issued before. For these reasons it appears to me that there was absolutely no evidence that there was any conspiracy between Hastings and Impey in reference to Nuncomar's trial."* The last of this group of charges is that Impey refused to respite Nand Kumár. Macaulay's remarks on this point will be found on p. 41, 2, and "That Impey ought to have respited Nuncomar...mercy or delay," and on p. 44, ll. 14-27, "Of Impey's conduct...to serve a political purpose." With reference to those remarks the first point to be borne in mind is that if the refusal to respite was wrong, all the four judges were equally to blame. Alone Impey had no such power. As to mercy, there is no evidence that Impey "would not hear of it"; as to delay, there was an interval of six weeks between conviction and execution. Whether the whole Court were wrong, can only be a matter of opinion. They had a discretionary power which they did not think fit to exercise for Nand Kumár's benefit. To impute motives is easy enough, but if they are to be imputed "we must either say that all four had motives for what they did, other than a wish to screen Hastings, or else that all four corruptly determined to withhold a reprieve in order to screen Hastings. To say that three were actuated by other motives and one by a desire to screen Hastings is to make an assumption as gratuitous as it is unjust." Moreover, Sir J. Stephen points out, the execution of Nand Kumár was not necessary to save Hastings. Had the Court respited him and recommended imprisonment for a term of years, with a heavy fine, Hastings would have been protected as effectually as by his death. Sir J. Stephen goes on to show that nearly all the

* *The Story of Nuncomar,* ii. 41, 2.

statements made by Macaulay in the former of these two paragraphs were incorrect, and finally sums up on the whole story from the accusation brought against Hastings down to the execution of his accuser. This summing up is in the main a recapitulation of conclusions already stated in following out the different points *seriatim*, and want of space prevents my giving it in full length. One small matter remains as regards the refusal of the Court to respite Nand Kumár. This refusal need not have been final, for the majority of the Council had it in their power to ensure a reprieve by addressing the Supreme Court on the subject. This they declined to do, and they, much rather than Hastings or the Supreme Court, are answerable for Nand Kumár's death.

It has already been mentioned that besides the charges against Impey which have now been considered, there were five other charges which, though not proceeded with, were originally a part of Impey's impeachment. These charges were, first, that Impey had misconducted himself in a cause known as the Patna Cause; secondly, that he had unwarrantably and for corrupt purposes of his own extended the jurisdiction of the Supreme Court; thirdly, that he had misconducted himself in a cause called the Kásijura Cause; fourthly, that he had corruptly accepted the office of Judge of the Sadr Diwáni Adálat; fifthly, that he had corruptly abetted Hastings in certain proceedings for which Hastings was then under impeachment, by improperly taking affidavits intended for his justification. With the first three of these charges we have nothing to do since no reference is made to them in Macaulay's essay. Out of the fourth and fifth, however, Macaulay has framed a powerful indictment against both Hastings and Impey. That this indictment has no basis in truth I shall endeavour to show. For this purpose I shall first quote Sir A. Lyall's succinct statement of the circumstances which led up to the appointment of Impey as Judge of the Sadr Diwáni Adálat, and then, with Sir J. Stephen's help expose the fallacies of Macaulay's diatribe.

"It should here be mentioned," says Sir A. Lyall,[*] "that in 1779 the dissensions between the Court and the Council in Calcutta had risen to the degree of actual collision between the two authorities; that in this quarrel Hastings had made common cause with Francis against the judges, and that he had consequently broken off his alliance with Impey, who much lamented this rupture of their personal friendship and reciprocal understanding upon public affairs. The Governor-General in Council had published a proclamation authorising disregard of the Court's process, and had supported it by an armed force. The Court issued warrants for apprehending the Company's soldiers; and summonses on a plea of trespass were served on the Governor-General

---

[*] *Warren Hastings*, pp. 113-116.

and his Council, which they refused to obey ... The Governor-General
in Council accused the judges of arrogating to themselves the right to
review the orders and proceedings of executive officers, and of the
provincial councils which disposed of the revenue and judicial business
in all the districts.   The judges retorted that the government expected
to indulge their subordinates with impunity in mere lawlessness and
licentious oppression ... Sir James Stephen has decided that the
Court was on the whole less to blame than the Company's officers;
and he discovers the real offenders in the authors of the clumsy and
ill-drawn Regulating Act of 1773, which bestowed powers without
circumscribing the jurisdictions, and which purposely left uncertain
the supreme jurisdiction, that is to say, the sovereignty of the country.
However this may be, the judges had so roughly handled the district
courts of justice, which were presided over by the revenue officers of
the Company, that Hastings saw the necessity of establishing separate
civil courts; and these courts were soon found to require proper
judicial superintendence.   There had for a long time existed a central
court of appeal in civil suits, called the *Sudder Diwáni Adálat*, whose
powers had since 1773 been vested in the Governor-General in Council,
but had never been exercised in any regular manner.   Hastings conceived the luminous idea of transferring these powers, with a salary
of £6000 yearly, to the Chief-Justice; and six weeks after the duel he
announced his project in Council, stating, what was perfectly true,
that the civil courts urgently needed the supervision and direction of
a trained expert, ... The office and salary were to be held during the
pleasure of the Governor-General in Council.   The measure was at
once politic, practical, and effective; it terminated by a master-stroke
the conflict of jurisdictions; it disarmed and conciliated the Chief-
Justice; and it undoubtedly placed the country courts, which had
been dispensing a very haphazard and intuitive kind of justice, for the
first time under a person who could guide and control them upon
recognized principles ... Impey accepted the salary subject to refund
if the arrangement should be disallowed at home; and he appears to
have undertaken the duties in an honourable spirit.   Any question as
to the morality of this transaction touches Impey rather than
Hastings; for even if Impey be held guilty of having compounded his
controversy with the government by accepting a lucrative appointment,
yet the plan of uniting the Chief-Justiceship with the superintendency
of the district courts, taken on its merits, was a good and practical
remedy of existing evils." ...

Sir James Stephen's history of the subject is probably the basis
of Sir A. Lyall's *resumé*, but it is too long and intricate to be
followed here.   His criticism of Macaulay* I give almost in
full.

   "Macaulay's account of the quarrel between the Court and the
Council deserves to be carefully noticed.   It supplies a strong instance
of the danger of breaking down the boundary between history and
romance ... It is a gloomy picture of horrible oppression, causeless,
purposeless, mysterious, and yet so tremendous that it almost justified

---

* *The Story of Nuncomar*, ii. 247-255.

the course taken by Hastings of buying off by an enormous bribe the infamous tyrant by whom it was carried on. The objection to it is that it is absolutely false from end to end, and in almost every particular, as the following instances will show. After stating truly that arrest on mesne process was the first step in most civil proceedings, he expatiates on its abuses. He says at great length that to a native woman of rank it is an intolerable outrage that her apartment should be entered by strange men. He then adds: 'To these outrages the most distinguished families of Bengal, Behar, and Orissa, were now exposed'; and he says that the effect of the attempt which the 'Supreme Court made to extend its jurisdiction over the whole of the Company's territories' was like an attempt in England to empower any one by merely swearing that a debt was due to him, to horsewhip a general officer, to put a bishop in the stocks, to treat ladies in the way which called forth the blow of Wat Tyler.' He then goes on as follows: 'A reign of terror began, of terror heightened by mystery, for even what was endured was less horrible than what was anticipated. No man knew what was next to be anticipated from this strange tribunal. It came from beyond the black water as the people of India with a mysterious horror call the sea. It consisted of judges, not one of whom was familiar with the ways of the millions over whom they claimed boundless authority. Its records were kept in unknown characters. Its sentences were pronounced in unknown words.' The general answer to all this is that the Supreme Court never did claim any such general jurisdiction as is alleged. Practically, the most important of its claims was jurisdiction over the collectors of the revenue and officers of the Provincial Courts, as being servants to the Company ... The nature of the jurisdiction claimed by the Court protected women from being sued before it. They could not be servants to the Company. The only writ against a woman was the writ against Naderah Begum, and that was in the Provincial Court at Patna, and not in the Supreme Court. How far zenanas were incidentally trespassed upon, I will examine immediately. To pass to the details. What sense is there in the language about the black water and the strange characters? Did not Hastings and the East India Company come from beyond the sea as well as the judges? Were not most of the records of the Company kept, and most of their orders given, in English, like those of the Supreme Court? When and where did the Supreme Court claim boundless authority over the natives? Its claims were quite distinct, but they cannot be stated in a picturesque way. 'No Mahratta invasion had ever spread through the province such dismay as this inroad of English lawyers. All the injustice of former oppressors, Asiatic and European, appeared as a blessing when compared with the justice of the Supreme Court.' In 1779 the Mahrattas had been kept out of Bengal for a considerable time, but[*] from 1742 to 1750 'these merciless hordes of miscreants devastated the country to the southward of the Ganges from October till June to extort their "chout." One incident of these invasions may be mentioned to show how far Macaulay's statement is just. The then Nabob Aliverdy Khan treacherously murdered many of their chiefs. Thereupon the Mahratta army wreaked their vengeance upon

[*] Talboys' *Wheeler*, p. 267.

the unoffending inhabitants. They ravaged the country with fire and sword, cutting off ears, noses, and hands, and committing countless barbarities in the search of spoil. The wretched Bengalis fled in shoals across the Ganges to take refuge or perchance to perish in the hills and jungles to the northward of the river.' What did the Supreme Court ever do remotely comparable to this? How many imprisonments on mesne process would it take to create more terror than the mutilation, torture, and robbery of hundreds, perhaps thousands, of innocent peasants? To come to something more specific. 'There were instances in which men of the most venerable dignity, persecuted without a cause by extortioners, died of rage and shame in the gripe of the vile alguazils of Impey.' The only matter to which this can refer is the case of Cazi Sadhi. He was one of the defendants in the Patna Cause, and was taken in execution after bail had been given for him by the Company. He died on a boat on the Ganges on his way to Calcutta whilst under a guard of Sepoys. He may have been hardly dealt with, but to say that he was persecuted by extortioners without a cause is to allege that the judgment in the Patna case was wrong, and of this judgment Macaulay takes no notice at all. The Cazi was sued for gross oppression and corruption, which the Court upon an elaborate inquiry thought he had committed. Macaulay does not suggest that there was even a question on the subject. ... At all events the Sepoys who had charge of the boat in which the Cazi died were not the 'vile alguazils of Impey,' or officers of the Supreme Court at all. They were a guard put over him by the Dacca Council, which had given bail for him, and which was specially directed to treat him as might be, which it was anxious to do ... This indefinite way of writing 'there were instances' is singularly unfair and inaccurate. Here is another instance of it :—'The harems of noble Mohammedans, sanctuaries respected in the East by governments which respected nothing else, were burst open by gangs of bailiffs, and there were instances in which they shed their blood in the doorway while defending, sword in hand, the sacred apartments of their women.' I have carefully gone through the whole of the evidence in the report and appendices referred to, in order to test the truth of these eloquent generalities, and I find as follows :—There was one instance in which one Mohammedan of some rank thought that his friend's zenana was likely to be broken open, and stood in the doorway sword in hand to defend it. The house, not the zenana, was broken open, and a fray took place in it, in which the father of the Mohammedan in question was endangered. The son left his position in the passage to the zenana, took part in the fray, and was hurt. It does not appear that the zenana was broken open, or that any attempt to do so was made. There is some though not much foundation for the introductory part of the statement. One zenana was broken into by a bailiff, and a slave girl was wounded, and the Advocate-General suggested that the matter should be laid before the Court, which would, if applied to, punish the bailiff. The Rajah of Cossijurah's zenana is said to have been entered, but no detail is given. Upon these three cases, and no other materials which I can discover, is founded all the eloquence about Wat Tyler, a reign of terror, and the cruel humiliation of all the nobility of Bengal. This way of generalising particular incidents is bad enough, but the following passage is, I think worse. 'The

Government placed itself firmly between the tyrannical tribunal and
the people. The Chief-Justice proceeded to the wildest excesses.
The Governor-General and all the members of Council were served
with writs calling upon them to appear before the King's justices and
to answer for their public acts. This was too much. Hastings, with
just scorn, refused to obey the call, set at liberty the persons wrongfully detained by the Court, and took measures for resisting the outrageous proceedings of the sheriffs' officers, if necessary, by the sword.'
This passage implies that Impey individually caused the Governor
and the members of Council to be 'served with writs.' Neither Impey
nor the Supreme Court did anything of the kind. They expressly
refused to issue an attachment against the Governor or the Councillors,
because they were by the Regulating Act exempt from the criminal
jurisdiction of the Court. The writs with which Hastings and the
Council were served were writs issued by Cossinauth, the plaintiff in
the action against the Rajah of Cossijurah, for preventing him by
armed force from compelling the Rajah's appearance. Neither Impey
nor the Court had any right to refuse to issue a writ on such a claim.
... It is not true that any one arrested by the Court justly or not, in
this matter was set at liberty by the Council. One person only—Naylor,
the Rajah of Cossijurah's attorney—was imprisoned, and that was for
contempt in not answering interrogatories. The Council never set
him at liberty. They authorised him to answer the interrogatories in
order to regain his liberty. The climax of injustice is, I think, reached
in the passage which follows the one just noticed. After saying that
Hastings 'took measures for resisting the outrageous proceedings of
the sheriffs' officers, if necessary by the sword,' Macaulay adds : 'But
he had in view another device, which might prevent the necessity of
an appeal to arms. He was seldom at a loss for an expedient, and he
knew Impey well. The expedient in this case was a very simple one
—neither more nor less than a bribe. Impey was by Act of Parliament a judge independent of the Government of Bengal, and entitled
to a salary of 8,000l. a year. Hastings proposed to make him also a
judge in the Company's service, and to give him in that capacity about
8,000l. a year more. It was understood that in consequence of this
new salary Impey would desist from urging the high pretensions
of his Court. If he did urge those pretensions, the Government
could at a moment's notice eject him from the office which had been
created for him. The bargain was struck ; Bengal was saved ; an
appeal to force was averted. The Chief Justice was rich, quiet, and
infamous?' This charge is inconsistent with the dates, and asserts
imaginary facts. No appeal to force was averted. On the contrary,
such an appeal was made. The sheriff's officers actually were resisted
and taken prisoners by two companies of sepoys in January, 1780.
Impey never did desist from urging the high pretensions of the Court.
The Council, by military force, restrained the jurisdiction of the
Court, and by a proclamation to all the natives informed them that
they were at liberty to set its process at defiance. No bargain was
struck. The Council and the Court respectively had done their very
worst by each other nine months at least before any sort of offer was
or could be made to Impey. Moreover, the Court was powerless to do
anything unless it was set in motion by a suitor, but after the course
taken in the Cossijurah Cause, who would venture to sue any one

whom the Council had taken under its protection? The plaintiff could not serve his writ. He could not execute his judgment if he got one. Nor was any redress to be had against the individuals by whom he was prevented from exercising his legal rights. The Governor-General and his Council had committed themselves to a forcible resistance to any attempt to make themselves or their inferior agents liable in damages to any one who suffered by their interference. This conduct was persisted in, and was never modified in the smallest degree. In that state of things it is difficult to see what the Court had to give for which it was worth the Council's while to offer a bribe. Hastings wanted nothing from Impey. There was nothing to be got from him except an admission that the Council had been right in their difference and the Court wrong, and this Hastings did not ask for, did not get, and did not want. If he had got it, it would have been useless."

The last charge in the impeachment of Impey, and one on which Macaulay hangs some of his bitterest reproaches, relates to the taking of certain affidavits. Macaulay's words are:—

"But we must not forget to do justice to Sir Elijah Impey's conduct on this occasion. It was not indeed easy for him to intrude himself into a business so entirely alien from all his official duties. But there was something inexpressibly alluring, we must suppose, in the peculiar rankness of the infamy which was then to be got at Lucknow. He hurried thither as fast as relays of palanquin-bearers could carry him. A crowd of people came before him with affidavits against the Begums, ready drawn in their hands. Those affidavits he did not read. Some of them indeed he could not read; for they were in the dialects of Northern India, and no interpreter was employed. He administered the oath to the deponents with all possible expedition, and asked not a single question, not even whether they had perused the statements to which they swore. This work performed, he got again into his palanquin and posted back to Calcutta, to be in time for the opening of term. The cause was one which, by his own confession, lay altogether out of his jurisdiction. Under the charter of justice, he had no more right to enquire into crimes committed by Asiatics in Oude than the Lord President of the Court of Session in Scotland to hold an assize at Exeter. He had no right to try the Begums, nor did he pretend to try them. With what object then, did he undertake so long a journey? Evidently in order that he might give, in an irregular manner, that sanction which in a regular manner he could not give, to the crimes of those who had recently hired him; and in order that a confused mass of testimony which he did not sift, which he did not even read, might acquire an authority not properly belonging to it, from the signature of the highest judicial functionary in India."

Now from Macaulay's account it would be implied that Impey volunteered his assistance, and came all the way from Calcutta to give it. Neither is the fact. Impey was on a tour of inspection of the provincial Courts and had reached Manghír when he received from Hastings several letters pressing him to come up to Benares, where Hastings then was. Impey understood that

Hastings wished for his presence on account of the difficulties in which he was then involved. He accordingly hastened to Chunár, whither Hastings had retreated. On his arrival he was consulted by the Governor-General as to the narrative of the Benares affair which he was then writing, and the facts of which he was anxious to have properly authenticated. Impey suggested affidavits, and at the request of Hastings proceeded to Lucknow to take them. It is not true that "a crowd of natives came before him with affidavits against the Begums, ready drawn in their hands." Of the forty-three affidavits presented, ten only mentioned the Begums, and those only slightly and incidentally. It is true that, as Macaulay says, Impey did not read them. But Macaulay's complaint on this point only shows ignorance of law. Sir J. Stephen * points out that "in the common course of business when an affidavit is sworn, even in a judicial proceeding, the person before whom it is sworn never knows its contents. He has as little to do with it as the attesting witness of a will or deed has to do with the contents of the document which he attests. To blame a man for swearing an affidavit in a language of which the person before whom it is sworn is ignorant, is as absurd as to blame a man for witnessing a will written in a language which he does not know. All that the judge or commissioner has to do is to satisfy himself that the deponent swears that the contents of his affidavit, whatever they may be, are true. All that he need know of the deponent's language is enough of it to ask him if the matter of his affidavit is true and to give him the oath." It has been proved that Impey knew much more Persian and Hindustáni than was necessary for this purpose, and he declared in his evidence on the subject that he did ask the nineteen deponents to the Persian affidavits whether the contents of their affidavits were true. If Macaulay had to characterize in another his own remark that Impey could not read some of the affidavits "because they were in the dialects of northern India and no interpreter was employed," we should, I think have had some very trenchant language. Sir J. Stephen deals very gently with the matter when he says, "All the affidavits were in English except nineteen in Persian, one Persian translation of a Hindustani original, and one in French. Not one was in any 'dialect of upper India.' This assertion is remarkable, because it is an error upon an error. In his original review Macaulay said, 'the greater part (of the affidavits) indeed he could not read, for they were in Persian and Hindustáni.' On learning from Mr. Macfarlane's work that Impey knew Persian, the passage was altered to the incorrect form in which I have quoted it, a false premiss being substituted for one which was half true, in order to suggest a conclusion wholly false —namely, that Impey was unable to read the affidavits." Impey's

* *The Story of Nuncomar, etc., ii. 265-7.*

action in the matter may have shown an undue eagerness to serve an old friend. But it may also have been due, as he himself asserted, to public spirit; and the circumstances in which Englishmen in India were situated at that period were very different from those as we know them now. Even if Impey be thought somewhat officious in the matter, it must be borne in mind that in those times "the taking of voluntary affidavits, not in any judicial proceedings, but for the purpose of attesting matters of fact which any one wished to authenticate was very common. Impey's act ... had no greater and no less legal significance than his asking the deponents whether what they said was true would have had. As far as the law went any private person might have administered the oath as well as he. His office and dignity no doubt put on record the fact that the oath was taken with more emphasis than Middleton or Hannay could have given to it, but an affidavit on such a matter sworn by either of them would be legally neither better nor worse than one sworn before Impey. I think indeed that the mere taking of the affidavits would not have been charged against him as an offence if it had not been regarded as an overt act of a conspiracy between him and Hastings to plunder the Begums."

I have now gone through all the controversial matters which were too long to be discussed in my Notes. But fully as I have endeavoured to set them forth in the limits allowed me, I am well aware that I have done very imperfect justice to the narratives of Sir John Strachey and Sir James Stephen. The work of the former is, however, an octavo volume of three hundred and more pages, while that of the latter extends to nearly six hundred pages of a not much smaller size. With such abundance of material before me—all of it thoroughly germane to the matter—it has been by no means easy to pick out what was most essential to my purpose, and it is quite possible that in other hands the work of selection would have been made with greater judgment.

APPENDIX IV.

THE RISE GROWTH, AND DECLINE OF THE MARÁTHA POWERS.

In Macaulay's Essays on Clive and Hastings mention of the Maráthas is necessarily frequent, and it will probably be convenient to students to have some connected narrative of the part they have played in Indian history. The following brief sketch, taken in the main from Mr. H. G. Keene's monograph on Mádhava Ráo Sindhia and Sir A. Lyall's history of the *Rise of British Dominion in India*, will, I hope, enable them to follow the fortunes of this race, more especially in regard to its points of contact with the British power.

Maháráshtra, a tract of country bounded on the west by the ocean, on the north by the Narbada, on the east by the Wainganga, and on the south by the Krishna rivers, was a Hindu kingdom in very early times, with its capital at Kalyán, near the modern city of Bombay. The name *Marhat* for its inhabitants occurs in the history of Muhammad Tughlak in the fourteenth century, and shortly afterwards we find mention of them in connection with the Musalmán kingdom of Bijápur, where they were known as light cavalry, and seem to have taught the Bijápur Musalmáns that system of guerilla warfare to which the kingdom owed its ability to resist its enemies for nearly two hundred years. But the growth of this extraordinary race dates from the reign of the Emperor Sháh Jáhán, and the period which will be dealt with in this sketch extends only from about 1650 to 1818. Sháh Jáhán's efforts to overthrow the Bijápur dynasty brought about the first troubles. At that time the nominal ruler of Bijápur was a minor, and the regency was held by a Marátha captain, Sháhji Bhonsla. Sháhji resisted Sháh Jáhán's attempts, and from this period the Maráthas began to assert themselves as a distinct power. Their activity was first shown in raids upon immediate neighbours, but these were mere spasmodic acts of plunder directed by no systematic policy. When, however, the Muslim power in the Dakhan began to crumble to pieces they adopted wider aims, and fully organized the practice of levying contributions on the subjects of other states, till at last their incursions came to spread over almost the whole peninsula. It was not territorial power, at all events until a much later period, that they desired. The elaborate requirements of ordered rule they gladly left to others, so long as a descent upon fertile provinces and rich hoards gave them booty to be squandered in reckless enjoyment, and means for the subsistence of an ever increasing host of free lances. The black-mail they modestly exacted was twenty-five *per cent.* of the revenue of the invaded territory, and so merciless was their style of warfare, and so swift and irresistible their swoop, that for the most part no serious effort was made to escape their exactions. The germs of an organization, which in its development made the Maráthas the most formidable power the English later on had to reckon with, were planted by Sháhji's son Siváji, who raised a regularly paid army, possessed himself of forts, and finally assumed the functions and insignia of a king. So large a stride towards consolidation was made under his rule that at the death of Aurangzeb, or shortly afterwards, the civil administration of the Hindus in Maháráshtra had developed into a well-knit

power. Under the Rája, its nominal head, was a council of
eight, whose president bore the title of Peshwa. The first of
these Peshwas was Báláji Viswanáth, who had entered the
service of Sáhu, Siváji's grandson. By his conspicuous business
abilities he shortly became the most important person in the
government, and vigorously addressed himself to the task of
confirming order and a settled system of rule in Maháráshtra.
The right to levy *chauth* in the six imperial provinces of the
Dakhan had been formally ceded to Sáhu in 1709. This concession was confirmed to Báláji, and in return the Rája of
Maháráshtra was bound to pay a fixed annual cess to the imperial
treasury, and to provide the emperor with a specified force of
Maráthas whenever called upon to do so. The Rája was in fact
to be nominally a vassal of the emperor, but the compact gave to
Báláji's schemes a firmness of foundation they had hitherto lacked.
In the midst of his efforts at consolidation of power, Báláji died
in 1720, and was succeeded by his son, Báji Ráo, a man even more
remarkable than his father, and with wider range of ambition.
He aimed, indeed, at supreme power in Hindustán, entered into
a long war with the Nizám-ul-mulk in the south, made himself
master of the rich provinces of Málwa and Orissa, and attempted
the conquest of the Karnátak. He also contrived to acquire for
his descendants the office of Peshwa as an hereditary dignity,
and the leadership of the Marátha confederation which was
shortly to branch out in four principal chiefships, that of the
Bhonsla Rája in Berár, the Gaekwár in Baroda, Holkar in the
south of Málwa, and Sindhia in the north-east of the same province. But a severe reverse was in store for the Maráthas. Success
had tempted them too far ; for the Mughal power being shattered, and Ahmad the Abdáli having retired to Afghánistán with
his plunder of Dehli and the Panjáb, Raghunáth Ráo, brother of
Báji Ráo, supported by the contingents of Sindhia and Holkar,
marched northward, seized Dehli, pushed on to Lahore, drove
out the governor left by Ahmad, and substituted a Marátha
administration in the Panjáb. This insolence was too much for
Ahmad. In the winter of 1759-60 he came sweeping down into
the Panjáb, retook Lahore, drove the Maráthas out of the northern country, and defeated Holkar and Sindhia with heavy loss.
The Peshwa despatched from Puna a large force to repair these
disasters, and in January, 1761, the Afgháns with their Musalmán allies met the Maráthas on the field of Pánipat. The result
was a decisive victory for the Afgháns, and the Maráthas were
for the time swept out of Northern India. The defeat was a
crushing blow to Báji Ráo, and he died in the following June of
a broken heart. His mantle fell on the celebrated Mádhava Ráo,
otherwise called Mádhoji, an illegitimate son of the slipper-bearer,
Ránoji Sindhia, who for his fidelity to Báláji Viswanáth had
obtained a fief in Northern Málwa and made Ujjain his head

He next inflicted a severe defeat upon the troops of the Nágpur Rája at Argáon, and took by storm the hill forts of Gáwilgarh. Lake was equally active in the north-west. He took Aligarh by assault, dispersed Sindhia's force before Dehli, besieged and captured Agra, and finally at Láswári routed the last of Sindhia's regular army. " The result," says Sir A. Lyall,* " of these well-contested and hardly won victories was to shatter the whole military organization upon which Sindia's predominance had been built up, to break down his connection with the Moghul court in the north, and to destroy his influence at Poona as the most formidable member of the Maratha confederacy. Both Sindia and the Nagpore Rája, finding themselves in imminent danger of losing all their possessions, acquiesced reluctantly in the terms that were dictated to them after the destruction of their armies. The treaty of Bassein was formally recognized; they entered into defensive treaties and made large cessions of territory. Sindia gave up to the British all his northern districts lying along both sides of the Jumna river; he ceded his sea-ports and his conquests on the west coast; he made over to them the city of Delhi and the custody of the Mogul emperor; he dismissed all his French officers, and accepted the establishment, at his cost, of a large British force to be stationed near his frontier. The Rája of Nagpore restored Berar to the Nizám, and surrendered to the British government the province of Cuttack, on the Bay of Bengal, which lay interposed between the upper districts of Madras and the south-western districts of Bengal." Holkar still remained to be reckoned with. He had been hoping to profit by Sindhia's discomfiture, and now thought to take advantage of his defenceless condition. He was, therefore, summoned by Lake to retire within his own territories, and on his refusal was attacked by the British troops. Although for a time Holkar had followed Sindhia's example of maintaining a staff of European officers and of drilling his troops after the European fashion, he had before this returned to the traditional Marátha tactics of rapid cavalry movements. His object was to evade a regular engagement, and it was not without a prolonged effort that Lake surprised and finally dispersed his bands. Holkar at last took refuge in the Panjáb, whence he returned only to sign a treaty on terms similar to those imposed upon Sindhia and the Nágpur Rája. For some years there was peace between the English and the Maráthas. But in 1816 the Bhonsla Rája of Nágpur, with whom Lord Hastings had concluded a subsidiary treaty detaching him from the Marátha confederation, repented an engagement which tied his hands, and began to concert hostile measures with the Peshwa, who also was impatient of the restrictions placed upon him by alliance with the English. The latter, however,

---

* *Rise of the British Dominion in India*, pp. 227, 8.

before actually plunging into another struggle realized the danger he incurred of being stripped of all his possessions, and again entered into negotiations with the English whereby, in exchange for an increased subsidiary force, he made further cessions of territory, and virtually renounced all pretensions to supremacy in the Marátha confederation. His good faith was of short duration. In the following year he broke into open hostility and attacked the British troops at Puna, the Nágpur Rája imitating him in his outbreak. Their combination quickly proved ineffectual. The Peshwa was routed and his forts seized. In 1818 he surrendered, and the greater part of his territories passed under the British sovereignty, he being allowed to reside at Bithúr on a pension of £80,000 a year, the non-continuance of which after his death made an enemy of his adopted son, Dhundu Panth, commonly known as "Nana Sahib." The Nágpur State had also to cede several important districts, and thenceforth the Marátha powers ceased to exist except as feudatories of the British rule.

INDEX TO NOTES.

232

GLASGOW : PRINTED AT THE UNIVERSITY PRESS BY ROBERT MACLEHOSE AND CO.

MACMILLAN'S
ENGLISH CLASSICS:
A SERIES OF SELECTIONS FROM THE
WORKS OF THE GREAT ENGLISH WRITERS,
WITH INTRODUCTION AND NOTES.

The following Volumes, Globe 8vo, are ready or in preparation.

ADDISON—SELECTIONS FROM THE SPECTATOR. By K. DEIGHTON. 2s. 6d.

—THE DE COVERLEY PAPERS. Selected from the Spectator. By K. DEIGHTON.

BACON—ESSAYS. By F. G. SELBY, M.A. 3s. ; sewed, 2s. 6d.

——THE ADVANCEMENT OF LEARNING. By F. G. SELBY, M.A. Book I., 2s. Book II., 4s. 6d.

BURKE—REFLECTIONS ON THE FRENCH REVOLUTION. By F. G. SELBY, M.A. 5s.

——SPEECH ON AMERICAN TAXATION ; SPEECH ON CONCILIATION WITH AMERICA ; LETTER TO THE SHERIFFS OF BRISTOL. By F. G. SELBY, M.A. 3s. 6d.

COWPER—THE TASK. Book IV. By W. T. WEBB, M.A. 1s.

——SELECT LETTERS. By W. T. WEBB, M.A. 2s. 6d.

——SELECTIONS FROM. By W. T. WEBB, M.A. 2s. 6d.

DRYDEN—SELECT SATIRES—ABSALOM AND ACHITOPHEL ; THE MEDAL ; MAC FLECKNOE. By J. CHURTON COLLINS. 1s. 9d.

GOLDSMITH—THE TRAVELLER and THE DESERTED VILLAGE. By ARTHUR BARRETT, B.A. 1s. 9d. THE TRAVELLER and THE DESERTED VILLAGE, separately, 1s. each, sewed.

GRAY—POEMS. By JOHN BRADSHAW, LL.D. 1s. 9d.

HELPS—ESSAYS WRITTEN IN THE INTERVALS OF BUSINESS. By F. J. ROWE, M.A., and W. T. WEBB, M.A. 1s. 9d.

JOHNSON—LIFE OF MILTON. By K. DEIGHTON. 1s. 9d.

——LIFE OF DRYDEN. By P. PETERSEN, D.Sc.

——LIFE OF POPE. By P. PETERSEN, D.Sc.

LAMB—ESSAYS OF ELIA. By N. L. HALLWARD, M.A., and S. C. HILL, B.A. 3s. ; sewed, 2s. 6d.

MACAULAY—ESSAY ON ADDISON. By Prof. J. W. HALES, M.A.
[*In the Press.*

——ESSAY ON LORD CLIVE. By K. DEIGHTON. 2s.

——ESSAY ON WARREN HASTINGS. By K. DEIGHTON. 2s. 6d.

——ESSAY ON BOSWELL'S LIFE OF JOHNSON. By R. F. WINCH, M.A. 2s. 6d.

MALORY—MORTE D'ARTHUR. Edited by A. P. MARTIN, M.A.
[*In the Press.*

MILTON—PARADISE LOST, BOOKS I. and II. By MICHAEL MACMILLAN, B.A. 1s. 9d. Books I. and II., 1s. 3d. each ; sewed 1s. each.

——L'ALLEGRO, IL PENSEROSO, LYCIDAS, ARCADES, SONNETS, &c. By W. BELL, M.A. 1s. 9d.

——COMUS. By W. BELL, M.A. 1s. 3d. ; sewed, 1s.

——SAMSON AGONISTES. By H. M. PERCIVAL, M.A. 2s.

——TRACTATE OF EDUCATION. By Prof. E. E. MORRIS, M.A. 1s. 9d.

POPE—ESSAY ON MAN. Epistles I.-IV. By E. E. MORRIS, M.A. 1s. 9d.

SCOTT—THE LADY OF THE LAKE. By G. H. STUART, M.A. 2s. 6d. ; sewed, 2s. Canto I., sewed, 9d.

——THE LAY OF THE LAST MINSTREL. By G. H. STUART, M.A., and E. H. ELLIOT, B.A. 2s. Canto I., sewed, 9d. Cantos I.-III. and IV.-VI., separately, 1s. 3d. each ; sewed, 1s. each.

SCOTT—MARMION. By MICHAEL MACMILLAN, B.A. 3s.; sewed, 2s. 6d.
——ROKEBY. By the same. 3s.; sewed, 2s. 6d.

SHAKESPEARE—THE TEMPEST. By K. DEIGHTON. 1s. 9d.
——MUCH ADO ABOUT NOTHING. By the same. 2s.
——A MIDSUMMER NIGHT'S DREAM. By the same. 1s. 9d.
——THE MERCHANT OF VENICE. By the same. 1s. 9d.
——AS YOU LIKE IT. By the same. 1s. 9d.
——TWELFTH NIGHT. By the same. 1s. 9d.
——THE WINTER'S TALE. By the same. 2s.
——KING JOHN. By the same. 1s. 9d.
——RICHARD II. By the same. 1s. 9d.
——HENRY IV. Part I. By the same. 2s. 6d.; sewed, 2s.
——HENRY IV. Part II. By the same. 2s. 6d.; sewed, 2s.
——HENRY V. By the same. 1s. 9d.
——RICHARD III. By C. H. TAWNEY, M.A. 2s. 6d.; sewed, 2s.
——HENRY VIII. By K. DEIGHTON. 1s. 9d.
——CORIOLANUS. By the same. 2s. 6d.; sewed, 2s.
——ROMEO AND JULIET. By the same. 2s. 6d.; sewed, 2s.
——JULIUS CÆSAR. By the same. 1s. 9d.
——MACBETH. By the same. 1s. 9d.
——HAMLET. By the same. 2s. 6d.; sewed, 2s.
——KING LEAR. By the same. 1s. 9d.
——OTHELLO. By the same. 2s.
——ANTONY AND CLEOPATRA. By the same. 2s. 6d.; sewed, 2s.
——CYMBELINE. By the same. 2s. 6d.; sewed, 2s.

SOUTHEY—LIFE OF NELSON. By MICHAEL MACMILLAN, B.A. 3s.; sewed, 2s. 6d.

SPENSER—THE FAERIE QUEENE. Book I. By H. M. PERCIVAL, M.A. 3s.; sewed, 2s. 6d.
——THE SHEPHEARD'S CALENDAR. By Prof. C. H. HERFORD, Litt.D.

TENNYSON—SELECTIONS. By F. J. ROWE, M.A., and W. T. WEBB, M.A. 3s. 6d. Also in two parts, 2s. 6d. each. Part I. Recollections of the Arabian Nights, The Lady of Shalott, The Lotos-Eaters, Dora, Ulysses, Tithonus, The Lord of Burleigh, The Brook, Ode on the Death of the Duke of Wellington, The Revenge.—Part II. Œnone, The Palace of Art, A Dream of Fair Women, Morte d'Arthur, Sir Galahad, The Voyage, Demeter and Persephone.
——MORTE D'ARTHUR. By the same, 1s.
——ENOCH ARDEN. By W. T. WEBB, M.A. 2s. 6d.
——AYLMER'S FIELD. By W. T. WEBB, M.A. 2s. 6d.
——THE PRINCESS. By PERCY M. WALLACE, M.A. 3s. 6d.
——THE COMING OF ARTHUR; THE PASSING OF ARTHUR. By F. J. ROWE, M.A. 2s. 6d.
——GARETH AND LYNETTE. By G. C. MACAULAY, M.A. 2s. 6d.
——THE MARRIAGE OF GERAINT; GERAINT AND ENID. By same. 2s. 6d.
——LANCELOT AND ELAINE. By F. J. ROWE, M.A. 2s. 6d.
——THE HOLY GRAIL. By G. C. MACAULAY, M.A. 2s. 6d.
——GUINEVERE. By G. C. MACAULAY, M.A. 2s. 6d.

CHOSEN ENGLISH—Being Selections from Wordsworth, Byron, Shelley, Lamb, Scott. By A. ELLIS, B.A. 2s. 6d.

POEMS OF ENGLAND. A Selection of English Patriotic Poetry. By H. B. GEORGE, M.A., and A. SIDGWICK, M.A. 2s. 6d.

MACMILLAN AND CO., LTD., LONDON.

www.ingramcontent.com/pod-product-compliance
Lightning Source LLC
Chambersburg PA
CBHW030804020726
47499CB00006B/1759